DERANGED
Love

A NOVEL BY

Honey

STREET *Essence*

ISBN 13: 978-1-9384429-1-9
ISBN 10: 1938442911
LCCN: 2013945547

Join us on our social networks
G Street Chronicles Fan Page
G Street Chronicles CEO Exclusive Readers Group

Follow us on Twitter
@GStreetChronicl

DERANGED
Love

Dedication

This book is dedicated to my son, my parents and the memory of my late Aunt Jackie. You were the inspiration behind the character Aunt Jackie in this story. I miss you so much.

Rest in Peace,
JRS
August 18, 1946 – September 27, 2011

Acknowledgements

First and foremost, I thank God for blessing me with the wonderful gift of creative writing. Everything I write is because of Him. I'd like to thank my son for his patience, understanding and cooperation while I worked on this project. Mommy loves you, Pooh Bear! ☺ A special thanks to my husband for holding me down always. I've been blessed with the world's greatest parents who have supported me in everything I've chosen to do my entire life. Thank you so much, Momma and Daddy. I thank God for my four siblings, especially my oldest and youngest sisters. NTR & DRK, you two keep me grounded and on track. Y'all are 100% team Honey ride or die. Thank you. My manager/cousin/confidant/consultant AK is my greatest source of support. I love you, chick. You're there when no one else is. I don't know what I would do without you. Thanks for everything. I love my attorney. SDH, you rock, sistah! Very few chicks can attribute anything *good* to their brother-in-law, but I can. I have two that always have my back. Thanks guys for believing in me. Shout outs to AWC, DR, CR, CMC, TJ and THP. You guys are the screeners of the century. Thank you, Korisha. You look fabulous, sweetie. Last but not least, I must give heartfelt thanks to Mr. George Sherman Hudson and Shawna A. Your faith in me has changed my life in a very positive way *forever*. G Street Chronicles will always be a part of my life.

DERANGED Love

Chapter One

Jill rolled her round hips perfectly from left to right, slowly and seductively to the funky rhythm of the reggae classic. She looked content and full of life on top of the bar, wiggling her tiny, curvaceous body with the smoothness of a ribbon floating in the wind. Tipsy from too much rum punch, she giggled and lifted her hands high above her head while sweat trickled down her milk chocolate face and on to her neck. It was apparent to all who saw her that Jill was braless as her dark, hardened nipples pushed against the white, cotton fabric of her tank top. Just about every brother in the crowded nightclub was mesmerized by her raw beauty and fluid moves, but Jill only had eyes for *Jay*. Fighting a growing erection with a healthy dose of strong, coconut-flavored Jamaican rum, and dwindling physical restraint, Zach closed his eyes and listened to Bob Marley's warning. He knew from experience it was nothing but the truth.

"*No woman, no cry!*" The late, reggae legend belted out over the drone of loud voices, foot stomping and hand claps.

"A lucky son of a bitch," Zach mumbled into his drink, now feeling the buzz from the alcohol. Jay was just *that*, lucky as hell. Jill was sweet, sexy and passionate. She loved hard and without limits. But she was young; innocent too and unaware of her real worth. And that's exactly how Jay wanted to keep her.

Jill was a trophy, a mere possession, a *kept* woman. She had been trained, tamed and molded by Jay to near perfection. The twenty-three-year-old girl from the rough streets of Kingston had been handpicked to satisfy Jay's every physical and emotional need. And she was *supposed* to help erase the memories of Venus back home in Atlanta, and the heartbreak she had caused.

The crowd roared when Jill hopped off the bar and did a shimmy in the middle of the floor. Her denim miniskirt had crawled high above her well-toned thighs, almost revealing her *diamond*. Jay's loose and cocky lips had bragged on countless occasions to Zach that nestled between Jill's thighs was the pussy that no other human being on earth had every touched, tasted or entered before they'd met. It should've been an honor, but to Jay it was more like a right or an entitlement; an achievement even.

The screams and applause swelled, and Zach looked up in time to see Jill gyrating in slow motion in the direction of the table he'd been sharing with Jay earlier. She had a mysterious glint in her eyes, and her smile was too damn sexy.

Jill drew closer, and began to curl her index finger at Zach, begging him to join her in a dance.

"Who me?" he asked, looking around. "Nah, baby, Zach has had one too many. Where is *Jay*?"

Jill tugged Zach's arm, and he pressed his tall, muscular frame firmly in the chair and refused to move. He shook his head, embarrassed that every eye in the club was now on him. The faces of jealous men who wished they were him, combined with the loud claps and cheers, made Zach want to spit and curse. Before he could jump up and run away to safety, Jill straddled him and began a slow grind on his crotch. The bulge in his pants met her wet core with only the denim fabric of his shorts separating them. Jill did not wear panties. That was another tidbit Jay often boasted about. Zach could smell the sweetness of her feminine center and it intensified his high.

Jay slid back inside the club after a stroll with some busty chick sporting a head full of blonde micro braids. Standing at the entrance, enjoying Jill's little show, Jay laughed and clapped along with the rest of the club patrons, fully aroused. Zach panicked when he noticed his younger sibling watching his public lap dance from Jill. Jay gave him the okay signal with a flimsy wave of the hand, and cheered and howled along with everyone else. Zach was relieved when the song ended and Jill eased from his lap to another eruption of applause and hoots.

"Did you enjoy yourself, big bro?" Jay asked and took a seat. She pulled Jill onto her lap, and rubbed her smooth, sweaty thighs.

"It was fun, I guess. Where did you go? I think that dance was meant for *you*." Zach wiped the perspiration from his face with his palm and willed his throbbing dick to soften.

"I had to make a phone call, check on a problem at the resort."

Jill smiled and kissed Jay on her lips. "I want to dance, Jay. I want to dance!" She stood and raised her arms in the air and rotated her hips provocatively.

Jay smacked Jill's tight, round ass playfully as her eyes swept around the club. It was a good night for their friend Desmond, the owner of the popular establishment, Caribbean Cove. It was standing room only, and there was a long, curving line of folks outside hoping to get in. Jay spotted dozens of attractive women, mostly visitors to the island, dancing and flirting with men for drinks. Her eyes fell on Charlotte, a woman she spent time with every once in a while. She was sitting at a table alone in a dark corner of the club smoking a brown label cigarette. Jay licked her lips when Charlotte leaned forward and exposed her ample cleavage spilling over the low neckline of her red, strapless top.

"Jay, I want to dance, baby," Jill whined.

"Zach, will you *please* dance with her? I need to call the resort again. I can't hear a damn thing in here. I'm gonna go in Desmond's office. I'll be right back."

Once again Jay left Zach and Jill alone while she went on a kitty cat call. It was just her lustful nature. Jayla Simone King loved women and she always had as far back as Zach could remember. Despite their five-year age difference, the King siblings had grown up very close. Zach had realized very early on that there was something unique about his little sister and how she interacted with other females. As beautiful as Jay had been as a young girl, she'd never fully embraced the significance or advantages of it. She'd much rather admire Zach's girlfriends or the gorgeous models and entertainers she saw on television.

By the time she hit puberty, feeling the painful absence of their mother, Jay confided in Zach that she was a lesbian with a healthy sexual appetite. He'd kept that secret, not knowing exactly what to do with it other than hide it in the far recesses of his young mind. He'd hoped she would somehow outgrow what he thought was an experimental phase. It threw their Aunt Jackie for a loop when Jay marched into the house one evening after cheerleading practice and announced she was gay and proud of it. The heartbroken woman couldn't understand how a girl so gorgeous and shapely could desire the affections of another girl. Of course, since then she'd learned it had nothing to do with the way you looked, how you were raised, or where you came from. It was a matter of the heart, and Aunt Jackie had ultimately accepted that and loved Jay more than life.

Jill's subtle tug on Zach's arm snatched him from the past just as he watched Jay disappear behind Desmond's closed office door with some voluptuous redbone.

"Dance with me, Zachary," he heard her say in her rich, singsong, Jamaican accent.

Zach did not want to dance with Jill. He didn't even want to be close to her. She was Jay's lover, and the physical attraction he had for her was *taboo*. The more time they spent together, the stronger and more overwhelming his attraction became. Since Zach had been in Montego Bay on vacation, he had been forced to spend the majority of his time with Jill while Jay worked as the executive manager of the luxurious Island Paradise Resort. Often times she *pretended* to work while really chasing skirts.

Refusing to be ignored, Jill slithered her body between the table and the chair Zach occupied, and wiggled her hips before him as if she dared him to take her. When she lifted her leg to straddle him again, he stood to his full six-foot-two-inch stature. His rigidness pressed against her softness. The torture of the contact caused Zach's breathing to become labored and choppy. He placed his arm loosely around Jill's waist and led her out onto the jam-packed dance floor.

* * * * *

"Wake up, party animal!" Jay hit Zach softly over the head with a pillow. "You danced to the wee hours of the morning. I've *never* known you to do that."

Zach rolled over in the bed and peered at Jay with one eye then drew the covers over his head. He was tired. He and Jill had danced to song after song waiting on Jay to complete her *business* inside Desmond's office. She must have been in there with the buxom, high-yellow chick for two hours before she emerged secretively and gave her a ride home in her black BMW 528i. By the time Jay got back to Caribbean Cove, Zach was exhausted, but Jill was still bouncing off the walls with the energy of a young child.

"Get up, Zach! I have two important meetings today." Jay looked at her gold, Movado watch. "Jill needs to go to Kingston to check on her little brother. He's been acting out in school. I never let her go there alone. Her family is a pack of hungry vultures. I want you to make the trip across the terrain with her. Roy, one of the resort's drivers will take you."

"Jill is an adult, Jay. She doesn't need a chaperone. She's going home to spend time with her family. Why do you want *me* to tag along?"

Jay sat on the bed and snatched the covers from Zach's head. He looked into her pretty face which was set in a hard expression. Everyone said she looked like Jada Pinkett Smith. He admired her flawless, caramel complexion which was exactly like his, and waited for her spiel. Whatever Jay was about to say was serious. Zach knew that by the flash in her eyes and the way she'd pursed her pouty lips.

"Zach, those people wanna suck me dry. They think I'm a wealthy American. They see the way Jill dresses, how well she lives and speaks. She gives her mother money for her siblings every month, but they always want more. They frown on our relationship, but their greedy hands want my *damn money*! Go with her for me. Make sure they don't get inside her head or my bank account. Will you?"

Chapter Two

On the bumpy ride to Kingston, Jill talked nonstop about her brothers and baby sister. In between tales of her family, whom she spoke affectionately of, she pointed out the amazing sights of her country. Zach loved the way her dark brown eyes twinkled whenever she laughed. She had a dazzling smile that was infectious. Her short natural afro accentuated her high cheekbones. Jill had the face and body of a model. Back home in the States she could easily be the next Iman or Alek Wek, Zach thought.

"Jillian! Jillian! Jillian!" A shirtless little boy in green tattered shorts shouted when the dusty blue Jeep Wrangler rolled to a halt in front of the small wooden house.

To Zach, the kid appeared to be around the same age as Nahima. A few chickens clucked and scattered about the yard and a skinny dog barked and ran in circles.

"Come," Jill said to Zach. "This is my family's home."

Zach's eyes wandered over to the rickety screened door in desperate need of repair. There stood a woman who looked like a heavier, more mature version of Jill. She was holding a baby in her arms. Zach exited the SUV and was met by the dry, scorching heat of the sun. Baskets, boxes, and crates along with an overflowing trash can, cluttered the unbalanced porch. Jill trotted up the few wobbly wooden steps with a great big smile on her face. The woman behind the screen door maintained an unreadable expression. The little boy hugged Jill around her legs and waved shyly to Zach.

"Mommy, how are you?" Jill asked and pulled the door handle. "It's so good to see you." She hugged her mother and kissed the baby in her arms on her tiny face. "Meet my friend, Zachary."

The woman smiled at Zach, displaying the decaying remains of a once lovely smile. "Hello Zachary. I am Faye. Welcome to my home."

"It's a pleasure to meet you, Ms. Faye." Zach shook her hand.

Jill followed her mother into the house with Zach close behind her. The whir of a space fan blowing in the window sill of the sitting room was loud but useless. It did nothing to cool the dim room filled with pictures of little boys in school uniforms on every wall and table. Jill sat on the yellow vinyl sofa draped with dingy, white, crocheted dollies and Zach joined her. There was an imposing picture of Jesus Christ on the wall opposite the sofa. Underneath it was a picture of Bob

Marley and one of Harry Belafonte, two of Jamaica's most famous native sons.

Faye smiled at her daughter and her male friend. "I'll get ya something cool to drink. You like ginger beer, eh?"

"Yes, ma'am, ginger beer will be fine," Zach said.

The screen door opened and shut three times, and the pounding of a few pairs of children's feet filled the house along with shouts and laughter.

"Jillian! So good to see you!"

"It's Jilly!"

"Jillian is home!"

One by one, a trio of little boys dressed in navy blue and white school uniforms ran into the room showering Jill with hugs. She squeezed them and held them close with tears threatening to spill from her eyes. Zach watched the warm exchange between Jill and her little brothers. Faye returned with two peanut butter jars filled with ice and a pale yellow liquid. She handed one to Zach and the other to Jill.

"Shoo now," Faye said. "On to your lessons right away. Oliver, *you* stay here. You must sit and speak with Jillian and Mr. Zachary. He is your sister's friend."

"Tell me, Oliver. Why are you so troublesome at school, eh?" Jill asked as soon as her mother left the sitting room.

"I'm vexed, Jilly, so very vexed!" The boy dropped down onto a chair across from his sister.

"And why so, Oliver, eh?"

Jill and Zach listened to Oliver tell them how he can't see the blackboard very well at school. He said the words in his books and test tablets appeared blurred and jumbled. He told Jill that he had reported his poor eyesight to his mother, teacher and headmaster many times, but none of them seemed to have believed him.

Zach looked at Jill. "I'd like to speak with your mother if that's okay."

"Go, Oliver. Bring Mommy to me."

Zach stood and removed his wallet from his back pants pocket. "Ms. Faye," he said when she entered the room. "There is a clinic here. It's called the Johnson Medical Center. I'd like you to take Oliver there. He needs to see a doctor about his eyes. He can't see well. I think he may need glasses." Zach held out several American bills to her. "This should cover the cost. If it isn't enough, please call Jill immediately and she will contact me. I'll send you the balance."

"No," Faye said and folded her arms across her chest. "You are *stranger*. Me no take money from strangers. It is not proper."

"He is my *friend*, Mommy. He wants to help you." Jill approached her mother. "Please, take it. Oliver needs to see a doctor. I will pay Zachary back for you, eh?"

Faye pointed her finger at Jill. "You must repay him, Jillian and I will help you." She took the money from Zach's hand. "Thank you, Zachary. You are a fine man. God bless you."

Chapter Three

On the ride back to Montego Bay, Jill slept most of the way with her head resting on Zach's shoulder. He wrapped his arm around her and her face fell onto his chest. He listened to her breathe lightly with a slight whistle each time she exhaled. Zach thought back to what Jay had told him about Jill's family that morning and the warning she had given him about them begging for money. Neither Faye nor her children had asked Jill for a dime, but she had voluntarily given them all a few dollars and they'd thanked her. The three hundred dollars he had given toward Oliver's doctor's visit had come from his heart. The Bessette family seemed nothing like the greedy ingrates Jay had described.

"We're home, Jill," Zach whispered.

Her eyelids fluttered open and she moved toward the open door where Roy stood waiting for them to exit the vehicle. As they walked toward the building, Zach looked around the grounds of the posh resort he'd enjoyed for the past few days. He'd grown accustomed to the flowing fountains and flashing bright lights of the casino. The rolling green lawn stretched for acres, and a colorful botanical garden was a magnificent sight. Rowland the evening shift concierge greeted Zach and Jill when they entered the elegantly decorated lobby.

"Ms. King is out for the evening," he announced. "She had an important dinner meeting with some vendors in Ocho Rios. She said you mustn't wait up for her."

"Let's go to the casino," Jill said and grabbed Zach's hand. "I have lots of complimentary chips. I never win much, but it is so much fun! I play to pass time whenever Jay has to work long hours. Let's go," Jill urged and pulled Zach's hand again.

"Nah, I'm really tired, Jill. I'm not much of a night owl. I think I overdid it at the club last night. I just wanna hit the sack tonight and catch some Z's. You go ahead. I'll hit the casino with you one night before I return home."

Jill looked disappointed, but she smiled over it. Zach got the distinct impression that her young life was filled with low moments. She adored her family, but she wasn't allowed to spend much time with them. And whenever she did, Jay was there keeping a watchful eye on their interaction. Jill only had a high school diploma despite the fact that she was very smart and could've done quite well in college. Although she was a talented dancer, her formal training on the island had been limited. She'd told Zach that she'd dreamed as a child about perfecting her dance skills at Juilliard or the San Francisco Conservatory of Dance. And one day she'd hoped to join the Alvin Ailey Dance Company.

"Okay," Jill whispered, trying to hide her disappointment. "We will go to the casino another time. Are you hungry?"

"I'm still stuffed from the lunch your mother served us. She's an excellent cook. I haven't tasted any jerk pork, and peas and rice that good anywhere else on the island. Can you cook like that?"

"Yes, I cook just like my mommy. She taught me. I cooked for my family every day when I lived at home."

Jill looked around the busy lobby. Zach knew she didn't want him to the see the sadness in her eyes. "You miss your family, don't you?"

"I miss them very much, but I talk to them a lot. Jay takes me to visit them as often as she can. She's always busy, ya know?"

"I know."

"Let's go to the penthouse and watch a movie."

Jill pulled Zach's hand much harder than he'd thought she had strength to. She led him to the private elevator at the far end of the lobby. On the long ascent to the twelfth floor she hummed and rotated her hips with a twinkle in her eyes. Zach turned to stare at the lights illuminating the numbers indicating each floor they passed as they road to their destination. The tightness in his groin crept up on him like a thief in the night. Jill was not touching him. She was on the opposite side of the elevator swaying in her own little world. His attraction to her was more intense than ever, but it wasn't just physical. Zach was drawn to her care free, fun loving spirit and pure heart.

"We're here," Jill sang when the elevator chimed and stopped. She hurried out and walked to the double doors of the executive penthouse suite with Zach dragging behind her. "I'm going to shower and order us some cheesecake. I want to watch "Pretty Woman." It is my favorite movie! Will you watch it with me?"

"Sure, why not?"

The cool breeze of the air conditioner greeted them when they entered the suite. The sitting area was bigger than the Bessette family's entire house in Kingston. Jill skipped around turning on lights as she headed to the master bedroom she shared with Jay. Zach trudged to his bedroom, not really wanting to come out again for the rest of the night. Sure, he was exhausted and sleepy from the long night of dancing at Caribbean Cove and the trip to Kingston and back, but Zach's primary reason for wanting to stay locked in his room was *Jill*. She was oblivious to the effect she had on him.

Zach genuinely cared for her. He wanted to rescue Jill and make her happy. He wanted to introduce her to a world where she could pursue her goals and dreams. Jay was keeping her in a closed box away from the people and activities she loved. Jill was a prisoner, but she didn't even realize it. She didn't long for freedom because she'd never tasted it before. Her entire existence revolved around Jay and the world she had created for them.

Zach stripped from his clothes and allowed them to fall to the floor around his feet. He went into the bathroom and turned on only the hot water in the shower and adjusted the stream to high pressure. He got inside under the pounding spray with thoughts of Jill flooding his mind. Zach reflected back to the lap dance she'd given him the night before and instantly, blood rushed to his shaft. It swelled to a thick, long rod of stone. As he relaxed in the shower he fantasized about Jill.

"Zachary," her soft voice floated through the steamy bathroom. "Would you prefer blueberry, raspberry or strawberry topping on your cheesecake?"

Suddenly, feeling self-conscious and vulnerable, Zach snapped. "You shouldn't be in here, Jill! I'll have whatever topping you're having. Leave now! I'll join you *out there* shortly."

As Zach dried his body he cursed himself for speaking so harshly to Jill. He hated whenever Jay yelled at her or blew her off. But he'd just allowed his emotions to overcome him, causing him to do the same thing. Zach snatched a white tank top from the drawer and slid into a pair of plaid pajama shorts. He rushed into the sitting area and found Jill on the sofa laughing at the movie previews before the feature film. She didn't appear upset at all for being chastised like a child. She was used to being scolded and told what to do. Kindness was foreign to her and to Zach that was a damn shame.

Chapter Four

"Are you ready? I can fast forward it if you'd like." Jill's eyes sparkled and her smile was just as bright.

Zach sat on the sofa next to her with a reasonable amount of space between them. She aimed the remote control at the DVD player and advanced the disc to the starting point of the movie. The doorbell chimed.

"I'll get it!" Jill hopped up and skipped to the door.

She wore a simple, pink, cotton dress with spaghetti straps which fell to rest at mid thigh. The silhouette of her body was clearly outlined underneath. Just like Jay had taught her, she pranced about free from undergarments. Zach heard Jill and the room service attendant exchanging pleasantries in Patois, their choppy Jamaican dialect. She seldom spoke it because Jay did not approve. He wondered what the young man had said to make her laugh so bubbly. Zach felt a twinge of jealousy and it annoyed him. He had no right to be possessive of Jay's lover, but for some unexplainable reason, the bitter green-eyed monster had sneaked into his psyche.

"Dessert is served, sir," Jill announced and rolled the small serving cart in front of Zach.

She removed the silver domed covering from a plate and reached over to hand him a fork and napkin. The sight of her perky breasts, with their chocolate drop nipples, partially blocked the screen where a hooker was chauffeuring a potential john down Hollywood Boulevard in a Lotus.

"Strawberry," Zach said and smiled. "It's my favorite. How did you know?"

"It's your favorite, eh? I honestly had no idea. It's *mine* too!" Jill lowered her voice and looked around as if she was about to divulge some classified, high security secret. "Jay absolutely *hates* strawberry, so I never order it when she's around. She loves bloody raspberry and I simply can't stand it. Strawberry topping will be our little secret." Jill flopped down on the sofa. Then she quickly turned to Zach with a conspiratorial grin on her lovely face. "I'll tell you another secret if you promise to keep it for life."

"Who would I tell, Jill?"

"You mustn't ever tell *Jay*."

Zach saw the seriousness in her eyes. The respect and *fear* Jill had for his sister was astonishing. No one person in the entire universe, other than Christ himself, should have been reverenced in such a manner. The poor girl's life was centered on Jay's. Jill lived and breathed to please her in any way she could, without limits or consideration for even her own happiness. Love and faithfulness bestowed upon any human being by another at such an immeasurable degree, in most circumstances, would be praiseworthy and inspiring; imitated even. But knowing Jay's heart and her outlook on love, life, and relationships, made it quite repulsive to Zach.

"You can tell me your secret, Jill and I won't tell Jay or anyone else. You have my word. I'll even share something deep and dark about myself with you to level the score. That way we'll each know something naughty about the other, but we'll take it to the grave." Zach held up his hand and wiggled his pinky finger. "Wanna pinky swear?" he asked smiling like a big kid.

Jill's eyes grew wide with excitement. She giggled like a giddy school girl and hooked her pinky around Zach's much larger one. His flesh tingled from her innocent touch. The contrast of their complexions was rather obvious. Her rich darkness against his smooth, pecan tan was metaphoric imagery of the sweet blending of chocolate and caramel in Zach's eyes.

"Sometimes when Jay is away on business for an extended period of time, I visit my old dance teacher at her studio. I help her instruct the young students. I've choreographed some routines for them and they've performed them at *Carnival*!" Jill swallowed a forkful of cheesecake. "Once, I bought show costumes for dancers who didn't have money to buy them. My parents sometimes couldn't afford to pay for my dance attire when I was a student, so I missed lots of performances. No little girl who's been blessed with the gift of dance should have to sit on a stoop and watch others twirl about joyfully, ya know?"

"And what about a young woman who's been blessed with that same gift?" Zach asked. "Why should *she* have to live idly in the penthouse of a five-star resort and abandon her dreams of perfecting her gift abroad? Why isn't she dancing with a prestigious dance company?"

"I…"

"Don't tell me she's got you watching "Pretty Woman." Jay had sauntered into the penthouse with an unlit cigar wedged between her index and middle fingers. "Jill, didn't I tell you not to watch that damn movie again this year?"

Jill lowered her head and discreetly placed the green cloth napkin over the remains of her barely eaten cheesecake. It wasn't lost on Zach. He realized she was hiding the strawberry topping from Jay because she wouldn't approve of her eating it. His eyes bore a hole through his sister as she walked toward them with the cigar now in her mouth. Jay lit it and blew out a cloud of smoke.

"I asked Jill what her favorite movie was, sis. She said it was "Pretty Woman" and I told her I hadn't seen it in years. *I* wanted to watch it."

"Are you thirsty, Jay?" Jill asked. "Do you need me to order you a bottle of

Disarrono?"

"Yeah, baby, please do that," Jay answered, puffing away on her Cuban cigar.

Zach stretched his long muscular arms in the air and yawned just as Jill reached for the cordless phone on the end table. He did it again with exaggeration after she'd placed the order to room service and hung up.

"This old man is about to leave you ladies. A brother is tired as hell." Zach stood and stretched one last time. "I'll see you both in the morning."

"You won't see me, bro. I have to be in Negril early for a breakfast meeting. The resort's lounge needs a new live act. Desmond told me about a band and I'm gonna go hear them. If they're any good, we'll talk business."

"Can I go with you, Jay?" Jill asked with pleading eyes.

"Um…nah, baby, that won't work. I have some more business in Negril after that and it might keep me there until after lunch. You stay here and hang out with Zach. He may get lonely."

"*No*, take Jill with you. I'll be fine. I plan to hit the gym and go to the beach for a swim. Then I'll catch a cab and do some souvenir shopping at the straw market. There're a few more things I'd like to buy Aunt Jackie and Nahima."

"Who is Nahima, Zachary? Is she your *sweetheart*? Do tell," Jill teased.

Zach and Jay's eyes met and locked in an awkward and telling moment. Tension-filled silence lingered between them as time ticked away. Zach could feel Jill's curious eyes on him while she waited for his answer to what had quickly transformed from a simple question into a million dollar one in a matter of seconds. Jay's eyes narrowed to slits and she held her brother's unshaken gaze. She dropped down casually on the loveseat across from Zach and Jill. Her jerky body language, and the visible twitch in her jaw, sent out a clear warning that the truth was not welcome in the room.

"Ah, Nahima is my…my…god daughter," Zach managed to say through his slow mounting anger. He'd spoken to Jill, but his eyes were shooting fatal daggers at Jay. "She's my heart," he added. "I'm *surprised* my sister never mentioned her to you. Remind me to show you some pictures of Nahima tomorrow. I'm going to bed. Good night, ladies."

"Remember, you won't see me until tomorrow evening, Zach," Jay spoke to his retreating back. "Jill will be here with you. I'm not taking her to Negril. But I'm gonna finish watching "Pretty Woman" with my baby tonight." Jay winked an eye at Jill and licked her lips suggestively.

"Good night, Zachary. I hope you have pleasant dreams."

"I hope you do too, Jill."

Chapter Five

Loud, passionate moans and muffled, lovers' dialogue pulled Zach from a restless sleep later that night. He knew right away it wasn't the television because he'd distinctly heard Jill say "Jay, *oooh*, Jay" several times before he became fully awake. Zach wondered why the hell Jay hadn't taken her into their bedroom to make love. Surely she knew he'd be able to hear them with his bedroom being so close to the sitting area. Jill's high pitch shriek shocked him. He hadn't expected anything like that. He was curious to know what one woman could do to another one that would make her cry out in such sexual fulfillment.

According to Jay, she'd never used the traditional strap on, or any other kind of toy for that matter, with Jill. She often bragged that she could take her, and any woman, to the stars with only the body parts she'd been born with. Jay told Zach repeatedly that if she relied on a fake dick to please her women, they could just go and fuck a man without any further thoughts of her. She claimed she had *special skills* to satisfy her lovers to the extent that any brother would find it hard to compete with her on a sexual level. Zach would never believe that because if it was so, Jay would still be with Venus, the love of her life. Venus had broken his sister's heart by leaving her after a four-year relationship; abandoning gay life to return to heterosexuality. Venus was now raising Nahima with her fiancé Charles, who she was scheduled to marry early next year.

"Mmm, mmm, Jay! Ah! Ooh!" Zach heard Jill yell from the other side of the wall.

He flipped over onto his stomach and covered his head with the covers. No brother wanted to hear to his sister and her partner making mad, passionate love; especially if that brother had an acute fondness and covert sexual attraction for said lover. As Jill's moans and cries of satisfaction heightened, Zach berated himself for fantasizing about the sights and sounds they could make together if her heart didn't belong to Jay. He made a sincere effort to steer his mind away from that forbidden, erotic, apparition, but Jill's moans of pleasure held his mind, body and soul prisoner. His lustful member betrayed him, adding to the physical and mental torment. Zach rolled onto his back with an enormous erection that lifted the cool crisp sheet away from his body. A severe case of inquisitiveness combined with sexual frustration yanked him from the queen size, four post bed before his capacity for better judgment could protest.

Honey

Zach wasn't sure if his heart was still beating or not when his eyes caressed Jill's naked body through the crack of his bedroom door. He tiptoed a few inches outside his room for a better view. The muted television in the sitting area provided sufficient light for him to see her exquisite profile from the right. There she stood, with a wide open leg stance over Jay, who was on her knees devouring her like a sweet and delectable fruit. Jill thrust her hips forward in rapid succession as if she were dancing to the beat of an African drum. Jay squeezed and massaged her tight, round bottom, and in response, she twisted her fingers in the soft, jet-black curls covering Jay's head. On the brink of a powerful climax, Jill lifted her hands from the curly locks and fondled her fully erect, dark nipples frantically. She threw her head back and screamed out her explosive release, causing Zach to convulse and spill warm seed down his thighs and legs. He ducked back inside his bedroom breathlessly and closed the door, unable to recall the moment his hand had slid underneath the waistband of his shorts.

* * * * *

"Where are you going so early, Zachary?"

"I'm on my way to the straw market to do some shopping," he answered with his back to Jill. "I thought you were still asleep. I didn't wanna disturb you. I'll be back around noon. We'll have lunch at the deli you like downstairs. And we'll order cheesecake and our secret topping."

Zach's hand gripped the door knob tighter, hoping the conversation was over. He refused to turn around to face Jill out of fear that she would be able to read the raw emotion in his eyes. In his mind, he had made love to her last night, and because she had not granted him permission to do so, it had been diminished to rape. Zach was ashamed and disturbed by the entire secret act. He didn't hear Jill's soft footsteps in the plush carpet, and it was impossible to see her while facing the door. The ginger and lilac scented body gel and oil she wore daily alerted him that she was near.

"Enjoy the shopping, Zachary," she said and placed her hand on his shoulder. "I'll meet you in the deli at noon."

The feel of Jill's hand continued to burn an imprint in Zach's flesh hours after he'd left the penthouse. As Riley, the cab driver, sped over the hilly, winding roads, his shoulder tingled with visions of Jill assaulting his thoughts. *What is it about that young, naïve girl that has captured your five senses, heart and loins?* Zach's macho male ego asked. And he pondered the question, even as he bartered and flirted with the wise and sassy old women at the straw mart for deals on his souvenir purchases.

"Where ya wanna go now, mon?" Riley, the friendly cabbie, asked Zach after he eased into the back seat of the car. He peered at his passenger's face through the rearview mirror and waited for instructions.

"Take me back to the resort, Riley," Zach said, noticing the time on his white gold Cartier watch. "I have a lunch date with a special friend that I gotta keep."

* * * * *

Zach spotted Jill immediately when he entered the swarming deli. She was sitting, sipping lemonade and watching the many faces in the bustling lunch crowd. Dozens of people were laughing and talking over their midday meals.

"I'm sorry I'm late," Zach apologized, sliding onto the bench inside the booth opposite Jill.

Her eyes lit up and she smiled that smile that made his heart skip a beat. "It's okay. I came early anyway. I was so bloody bored in the penthouse. I wrote my father a letter and organized Jay's clothes and shoes in her closet. Then I went to the pool to people watch.

"How would you prefer to spend your time? Isn't there something else you'd rather be doing with your life besides taking care of Jay?"

"Mmm," Jill moaned, obviously rolling the question around in her head. "I wish I had an important job such as a teacher or business owner like Desmond. Maybe I could become a nurse like you. What's it like, Zachary, taking care of sick children and saving their lives?"

"It's very rewarding. When you meet a child who's close to death, and you and your team make them well again, there's no greater feeling. You know that your life has a wonderful purpose."

Zach witnessed the impact his words had on Jill right away. He hadn't meant to make her feel small or worthless, but he clearly had. Her eyes revealed it. Zach regretted his last statement, and he wished he could take it back. But Jill had asked him his feelings about the profession he had loved and cherished for over a decade now, and he had only told her the truth. It was unfortunate that his words had somehow stung her fragile feelings.

"I've not yet found my purpose," Jill explained. "Jay says I'm still young and have lots of time to decide what I'd like to do with my life."

"I think you should go to school, Jill. You're smart, ambitious and well spoken. I honestly believe you'd do well in any field you choose to study. I think you'd do *exceptionally* well if you concentrated on what you love most. You were born to dance Jillian Bessette."

"My mommy has said that since I was a little girl, but she and Papa could not afford to send me away to New York or Paris or London to be formally trained. It is *very* expensive, Zachary."

The server came to take their orders. Jill wasn't used to having the liberty of selecting her meals in public. Jay usually ordered for both of them. Zach waited patiently while she carefully perused the menu. The young, attractive, female server tossed her long braids over her shoulder flirtatiously and smiled at him.

Jill finally settled on a grilled chicken sandwich on wheat bread with a side order of potato salad. Zach's king size appetite called for a twelve-inch Mediterranean sub, vinegar and garlic potato wedges and pasta salad.

"Could you please put our dessert orders in as well? We'll both have cheesecake with strawberry topping."

"We'd like *lots* of strawberry topping," Jill added and giggled hysterically.

Zach couldn't help but join in on her silly laughing fit. He shook his head, thinking just how often she made him laugh without even trying. There was something about her bubbly personality that stole his heart and gave him permission to throw caution to the wind. Jill was a woman, physically and intellectually so, but her childlike spirit and generous heart allowed you to glimpse inside her soul. She was an unassuming and compassionate woman, one with an abundance of love to give even to those who didn't deserve it. That was the best way Zach could describe her. She was as close to perfection as any human being could ever be.

His countenance became serious without warning and he gazed deeply into Jill's enchanting eyes. "You didn't *fully* answer my question. If you could wave a magic wand and change your life to do *anything* you wanted, what would you be doing every day?"

"I'd be in school somewhere in the United States studying dance and I would teach little girls how to dance too. With the money I earned, I would help take care of my parents and siblings." Jill closed her eyes and paused. "I would have some *babies*! Two or three little boys and perhaps a girl too, is what I'd like. And I would love them plenty and give them the world." She opened her eyes and found Zach staring at her with a mystifying look.

"You wanna have *children*? I never would've guessed it. How...I mean... you can't...Jay..."

"I know, but you asked me if I had a magic wand, what I would do. I've told you, Zachary. You didn't say it had to make sense."

The server came with their food and they ate in comfortable silence. Jill seemed totally detached from their earlier conversation. It baffled Zach how she had mastered the technique of separating reality from fantasy without a smidgen of regret or longing. She embraced her unfulfilled life and functioned, day in and day out, like it was a perfect existence. In actuality, it was anything but what she desired or dreamed of. Jay had somehow convinced Jill that *she* had been brought into her life as a suitable replacement for all the ambitions, hopes and dreams she'd once had. If Zach didn't know better, he would swear his sister really did have a magic wand, and had cast a wicked spell on Jill that made her hopelessly loyal to her and her selfish agenda.

"You're absolutely right, Jill. It doesn't make sense," Zach finally said. He pressed forward cautiously with the best of intentions, hoping not to offend her again. "You wanna be a professional dancer and instructor, yet you've abandoned those dreams without ever making any attempt to make them come true. You've told me you'd like to have children someday, but you're in a relationship that makes that impossible. Are you gonna throw that aspiration away too? Will you be content with being a domestic partner to Jay for the rest of your life without experiencing the joy of motherhood?"

"Jay says we'll adopt children. There are lots of little ones around the world who are in need of a loving home. Jay and I can give them that."

Zach reached for his dessert and began to eat it slowly. He knew Jay's adoption promise was a big lie. His sister didn't want children. Venus could most definitely attest to that. Jay had only told Jill they would become adoptive parents to appease her. There was nothing Zach could say that would open Jill's eyes without exposing his sister for the cold, calculating master of deception she was. He also didn't have the heart to hurt her with the truth either. His compassion for Jill increased tremendously because he knew within time she would have to face some harsh realities about her life with Jay. A day would come when she would realize how steep a price she was paying to be with her.

"Well, I hope your every dream will come true, Jill. You're a very special young lady, and you deserve a wonderful life filled with many blessings and happiness." Zach removed his wallet from his back pants pocket. He opened it and handed it to Jill. "That's Nahima. She'll be five years old in November."

"Wow, Zachary! She is very beautiful. Her skin is flawless. You and her share the same complexion, ya know? And her smile is just like yours too. This child could be mistaken for your daughter."

Zach closed his eyes and ordered his racing heart to slow down. Jill had keen perception. She was much smarter than Jay gave her credit for. She had picked up on his and Nahima's similar facial features in a matter of seconds. A little girl that pretty and adorable was way too precious to be kept a secret. *Damn you, Jay!* Zach wanted to scream.

"She's just like my daughter. We spend a lot of time together and she loves me like there is no tomorrow. I'd rather take Nahima to Chuck E. Cheese's for the evening than go on a romantic weekend getaway with Tyra Banks."

Jill lifted her eyes from the picture and shot Zach a confused look. "I know who Tyra Banks is, but who is this Chucky person? Is she a model as well?"

Zach cracked up and Jill stared at him as if he had lost his mind. Several diners in the deli were watching them. Zach's outburst had obviously embarrassed Jill.

"Zachary, please stop laughing at once," she whispered. "People are staring at us."

"I'm sorry, Jill. *Chuck E.* isn't a person. He's a giant *mouse* actually."

"So you'd prefer taking your god daughter to see a rodent instead of making love to Tyra Banks? Zachary, that is *absurd.*"

"Listen, Chuck E. is not a real mouse. He's this *character* at a popular fun place for children in America. They go there to play games and enjoy music and puppet shows. There are rides, games and food there that kids love. Sometimes I take Nahima there on a Saturday afternoon and we stay until the place closes."

"Whenever Jay and I visit you in Atlanta, you must take me there. I will go with you and Nahima to meet this Chucky mouse."

Chapter Six

Jill cried the entire cab ride to Sangster International Airport. She had insisted that she give Zach a proper sendoff since Jay was unable to. There had been a shipping mishap with one of the resort's major suppliers that required Jay's immediate attention. Zach had told Jay that he understood and would be fine going to the airport alone, but Jill would not consider it. Now she was in the back seat of Roy's van from the resort with her head resting on Zach's shoulder bawling. His heart was heavy too and he felt like crying himself, but like his other newfound feelings for Jill, he suppressed the sadness. When she reached over thoughtlessly and rubbed his chest, his heartbeat accelerated three times its normal rhythm. If only Jill was aware of the physical and emotional affect she had on him.

When the van came to a stop in front of the United Airlines curbside terminal, Roy exited the van and gathered Zach's luggage. Jill began to whimper louder and more pitifully. She tightened her hold on his body and kissed him softly on his cheek and neck repeatedly. Zach sat completely still, unable to move. He didn't know whether to stop Jill because the way she made him feel was wrong, or to allow her to continue because it felt so right. The defining moment came when she covered his lips with hers and smacked once, twice, and then again. Defenseless and weak, Zach was a hot second away from slipping his tongue inside Jill's mouth, but thank God for Roy. He pounded on the window and tapped the face of his watch with his finger.

"I have to go, Jill," Zach whispered. "I don't wanna miss my flight."

He eased out of her clutches and stared down into her gorgeous, tear-streaked face. She caused Zach's blood to simmer even as she cried. He wanted to comfort her and tell her everything would be okay, but he knew better. She would never have the kind of life she deserved as long as she was with Jay. Zach wished, above all things, that he could take Jill home to Atlanta with him and introduce her to his world. He could make her happy, and give her the desires of her heart.

"I'm going to miss you, Zachary," Jill cried. "I'll be so lonely without you. Please promise that you'll come again soon."

"I'll try, but I can't promise you anything. Maybe you and Jay could come to Atlanta for Christmas. Aunt Jackie would love that."

Jill nodded her head with tears in her eyes and watched Zach exit the van and walk away. She broke down as Roy sped off, taking her back to the cold, lonely world of the resort and her uneventful life with Jay.

* * * * *

"So how was your trip, dude? Did you meet any hot honeys? Did you get some *Jamaican trim*?"

Zach laughed at his best friend Dex and rolled his eyes to the roof of Dex's Ford Explorer. "I went to visit my sister, man and get some R and R. I wasn't on the prowl, but there are some beautiful sisters in Jamaica, *mon!*"

Dex took his eyes off the road for a few seconds and looked as his boy. He and Zach had been best friends since their days at Florida A & M University. They'd met as freshman in Gibbs Hall, having never crossed paths in their hometown of Atlanta. They'd clicked instantly and had been thick as thieves ever since. After Zach completed the nursing program, and Dex became a licensed respiratory therapist, they returned home and landed jobs at Grady Memorial Hospital. They were like brothers and knew each other well. That's how Dex was able to detect that something wasn't quite right with Zach.

"What's *really* up, dude? Something happened in Jamaica. Don't deny it. I know you. Please don't tell me you fell in love over there."

"Man, please!" Zach snapped. "You know your boy loves em' and leaves em' wherever he goes. Ain't *nobody* in love."

"Well, you're in *strong like*. What's her name? How good was the pussy? And what lie are you gonna tell Ayla when you have to rush back to Jamaica for a tune-up?"

"Number one, I kept my dick on ice and I don't have to tell Ayla a damn thing because it's not like that between us. We're just kicking it and I can do whatever I wanna do. You know this, Dex, and so does Ayla."

"Who is she, Zachary Sean King?"

Zach ignored Dex's inquiry. There was no way he'd ever tell him, or anyone else, that he'd fallen hard for his sister's lover. He'd had a difficult enough time admitting it to himself. Things like that weren't supposed to happen. It was a cardinal rule. You were to never fool around with a broad who had smashed a family member or a friend. That was the law in the hood. White folks did that stupid shit all the time, but black folks didn't get down like that.

"Who is she?" Dex asked again with a little impatience in his voice.

"I didn't meet anybody. I'm just tired and it feels like I may be coming down with something." Zach removed his cell phone from his carry-on bag and smiled mischievously. "Ain't nothing wrong with me that a buck wild ride in the sack with Ayla can't cure."

* * * * *

"Wow! Somebody missed *me*," Ayla purred naughtily and collapsed from a high perched, straddling position on top of Zach. She rested on him evenly.

Zach had not missed her at all. He missed *Jill* and he had thought of her every minute he'd been fucking Ayla's brains out. All of his energetic, expert moves had been inspired by his secret Jamaican sweetheart. Zach had done to Ayla what he wished he could do to Jill. The good loving he had just put on her was compliments of Jillian Bessette. He almost cracked up when he thought about sending Ayla a bill for services rendered on Jill's behalf.

Zach rolled onto his right side, lowering Ayla to the bed to face him. He could feel her gaze on him even in the thick darkness. Zach closed his eyes with no desire to talk or cuddle. He wanted to fall into a deep sleep so his mind could whisk him away to the fantasy land reserved for him and Jill.

"How was Jamaica?"

"Fun and relaxing," Zach replied softly.

"What did you do over there?"

"I got plenty of much needed rest, ate delicious Caribbean cuisine, swam and toured the island."

"Mmm," Ayla hummed. "Next time you'll have to take me with you."

That will never happen, Zach thought as he tried with all his will to drift off to sleep. One thing he'd learned very early as a young, handsome, smart teenager: never take sand to the beach. And in Jamaica there was an abundance of sand. There were stunning native women and globs of pretty female tourists roaming about the tropical island looking for a good time. Zach had had every intention of giving a select few of those sistahs a hell of a good time during his ten-day vacation. But from the moment he laid eyes on Jill, and became spellbound by her passionate presence, his plans to chase and conquer crashed.

Ayla had big nerve to suggest they take a trip together anywhere anyway. Their fourteen-month friendship, bed buddy situation, or however she chose to classify it, had been established with no strings attached. Sure, they made the occasional public appearance and their respective sets of friends, family members and coworkers knew they were linked in some way, but not once had Zach ever indicated that they were exclusive, or an item. Ayla knew damn well he wasn't ready to settle down with her or any other chick. She and Zach had met at the disastrous ending of the two-year relationship with his ex, Tara. She'd called it quits when she finally realized marriage was not a part of his agenda in the near future. Zach had cared deeply for Tara, and she could have easily become his wife if she'd been willing to hang around for another five to seven years. She wasn't.

Ayla entered the scene right after that, and eased her way into Zach's life and his bed as merely a rebound. The cute and well-stacked neonatal resident had drawn lots of attention from male medical professionals all around Grady Hospital. None of them had made her juices flow. When the five-foot-six redbone with curly, sandy brown hair and doe-shaped eyes met the handsome male nurse who could hold a premature infant in the palm of his hand, she was *done*. You could've stuck a fork into the lovely Doctor Ayla Fitzpatrick and served her on a plate. At the end of their first date, she nearly sucked Zach's brains down through Mr. Wonderful, his *dick,* inside his Plymouth Prowler. She proceeded to mount him, wearing leopard print, *Wicked Temptations*, crotchless panties. The sistah had every intention of riding him like a rodeo queen until the cows came home. It took lightning speed, Herculean strength, and magician's hands, all motivated by the fear of an unwanted pregnancy or worse for Zach to protect himself. He thanked his lucky stars for the single condom he'd conveniently stashed in his glove compartment. That night in the parking lot of Ayla's gated townhouse community sealed the deal on their fourteen-month liaison and all the perks that came along with it.

Zach enjoyed Ayla's company and the sex was *bananas*! She was a decent cook for the most part, as long you didn't request anything fancy. And her hectic work hours made it less complicated for Zach to do his thing whenever he felt like it with whomever he chose to do it with. Although Ayla was high maintenance, she had her own money and resources. Basically, Zach was content with their arrangement and didn't see the need to change a damn thing. Ayla knew their situation was casual and she seemed okay with it. Most important of all, they'd agreed at the very beginning of their association that marriage would not be the end result, and Zach constantly reminded Ayla of that at least once a month.

DERANGED Love

Chapter Seven

"Uncle Z! Uncle Z! Uncle Z!" Nahima shouted and ran toward Zach with outstretched arms. "I missed you!"

Zach scooped her up and spun her around, and like always, she laughed and squealed. "I missed you too, pumpkin. Who is Uncle Z's favorite girl?"

"I am!"

"Who has the key to Uncle Z's heart?"

"I do and it's right here," Nahima said, reaching for the key-shaped diamond pendant Zach had given her when she turned a year old. She held it up and smiled.

Zach fingered it with care and gently nuzzled Nahima's neck with his nose. She wiggled and laughed. Then he pulled one of her thick, long pony tails and she laughed even more.

Venus stood in the middle of Zach's spacious den, holding her daughter's pink overnight bag, and watched them with a smile on her face. The love they had for each other was special and it ran deep. Venus was grateful to Zach for playing such a huge role in Nahima's life. He had been the only father figure in her little world until Charles came along, and even with his involvement, Uncle Z was still her main guy.

Zach lowered Nahima to the floor. "You should go check out your room, pumpkin. There are lots of surprises on your bed. Uncle Z bought you some souvenirs from *Jamaica*, and you have a new friend from Heritage World who's been crying to meet you."

"Did you buy me Imani or Timia?"

Nahima's smile and wide, curious eyes made Zach's heart do a flip. He loved her like she was his very own. "Go and see for yourself," he said and swatted her playfully on the bottom.

Nahima tore off down the hallway toward her "Princess and the Frog" inspired bedroom, leaving Zach and Venus alone. He motioned for her to sit with him on the brown Italian leather sofa. Their relationship could have been awkward and forced, but it wasn't. Whatever had gone down between Venus and Jay had not involved Zach whatsoever. It wasn't until Nahima was born that he rowed into the flow and he'd had every right to do so. Since then, he had committed his life to the little girl with no intentions of ever turning back.

"How are you, Venus?"

"I'm well. How are you?"

"I have no complaints."

"How is Jay?"

"My sister is fine. I enjoyed my visit with her. The resort she manages is off the chart!"

Venus touched Zach's thigh and searched his eyes. "Did she even ask about Nahima?"

This was a sensitive subject for all who were involved. It had been that way since the day Nahima entered the world. It was all Jay's fault and Zach would forever hold her responsible for the mess she'd made and left behind.

"Um…*no,* she didn't. I showed her some new pictures and gave her the framed one you sent for her desk. She placed it in a drawer and kept right on doing whatever she was doing. That's Jay, Venus. You know her better than anyone. You can't share four years of your life with someone and not learn who they really are."

"Did you tell her about Charles and me? Does she know we're getting married?"

"I couldn't come up with one reason why she needed to know. It's been four years, Venus. You don't owe Jay anything. I appreciate you trying to keep her in the loop, but the truth is my sister isn't interested whatsoever. She's still bitter although she'll never admit it."

"I did love her, Zach. I want you to know that. I never meant to break her heart. I hope Jay will forgive me someday and find happiness. There's a woman out there somewhere who will love her the way she wants to be loved, and who's willing to live by her rules."

Zach wanted to tell Venus about Jay and Jill, but for what? He asked himself. Their lopsided relationship wasn't worth mentioning. It was one hot mess as far as Zach was concerned. Jay couldn't be faithful to Jill if her life depended on it. Six months from now, he wouldn't be surprised if he got a call from his sister talking about her new woman. That thought bothered Zach because it would crush Jill. She had given up everything to be with Jay and would be left with nothing in the end.

"Mommy, look at my brand new baby doll! Uncle Z bought me Timia! Isn't she *pretty*?" An excited Nahima came bouncing into the room with the latest addition to her Heritage World doll collection. Zach had bought her very first one for her second birthday. Since then, he'd given her a grand total of eleven, out of the thirty, expensive brown dolls created especially for little girls of color.

Venus removed the doll from Nahima's hands and examined her closely. "She sure is pretty, sweetie. What should you say to your uncle?"

Nahima hopped on Zach's lap and threw her short arms around his neck. "Thank you, Uncle Z for my new baby doll! I love you *sooo* much." She placed a tender kiss on his face. Then she filled her cheeks with air and blew it out all over the right side of his face. "That's a bubble kiss! Did you like it, Uncle Z?"

Zach smiled and pinched Nahima's cute nose that bore a striking resemblance to his own. He gave her two bubble kisses, one on each cheek and she chuckled and screamed.

"I loved your bubble kiss. Did you like both of mine?"

"Yeah!" she shrieked. "Do it again."

* * * * *

A few mornings later, an early telephone call yanked Zach from a peaceful slumber. His hand roamed across the nightstand with his eyes closed against the rising sun until he found the receiver. He snatched it up quickly, hoping it wouldn't wake Nahima who was lying next to him upside down.

"Hello," Zach whispered into the mouthpiece.

"Good morning Zachary! How are you?"

He sat straight up in bed at the sound of Jill's angelic voice. Nahima did a flip onto her back and kicked Zach in his lower abdomen just inches away from his *jewels*.

"Whoa!" He drawled out and removed the tiny wayward foot. "Jill, is that you?"

"It is me. Did I call at a bad time? If you are busy I could call you later, ya know?"

"I'm not busy. I was sleeping and my bedfellow is a wild one."

"Oh…"

"It's *Nahima*, Jill. She's here with me for the next few days before I return to work. I tucked her in her bed last night and stayed in her room until she dozed off. When she got up and came in here is a mystery."

"Did I wake her too?"

"No, she's still asleep. It'll take a tornado to wake this one."

"I miss you, Zachary. Things haven't been the same since you left. I'm lonely. Jay has been in Ocho Rios for the past two days, but she may return home tonight. I wanted to go to Kingston to spend some time with my family while she's away, but…"

"But Jay said you couldn't. She doesn't want you to go there alone."

"She's going to take me to Kingston for a visit one day next week. She promised, Zachary. I spoke with my mommy and brothers on last evening. They are all fine. Oliver has his glasses, and he's doing much better in school. Edgar and Paul are playing football…I meant *soccer*. Christian is keeping Mommy very busy at home. Angelina has two new teeth and Papa will come home from the ship in three weeks. What have you been doing since you returned home, Zachary?"

Zach wanted to tell Jill he'd been thinking about her every waking moment of the day, but he knew that was inappropriate. Instead, he told her all about the activities he and Nahima had been enjoying on the final days of his twenty-one-day leave from work. Jill was in awe when Zach recapped their visit to the Georgia Aquarium and the day they'd spent at Six Flags riding every ride possible. When he mentioned their afternoon at Chuck E. Cheese's the day before, Jill asked a million questions. She wanted details and Zach obliged her.

"You and Nahima have been having lots of fun. She's a lucky little girl to have a god father like you, Zachary. I hope to meet her someday. Please give her a kiss for me."

"I'll do that. Take care of yourself, Jill and tell Jay I said hello."

Chapter Eight

Zach held Nahima's hand and strolled composedly down the center aisle of Refuge Pentecostal Temple, his lifelong house of worship. Jackie Dudley Brown, his devoted maternal aunt who had singlehandedly raised him and Jay after death and incarceration robbed them of their parents, spotted them right away. She smiled brightly from her front row seat of the soprano section in the choir stand. They waved and smiled back. Zach's relationship with the Lord was nowhere near what it should've been, but he did attend church regularly. It had been a weekly tradition when he was growing up and he continued it as an adult. He had sung in the youth choir and served on the junior usher board right up until he left for college and so had Jay. Their father, Reverend Wallace F. King, had been the pastor at Refuge Pentecostal Temple back then. He probably still would be today if it hadn't been for that unforgettable, tragic day one week after Zach's seventh birthday.

"Let the church say Amen!" Reverend Broadus shouted. "Clap your hands if you love the Lord this morning! At this time, we'll be blessed with a selection from the choir. Say Amen, church!"

Zach guided Nahima to their seats on a pew close to the front on the right side of the aisle just as the musicians ripped into an upbeat song. The little princess flopped down with her new baby doll and pink patent leather purse in tow. Zach stayed on his feet and started clapping his hands and swaying to the dynamic music along with many other worshippers. The small band, made up of an organist, keyboard player, drummer, bass guitarist and a saxophone player, was jamming. When Aunt Jackie grabbed the microphone and belted out the first line of her solo, folks instantly started dancing, jumping and shouting all over the sanctuary.

"I've got a reason to praise the Lord!" The choir answered in perfect three-part harmony to each one of Aunt Jackie's leading lyrics. She had an amazing, soul stirring voice that brought the house down Sunday after Sunday at Refuge Pentecostal Temple. Zach's face beamed with pride as he continued to clap and rock his body to the rhythm of the music. Aunt Jackie was singing her heart out to God, strutting back and forth across the pulpit. The saints were having a hallelujah good time. The V-shaped collar on Aunt Jackie's red and black choir robe had turned completely around, but she kept making a joyful noise like it might be her

last time. The audience danced and shouted to the musician's lively instrumental composition long after the choir had sat down.

* * * * *

"You don't have to serve me, Auntie. I can fix my own plate and Nahima's too. Sit down. I got this."

Zach pulled out the chair at the head of the dining room table. Aunt Jackie smoothed the lower part of her bright yellow muumuu against her thick thighs and eased her plump body down. She and Nahima watched Zach fix three plates of fried chicken, collard greens, cornbread muffins and potato salad. The overflowing plate with two breasts belonged to him. Nahima quickly pulled the one with a drumstick and no potato salad onto her placemat. Aunt Jackie loved chicken wings, no matter how you cooked them, so Zach put two on her plate with a double serving of greens.

"I'll get the tea from the refrigerator and then when we can eat," Zach said. When he returned to the table he poured the sweetened, Southern liquid delight into each glass of ice. Aunt Jackie offered a short blessing and the threesome dug into the mouth-watering meal.

"Jay called me yesterday," Aunt Jackie announced with her mouth filled with food. "She wired me some money. I'll go down to Western Union in the morning to get it. I don't understand why she insists on sending me money every month." Aunt Jackie pinned Zach in place with her eyes. "I don't know why you do it either. I can make it on my disability and Julius's pension."

"We love you, Auntie. You took us in at a time in your life when you should've been having fun without a care in the world. But instead you were strapped down with a toddler and a first grader at the age of twenty. You put your life on hold and missed out on so much because of Jay and me."

"I didn't miss nothing but my *sister*. God rest her soul. I only did for you and Jay what Belva would've done for my children if I'd had some. Your momma would've taken my babies and raised them too if I had died and left them behind. You and your sister added meaning and purpose to my life."

"You always say that, but you could've had a different life if you hadn't been stuck with us. I remember when you dropped out of nursing school and went to work at Cascade Convalescent Home. You would've made a great nurse, Auntie. Jay and I know you turned down Larry's marriage proposal because of us. He loved you with all his heart and he promised to adopt us and become our father. We heard him that night he gave you the ring."

"Oooh weee! Y'all were some nosey, sneaky children!" Aunt Jackie snapped and threw a meatless chicken bone onto her plate. "I ought to beat your behind *right now*, Zachary King. I didn't marry Larry because he wanted children of his own and I didn't. You and Jay needed all my attention, and if I'd had kids...I...I don't know how it would've affected y'all."

Zach gazed into Aunt Jackie's eyes glossed over with unshed tears. He and Jay had always wondered if she'd ever wanted to birth her own children. Now, he had finally learned the truth. Zach didn't think it was humanly possible to love and respect her any more than he already did, but at that moment his heart was about to burst. He leaned over and kissed her smooth brown cheek.

"I hope you ain't over there feeling sorry for me, boy. God blessed me with two wonderful children. Y'all may not have come from my womb, but I couldn't love you or Jay more. Larry wasn't the man I was supposed to marry. *Julius* was and we had a good life together until he passed away."

"Uncle Julius was a cool cat. I didn't get a chance to spend a lot of time with him being away at school and all, but I liked him. You two seemed so happy together. I was at peace knowing Uncle Julius was here taking care of you and Jay."

Aunt Jackie rose from her seat and started clearing the table. "Julius was sweet to me and Jay. Those few years God gave us together were amazing. I miss him terribly." She waddled into the kitchen with her ample hips swaying from side to side.

Zach removed Nahima's empty plate from her placemat and gave her a pat on her head for eating all of her food. "Good job, pumpkin. Now we can eat a slice of Aunt Jackie's pound cake with a scoop of ice cream."

"Yeah!" Nahima shouted and pumped her small fist in the air.

For the remainder of the afternoon, Zach, Aunt Jackie and Nahima relaxed in the den and watched movies on BET. They chatted and laughed during commercial breaks about weird Mrs. Taylor next door, Sister Talton's new, jet-black wig and the young gal down the street who had ten kids. Nahima soon fell asleep on the loveseat, allowing Aunt Jackie the opportunity to ask Zach something she'd been itching to from the moment they'd walked in the house.

"Did you know Jay had applied for a job here in Atlanta?"

Zach sat up from his slouching position on the sofa and rubbed his goatee thoughtfully. He shook his head.

"Well, she told me yesterday that she was interested in managing a new hotel in the convention center the city is building here near the airport. You've seen it. They're almost finished with it. It's supposed to be a multimillion-dollar complex with an auditorium, sports arena, a mini mall and dozens of restaurants. Jay wants to manage the *hotel*. You sure she didn't mention it to you while you were over there?"

"I would've told you, Auntie. I can't understand why Jay would wanna leave that gravy job in Jamaica to come back here. That's whack!" Zach frowned and shook his head.

Aunt Jackie started rocking nervously in her big burgundy recliner. "Well, I think her decision may have been influenced by something I *accidentally* slipped and said." She raked her stubby fingers through her short, salt and pepper sister locks.

"Aw man, Auntie, what did you say?"

"A few weeks ago, I told Jay that Venus was engaged. I didn't mean to, Zach. One minute we were talking about you and Nahima and then Venus's name popped up somehow."

"Why were you discussing Nahima with *Jay*? She doesn't give a damn about her!" Zach covered his lips. "Oops, I'm sorry, Auntie. I meant no disrespect. It just irks me how Jay pretends like the child doesn't even exist. Whenever I mention Nahima, she flinches."

"You know, as well as I do, that there are some painful memories for Jay surrounding that precious baby." Aunt Jackie's eyes floated over to the loveseat where Nahima lay sleeping. "I've been praying about it, and I believe one day your sister will come around."

"It's too late for that now. Nahima is almost five years old. The truth will be too much for her to handle. Jay needs to keep her ass in Jamaica and leave well enough alone. I'm sorry again, Auntie. This whole situation just brings out the worst in me."

* * * * *

On the way to Venus's house, Zach mentally hit the replay button on his conversation with Aunt Jackie. The thought that Jay was considering moving back to Atlanta was disturbing. What would it mean for Nahima? Would Jay suddenly want to play a role in her innocent life and if so, who would she tell the child she was? Zach shook his head and blew out a hard, frustrated breath. Poor Jill, he thought. She would be devastated if Jay got up one morning and announced she was moving back home.

Zach dreaded it, but he had to give Venus a heads-up. He owed her that much. Then he'd have to call Jay to see what was really going on. Nothing could be left to assumption. Zach needed to know the real deal and he could only get it from the horse's mouth. He gunned the engine of his black Mercedes GL450 and headed eastward on I-285.

* * * * *

Zach dropped the pink overnight bag on Venus's stoop and rang her doorbell. Nahima was hoisted over his shoulder limp as a ragdoll. She had slept through the entire conversation with Aunt Jackie and the ride to her house.

"Hey," Venus whispered when she opened her front door. "Look at my baby girl. She's out like a light."

"Yeah, she ate some of Aunt Jackie's good old soul food and fell asleep." Zach took in Venus's appearance. He'd always thought she was an attractive brown skin girl. Her smooth dark skin glistened against the off-white caftan she had on. Zach could hear Teddy Pendergrass in the background begging her to *turn off the lights*. "Do you have a minute?" he asked, hating to interrupt whatever plans she and Charles may have had.

Venus turned and looked inside the house. "Sure, come on in." She stepped aside and allowed Zach to enter the foyer of the stucco ranch style home. He followed her down the hallway to Nahima's bedroom.

"Is it okay for us to talk here? I wouldn't want Charles to hear our conversation. It's of a sensitive nature." Zach carefully placed Nahima on her bed and faced Venus.

"You're scaring me, Zach. What is it?" She peeked in the hallway before she closed the bedroom door. "Just spit it out."

"I have reason to believe Jay may be considering moving back to Atlanta."

Venus dropped down on the pink, lace covered bed. "Oh no," she whispered, shaking her head. "She can't be. Why the hell would she do that?"

"Don't panic. I'm not sure yet. I'm gonna give her a call as soon as I get home. I'll ask her and demand that she tell me the truth."

"Ain't nothing that damn simple with Jay. She'll string you along with a bunch of bullshit just for the hell of it. That's her style," Venus spat with anger in her voice.

"Nah, she'll tell me the truth. She *has* to. Jay knows not to run game on me when it comes to Nahima."

Chapter Nine

Zach welcomed the hustle and bustle at work that Monday morning. The fast pace helped keep his mind off the big blowup he'd had with Jay the night before. It was the worst argument they'd ever had. Jay had cut right to the chase. She admitted that she had indeed applied for a job at the Georgia Global Cultural and Exchange Center. She told Zach that she had been in negotiations with Atlanta's mayor and city council, as well as the executive board of investors, about managing the five-star, Seven Seas International Hotel. The shit hit the fan after her confession. Zach went in for the kill, provoking Jay to take off her gloves and swing back hard.

The conversation had wrecked Zach's nerves so bad that he had thought about calling in sick for the day just to cool off. But staying at home would have only made matters worse. He sat at the table in the hospital cafeteria, waiting for Dex's slow ass to come through the line so he could vent. Zach badly needed his boy's support and advice.

Dex approached the same table, in the exact same spot he and Zach had been sharing lunch together for the last nine years. Before then, they were young and stupid. They used to spend hundreds of dollars a week going out to restaurants in the area. Now, they either brought their own food from home, or used their employee discounts in the cafeteria.

"You look like shit!" Dex placed his tray on the table and took the seat opposite Zach. "What the hell is going on with you?"

"Everything is going on, man. I spoke with Jay last night. Can you believe her trifling ass is talking about moving back here to Atlanta?"

"Whoa!" Dex stretched his eyes. "For real, man?"

Zach nodded. He drained the Styrofoam cup of lukewarm, black coffee and dropped it on the table. "She claims she wants to be here to take care of Aunt Jackie and be near the rest of the family. Jay is lying, Dex. She wants to come here and stir up some shit. Aunt Jackie *mistakenly* mentioned that Venus and Charles are engaged and I'm sure you can pretty much figure out the rest."

Dex grunted and shook his head. "Your sister is a *pimp*, dog! She's gonna try to stop that wedding. I hate to say it, but she'll probably use Nahima to do it too. That's some foul shit…even for Jay. I knew she was gangsta, but *daaamn*…"

"She's so damn selfish, Dex. Jay only cares about Jay. She has the sweetest, most beautiful woman in the world who loves her to death. Her name is Jill. She's a young native from Kingston. Man, that girl is fine as hell! Jay treats her like a piece of property. Jill deserves so much better."

Dex chewed his turkey sandwich and watched Zach's eyes and body language. Talking about this Jill chick had brought out a mellow and gentlemanly side of Zach. A side that Dex hadn't seen since Zach's early days with Tara. Could his boy be in love with Jay's woman? Had he tapped that ass while he was on the Caribbean island? Dex wondered. After all, they'd been talking about Jay possibly moving back to Atlanta to turn Venus and Nahima's world upside down. Jill had nothing to do with that.

"What the hell happened between you and this *Jill* girl?" Dex cocked his head to the side and fingered the neatly trimmed beard on his chocolate-colored face.

"Nothing happened. I'm just saying she's a nice girl who happens to be in love with the wrong woman."

Dex's brows furrowed. "It's *me*," he said, slapping his chest with an open hand. "I'm your boy. I know you, Zach. Did you hit that while Jay was counting pillow cases and silverware?"

"Nah, man, I would never do that. I like Jill. We spent a lot of time together because Jay was always busy working or chasing ass. Jill and I got close. That's it."

"Yeah right," Dex mocked, sitting back in his chair. He looked Zach square in his eyes. "Did you *wanna* hit it? I know you thought about it."

"Nope, I never even thought about it. That's enough about Jill. What do you suppose I do about Jay?"

* * * * *

Venus had agreed to meet Zach at a small rib joint near the school where she taught fifth grade. Charles had promised to pick up Nahima from preschool on his way home from work to give them a chance to talk alone. Once Zach dropped the bombshell, Venus became upset, and started crying.

Zach reached his hand across the table and grasped her trembling hand in an attempt to soothe her. He couldn't remember ever seeing her more distraught. "Venus, we will get through this, but it's time to come clean. You'll have to tell Charles the whole truth. There's no getting around it now."

"He will leave me!" She shouted and snatched her hand away. "Do you know how many lies I've told him to protect my little girl? The only *honest* thing I've ever told Charles about my past with Jay is that we were lovers for four years. He didn't have a problem with that, but once he finds out everything else, he'll…oh my God…Zach…I can't lose him! I love Charles and he loves me and Nahima."

"And because he loves you, Venus, Charles will eventually understand. It may take some time, but he *will* come around and forgive you. You'll still become his wife…and you, Charles and Nahima will live happily ever after. Of course Uncle

Z will too."

Venus looked up at Zach's face. She wanted to believe him, but her heart was aching, and her mind was twisted. What he had advised her to do sounded simple, but it was very complicated.

"I never thought this day would come, Zach. I guess I was a tad bit naïve. Now we're staring reality in the face. I will tell Charles, but not until it's absolutely necessary. I'll tell him *if* Jay gets the job and is on a flight headed for Atlanta, and not a moment sooner."

* * * * *

The thought of moving to Atlanta both thrilled and frightened Jill. Jay had been talking about it for a couple of weeks now, and the more she talked, the more anxious Jill became. The idea of living in a big city overflowing with culture, history and opportunity was exciting to her. On the other hand, there was the dread of leaving her family behind. Although Jill wasn't able to spend as much time with them as she would've liked to, she was comforted by the fact that they were just across the terrain. She wasn't sure how far Atlanta was from Jamaica, but she was certain she couldn't hop on a van and be home within an hour or so.

Jill picked up the cordless phone and went outside on the terrace of the penthouse. She dialed Zach's home number which was now fixated in her memory. The last time she had spoken with him, his voice sounded distant and he seemed distracted. Jill still didn't know what to think of that weird conversation.

"You have reached Uncle Z's house. This is Nahima Angelique Lawson. What's your name?"

Jill laughed out loud. "My name is Jillian Josephine Bessette. It's so nice to hear your voice, Princess Nahima."

Zach stood in the doorway listening to Nahima chat with Jill. He'd seen Jamaica's country code and the resort's number flash across the caller ID in the kitchen. He was impressed with how well-spoken Nahima was, even when conversing with a complete stranger who had a thick Caribbean accent.

Nahima's jaw dropped and her bright eyes grew wide. "How did you know I was a *princess*?"

"Your uncle told me so. May I speak with him please?"

"Yes, you may."

Nahima let the phone fall onto the sofa when she hopped down from it. She was about to yell to Zach that the phone was for him, but she slapped her hand over her mouth when she saw him standing in the doorway staring at her.

Zach sat on the sofa and grabbed the phone. "Hello," he said as calmly as he could. His cool demeanor defied the excitement within. The sound of Jill's voice quickened his pulse.

"Oh Zachary, Nahima is simply *precious*! She's awfully smart too. I know you and her parents are so very proud of her. I can't wait to meet her. I'm sure your sister has told you she has applied for a job in Atlanta. Isn't it great, Zachary?"

"It's *something*." Zach propped his long legs on the coffee table. Nahima sat next to him and rested her head on his shoulder.

"Jay is downstairs on an important conference call with some executives in Atlanta as we speak. If she gets the job, I'll be relocating with her! How wonderful is that?"

Zach's body jerked forward involuntarily from the shock. Nahima toppled sideways, and she laughed like a goofy rabbit. Zach reached over and pulled her onto his lap. "Did Jay tell you you'd be joining her in Atlanta if she gets the job?"

"Of course she did, Zachary. Why else would I have said it? I asked Jay if I could attend school in Atlanta, and she's considering it. Oh Zachary, I'll get to study dance and soak up the American culture! Do you know what the best part about moving to Atlanta will be?"

"What?"

"I'll get to see you *every day*!"

"Yes, that would be nice, Jill," Zach lied. Seeing her every day and not being able to have her would make his life a living hell.

He sat quietly for the rest of the conversation and listened to Jill's continuous chatter about Atlanta, Jay and her family. He appreciated her enthusiasm, but he was still stuck on her earlier statement about Nahima's *parents*. Zach knew Jill was ignorant to the truth, and had not meant any harm, but he couldn't shake the sinking feeling in his gut. Jill had stumbled onto an off-limits subject. As far as Nahima knew, Venus was her mommy, her father was dead and Zach was her uncle. She called Aunt Jackie her Nana, and soon Charles would become her stepfather. That was the world according to Nahima, but Zach had no idea what changes Jay's entrance on the scene would bring to the situation.

Chapter Ten

Zach stood over Nahima watching her sleep. She looked so peaceful and comfortable. It had been his prayer for her since the day she was born to live a happy and secure life surrounded by all the people who loved her. Zach believed that no child should have to grow up without their mother and father the way he and Jay had. Aunt Jackie had been an incredible substitute, and she had showered them with all the love and affection in her heart. But she wasn't Belva King. Uncle Bubba and Aunt Hattie Jean had done their part too, as well as Aunt Bertha, Cousin Phoebe and Dolly Mae.

After the murder of Zach and Jay's mother, and the twenty-year prison sentence imposed upon their father for shooting her, the Dudley clan came together. They formed a protective village around the two orphaned King children. They did their best to ensure that all their needs and most of their desires were met. But because Zach had been seven years old at the time while Jay was barely two, Zach had been affected more by his parents' absence. Even to this day, he had not been able to maintain a healthy, monogamous relationship with any female for an extended period of time. Zach was afraid of falling deeply in love out of fear that he'd be driven to kill in a fit of jealous rage someday; just like his father had.

Newspaper clippings, court transcripts and loose talk among family members, all indicated that Reverend Wallace King did not mean to kill his wife of ten years. But a horrendous murder did take place in room 214 at the White Cloud Motel that night twenty-eight years ago. The popular Atlanta pastor had been aiming his .45 automatic pistol at his best friend Claudius Henry, not the first lady. That lowdown bastard caught bullets in the right leg and buttocks; but Belva, the preacher's adulterous wife, took a fatal shot in the heart which killed her instantly.

Zach didn't realize he was crying until he tasted salty tears on his lips. He wiped his face with the back of his hand and leaned over to kiss Nahima one last time before he left her room. He smiled at what had become her late night ritual as he closed the door quietly. He was willing to bet his whole paycheck that he would wake up with one of Nahima's small feet in his face. It amazed him how much more he preferred that over one of Ayla's professionally pedicured feet rubbing affectionately against his legs. She'd been bugging him all day about them spending the weekend together. But Zach had told her the truth about his plans with his favorite girl in the whole world, and it had pissed her off. It wasn't like Ayla didn't know the drill when it came to Nahima. He'd told her from the jump that no woman was allowed at his house whenever she was there.

* * * * *

"Nah, nah, Ramona," Zach said and waved her off. He threw his napkin over his empty plate. "I can't eat anything else. I'm thirty-five now. My metabolism is on the decline. I have to hit the gym at least three times a week so I won't grow hips and a bubble ass like your hubby." He laughed hard at his own joke.

Ramona rounded the table and kissed Dex softly on the lips. "I like a man with meat on his bones. No light weight brother can handle *all of this*." She placed the serving dish on the table and did a slow snake like move with her curvy size fourteen hips. She blushed when Dex grabbed a handful of her big ass and squeezed it. She slapped his hand away and hurried into the kitchen to check on dessert.

"I'm leaving." Zach stood and frowned at Dex. "Why y'all gotta get all freaky while I'm here? I know Ramona still got stitches. You're *nasty*. Keep it up. When she goes back for her six-week checkup, she'll have another bun in the oven. Little Abriah Nicolette won't like that very much. She'll have a sibling before she can even walk."

"Shut up and sit your ass down! You know you ain't going nowhere before dessert. Ramona baked that mixed fruit cobbler you like."

Zach sat back down. "I'm only staying to help *you* out. You don't need to eat a lot of that cobbler, man. All the weight you gained while Ramona was pregnant ain't sexy, Dex."

"Don't worry about my weight. You've got problems of your own. I ran into Ayla today in the parking deck. She was *pissed*. Honey said you've been missing in action since you've been back from Jamaica. Is it true y'all have only hooked up twice over the past six weeks?"

Zach nodded his head. "Yeah, she's right. I've got a bunch of heavy shit on my mind, man. With Jay talking about moving back home and Venus calling me every day tripping about it, I ain't got time for Ayla. I get Nahima every weekend now, and she's the best part of my life. Anyway, Wallace called."

"For real, Zach? How is he?"

"He sounded good. He's got a small church in Raleigh, North Carolina. I'm thinking about going up to visit him and his wife. I think it's time for me to meet Wallace Junior. He's six years old. Nahima and I sent him some gifts for his birthday."

Ramona came back into the dining room carrying the piping hot cobbler in her mitten-covered hands. She sat it on the table and left, but returned quickly with a gallon of French vanilla ice cream and dessert bowls. She served her husband first and then Zach.

"Does Jay or Aunt Jackie know you and Wallace keep in touch?"

"Nope," Zach said, scooping up a spoonful of cobbler and ice cream. "I'll tell Auntie soon. I can't keep it from her much longer. Jay and I aren't on good terms right now. We haven't spoken since I cussed her ass out three weeks ago. But she's fine. She's still going through the evaluation process for the job at the Georgia Global Cultural and Exchange Center. She made the top twenty-five candidates out of eight hundred and seventy-nine."

Dex shot Zach a suspicious look. "If y'all ain't speaking, how do you know that?"

"Jill told me."

"Mmm, so how often do you speak with *Jill*?"

"What difference does it make? She calls sometimes and we talk. What's wrong with that?"

"There's nothing wrong with it *if* that's all to it. But if you have any romantic or sexual feelings for this girl, Zach, it could be explosive."

"I *don't*!"

Dex kept a straight face. He knew Zach was lying through his teeth. His boy had the hots for Jill. Dex's instincts told him so. He wasn't sure what had taken place in Jamaica during Zach's vacation, but *something* had definitely jumped off between him and the mysterious Jill. If Jay landed the job with the GGCEC and relocated her Jamaican lover to Atlanta with her, all hell was gonna break loose.

"I hope you don't," Dex said a few seconds later. "I seriously hope you don't.

* * * * *

Zach's friend, and coworker, Emily Anne spotted him through the window of the neonatal intensive care nursery. He was using a respiratory apparatus to carefully suction mucus from the nostrils of a tiny baby boy who had been born three months prematurely. The infant was battling pneumonia, and his prognosis was dim. Zach was determined to do all he could to make his life as comfortable as possible. The frail baby squirmed and cried as his dedicated nurse continued to clear his nasal passages.

"Hold on, little dude. I'm almost finished. You'll feel better when it's all over."

"Hey," Emily Anne said softly, walking up beside Zach. "There's a phone call for you at NIC-5. The unit secretary said it's an international call."

"Thank you, sweetie, I'll be done here in a minute."

The blue-eyed nurse blushed at Zach's innocent endearment. She and all the other nurses thought he was drop-dead gorgeous. She flung her blonde locks over her shoulder and made goo-goo eyes at him. "You're welcome."

Zach finished his task and left the warm, sterile nursery. He was anxious to know why Jill would be calling him on his job. He hoped nothing bad had happened to her or Jay. He picked up his pace as he rounded the corner. Ayla was standing near the nurse's station looking over a chart with another doctor and a nurse. She rolled her eyes and sucked her teeth after he acknowledged the group with a subtle smile and a slight nod of his head. Zach pressed the flashing light on the phone and lifted the receiver.

"This is Zachary King."

"Zach, it's me, Jay."

A pregnant pause filled the phone line before he was able to respond. "What's going on, Jay? I can't remember the last time you called me at work. Is something wrong?"

"Nothing is wrong. In fact, things are quite well. I got the job, Zach. Jill and I are moving to Atlanta in two months. I know things are kinda crazy between us, but I need a favor."

With the shock still radiating through his body, Zach inhaled and exhaled slowly. "What do you need, Jay?"

"I was hoping Jill and I could stay with you for a few weeks until we can find a place."

Chapter Eleven

Zach glanced down at the timer on the treadmill's control board. He had four minutes and twenty-seven seconds before he would complete his sixty-minute jog. With sweat pouring down his face and body, his feet pounded hard against the rolling track. He had driven straight to the gym when he left the hospital with the intention of working off some of the stress he was now under. In two months he, Jay and Jill would be living under one roof, *his* roof, for an unspecified period of time. As if that wasn't nerve-racking enough, Venus had asked him to be present on the day she would tell Charles the truth about her, Nahima and Jay. Zach didn't give her a definite answer, but he was pretty sure he would be there to hold her hand. He felt it was his duty to support Venus out of love for Nahima.

The treadmill's speed automatically decreased to cool down mode. Zach grabbed the white towel from the safety rail and wiped his sweat drenched face. His feet glided across the slow moving rolling track with ease. He felt his cell phone vibrating inside his pocket and he removed it to check the caller ID. It was Ayla.

"What's up, Doc?"

"You have big nerve! We haven't spent any time together in weeks. The only place I see you is at work. You could at least call me every now and then, Zach. That's what *friends* do."

"I'm sorry, Doc. Let me make it up to you."

As much as she wanted to be mad at him, she softened under the sound of his sexy voice. Zach's rich baritone timbre made Ayla's nipples tingle. An instant pool of love juice saturated the crotch of her red lace panties, causing her to squirm on the sofa. Ayla crossed her legs against the dampness and her pulsating clit. "How do you plan to make it up to me? You've been ignoring me and *Ms. Kitty* too long, and we feel sad."

Zach smiled and jumped off the treadmill. He could hear Ayla's rugged breathing. She wanted Ms. Kitty and Mr. Wonderful to have a coed slumber party. Zach was down with that, but it would have to take place at her townhouse because he wasn't in the mood for an all-nighter. He made it a practice to never spend the night at Ayla's spot. The only reason he allowed her to stay overnight at his house was because he liked the French toast breakfast she always served him in bed the morning after.

"I could be there in a half hour. Ask Ms. Kitty if that's cool."

Ayla had already stripped off her clothes and was headed to the shower, grinning like she'd hit the lottery. "Ms. Kitty said she'd like that very much."

* * * * *

Jill bounced Angelina on her knee and tried hard not to cry. Oliver had both his arms wrapped securely around her. Edgar, Christian and Paul sat to her left on the old vinyl sofa, sobbing out loud.

"Why must ya leave, Jillian?" her father asked. He and Faye were seated in a pair of folding chairs across from their six children in the hot sitting room.

"I *must* go, Papa. Jay loves me and she wants me to be with her wherever she goes. I can enroll in college in America and enhance my dance skills like you and Mommy have always wanted. I will have a better life and learn new things. There are no opportunities for me here. I can make money and send it to you to help the family."

"Keep ya bloody American money!" Orville Bessette shouted, and sprang from his chair. "I forbid ya to leave this country with that *sinful* woman! It is humiliating enough that she makes ya lie with her in an ungodly and unnatural manner! You *will not* leave Jamaica with her!"

Jill dropped her head and rocked Angelina in her arms. Her tears fell into the baby's hair. Oliver was crying louder and still clinging to her. Jill leaned over and kissed him on his forehead.

"Please don't leave us, Jilly," Edgar begged. "We love you."

Jay blew the horn and everyone looked toward the window. All four of Jill's brothers were now crying desperately. She pried Oliver's hands away from her body and placed Angelina on her shoulder. Jill got down on her knees to face the boys.

"I love you all so very much, but I must leave to be with Jay. She has a new job in America and she wants me to go there to live with her. I will send you money and buy you lots of nice gifts, eh?"

Jill kissed each boy and wiped their faces with the palm of her hand. Jay started blowing the horn aggressively. Jill knew it was time to end her visit. She had said what she'd come to say and her family had reacted exactly the way she had expected them to. She stood and faced her parents. Her mother's tears and her father's anger broke Jill's heart, but she loved Jay and she was going to Atlanta with her. She crossed the small room to stand directly in front of her parents.

"I will make a new life for myself in America and make you very proud." Jill handed Angelina to her mother. "I love you, Mommy and Papa." She kissed her mother softly on her cheek. She wanted to touch her father, but the cold look in his eyes told her he wouldn't allow it.

DERANGED LOVE

*****

Aunt Jackie had prepared all of Jay's favorite dishes and stored them in Tupperware bowls. Zach stacked them neatly in his new deep freezer. There had never been so much food in his house before. His kitchen smelled heavenly with the scent of good Southern cooking wafting all around.

"These are for you, Zach." Aunt Jackie said, placing a medium-size bowl on the counter. "I know how much you love fresh turnips."

"Hell yeah, I do."

Aunt Jackie rolled her eyes and planted her hands on her wide hips. "Watch your mouth, Zachary King. You ain't too old for me to whip your behind."

"Are you really gonna whip Uncle Z's behind, Nana?" Nahima looked up at Aunt Jackie with worry in her eyes.

"I won't whip him this time, sweet pea, but I will if he doesn't stopping saying bad words."

"He won't say any more bad words, Nana. I promise."

Zach pulled Nahima's giant pony tail at the back of her head. "Why don't you go to your room and play with your new doll house so I can talk to your nana in private?"

"Okay."

When Zach and Aunt Jackie were alone in the kitchen, he told her all about his yearlong telephone relationship with his father. He showed her some pictures Wallace had sent of him and his family, and he told her he'd been thinking about visiting him in Raleigh. Zach said he thought it would be a good idea to take Nahima with him.

"Are you okay, Auntie?"

"I'm fine." Aunt Jackie examined her fresh manicure. "I don't hate your father, Zach, because I'm a Christian. God says I gotta love everybody, and that includes *Wallace King*."

"So you don't mind that we're in contact. But would you be upset if Nahima and I flew to Raleigh to visit him?"

Aunt Jackie looked head-on at her nephew whom she had raised as her son. "No, baby, I don't mind that you and Wallace have a relationship. You *should* go and visit him. If Venus will approve of Nahima going with you, so will I. Now, I would like to know when you plan to tell Jay about your relationship with Wallace."

Zach snorted and rubbed his goatee. "I don't think she can handle anything that heavy right now with all she's got going on. After she gets settled here and on her new job, I'll tell her. I'm not sure how she'll react, but I'll tell her anyway. She has a right to know."

"Wallace loved Belva. Never forget that, Zach. He adored her and he was crazy about you and your sister. He'd heard rumors about your mother and other men before, but he never took them seriously. But when gossip about Belva and Claudius Henry started spreading like wildfire, your daddy got real suspicious."

"Did you know my momma was having an affair, Auntie?"

"I *think* I did, but I just didn't want to believe it. Claudius Henry had money and my sister *loved* money. You wanted a green bicycle with a bell on it for your birthday. I'll never forget it. Wallace was in seminary working on his master's degree. Money was tight. Belva must've made Claudius Henry speak in tongues in bed one day because he bought you the most expensive green bike I'd ever seen. It was a Schwinn."

"I remember that bike. It was shiny and had a water bottle inside a holder under the handle bars. I was the coolest kid on the block because of that bike."

Aunt Jackie blew out a shaky breath at the memory and popped her lips. "Unfortunately, that same bike caused your daddy's suspicions to go through the roof. He did a little digging around, and found out Claudius Henry had bought that bike for you. The very next week Wallace brought you and Jay to my little old apartment and asked me to watch y'all while he ran some errands. Belva was *supposed* to have been at Clara Anne's House of Curls getting some finger waves. Even during his trial, Wallace never said how he'd found out where she actually was. Whoever tipped him off sent him flying over to that motel and the rest is painful history."

"I'm gonna ask Wallace how he found out when I visit him. He promised to tell me anything I wanna know. I was a little boy when my momma died, and now I'm a man with serious commitment issues. I need answers and closure, Auntie, and only Wallace can help me with that.

Chapter Twelve

Zach and Dex scanned the baggage claim area thoroughly. According to the flight schedule monitor, Jay and Jill's flight had landed thirty minutes ago. Zach dialed his sister's cell phone number again and got her voicemail. Dex pushed the luggage cart through the crowd, and walked to the far end of the baggage area. Zach leaned on another cart right by the baggage carousel where Jay and Jill's luggage was expected to come out.

"Zachary! Zachary!" yelled the voice that invaded his dreams nightly. Jill was smiling and waving her hand. She looked like a fashion model in an orange sundress and strappy, metallic gold sandals. Jay was dragging behind her in a pair of faded jeans, a white t-shirt and an Atlanta Braves baseball cap.

Dex was making steps in Zach's direction when Jill threw herself into his buddy's arms and kissed him firmly on the lips. There wasn't any tongue action in the kiss, but it lasted longer than a friendly peck. Zach's hands rested comfortably in the arch of Jill's back inches above her ass. Dex closed his eyes having witnessed the confirmation of what he'd hoped was just foolish speculation. All bets were off. Zach had a thing so powerful for Jill that Dex could smell the fragrance of lust in the air as he got closer to them. And Jill was smitten by Zach too, but she just didn't know it yet.

"What's up, family?" Dex said, smiling from ear to ear. He grabbed Jay's slender frame in a bear hug and released her.

"Dex, this is Jill." Jay tossed her hand back and forth. "Baby, this is Dexter Cruz, Zach's best friend. He's like a big brother to me."

Jill was so excited. She flung her arms around Dex's stocky body. "It is my pleasure to meet you, Dexter Cruz."

"It's nice to meet you too, Jill. Please call me Dex."

The baggage carousel came to life, humming and dispensing luggage of all shapes, colors and sizes. Jay and Jill pointed out their many pieces while Zach and Dex loaded them onto the carts.

"Are y'all hungry?" Zach asked as they exited the airport

"I'm not," Jill said. "Are you hungry, Jay?"

"Nah, I'm tired. I just want a hot shower, a glass of Disarrono and cranberry juice and some rest."

"I'm not sleepy. I want to see Atlanta!"

Jay looked at Jill and rolled her eyes. "You need some rest too. You haven't slept in hours. We're going to Zach's house to relax. You'll have plenty of time to see the city."

* * * * *

"Yes, she's here, Venus," Zach whispered. He turned off the television so he could hear her faint voice. She was whispering through her tears. "I want you to calm down. Have a glass of red wine. Go make love to your man. There's nothing for you to worry about right now. Jay is tired. She won't make any moves tonight. We'll talk tomorrow."

A light knock at the door caught Zach off guard. It was ten minutes after eleven and his house was dark and quiet. Jay and Jill had been in the upstairs guest room since they'd first arrived around five-thirty. Zach had prepared the guest suite with a private bathroom downstairs for them. But for some reason Jay preferred to be upstairs.

"Come in."

Jill stuck her head inside the room and smiled. Zach placed the phone on the dresser and reached for his red t-shirt on the bed. He slipped it on and motioned with a curl of his finger for Jill to enter. Zach stood in the middle of the master suite and watched her tiptoe toward him wearing a soft, blue cotton dress with spaghetti straps. He could see her nipples pressing against the light fabric and her hourglass figure outlined underneath it. He swallowed hard when the scents of ginger and lilac tickled his nose. Zach was grateful Jill had left the door slightly ajar. The throbbing in his groin was tempting him to break the hood rule about touching a family member's lover.

Without warning, Jill hugged Zach and he froze. She released him and stepped away clueless of the fire she had ignited. "It is so good to see you, Zachary," she whispered. "I am very excited about being in America. Your house is magnificent! Why do have so many rooms when you live alone?"

Zach shrugged his shoulders and looked directly into Jill's eyes and got lost. "I don't know. I just fell in love with this house at first sight and I had to have it."

"Oh, I understand. May I ask you another question, Zachary?"

"Sure, go right ahead."

Jill took a seat on Zach's bed and casually slouched onto her side. She pressed her elbow into the mattress and rested her chin on her fist. "Tell me, Zachary, what must I do to enroll in school? I have brought all my records here from Jamaica. They are sealed and can only be opened by officials at the schools of my choice."

Zach sat in the black La-Z-Boy across the room. "I think this is something you should discuss with *Jay*. She'll be responsible for your tuition, books and transportation. Don't worry about school just yet anyway. Fall semester will begin next week at most colleges so you'll have to wait until the spring. Right now you need to see the sights of our great city."

"Jay has no time for that. She starts work tomorrow and she won't have a day of rest until Tuesday. Someone is picking her up in the morning to take her to get a rental car. Her car should be here by next week."

Zach had no idea Jay would be out of pocket for the weekend. She hadn't mentioned anything about her schedule to him. He and Venus had agreed that it would be best if Nahima stayed home with her and Charles until after he had spoken to Jay about her intentions regarding the child. Zach did not want to be left to babysit Jill. He needed to keep his distance from her as much as possible.

"Zachary," Jill said snapping her fingers directly in his face. "Did you hear what I said?"

Zach had been so deep in thought that he hadn't noticed Jill had left her comfortable position on his bed. "I'm sorry, Jill. What did you say?"

"I'd like to call home tomorrow if that's okay with you. Jay mustn't know, though. She wants me to wait a couple of weeks before I contact my family, but I simply can't wait that long. May I please call them tomorrow when Jay leaves for work?"

"Sure."

"We'll have another secret. You never told me yours, Zachary."

"I sure didn't. Mmm, let me see. I fell in love…"

"*Man*, how long did I sleep?" Jay walked into the room, yawning and stretching her arms in the air. "I'm starving."

Zach and Jill turned to watch her take a seat on the bed. Her eyes darted between them. Jill hurried over to Jay and sat on her lap.

"You got any food around here, bro, or do we have to call and order takeout?"

"I have plenty of food. Aunt Jackie came over Sunday after church and cooked all your favorites. Most of it is in the freezer, but I took out some roasted chicken and dressing last night. It's in the refrigerator. Let's go downstairs, and I'll heat it up for you."

* * * * *

Jill was bored to death sitting around Zach's big house with nothing to do. She had explored each room and closet on both floors like an adventurer. She had taken her time in Nahima's room admiring her unique furniture, clothes and baby dolls. It was the type of room she wished Angelina could sleep in one day. Jill had sat in the pretty white rocking chair and studied the big picture of Zach and Nahima she'd removed from the dresser. The exquisite crystal frame was heavy and no doubt expensive. Jill once again took note of the similarities in Zach and Nahima's facial features. They shared the same caramel complexion and full lips. Each had a pair of dark brown eyes and wavy black hair. Their smiles were identical. It was fascinating how much they resembled each other.

Jill had seen dozens of pictures of Nahima all over the walls and marble mantle in Zach's all- white formal living room. They ranged in date from her newborn portrait all the way up to the present. She assumed the striking young couple in the black and white portrait on the coffee table was Zach's parents. Jay had told her their mother had died when they were very young and their father had left them with their aunt. Other than that, she'd never spoken of her parents again.

Jill's attention was drawn to the picture window where she could see some neighborhood children roller skating around the cul-de-sac. She laughed and clapped her hands when a dog ran down the street and started chasing the children. She could hear them screaming. A little girl fell down and Jill felt sorry for her. She got back up and skated away. Seconds later the phone rang, and Jill went to search for it in the kitchen.

"This is the King residence," she said cheerfully. The caller hung up. She frowned at the hum of the dial tone in her ear. Before she could return the cordless phone to its cradle, it rang again and frightened her. Jill pressed the power button and repeated her greeting.

"Who is this and why are you answering *Zach's* phone?"

"I beg your pardon, ma'am," Jill said politely.

"Where is *Zach*?"

"I'm not sure, ma'am. Is this Aunt Jackie?"

The caller slammed the phone down in Jill's ear again.

Chapter Thirteen

Ayla was pissed off as she whipped her red Mustang convertible out of the hospital parking lot. The Jamaican chick who had just answered Zach's phone was more than likely the reason why he'd been so distant since returning from vacation. Ayla couldn't believe he had gone all the way to the island and hooked up with some tramp and sent for her to visit him.

"That lowdown, dirty bastard!" she yelled. "Who the hell does he think he is?" Ayla picked up her phone and pressed the number two on her speed dial list. Zach answered on the second ring. His voice sounded muffled.

"Where the hell are you, Zach? And who is that Jamaican bitch answering your damn phone?"

"I can't talk right now, Doc. Let me get back with you later." Zach ended the call.

"Ugh!" Ayla screamed as she headed down Jesse Hill, Jr. Drive.

* * * * *

"Was that Jay?" Venus asked.

"Nah, it was Ayla acting like a damn fool. She's been bitching lately because I haven't been able to kick it with her as much. She doesn't have a clue what I'm going through. We're just friends and she knows that. I've told her to move on and find a brother who wants to settle down and do the marriage and baby thing, but she won't. She called my house and Jill…"

Nahima ran past her mother and Zach, along with some friends she had met in the park. They stopped at the swings and each little girl slid into one and started pumping her legs.

"What were you about to say, Zach?"

He hesitated, unsure if he should tell Venus that Jay had not moved to Atlanta alone. She would be thrilled about it, but Zach didn't want to give her false hope. It didn't matter if Jay had one or one thousand women. She would always love Venus, and because of that, there were serious unresolved issues lingering between them. Zach rubbed his hands together and stole a glance at Venus with his peripheral vision.

"Jay didn't move here alone. She brought her lover Jill with her."

"That's wonderful! She *has* moved on." Venus smiled for the first time since they'd been at the park.

Zach held up both hands and shook his head to shut down her celebration before it even started. "Pump your breaks. Jill is gorgeous, sweet and generous, but Jay isn't in love with her. I think she cares about her in her own peculiar way, but it's not love."

"I see." Venus folded her arms across her chest. She leaned back on the metal bench and looked up into the sky. "I was hoping she had fallen madly in love like I have. Then maybe she wouldn't remember what we once shared. We were so happy back then, Zach. I thought it would last forever. I really did."

Zach threw his arm casually around Venus's shoulders. "But you wanted a baby and Jay didn't."

Venus nodded and turned her attention to Nahima swinging high into the air. She was having fun like all little girls should. "I had always wanted a child. Jay knew that. We'd discussed it very early on in our relationship. Your sister promised me we would have a family. Obviously, at the time, we weren't aware of certain things. But even so, Zach, she made me believe she supported my dream of having a baby. If only I had known she was lying." Venus waved and smiled at Nahima. "I don't regret giving birth to my daughter at all. She is not a mistake. I just wish the circumstances had been different. Why couldn't Jay bond with her? I think she could have if she had just tried."

"I'm not so sure about that. I honestly believe Jay only went along with the plan because she loved you and wanted to make you happy. Things changed quickly after that as they often do. But that's all in the past, Venus," Zach said, looking at her worried face. "We have a situation now that we have to deal with. Give me a day or two to talk to Jay and we'll take it from there."

* * * * *

It was just like old times at Aunt Jackie's house. Uncle Bubba and Aunt Hattie Jean and Aunt Bertha had come over after church for Sunday dinner to welcome Jay home. Dolly Mae had come too with all *six* of her bad ass grandchildren. Cousin Phoebe was at work, but had sent her love. There was an abundance of good food and lots of lively trash talking going on. Jill was in awe. She had never experienced anything quite like it. Zach watched her interact with his family. He was grateful that they were going out of their way to make her feel right at home. When she offered to help clean the kitchen, Aunt Bertha ran her away.

"Zachary, I love your family. Everyone is so very nice. Your auntie is the world's greatest chef! I ate two pork chops."

Jill rubbed her stomach and leaned back on the sofa. She was in Aunt Jackie's den with Zach, Uncle Bubba and two of Dolly Mae's teenage grandsons. The men had gathered in front of the big screen television to watch an Atlanta Braves baseball game. All the other women except Jay were in the kitchen washing dishes and putting away the leftovers. She was on the front porch talking on her cell phone.

"I'm glad to see you enjoying yourself in America. I still have to take you sightseeing. Maybe we could go this coming weekend, but it'll have to be our secret."

Jill sat up and gave Zach a sly grin. "Oh, I can keep your secret, Zachary," she whispered. "You have kept all three of mine and I will keep yours *forever*. I promise."

* * * * *

True to his word, Zach got up early the following Saturday morning to take Jill to see the city. Jay was spending the weekend at the hotel, claiming she was up to her eyeballs with paperwork. Getting out of the house was the perfect idea to avoid temptation. Jill had strolled downstairs practically nude the night before to get a bottle of water. She didn't know Zach had fallen asleep on the sofa in the den. He woke up when he heard her footsteps and found her in a simple white t-shirt that barely covered her ass. As usual she wasn't wearing panties, and the sight of that had kept him awake for three agonizing hours afterwards.

As they exited Zach's quiet, middle-class subdivision, he told Jill he had another secret. "You're gonna meet Nahima today."

"Are you telling me the truth?"

Zach laughed at Jill's enthusiasm. "I swear. We're about to pick her up right now as a matter of fact. But Jay can't know anything about this, Jill. Do you understand?"

"No, I don't understand, Zachary. Will Jay think it is a *bad* thing for me to meet your god daughter?"

When they paused at a stop sign, Zach faced Jill and reached his hand across the console to touch hers which was lying on her lap. "It's a very complicated situation that doesn't concern you, Jill. I just need you to promise me that you won't tell Jay that you've met Nahima until I say it's okay."

"I promise."

* * * * *

It was dark by the time Zach finished showing Jill around Atlanta. He and Nahima had been great tour guides, and Jill had enjoyed every minute of hanging out with them. They'd taken her to the King Center, Olympic Centennial Park, Underground Atlanta, and the Coca Cola Museum. The highlight of Jill's day had been spending time with Nahima at Chuck E. Cheese's.

Zach's cell phone rang as he pulled up at a gas station to fill his tank. It was Venus. "I know we're late," he offered as a greeting. "I'll have her there in thirty minutes."

"No, Zach, don't bring her home. Things are chaotic around here. Jay called the house, and left a message on the voicemail while Charles and I were out. She said she wants to see me! Why would she do such a thing, Zach?" Venus cried. "Charles lost it when he heard Jay's voice. She sounded all nonchalant like everything was normal. Can you believe she asked me to meet her at the hotel? She's an evil, psychotic *bitch*!"

"Calm down, Venus. I'll keep Nahima. That's not a problem. Jay will be at the hotel until Monday afternoon. Are you gonna be okay?"

"I...I...I'm not sure. Charles is asking all kinds of crazy questions and making irrational accusations. I'm afraid he's gonna leave me. He can *never* know about Nahima now, Zach, *never*!"

Zach could hear Charles shouting in the background. His voice was getting louder by the second. He was one mad brother. Zach's heart went out to Venus, but he was livid with Jay. He wanted to strangle her with his bare hands. She had only been back in town for a few weeks, yet she had already started some shit. Zach was about to speak when he heard Charles ask Venus who was she on the phone with.

"I gotta go," she said and hung up.

"Was that Jay, Zachary?" Jill asked when he entered the vehicle after pumping the gas.

"Nah, um...it was Venus. She's not feeling well. She needs me to keep Nahima tonight." Zach turned and looked over his shoulder at the sweet, innocent, little girl who had been born into a world of turmoil. She was sound asleep in her car seat. "Since Jay isn't coming home until Monday, I told Venus she could stay."

* * * * *

"Open this damn door, Zach!" Jay banged her fist against his bedroom door. "I need to talk to you *right now*!"

Zach sat up and looked at the clock on his nightstand. It was two-forty-eight in the morning. *Nahima!* He suddenly remembered she was there. Jay was supposed to have been at work. Zach jumped out of bed and ran to the door. As soon as he opened it, Jay rushed right past him.

"What the hell is going on?' She screamed. "Why is *that child* here? What kind of bullshit game are you trying to pull?"

"This is *my* house, Jay," Zach said as calmly as he could. His emotions were running gamut and they had been since he'd spoken to Venus. "I can bring anybody I want to up in here. You need to back the hell up and chill." He sat down on the foot of his bed.

Jay stood over him. She was mad as hell. Both her fists were clenched as if she were about to go to blows with him.

"What did you say to Jill? Who did you tell her that child was?"

"I told her the same damn *lie* I told her in Jamaica! I said she was my god daughter! What the hell is wrong with you, Jay, huh? Why did you bring your selfish, heartless, trifling ass back here anyway? Did you come to ruin Venus's life? Are you gonna try to stop her and Charles from getting married? Is that why you called *their house*, Jay?" Zach was up and in his sister's face now.

"You dirty son of a bitch! You're my brother, damn it! You're supposed to have my back! It has always been you and me against the world," Jay shouted. "We were two little orphans trying to make it without our parents."

"We ain't victims anymore. We're *survivors*. We made it, Jay. Let it go. You're victimizing people who love you." Zach reached out to embrace his sister, but she snatched away.

"Venus never loved me! If she did, why did she leave me? She took what she wanted and…and left me. All she wanted was *that child* in there!" Jay stomped her foot and pointed in the direction of Nahima's room.

"*That child?* Did you hear yourself? You are the most evil and emotionally detached human being ever to walk the face of the earth. Nahima is *your child*, Jay! I know you hate to hear it, but you need a reality check. You are her *mother*, but you just referred to her as *that child*." Zach ran both hands down his face wiping away tears. "What kind of damn monster are you? You may not have carried her or nursed her, but it was *your egg* that Whitaker's sperm fertilized. Venus most definitely birthed her, but *you* created her! That's *your* face Nahima has!"

Jay pressed her hands over her ears and shook her head from side to side like a deranged person. Tears and snot poured down her face as she panted for air. "No! No! No!" She screamed hysterically. Then, as if she hadn't heard a word Zach had just spoken, Jay composed herself and stepped to him. "I *hate* you," she hissed. "Jill and I will be outta here by the end of the week. I have to go back to work now."

"Wait, Jay. We haven't finished this."

She spun around quickly, and flashed fiery eyes on Zach. "Oh, I'm done, big brother. I am *done*."

Chapter Fourteen

Jill had felt like her heart was about to explode when she jumped inside the linen closet in the hallway. All the banging and screaming in Zach's room had interrupted her sleep. She had left her bed to see if there was something wrong with Nahima, but instead, she was totally blown away when she discovered Jay had come home in the middle of the night. Zach's bedroom door was cracked, making it impossible for Jill to ignore the loud, heated exchange. She had heard *everything*. She suddenly felt cold in the closet, and shivered like the temperature had dropped below zero degrees. In actuality, she was experiencing emotional shock. Jay had run down the steps and out the front door several minutes ago, but Jill could not mobilize her weak and stunned body.

She fell to her knees in the closet when she heard Zach leave his bedroom. She heard his fast footsteps heading toward Nahima's room. That was her cue to get out as quickly as possible, and run to her bedroom. Jill turned the knob slowly and quietly. Just as she gave the door a gentle push, Zach rushed back down the hallway. She panicked and gasped. Her breath caught in her throat, and her eyes clamped shut. Jill could feel her heart pounding erratically in her chest.

Zach's footsteps paused right outside the closet. He stood there quiet and still, wondering if he had heard movement inside or if he had only imagined it. He laughed and shook his head. "I must be losing my damn mind," he mumbled and started to walk away. But some invisible force held him in place. Zach stretched out his right arm and pushed his bedroom door closed with a boom.

Jill stood, pushed the closet door open and bolted out, but collided with Zach who was still standing there. They stood toe-to-toe in silence, neither knowing what to say. He felt her soft body trembling against his. When Jill lifted her face to look into Zach's eyes, he could tell instantly that she had heard every word spoken between him and Jay. She was crying through red, swollen eyes as if she were in mourning. Without forethought, and only for the purpose of comforting her, Zach enfolded Jill gently in his arms. Physically and emotionally drained, she collapsed in his embrace, and he lifted her off her feet.

When Jill's feet left the floor, she raised her legs and wrapped them around Zach's waist exposing her bare bottom. He slid his clasped hands to rest on her backside and started a methodical, flesh singeing massage. With yearning, Jill's lips found Zach's and covered them in a kiss so slow and tantalizing that his knees buckled. Careful not to drop her, he regained his footing, and eased his tongue deep inside her mouth, and she received it as if were nourishment to sustain her for days to come. Zach's right hand found the knob on his bedroom door and turned it. He entered the suite with Jill clinging to him as he kissed her senseless. A side kick closed the door, and Zach steadied his lustful mind long enough to lock it with his free hand.

Jill hummed out her passion as wave after wave of pure ecstasy washed over her. Zach sat at the top of his king size sleigh bed and propped his back against the headboard with Jill now straddling him. He slid the white t-shirt over her head, and she sat naked with her smooth, dark skin glistening under the light of the crescent moon shining through the window. Alternately, Zach tasted each nipple with the tip of his tongue, taunting and teasing both hardened buds to Jill's delight. She whimpered and threw her head back, intoxicated by the scent of foreplay invading the air. Jill pressed her feet deep into the mattress, and stood where her wet diamond sparkled brightly before Zach's eyes. He palmed her bottom, and buried his face into her feminine essence; where he drank her sweet nectar with fervor like a starving newborn suckles milk from its mother's tit.

"Mmm, Zachary, Zachary," Jill began to sing his name in high pitch.

Zach felt her body beginning to take flight toward the mountain top, and he stopped abruptly to delay her ascent. Jill squirmed, moaned, and begged for more of what he had given her, but he refused. Zach wanted her to experience ultimate sexual gratification, which had been the first coupling of any kind passed down from Adam and Eve over thousands of generations to the present. It was the traditional physical fulfillment reserved only for *man* and woman. He guided Jill's body lower to her knees and directed her hand slowly to the fully erect member of his anatomy. She explored, squeezed and caressed it, finding satisfaction as it expanded and pulsated in response to her touch.

Zach lifted his muscular thighs, and slid out of his boxer shorts. Jill freed him of his tank top and kneaded his chest with her right hand, while stroking his now bare penis with her left one. Unable to prolong the inevitable, Zach took hold of Jill's hips and elevated her body slightly. With perfect aim, he thrust his hips upward and brought her hot wetness down as he looked into her hazy eyes.

Her tight, virgin walls felt pain, but also pleasure, upon his entry. Gradually, Jill took in the full length and breadth of Zach, allowing him to touch a part of her that had never been touched before: her soul.

It was a gentle and unhurried ride toward euphoria. Zach rocked and moaned. Jill bucked and hummed. Each lover determined to give the other their very best without limits or inhibitions. They soared high to unknown dimensions with reckless abandon. Ripples of unfamiliar fulfillment overtook Jill, starting from within and spilling outward. The sound of a melodious love song, the scent of delicate flowers, rapturous sensations, the sweet taste of honey and the sight of sparkling stars all bundled into one life-changing release. Jill had now heard, smelled, felt, tasted and seen love for the very first time.

Seconds later, Zach followed her into that special, secret place and closed the door on the world and all its inhabitants. Nothing and no one else mattered outside of the haven they'd created for themselves with desire, passion and need.

Their eyes met and they became fully aware of what they'd just experienced. Zach and Jill were now connected in a way that could never be reversed. It would be impossible for them to go back to their separate worlds having touched the innermost part of each other.

"Zachary," Jill said softly, and closed her eyes. She lowered her head onto his shoulder.

"Jill, please don't cry." Zach whispered, rubbing her back in a gentle, circular motion. He could feel her warm tear drops trickling down his shoulder and back. "Sssh, everything is gonna be okay."

Zach eased onto his back with Jill still straddling him. She relaxed her legs and lay flat on his body. He rocked her gently and cooed in her ear until she fell asleep.

* * * * *

"Uncle Z!" Nahima tapped on the locked bedroom door. "Uncle Z, let me in! The sun is shining."

With care, Zach rolled onto his side with Jill in his arms. He eased her to rest on her back, trying his best not to wake her. He found his shorts on the bed and slid into them. He hurried to the door and cracked it open.

"Good morning, Uncle Z, how did you sleep?"

"I slept fine, pumpkin. Why don't you go downstairs to the kitchen and grab a juice box from the refrigerator? I'll be there shortly to get breakfast started."

"Okay."

Zach closed the door and looked at Jill sleeping on his bed. Her naked body was exquisite in every way, and even more so now since he had christened it. He tore his eyes away from her, and went to the closet to get a blanket. Zach covered Jill, and rushed into the master bathroom and showered in record time. The face he saw in the mirror as he brushed his teeth was that of a troubled man. How could something that felt so amazing have been so immoral? Zach marveled at the contradiction.

He left the bathroom and clutched his chest when he saw his empty bed. Jill was gone, and so was the blanket. Zach ran out of the room and down the hallway to the guest room with only a towel covering his lower body. He tapped on the door.

"Jill, are you alright?" When she didn't answer, he tapped again, but harder. "Jill, I need to know if you're okay. Please answer me."

Zach turned the knob. The door was locked. He panicked. He continued to knock and call out to Jill in desperation. She didn't answer. Zach walked away, with jumbled emotions, to give her the time she needed to process what had taken place between them.

DERANGED
love

Chapter Fifteen

Jill had heard Zach, but she was too ashamed to face him. She had no idea what to say to him anyway. Nothing made sense to her at the moment. She had enjoyed making love with Zach, but the guilt of betraying Jay weighed heavily on her heart. Even after learning the agonizing truth about Nahima, and hearing Jay's ill feelings toward the child, she still felt a sense of loyalty to her. Jill would forever be indebted to Jay, but she'd placed her heart in Zach's hands last night. She pulled the blanket over her head, and pressed her face into a pillow and cried tears of confusion.

* * * * *

By noon Zach's concern had driven him over the edge. He and Nahima had gone to Jill's room several times to check on her. Each time she'd told them she was resting because she was extremely tired. She had refused to eat breakfast although Zach had offered to serve it in her room. Nahima had just returned to the kitchen with a plate of food that she had tried to give Jill, but she had sent the child away.

"Ms. Jill said she's not hungry, Uncle Z. I think she's sick. Maybe her tummy hurts or she's got the flu." Nahima placed the fork and the plate of pasta salad and chicken tenders on the counter. "I'm gonna go watch the Disney Channel."

Zach climbed the stairs with every intention of speaking with Jill no matter what. He wanted to respect her privacy, but he had to see her to make sure she was okay. He'd promised himself that he wouldn't pressure her to talk about what they'd done, but he would certainly take full responsibility for his actions. He had to convince Jill that she had nothing to feel bad about and that everything would work itself out.

Jill sat up and adjusted the blanket across her body when Zach entered the room. He'd had no other choice but to use his master key to let himself in. He pressed his back against the closed door, and shoved his hands into the pockets of his denim shorts. All morning he had been anxious to see Jill, but now that he was in her presence, words escaped him.

"I am so very sorry, Zachary! Please forgive me. What we did was wrong, and it was all my fault. Jay will hate me if she ever found out. Can't it be another secret for us? *Please*, Zachary."

Honey

Zach rushed to the bed and kneeled against it. He touched Jill's face and stroked it gently. "It wasn't your fault, baby. If there's anyone to blame, it's me. I should've stopped things before they got out of hand, but I *couldn't*. What happened between us…the love we made…it was beautiful. Yes, Jay will be very angry, but not just with you. She'll probably be more upset with me. Don't worry. She'll never find out, okay?" Zach pressed his palm against Jill's cheek and smiled.

"Thank you, Zachary." She dropped her eyes.

"Look at me, Jill."

Slowly she lifted her eyes, filled with tears, and met Zach's gaze.

"Maybe we shouldn't have made love, but I don't regret it. Do you?"

"No," she answered without hesitation.

* * * * *

For the rest of the day Zach kept his distance from Jill, aside from that evening when he'd served her dinner in her room. She needed time and space to deal with her emotions. So much unexpected drama had unfolded over the past twenty-four hours, and the impact of it all must have been devastating. Jill had learned that Jay was Nahima's biological mother and that she had attempted to make contact with Venus, her ex-lover. And then Zach had made love to her while she was confused and vulnerable, which had only complicated her life further. But Jill had confessed to him that she had no regrets, and neither did he.

"Uncle Z, I'm ready!" Nahima came bouncing around the corner snapping Zach from his thoughts.

"Come on, pumpkin. Let me take you home to your mommy. I'm sure she misses you."

* * * * *

"I knew it! Damn it, Zach! What were you *thinking*?" Dex slammed his hand on the dashboard. Instead of having lunch in the cafeteria, he and Zach were eating in his Ford Explorer for privacy.

Zach refused to look at his friend. He stared straight ahead out into the packed parking lot. "It just happened, Dex."

"Yeah, I bet it did. That innocent girl has only been in this country two months and you and Jay have already turned her life upside down! I knew as soon as you got back from Jamaica that you had a thing for Jill. I tried to get you to talk about it, but no, no, no! You were in denial. Now what are you gonna do? You can't keep boning your sister's woman, Zach."

"I'm hoping she won't be Jay's woman much longer."

"What the hell is that supposed to mean?"

Zach looked directly at Dex. "I want Jill. I love her, and I wanna be with her."

DERANGED LOVE
*****

The tension in Zach's house was *insane*. Jay had big nerve. She wasn't speaking to Zach at all in his own house, but he didn't give a damn. One evening, they sat in the den a few feet away from each other and watched an entire episode of CSI in complete silence. And as the closing credits began to roll, she removed her keys from the coffee table and left the house without a word. The next morning Zach found a note Jay had written and taped onto his bedroom door. It said her plans to move out had been pushed back indefinitely because she was in the process of working out a deal to purchase a condo at the Seven Seas rather than a house in the city. Zach laughed at his sister's cockiness. At the bottom of the note she added that he should be pleased to know she'd be spending as much time as possible away from his house so she wouldn't have to see his precious *Nahima*.

Things were a bit awkward between Zach and Jill also. They were always cordial to each other, but cautious not to make any physical contact. Their conversations were pleasant, but nothing deep or thought provoking. Since the morning after they'd made love, neither of them had mentioned it. Zach wanted to discuss it, and he was curious about what was going on between Jill and Jay. He knew for certain that they hadn't been intimate. Jay had only spent one night at the house since the big argument. On that particular night, Jill was suffering from a migraine headache that she'd been complaining about all day.

Zach had been patient and understanding, but it was time for him and Jill to talk. He trotted up the stairs and went straight to the guest room.

"Knock, knock," he said, and stuck his head inside. "May I come in?"

Jill sat up on the bed and picked up the remote control to turn off the television. She self-consciously tugged at the hem of her red dress, and checked her neckline.

Zach didn't want her to feel uncomfortable, so he sat in a chair in the corner of the room instead of at the foot of the bed like he had planned. "I don't want you to be afraid of me, Jill. I would never intentionally do anything to hurt you."

"I know that. It's just that I'm very confused right now. So much has changed between us. Things aren't the same between Jay and me either. I don't know how I feel about her anymore, Zachary." Her eyes watered. "How can she love *me*, but hate her own child? Why didn't she tell me she had a daughter? And why did she bring me here if she is still in love with Venus?"

"You'll have to ask Jay that, Jill. I can't answer those questions for you. Have you spoken to her about anything you heard us arguing about?"

Jill shook her head. "She doesn't even know I heard the fight. She would be vexed if she learned I eavesdropped on the two of you. But I couldn't help it. Jay was so loud." Jill got up and walked across the room. She stood directly in front of Zach. She cupped his face with her hands and looked into his eyes. "I need to know the full story about Jay, Venus and Nahima."

Zach pushed her hands from his face and shook his head. "It's not *my* story to tell. If you wanna know anything about Jay's past, you'll have to ask *her*, Jill. I've already crossed the line by making love to you. I won't tell you anything about my sister without her permission."

"I need to know, Zachary! Don't you understand? I have given up everything to be with Jay. I left my family, my country and abandoned my dreams for her. And I've since learned it may have all been in vain. My God, Zachary, don't you think I deserve to know the truth?"

Zach stood and wrapped his arms around Jill. When he broke the embrace, he took her by the hand, and led her downstairs to the den. They sat face-to-face, and he told her everything he felt she needed to know about Jay and Venus's relationship. Some things had been hurtful to hear, but she had insisted that he tell her. Before Zach left the room to leave Jill with her thoughts, he placed a soft kiss on her lips and wished her a good night's rest.

Chapter Sixteen

Jay left Julio's Bar around two o'clock in the morning, and headed for Zach's house. The Disarrono had her feeling light and mellow. All she could think about was Jill sitting on her face once she hit their bedroom. That would be the perfect night cap before *Mr. Sand Man* carried her away. Jay hadn't been in the mood for sex lately after hearing Charles's cheerful greeting on Venus's voicemail. It was hard to believe her ex had moved on and was happy with a *man*. Back in the day, Venus used to constantly say that all men were dogs, but now she was engaged to marry one, and raising Nahima with him.

"Nahima," Jay growled and sucked her teeth. Zach had been thoughtless and cruel to bring her to his house while she was still living there. And he'd had the audacity to let Jill meet her. He was a dog just like all other men. He was no better than Wallace, Claudius Henry or that Charles clown. Jay killed the engine in front of the house and rubbed her temples. When she thought about making love to Jill again, she hurried out of the car and went into the house. She headed straight to the upstairs' bathroom.

* * * * *

"Jill, wake up, baby." Jay had taken a quick shower and was standing over the bed in her birthday suit. She reached under the covers and pinched one of Jill's nipples, and then the other one. "Wake up baby."

"Go away, Jay. I'm tired." Jill turned over on her side and pulled the covers up to her neck.

The word *no* was not an option for Jill, as far as Jay was concerned. Jill had never denied Jay sex, even when she was sick back in Jamaica. It was the second time since they'd moved to Atlanta that she had brushed her off in the bedroom. Jay snatched the covers from Jill's body. She wrestled her onto her back and got on top of her.

"Stop it, Jay! Get off me!" Jill struggled against Jay's weight. She folded her lips inward to keep Jay's tongue from entering her mouth.

Jay got a twisted rush out of Jill's resistance and her arousal flew off the chart. She ran her tongue down her face and neck and even lower. Jay then grabbed both of Jill's wrists and pressed them to the bed, high above her head. She dipped her head below Jill's neckline and caught one dark nipple between her front teeth and bit it.

"Ouch! Jay, you're hurting me! Please stop! Get off me! Why are you doing this?"

"You like it. Stop pretending," Jay growled low and emotionless. "She bit down on Jill's nipple again with more pressure."

"Ah! Stop, Jay *please*! I'm begging you to stop. You're hurting me!"

Jay maneuvered her hand down Jill's body and lifted her t-shirt. When she ventured between her thighs, Jay was shocked to feel fabric. Jill was wearing *panties*. Jay went off! "What the fuck?"

"What the hell is going on in here?" Zach had burst into the room, and flipped on the light switch. He stood in the middle of the floor with his eyes shifting back and forth from Jill's horrified face to Jay's annoyed one."

Jay yanked the covers over her body and Jill's. "It's all good. We were just doing a little role play. You know how it is, bro. Couples have to keep it fresh and spicy. Go back to bed. We're fine.

Zach instincts told him that wasn't the case. Jill was not fine. She looked like a terrified child with tears in her eyes. As usual, Jay was lying. From the way Jill had been crying and screaming, it was obvious they hadn't been playing some kinky sex game. He had just walked in on Jay forcing herself on Jill. Zach was tempted to drag Jay from the bed and kick her ass out of his house, but Jill would suffer her wrath if he did.

"It just sounded kinda strange in here," Zach finally said. "It was pretty loud. I thought Jill was crying. Maybe you were being too rough with her, sis."

"She's *fine*," Jay hissed annoyed as hell. She looked over at Jill. "Aren't you, baby?"

Jill nodded her head, but kept her eyes on Zach. Her eyes were sending out a conflicting message from what Jay had just said. She was anything but fine. Zach sensed that Jill didn't want to be in that bed or even in the room.

He wished he could do something to help Jill. Obviously, she was in distress, and it was eating him alive. But his hands were tied at the moment. One wrong move, or word, could send Jay over the edge, and she would take Jill away from the house and make sure Zach never saw her again. He had to be careful not to provoke her to go there, but he had to do something soon. Jill didn't deserve the harsh treatment Jay was inflicting on her. And she shouldn't have been subjected to the last four years of emotional and verbal abuse she had endured from Jay either. Zach would confront Jay about a few things, before long, concerning her mistreatment of Jill and her obsession with Venus.

Zach looked at Jill one last time before he turned off the light. "Good night, ladies," he said and closed the door.

Minutes after he had returned to his room, he heard Jay running down the stairs. The front door slammed shut with a bang. Then the engine of her BMW came to life and sped recklessly away from the house.

* * * * *

Jay's sexual aggression had shaken Jill up. She rubbed her sore nipple and cried silently. If Zach had not come into their room, God only knows what might have happened. Jill had smelled alcohol on Jay's breath which wasn't unusual. She had at least four or five drinks of Disarrono every night before she went to bed, but tonight she reeked of her favorite liquor. Why had she been drinking on the job? Had she even been at work at all? Suddenly, thoughts of Jay hugging and kissing Venus or another woman popped inside Jill's head.

Oddly enough, the thought didn't disturb her. It used to break her heart whenever Jay stumbled into the penthouse at all times of the night with the scent of another woman on her skin. Jill had been no fool. She'd known back then that Jay had been with several women around the island. Charlotte, the voluptuous chick with the size 44DD breast, had been one of her flings. Roy, the driver at the resort, had told her about Jay's outside sexual indulgences, but Jill had been helpless to do anything about it. Now, in light of everything Zach had shared with her about Jay, and the way Jay had just treated her, Jill no longer wanted to be in a relationship with her.

The story had paralyzed Jill to the point that she sat alone in the dark for two hours downstairs that night after Zach had gone to bed. She was shocked to learn that it had been Jay's idea for her and Venus to have a child together. She'd been fully aware that they would have to conceive by in vitro fertilization. During that time, they'd learned that Venus had a rare condition that limited her ability to ovulate. Jay had volunteered her eggs to be fertilized by a sperm donor, and she promised to underwrite the cost of the entire procedure. All Venus had to do was find a male family member to donate his sperm so the child could be biologically related to her. And of course, she was expected to carry and give birth to the baby because that part was definitely out of the question concerning Jay. Venus's first cousin Whitaker, the worthless jailbird that he was, agreed to give them all the sperm they needed for a one-time payment of two thousand dollars. He signed all his paternal rights away long before the child was even born. He was more concerned with dollar signs than the future of his seed.

Zach said initially Jay was ecstatic when Venus became pregnant, but her emotional high nosedived right after the doctor told them they were having a girl. Jay had made it known to everyone who would listen, that she wanted a little football player. That disappointment was magnified for Jay when certain legal issues surfaced, drastically complicating the matter even more. Jay felt slighted because she had made major sacrifices for Venus to become pregnant, yet all of her involvement had been reduced to little or nothing under the laws of the state of Georgia. Jay found herself on the losing side of the judicial system. It was her egg, but she could only be recognized as the child's legal and natural mother if she took Venus to court once the baby was born and established her maternity while stripping Venus of her rights. To avoid a legal battle, and to save their troubled relationship, Jay demanded that Venus terminate the pregnancy or give the baby up for adoption immediately after birth.

Quite naturally, Venus refused to entertain either option. She was stunned that Jay had even suggested that *they* do away with the baby by any means. Then Whitaker met his untimely death from an accidental cocaine overdose. The news sent Venus into premature labor in her thirtieth week of pregnancy and she gave birth shortly thereafter. While Nahima fought to live with under-developed lungs, weak kidneys and severe jaundice, Jay kept her distance from the hospital. Venus camped out at Grady Memorial's neonatal intensive care unit day and night even after undergoing an emergency C-section just three days before. Early one morning, out of desperation, Venus called Jay and asked her to bring her a change of clothes and a pillow to the hospital. In an angry and drunken state of mind, Jay was led to tell Venus that she would not bring anything to her and that she hoped the baby would die because their lives would be better off without her.

When Nahima was finally released from the hospital, she and Venus went home with Zach. He took off six weeks from his job to take care of both of them. Surprisingly, Jay came over to check on them every day. She and Venus had begun to work on their relationship. Things seemed to have improved, and they were getting along well. But not once did Jay hold Nahima. She wouldn't even look at the poor baby. It was too much for Venus. She refused to raise her daughter in a home with a woman who didn't want the child there.

When Nahima turned three months old, Venus took her to the house she had shared with Jay for four years. It was *her* home. She had purchased it before they had ever met. Venus asked Jay to vacate the house and take all her belongings with her. Venus offered Jay a financial settlement to cover whatever expenditures she had incurred during the course of their relationship. In retaliation, Jay sued Venus for two million dollars; citing abandonment, mental anguish and breach of verbal contract as the basis. Additionally, Jay sought reimbursement for her portion of the mortgage, half of all the household bills over the period of four years, the cost of the in vitro procedure, and her relocation costs. The judge ordered Venus to pay Jay twenty-five thousand dollars, which was the amount she had initially offered her. When the issue regarding custody of Nahima was raised, Jay left the courtroom, and Venus was awarded sole permanent custody of the child.

Chapter Seventeen

"**H**ave you heard from Jay?"

"No," Jill said, opening a pot on the stove to stir its contents. "She was *vexed* when she left that night, ya know?"

Zach took a seat at the kitchen table and began sorting through the mail. It was almost the weekend, and he, nor Jill, had heard a single word from Jay since she'd left the house angry Monday night. In her absence, Zach and Jill had spent a lot of time talking and getting to know each other as *friends*. They had not shared anything intimate other than a kiss here and there, although the sexual tension between them was damn near explosive. Zach wanted to make love to Jill again, but he needed to know her expectations and intentions. For the first time in his life, he wanted something more than just a casual physical relationship. With Jill, Zach wanted it all.

He'd helped her complete two college applications for the spring semester. The dance programs at Spelman College and Emory University were quite impressive. Zach was willing to pay whatever portion of Jill's tuition that grants, scholarships or financial aid would not cover. He loved her and wanted the best for her. Jill wanted to dance. It was what she'd been born to do, and Zach wanted to help her pursue her dream.

"This letter is for you, Jill." Zach held it up and waved it.

Jill washed her hands quickly and dried them on the red and white checkered apron around her waist. "It's from Oliver!" she said as soon as she saw the penmanship. She sat down in the chair next to Zach and read the letter. She ran her fingers across her brother's handsome face in a picture he had sent. "He wants to know if I am happy."

"Are you?"

Jill sighed and stared into space. "I could be."

"What would make you happy, Jill?"

"If my life had a wonderful purpose I would be very happy, Zachary. Remember when you told me how taking care of sick babies was very rewarding? I want to know what that feels like. My life lacks purpose. I must find it. And one day I want to be loved and respected by someone I can trust with my heart. What Jay did to me was so very unfair."

"What do you mean?" Zach knew exactly what Jill was talking about, but he needed to hear it from her mouth.

"I was only *nineteen* when I met Jay. I knew nothing about life. Papa had said I could not have a boyfriend until I turned twenty-one, and I had never been exposed to…um… ya know…"

"Lesbianism," Zach interjected. "You had never been exposed to lesbianism."

Jill nodded. "I was young and stupid. I knew it was different, but Jay was so kind to me and my family *at first*. She made me believe she was genuinely interested in my dream to become a dancer. Jay gave me fool's hope with many broken promises. By the time I discovered I had been deceived, it was too late. I had already left my parents' house to live with her at the resort. I was too ashamed to go back home. So I stayed and pretended as if everything was great."

"Do you still love her?"

"A part of me will always love the woman I met walking home from dance class that evening nearly five years ago. But I can only see Jay and me as *friends* now. So much has happened. I am not the same person I was back then. I've learned a lot thanks to you, Zachary."

Zach and Jill feasted on a meal of curry chicken, peas and rice, fried plantains and steamed cabbage. The atmosphere was relaxed and pleasant. Jill appeared content. She didn't seem the least bit uneasy being there with him alone as she had been right after they'd made love. Zach was relieved.

"After I wash dishes, I'd like to take you dancing. Go change into a party outfit and we'll head out to this reggae spot in Buckhead called Club Colony. I think you'll like it."

"Are you sure, Zachary? You have to work tomorrow, ya know?"

"I'm very sure. I wanna take you out tonight."

Jill rushed toward the stairs, humming a happy tune and snapping her fingers.

"Jill," Zach called out.

She turned around. "What is it?"

"The climate in Atlanta is nowhere near as hot and muggy as Jamaica. It'll be okay if you wear undergarments. You do own a bra and some panties don't you?"

"Of course I do, silly Zachary. I have one bra and one panty. I must go shower now, we're going *dancing*!"

And dance they did until two o'clock Friday morning. On their way home, Zach took out his cell phone and called his supervisor's desk. He left a message saying he wouldn't be in before noon. There was just no way he could make his regular seven o'clock shift. Jill had worn him out. She'd pulled him out on the crowded dance floor on just about every upbeat tune the Deejay or live reggae band had played. And whenever the music slowed down, it was Zach who'd led Jill out onto the floor to hold her in his arms as they swayed to the smooth melodies of love songs.

"Thank you so much, Zachary," Jill said the moment they entered the house. "I had an absolutely *wonderful* night! I can't remember the last time I had that much fun." Jill turned abruptly and threw herself into Zach's arms and kissed him on the lips.

Zach slid his arms around Jill's tiny waist and responded with fervor. He deepened the kiss when she parted her lips and granted his tongue full access inside. Zach felt himself getting caught up in the moment. He had promised in his heart that he wouldn't make love to Jill again unless she came on to him. For too long, she had been coaxed and bartered for her affections. Zach wanted her to be liberated to seek pleasure at her will. If Jill wanted him, if she *needed* him, she would have to take the initiative and express her desires with words as well as actions.

Zach mustered up restraint he didn't even know he had, and released Jill from his hold. With staggered breathing and in a voice so deep it could've easily put James Earl Jones to shame, he told her good night. Then he kissed her on her forehead, climbed the stairs and went to his room.

Jill was left at the bottom of the staircase chilled to her bones. She rubbed her hands up and down her bare arms and shivered. She longed for Zach's warmth. Jill wanted him to take her to his bed and make her body sing and dance again like he'd done that night he'd introduced her to womanhood. What she had experienced with him was indescribable. Never in the four years she'd been with Jay had her soul taken flight and mingled amongst the stars. No woman, or any other man alive, could make her feel the way Zach could.

"Zachary!" She called and bolted up the stairs. "Zachary, I need you!" Jill pounded on the door. "Zachary, please let me in!" She burst into his bedroom and heard the spray of the shower in the bathroom. "Zachary!" She snatched the glass shower door open and hopped inside with Zach fully clothed. Water poured down over her chic red mini dress, five-inch silver sandals and yes, her bra and panties.

No words. No contemplating. No hesitation. There were just passionate kisses, gentle caresses, and moans of pleasure under the spray of warm water and rising steam. With speed and expert hands, Zach slid Jill's dress over her head and it floated to the shallow pool of water at their feet. She kicked off her high heels as he relieved her of her bra. Extreme anticipation caused Zach to rip the left string on the only pair of panties Jill owned. He pressed her back against the black and white tile in the shower stall.

"I'll buy you a thousand pairs," he whispered with his lips pressed against hers.

Jill nodded and sucked his bottom lip. Her entire body trembled with need. Zach inserted one, then two fingers, into the damp place he wanted so desperately to bury himself in, and remain in for a lifetime. Jill whimpered, squirmed and thrust her hips against Zach. Using both hands he lifted her effortlessly, the tile still their base. And in one fluid motion they became one *again*. It was a sweet reunion, a homecoming; an old fashion rekindling of a flame.

"Jill. Jill. Jill." was Zach's chant. Her name had become his one-word love song.

She responded with a wordless ballad of hums and sensuous moans. Jill was on the ride of her life. After several moments of the most exhilarating, sexual give and take moments she had ever experienced, pleasurable sensations washed over every inch of Jill's flesh. The feelings she felt took her breath away. She closed her eyes and purred like a kitten in Zach's ear when she felt the first spasm in her core. It shook her with sensations that made her tingle inside. Then a series of invigorating waves of sheer ecstasy captured her and took her as a willing prisoner.

Zach surrendered to his passion as well, and released drops of priceless treasure into Jill's contracting walls. Then he turned off the water, which had become cold, and cradled Jill close to his chest. He stepped over her clothes and shoes and carried her to his the bed as water from their naked bodies created a wet trail behind them on the carpet. Zach searched the closet and found the blanket he'd covered Jill with the first time they'd made love. They settled under it, spooning one another as they fell asleep in each other's arms.

The next morning when Jill woke up in Zach's bed, he was standing in front of the mirror combing his shiny black curls. He was shirtless; wearing just a pair of green scrub pants and white leather Adidas tennis shoes. Jill thought he looked too damn sexy for words. Then the shower scene from the night before replayed in her memory and she smiled. "What time is it?"

"It's ten-fifteen." Zach left the mirror and sat on the edge of the bed. He kissed Jill on her lips. "How did you sleep?"

"Quite well," she said and blushed. "What about you?"

"Mmm, I've never slept better in my life. I cooked breakfast. Your plate is in the microwave. I'll be home around five. I have to swing by to pick up Nahima from her mother. Do you need me to bring you anything?"

Jill laughed and sat up in the bed. "You owe me a pair of panties."

Chapter Eighteen

Ayla stormed into the employee's break room with her nose in the air. The small group that had gathered around the television was surprised to see her because she normally didn't mingle with the support staff at all. The technicians, nurse's assistants and orderlies thought she was a snob; and that assumption was justified, as far as they were concerned by her actions. The environmental services team stayed out her way, and so did almost everyone else.

Ayla did a sweep around the room with her eyes. "Has anyone seen Zachary King?" She asked no one in particular, but everyone in general. She turned slowly, an eyed each person, but they all ignored her. She rolled her eyes to the ceiling and sighed. Then she rushed out of the room in a huff.

A table full of housekeepers started laughing and slapping hands. Mrs. Ida Bell Black was the ring leader. She was a member of Refuge Pentecostal Temple. She had known Zach all his life, and she couldn't stand the uppity Dr. Ayla Fitzpatrick at all. She was beneath him as far as Ida Bell was concerned.

"*Humph*," Ida Bell said. "Ain't nobody seen Zach today, but my daughter Tina said she saw him *last night* doing a two-step with a beautiful chocolate girl at the reggae club. It's the same girl I told y'all he's been bringing to church with him for weeks."

Ayla's blood began to boil. She had been on her way back inside the break room to get a diet soda from the drink machine when she heard Ida Bell's announcement. She rounded the corner and headed for the elevators. She pressed the lighted arrow pointing down so she could get a decent cup of black coffee from the cafeteria a few floors below. And low and behold, Mr. King, in the flesh, emerged from the center elevator just as she was about step inside of it.

"Good morning," Zach offered and flashed a friendly smile.

Ayla checked her watch and looked him up and down. As always, Zach had a bagged lunch in his hand. "Mmm, it's twelve minutes after twelve. I think morning has definitely passed. The proper greeting would be *good afternoon*." She folded her arms across her chest and pinned Zach with questioning eyes.

"Good afternoon, Dr. Fitzpatrick. Isn't it a lovely fall day?" Zach pushed past Ayla, with her marching right behind him, and headed for the break room to place his lunch inside the refrigerator.

"Hey Zach!" Ida Bell shouted when he strolled in. "Dr. Fitzpatrick was hunting for you earlier. Dr. Fitzpatrick, there's Zach!" She smirked at her own cattiness, and the entire break room erupted with laughter. Ida Bell and her crew vacated their table and left, still giggling and shaking their heads at the events unfolding before *Ms. High and Mighty,* Dr. Fitzpatrick.

"Where have you been?" Ayla demanded as she closed the distance between her and Zach. "I've been looking for you all morning. I have playoff tickets for tomorrow night. I know, I know," she said raising both hands into the air. "I *detest* baseball, but I know how much you love it so I got tickets. Dinner and a private after party in my bedroom are included."

"No can do. I'll have Nahima as I do every weekend."

"You'll have Nahima, Zach…but who will have *you*? Is it that Jamaican slut you brought here that everyone is talking about? Is she the reason why you can't make it to work on time? Were you too tired from dancing with *Ms. Jamaica* all night that you couldn't get your ass out of bed this morning? And you take her to church with you too! What's that about? *She* can be around Princess Nahima, but I can't! What the hell is going on with you, Zach?"

"We will not discuss my personal life here, Ayla." Zach glanced around the break room and saw curious eyes watching them. "If you have time around two o'clock, I'll gladly meet you in the cafeteria where we can have a civilized conversation. Until them, stop riding my back! It's not a good look for you. You don't wear desperation well, Doc."

* * * * *

Venus closed her grade book and removed her reading glasses. The peace and quiet of her planning period was greatly appreciated on a busy Friday afternoon. She'd been under so much stress lately. Since that phone message Jay had left on her voicemail, things at home between her and Charles had become strained. He wanted to know her every move, and he had begun to question her relationship with Zach, the man who Charles *believed* was Nahima's biological father. When Venus had first met Charles, her heart told her he was a special guy. He hadn't judged her when she shared her past with Jay with him and he had readily accepted Nahima as if she were his own.

No one, not even Zach, had expected Jay to ever move back to Atlanta. She had sworn off her hometown, and jumped at the opportunity to work abroad, wishing to put as many miles between her and Venus and Nahima as possible. Jay's return couldn't have come at a more inconvenient time. Three months away from her wedding day, Venus was struggling with Charles's insecurities and distrust. He'd never had an issue with Zach before, and there was no reason for him to have one now. Charles had been led to believe that Nahima was the product of artificial insemination. Venus had explained that because Jay wanted to have biological ties to the child, Zach's sperm had been used to fertilize *her* eggs.

Charles had been deceived on so many levels that it was scandalous. He had no idea that the chance of Venus giving him a child was slim to none. And he was totally oblivious to Nahima's true pedigree. He believed she belonged to Venus and Zach when she was actually Jay and Whitaker's daughter.

"Ms. Lawson, you have a delivery in the office. Ms. Lawson, please pick up a delivery in the office."

Venus's mind snapped from the troubles of her complicated life at the sound of the secretary's voice over the intercom. The clock on the wall said she had fifteen more minutes before her twenty-five rowdy children would return from PE. Venus did a power walk out of her classroom and down the hall. When she reached the office, some teachers and Mrs. Wilcox, the secretary, were oohing and aahing over a beautiful bouquet of fresh flowers in a crystal vase. The ladies turned and smiled when they noticed Venus standing behind them.

"Well, somebody must have certainly done something right last night to get these," Mrs. Wilcox whispered. She lifted the vase from the counter. "These are for you, Ms. Lawson."

Venus was stunned. She had no idea why Charles had sent her flowers. After he'd pitched a fit last night because she had forgotten to record a purchase in their joint checking account, he slept on the sofa in the den. And they hadn't even acknowledged each other's presence this morning in the kitchen before she left for work. Venus smiled with a dreamy look in her eyes because she figured Charles had sent the flowers as a piece offering after his unnecessary tirade.

"Wow," she said reaching for the vase. She held the gorgeous arrangement to her nose and took in its sweet fragrance. "My Charles is so thoughtful. Thank you, Mrs. Wilcox."

Venus had a bright smile on her face and a little pep in her step as she rushed back to her classroom to read the attached card. Her heart was thumping fast and she felt tingly all over. As soon as she sat in the chair behind her desk, she tore the small envelope open and removed the single panel card.

"Oh my God! No!" She yelled and dropped the card. "Why is this happening?"

Jay had sent the flowers to Venus. On the card she had requested that they meet in one of the restaurants at the Seven Seas at six-thirty that evening. Jay promised if Venus would meet with her just once, she would never contact her again.

* * * * *

At two o'clock sharp, Ayla sat restlessly at the table in the hospital cafeteria that Zach and Dex claimed as their personal property. She looked toward the door and glanced down at her watch wondering where the man of the hour was. Impatient and annoyed, she stood up to leave. Zach strutted in, exuding raw swagger. Ayla drew in a quick intake of air to steady her pulse. It was going to be hard for her to stay mad at him because he was so damn fine. But she was about to give it her best shot.

"So you came."

"I invited you to meet me here so we could talk. Why would I not show up? Besides, a brother has to eat." Zach took the seat opposite Ayla and opened his lunch bag. He pulled out a Tupperware plate with a lid on it. Steam rose from his food when he opened it. "What's up, Doc?"

Ayla was too busy checking out Zach's Jamaican meal of jerk pork and peas and rice. She wanted to nut up right then and there, but she held it together. She didn't need to show her ghetto side in a cafeteria full of nosey ass people. After all, at the end of the day she'd still be a doctor with a reputation to protect.

"I'm just trying to figure out what's going on with us, Zach. We don't even talk anymore. And it's been months since we…you know, *hooked up*. You don't have time for me, but the buzz around here is you've been seen all over town with your sister's lover. What's up with that?"

"Like I told you before, Jay and Jill have moved to Atlanta, and they're staying with me indefinitely. My sister works a lot. She's the executive marketing manager at the Seven Seas hotel in that huge international complex near the airport. That's a big deal for a black woman, so her shit has to pop at all times. I take care of Jill. She's new to this country. I'm all she's got."

"And how do you take care of her, Zach?" Ayla's eyes narrowed and she cocked her head to the side, challenging him.

In every damn way! Zach was tempted to say. But instead he placed his fork on the edge of his plate and held Ayla's gaze. "You're attractive, smart and independent to a fault. I see how brothers around here watch you strut your stuff. Even the Asians and dudes from the Middle East do a double take when you're on the stroll. You've got a fan club full of men sniffing at your heels, Doc. I'm not the guy for you. What we were doing for the past year and a half was cool, but it's time to pull the plug on it. We've talked about this before."

"Damn it, Zach, I don't want to *marry* you! I just want things to go back to the way they used to be. Remember how we used to smash once or twice a week? You'd cook dinner and I'd take care of breakfast. We'd take in a movie here or dinner there. That's all I want. I miss our friendship."

"We'll always be friends, Doc, but just not *friends*. I'm sorry. I'm not in the same place I was when we first met. I told you I wasn't gonna hold you down, and you promised me the same. A lot has changed for me."

"I see," Ayla said flatly. "You don't want to screw me anymore so that means you're screwing some other chick. I know you, Zach. Mr. Wonderful is definitely thrashing his thunder on someone. You're not the kind of man who'll go without. Do you know what I think?"

"I have no idea." Zach leaned back in the chair and folded his arms across his chest.

"I smell some shit in the air and it is foul as hell. I think you're screwing *Jamaican Jill* behind your sister's back. Mmm, mmm, that's it! Your nasty ass is sticking what Jay's been licking. That Jamaican bitch..."

Zach reached across the table and grabbed Ayla's hand as she pointed an accusatory finger in his direction. "You don't know what the hell you're talking about. Lay off Jill. She's innocent. You don't know a damn thing about her. All you know is I won't ever fuck *you* again. I'm out."

Zach released Ayla's hand and gathered his lunch utensils. Then with coolness, he exited the cafeteria without a fleeting backward glance.

Chapter Nineteen

Venus opened the door before Zach had a chance to ring the doorbell. She looked stylish and sophisticated in a lavender pants suit. She smelled good too. But Venus seemed distracted and in a rush to get rid of Nahima. The customary small talk between her and Zach was cut short and she kept checking her watch. He got the unspoken message that there was someplace she needed to be soon.

"Have a good time wherever you're going tonight, Venus. Remind Charles again why he's such a lucky brother. We men need a shot of reassurance every now and then." Zach kissed her on the cheek and left her on the stoop waving at him and Nahima.

"Do you know where my mommy is going, Uncle Z?" Nahima raised her arms so Zach could secure her car seat.

"She's going on a romantic date with Charles, pumpkin."

"No she's not, silly goose." Nahima giggled at her uncle's wrong answer. "She's going to the meeting at the hotel. I heard her telling her BFF Janice on the telephone. Mommy said she's gotta go to *one* meeting at the hotel, and she won't ever have to go again."

Zach closed Nahima's door and looked back at Venus's now empty stoop. He didn't like the sound of what he had just heard, but it all made sense. Venus *was* acting strange and seemed anxious for them to leave. Zach needed to know if she was going to the Seven Seas to meet with Jay, and if she was, he wanted to know why. He got into the SUV and took out his cell phone to dial Venus's number. She came out the front door at the same time Charles pulled into the driveway. Zach pressed the phone to his chin, realizing the matter was out if his hands.

* * * * *

Pizza, ice cream and Disney movies were on the agenda for Friday night at Uncle Z's house. He'd ordered a large pizza with double pepperoni for himself and Nahima. And for Jill he'd ordered a small one with sausage and mushrooms.

"Can you please pay the delivery guy when he comes, baby?" Zach handed Jill a couple of bills. "I'm going upstairs to give Nahima a bath." He snapped his fingers and faced her again. He pulled more cash from his wallet and a piece of paper. "This is for you. I think you should have money in your purse at all times, and you need your own account. We'll go to the bank one day next week and open one for you, *Ms. Bessette*. The cash is for your family. Tomorrow we can swing by Western Union and make the transaction."

"I don't know what to say, Zachary. You are very kind to me. Thank you."

"You're very welcome. Let's go, pumpkin! It's time for a bubble bath and your princess pajamas!"

"I'm coming! I'm coming! I'm coming!"

Jill watched Nahima hop like a bunny up the stairs behind Zach. They were so in love. He was a caring and committed uncle to his niece and he was also a nice man. Jill wanted Zach to be *her* man, but she didn't know how to tell him. If only she could speak with Roy back at the resort. He could teach her how to tell him what she felt in her heart. She would give him a call early in the morning before sunrise.

* * * * *

Jay stood and pulled out the chair for Venus, and then took the seat across from her.

"You're just what the doctor ordered. Life must be good for you, V. You look amazing."

"Hello Jay," Venus said coolly. "I'm here. What do you wanna talk about?" She took in her surroundings.

"Let's have something to drink first." Jay snapped her fingers at a passing waiter. He stopped at their table. "Alonzo, give me the usual please and the lady will have a glass of merlot."

Venus looked at the entrance of the restaurant and smirked. "I'll also have a Hennessey and Coke and a glass of water please, Alonzo. Thank you."

Jay placed both elbows on the table and leaned forward. "I've never known you to drink anything heavier than wine. Go ahead and get drunk, baby. I can put you up in a fabulous, complimentary suite for the night."

"That won't be necessary," said a deep male voice. "She's not staying here." Charles reached down and placed his hand on Venus's shoulder. She touched his hand and rubbed it gently.

A white man in a gray Versace suit had approached the table alongside Charles with a brown Coach briefcase in his hand. "May we?" The Richie Rich look alike asked, already moving toward the chair beside Jay.

Charles sat next to his fiancée and draped his arm around her shoulders. A few moments of uncomfortable silence hung over the table like a cloud. Diners filed into the restaurant just ahead of the seven o'clock dinner hour. When Alonzo returned with the drinks, Charles lifted the Hennessey and Coke to his mouth and took a long swig. He smacked his lips and glared at Jay. The chandelier cast a glow on his bald head and golden complexion.

Venus took the initiative to get the party started. "Jay, I'd like you to meet my fiancé Charles Morris Junior. Charles, honey, this is Jay King, my *ex*."

Jay grunted something in the form of a greeting to Charles, and drained her drink. She raised the empty glass and signaled for Alonzo to bring her another one.

"And I'm Kirk Orowitz, their attorney." The white dude motioned toward Venus and Charles with the glass of merlot in his hand. "I'll just jump right in, Ms. King," he said tossing his blue eyes at Jay. "Ms. Lawson does not wish for you to contact her ever again by any means. She and her fiancé over there are in the process of having restraining orders issued against you. We all just dropped by to have drinks and give you a heads-up. That's how we *roll*. As their legal representation, it is my obligation to let you know if the restraining orders aren't persuasive enough for you, they're prepared to sue you for harassment. Lawsuits…my how awful they can be. You remember, Ms. King, the one you filed against Ms. Lawson was messy." Kirk reached inside his briefcase and removed some documents. "Anyway, here's a copy of the notes from this cozy soiree. And just in case you're a little *iffy* about what constitutes contact, I've included a list you can refer to. From this day forward, you should not come in physical contact with, call, text, email, write letters, send flowers or any other gifts to Ms. Lawson, Mr. Morris or little *Nahima*. Should I forward documentation of anything we've discussed here this evening to your attorney?"

"Nah, that won't be necessary." Jay guzzled down her second drink and slammed the glass on the red linen table cloth.

"Whew! That's good. We're all on the same page." Kirk finished the glass of merlot, sat it down and gripped his briefcase. "I guess we're done here," he said rising to his feet.

Charles stood and helped Venus from her chair. He held her hand and they both stared at Jay with victorious smiles on their faces.

Jay was not to be bested. "I ain't done yet," she said. She turned wicked eyes on Venus. "It's funny that old Kirk here covered *Nahima* under the restraining order. What do you think is gonna happen when she gets older and starts asking questions? She doesn't look anything like you, V and I bet she's never even seen a picture of Whitaker. What are you, Uncle Z and step daddy gonna tell the little princess?"

Venus dropped Charles's hand and stepped closer to Jay. "We will tell her the truth about *everything*, including how her biological mother wanted me to abort her in my nineteenth week of pregnancy. And we'll also tell her how she wanted her to die in the hospital after she was born prematurely. What will *you* tell her, Jay, if she reaches out to you?"

Charles placed his hand in the small of Venus's back and led her away. Kirk gave Jay a quick courtesy nod, and followed behind them.

Honey

*****

Jay was tired of driving around aimlessly. It was too late to visit Aunt Jackie, and she didn't need another damn drop of alcohol in her system. She had already exceeded the legal limit to operate a vehicle in the state of Georgia. She yawned and blinked her eyes against her fatigue. Jay figured she might as well go back to the one person who loved her in spite of herself. Jill had never been able to stay mad at her for more than a day or two. Poor thing was probably going crazy without her.

The light in the guestroom upstairs was off when Jay pulled into the driveway. She guessed Jill had already turned in for the night. Cuddling, instead of hot, wild sex would just have to do. It was better than nothing after the humiliation Venus had put her through. Jay needed Jill more than ever before. And it wasn't for anything physical. She was in need of love. She planned to go into the den where Zach was probably watching the Braves play. She would be cordial to him before she headed upstairs to Jill.

Nothing could have prepared Jay for the scene she discovered on the floor in the den. At first she thought her eyes were playing tricks on her. She had thrown quite a few drinks back after Venus and company had left her at the table in the restaurant pissed and embarrassed. But Jay was not too drunk to make out the bodies sprawled out over a blanket on the floor. The sight was sobering. Zach and Jill had fallen asleep with Nahima snuggled between them. The television and DVD player were on. A couple of frogs and a big alligator were singing and riding a log down a river headed for the Louisiana bayou.

Jay backed out of the den and ran outside to her car. Her emotions surprised her. She hadn't cried since her breakup with Venus. The day Venus had told Jay to pack her shit and get the hell out of her house had been Jay's darkest moment ever. Since then, she had coasted through life with a brick wall around her heart, protecting it from anyone who dared to care. Not even sweet Jill had been able to penetrate through it with all the love she had showered on Jay. Jill had dedicated her entire life, and turned her back on the world, to be with her. But it wasn't enough to win Jay's heart.

Jay started the Beamer's engine and drove toward the interstate. She was too exhausted and upset to make it to the hotel. The cheap motel two exits south of Zach's subdivision would suffice for the night. In the morning she would pick up Jill and take her to breakfast to apologize for being such a bitch the other night. And because her naïve lover adored her so, she would forgive her without a second thought. Then things would return to normal between them. Finally, Jay would make the necessary arrangements to get Jill out of Zach's house before she became too attached to Nahima, and started asking questions. All her past and present skeletons needed to remain in her closet. But how could she pull it off? Several ideas begin to roll around inside her head.

Chapter Twenty

From her stakeout point two blocks away, Ayla watched Zach and Jill exit his two-story brick home. Her curiosity piqued. Where the hell were they off to so early on a Saturday morning? Ayla's eyes zoomed in on Nahima. The little girl was twirling and waving her arms in the air like a ballerina. Jill stopped her and adjusted her short arms in another position, and instructed her how to point her toe correctly. The child mimicked the move, and Zach applauded like she had just landed a spot on "Dancing with the Stars." Ayla grimaced and cursed when the trio held hands and walked to the Mercedes SUV and hopped inside.

The pretty doctor sat behind the wheel of her red Mustang convertible, pouting like a bratty kid. She was tempted to trail them, but quickly decided against that juvenile move. She started her engine, and was about to do a quick U-turn, when a black BMW whipped into the driveway. Ayla leaned forward for a better view and held her breath. When the woman that exited the car used a key to enter the house, she knew instantly it had to be Jay. Ayla eased her car down the street, and stopped behind the Beamer. She killed the engine and waited.

* * * * *

Jay did a speedy but thorough inspection of the house, and discovered nothing out of the ordinary. She searched the refrigerator and was pleased to find leftover double pepperoni pizza. She gathered two slices and a bottle of guava juice and sat down at the table. Jay had been a fan of cold pizza since her days at Howard University's School of Business. She gulped down the food and juice and discarded the bottle and plate in the trashcan. On her way out, she looked inside the den and fresh memories of the night before came floating back. She did some lightning fast math inside her head and came up with the magic number of thirty-six hundred dollars. That was the amount of money she needed to get her hands on before she could move into the condo at the Seven Seas. Zach was the only person who would be stupid enough to lend it to her.

"Ms. King?" Ayla called out as soon as Jay walked outside. "Ms. King, I'm Ayla Fitzpatrick. I'm a very close friend of your brother's. We also work together."

Jay took Ayla's offered hand and shook it. She held on to it for a few seconds as she checked her out from head to toe. "It's a pleasure to meet you, Ms. Fitzpatrick."

Honey

"Actually, it's *Doctor Fitzpatrick*." Ayla corrected. She eyed Jay closely and was stunned by the arresting facial similarities the King siblings shared. Ayla thought Jay was much too pretty and curvy to be a lesbian, as was Jill. Jay was quite feminine too, not butchy at all.

"So you're a *doctor*, huh? That's cute. I bet my brother loves playing doctor with you. I damn sure would."

Jay's last remark threw Ayla off a bit, but she recovered fast. "I decided to pay Zach a visit after I left the gym this morning. It hit me after I got here that he told me last night he'd promised to take your friend to run some errands today." Ayla tapped her finger against her chin several times pretending to recall her last conversation with Zach. "I forgot where he said they were going. With all the stuff I have to remember about my patients, I guess it slipped my mind."

"I'm sure," Jay mumbled gawking at Ayla's breasts. "I'll tell my brother you made a house call, Dr. Fitzpatrick."

"Oh no, you don't have to do that. We'll just hook up some other time, although it hasn't been easy for us lately. Zach told me how much you work and that most times he's left to entertain Jill. She's so lucky to have him. The sweet girl would be bored to death if my Zach wasn't around to take her to church, grocery shopping and *dancing*. They partied so hard the other night that he was five hours late to work the next morning!"

"Yeah, Jill told me about that."

"Well, I better let you go now, Ms. King," Ayla said confident she had done her job.

That tidbit about Zach and Jill's night at the club had surprised Jay. Her poker face was terrible. Ayla had seen her flinch from the shock, and she couldn't have been more satisfied.

"Please call me Jay. Any friend of Zach's is a friend of mine, especially one as fine as you." Jay reached into the breast pocket of her suit jacket and removed one of her business cards. "If you ever need *anything*, Dr. Fitzpatrick, please don't hesitate to give me a call."

Ayla took the offered business card before she and Jay parted ways. She was ninety-nine percent sure she had just been hit on by Zach's sister, but she was certain beyond a shadow of a doubt that she'd just made an ally. Jay had been working too hard and too long while Zach and Jill had been *playing* equally as much, if not more, behind her back. Ayla had just cast the rod and now it was up to Jay to take the bait. She read the card and placed it inside her purse for safe keeping. She would indeed give Jay a call in a few days to add a little fuel to the fire she'd just started.

* * * * *

Jill's insides started bubbling with anticipation when Zach went upstairs to put Nahima to bed. Once he returned to the den, she was going to put Roy's advice into play. Their private conversation right before sunrise had lasted thirty minutes. The middle-aged driver had been thrilled to learn that Jill's relationship with Jay had taken a wrong turn, and now she was in love with Zach. Roy was even happier to know they were living under the same roof while his former boss was off working and collecting women as usual. Jill heard Zach's footsteps coming down the steps. She closed her eyes and tried to recall every word Roy had told her, especially the test he had prescribed that would determine if Zach truly loved her or not.

Zach sat close to Jill on the sofa and snaked his arm around her waist. "Did you have fun today?"

"Yes, I did. Thank you for everything, Zachary. Breakfast was delicious. I enjoyed the movie and lunch. I can't believe you bought me a cell phone. It was kind of you. I loved shopping for Nahima. She was so excited."

"Did you like the clothes *we* picked out for you?"

"Of course I did. Why do you ask?"

"You seemed distracted and very indecisive. I wanted you to select the pieces, but you kept asking my opinion."

"I wanted to know what you liked. I didn't want to choose the wrong color or fabric. You wouldn't have approved."

"I'm not Jay. I don't want to control you. It's not necessary for you to hide your feelings or opinions from me. Sometimes we'll disagree about certain things, but it won't be the end of the world. Your feelings really matter to me, Jill. This relationship isn't just about me. It's about *us*."

"So we are in a *relationship*, Zachary?"

"I thought we were, but I may have assumed too much. I'd like to hear your opinion."

"I don't want to be with Jay anymore. That I know for certain. I am happy here with you. I don't ever want to leave. I love you very much and I think Jay needs to know immediately, Zachary."

Zach pulled Jill's body closer to his. He kissed her eyelids, her nose and then her lips.

Jill melted into Zach and responded to his kiss with zest, but Roy's voice ringing in her ears caused her to pull back. She ended the kiss suddenly.

"What's the matter?" Zach asked, frowning.

Jill had purposely poured water on the flame. "Did you not hear what I said?"

"I heard you. I love you too, Jill. You know that." Zach kissed her lips. "But I'd much rather *show* you than tell you right now." He kissed her again more passionately than before.

Words and thoughts were flying out the window. Jill had to fight the fire burning within in order to stay on course. She pushed away from Zach again.

"Mmm," she said trying to reel in her raging hormones. "If we are going to be together we must tell Jay at once, Zachary. It is only right. If it is truly love, why must we hide it? She will be vexed, but I don't care and neither should you. Jay and your friend Ayla must be told that we are in love, if it is really the way you feel. I'm sleepy. Let's go to bed."

* * * * *

When Jill had suggested they go to bed, Zach hoped she meant to make love. But when he finished showering he was disappointed to find her in his bed sound asleep. He gathered her in his arms and she threw her right leg mindlessly across his lower torso. Against his better judgment, he slid his hand down her waist and on to her hips. Her bottom was bare. On their shopping spree Zach had bought Jill over a dozen pairs of panties in all colors, prints and styles. He was aggravated because she had chosen this particular night to backslide to her old habit. He had to laugh to keep from crying.

Jill opened her eyes in the darkness when Zach kissed her on the forehead. She smiled when he whispered "I love, Jill." She couldn't wait to report back to Roy. Zach had passed parts one and two of his three-part test. Once he told Jay, and his friend Ayla whom he had warned her about, that they were in love and involved in a romantic relationship, everything would be perfect.

Chapter Twenty-One

Ramona picked up Jill from Zach's house at ten o'clock Wednesday morning as she had promised. Her younger cousin Zariah was an aspiring dancer and student at Umoja Academy of the Performing Arts in Midtown. She'd told Jill about an opening for a dance teacher at the school after meeting her at Ramona and Dex's house Sunday evening. Zach and Jill had stopped by to see little Abriah after they'd taken Nahima home. Zariah was there getting her hair braided by Ramona's sister Felicia, and talking nonstop about her upcoming audition for the lead in a dance recital. Quite naturally, when Jill heard the word "dance" she got excited, and offered Zariah a few tips. The two dancers made an immediate connection which resulted in an upcoming job interview at the academy.

* * * * *

For weeks, Umoja Academy's founder and director, Helena Bingham Scott, had been in desperate search of a replacement for Sister Asatta, the previous instructor for the senior women's dance class. The sixteen silver foxes had been abandoned for the bright lights of New York City. Asatta had landed a spot in the off Broadway production of "Angels with Black Wings." Helena was proud of her former student's accomplishment, but Asatta's sudden departure had left Helena in a bind. She read over the profile of Jillian J. Bessette, the Jamaican dancer that one of her female intermediate dance students had been raving about. Her training was inadequate, but her references and reviews from critics on the small Caribbean island were impressive. Helena shuffled through the thin stack of pictures again. She thought Ms. Bessette was a natural beauty who could do very well on catwalks with the proper training.

The intercom on Mrs. Helena's desk buzzed. Petra, her administrative assistant, announced that her eleven-fifteen appointment had arrived.

"Send Ms. Bessette right in, Petra. Thank you."

Jill bounced into the office smiling. She looked radiant in her bright orange, single-breasted, Michael Kors pants suit with brushed gold buttons. The multicolor silk scarf draped around her shoulders and neck was a nice touch and so were the gold Jessica Simpson sling backs.

"Good morning, ma'am, how are you? I am Jillian Bessette, but you may call me Jill." She extended her hand.

Jill's lovely smile was infectious. Mrs. Scott offered her one in return, and grasped her hand in a friendly shake. "Please have a seat, Jill," she said, motioning to the chair facing her desk. "Tell me about yourself. What brought you all the way to Atlanta from *Jamaica*?"

"I moved here with a friend, an American friend who wanted to move back home. I came to Atlanta so I could study dance. And I'd like to teach as well. Back in Jamaica I taught and conditioned young girls for performances. I choreographed group and solo routines for *carnival*. It is a very special time on our island. Thousands of people come from all over the world each year to Jamaica for Carnival."

"I can tell by the glint in your eyes and the cheer in your voice how much you love to dance. It's an amazing art form. What is your favorite part, Jill?"

"It is the discipline. You see, in Jamaica we don't have big, extravagant schools such as this one, or huge studios like those in New York and other major cities. Most girls learn to dance like I did- in small crammed rooms with warped music boxes and no mirrors. I had to use my imagination, and rely on my memory of performances by professional dancers I'd seen on television, in order to develop my craft. In classes, my dance mates and I had to work five times as hard to develop skills and techniques because we did not know if our parents would have money to pay next week's fees. So I used to practice at home *every day* just to stay ahead. My love for dance and the discipline became my driving force. Because of it, I became a very fine dancer. After a while, there was nothing else my instructor could teach me. Thank God I am here in America where I can learn more."

Mrs. Scott rose from her chair and walked over to a shelf where a portable stereo sat. She pushed a button and the Fugees version of "Killing Me Softly" filled the room.

"May I?" Jill asked, removing her scarf.

Mrs. Scott reclaimed her seat and smiled. "I was hoping you would."

Jill waved her scarf in the air and did a smooth pirouette. She then moved into a series of forward lunges and shoulder rolls. A perfect left leg side lift followed by a cha-cha earned her a round of applause from her audience of one. Jill took her impromptu performance to another level by mixing some hip-hop and tap moves into the routine.

"You're a very talented dancer, Jill!" Mrs. Scott pressed her hand to her chest in awe. "The job is yours if you want it. I know you're used to teaching youth, but the senior ladies are a wonderful group. They meet Monday, Wednesday and Friday from ten o'clock until noon. And if you can, I would love for you to spend an extra hour, or two, here on Wednesdays to help me work on some choreography for our Christmas production. I can only pay you fifteen dollars an hour until my grant is renewed, but after that, we'll sit down and negotiate a better deal. I have great plans for you, Jill!"

"I'll take it! Thank you so very much, Mrs. Scott. I will not disappoint you.

* * * * *

"Oh my God, Zachary," Jill whispered. She covered her mouth with both hands and stared at Jay's car parked in the driveway. "I don't want to see her! You told me you were going to the hotel to tell her about us. Why haven't you kept your word?"

Zach looked at his house. The only light on was in the upstairs guest room. Jay, the control freak, had returned and was sending a bold message to Jill. After being away for over a week without as much as a phone call, she was now back, and expected Jill to share a bed with her. Zach was highly pissed off, and he wanted nothing more than to go inside and tell Jay that he and Jill were in love. But it wasn't as simple as that. For days he'd been trying to make Jill understand that Jay could make their lives a nightmare if they didn't handle the situation with extreme caution.

"I'm taking you to Dex's house. You can't stay here tonight."

"No, I won't go, Zachary! Why can't you just go into *your* house, tell Jay you love me, and demand that she leave?"

"Damn it, Jill, it ain't that simple! If I do that, Jay will pull the plug on your paperwork with the immigration department and send you back home. You know what she's capable of. Look at what she tried to do to Venus out of spite! We are dealing with a woman who hates her own child. I ain't gonna give her an opportunity to hurt you. You'll stay with Dex and Ramona tonight. I'll make up something to tell Jay. Give me a little more time to work this out...*please.*"

* * * * *

Jay was in the kitchen when Zach returned from Dex's house. He had stayed for a while to explain the situation to his boy and Ramona. Then he spent some time with Jill, and helped her get settled before he left. On his way home, he thought about how he had hoped he'd be spending the rest of his night with him and Jill continuing the celebration of her new job in bed. He had taken her to Rays on the River for dinner, and she'd promised to thank him for it all night long. Now, instead of making love with Jill, Zach was standing in his kitchen about to have a bullshit conversation with Jay before going to bed with a hard dick.

Jay looked up from the bowl of grapes she was eating and stared past Zach. "Where is Jill?"

Zach loosened the knot in his red necktie and leaned against the counter. "She's at Dex's house. His wife Ramona has a job interview in the morning, and Jill is gonna babysit their daughter. When did you get here?"

"I took off around five o'clock and drove straight home. I'm off tomorrow too, so I thought I'd spend some time with my baby."

Zach saw red, but he was cooler than that. He held his anger in check. "You haven't seen Jill or called her since you stormed outta here over a week ago, Jay. What's up with you?"

"I've been *busy*. This ain't Jamaica. White folks will eat your ass alive if you miss a step. You know how it is. I've finally got the marketing department running smoothly at the hotel, so I took some time off to take care of my personal life, which reminds me. I need a loan, Zach."

Bitch, you've got some damn nerve! The words almost rolled off Zach's tongue, but he swallowed them. He dropped down in a chair at the table and eyed Jay suspiciously. "What do you need money for and why the hell should I lend it to you? You've treated me like shit in my own home since the day you moved in, and I've taken it. And now you have the audacity to ask me for money."

"I need to *borrow* about four thousand dollars so I can secure Jill's permanent resident status here," she rushed to say. "I'm having everything expedited so she can apply for school, and maybe get a part-time job. I want her to be able to take advantage of the opportunities Atlanta has to offer. I owe her that."

Zach nodded, knowing full well he had just been fed a load of bullshit by his sister. After all these years, Jay still thought he was stupid. She was up to something. Zach could feel it in his gut. Jay needed money for some reason she didn't wish to share with him, and she was using Jill as an excuse to get it.

"Give me Jill's file and I'll take care of it. I've got a friend who has juice in the immigration department. He can get things done quickly, and it damn sure won't cost four grand. I'll pay for everything as a favor to you, sis. You won't have to worry about a thing."

Zach got up feeling like a million bucks. He smiled down at Jay. She wanted to say something, but he had shut her down. If looks could kill, he would've been a dead man. He patted her shoulder before he walked out of the kitchen, but quickly turned around.

"I almost forgot. Jill has a part-time job. She'll be teaching dance and doing a little choreography at a performing arts school in Midtown. She starts Monday."

Chapter Twenty-Two

Jill was too upset and disappointed in Zach to sleep. She'd been crying since he'd left her at Dex's house. She was comfortable in the guest bedroom next door to Abriah's nursery, but it wasn't where she wanted to be. Jill wanted to be at *home* with Zach, but he had sent her away because of Jay. By now, he should have told his sister about them. In Roy's opinion, that would indeed be his most difficult task, but he'd said Zach would do it if he truly loved her. Jill sat up and looked out the window. It was a beautiful starry night. Her eyes found the brightest star in the sky and she made two wishes: That Zach would tell Jay that he loved her, and that they would be together forever.

Jill's cell phone rang, startling her. She knew it was Zach. No one else called her except him. "Zachary?"

"Yeah, it's me. I just wanted to make sure you're okay. And I want you to know I love you, Jill. I love you more than I thought I could ever love a woman. Please don't ever doubt that. You have to trust my heart and believe I'm making the best decisions for us right now. I'm gonna start working on your resident status tomorrow with the immigration department. Once I take care of that, I'll tell Jay everything. I promise. I love you."

"I love you too, Zachary."

* * * * *

"Jay is giving you the runaround, Zach. Clive has already told you that Jill's application doesn't exist. You need to get your hands on her passport and other documents so you can get the ball rolling. She's gonna need them for school and for tax purposes anyway. She's a working girl now." Dex eyed his boy with concern.

"I've called Jay every single day since I told her I'd take over the process, but she's always too busy to talk. I offered to stop by the hotel to pick up Jill's file. Jay had a million excuses. She's got me the by the balls and she knows it."

"I have an idea how to get everything you need from Jay, but I'm not sure you'll go along with it."

Zach took his Heineken to the head and sat the empty bottle on the bar. Floyd, the bartender, replaced it with another one right away. "I'm desperate, Dex. I'll go along with just about anything."

"Send Jill to the hotel to get it."

"Are you *crazy?* You expect me to let Jill sleep with Jay for a passport and some damn documents? That's some twisted shit even for you, Dex. I'd rather move with Jill back to Jamaica. Besides, she wouldn't do it. She won't let anybody touch her except *me*."

"I didn't say anything sexual *necessarily* had to go down. But if Jay *thought* Jill was about to break her off…" Dex raised both palms in the air. "Jill could pretend she needs her file for her job which I'm surprised really isn't the case. Anyway, we could take her over there and wait for her to get Jay all hot and bothered. Then as soon as she gets the goods, we get her outta there before anything jumps off."

"Don't you think that's cutting it kind of close, Dex? Would you want Ramona all up in a hotel room with her ex trying to seduce him outta some old pictures or something?"

"I wouldn't mind if it was something very important. And as long as she accomplished the goal without taking off her clothes, I'd be okay."

"Jill doesn't even wanna be in the same room with Jay."

"Ask Jill if she wants to continue to live in the same house with *you* in *this* country."

* * * * *

"*Nooo*, Zachary, I won't do it!" Jill cried and waved her hands before his face. "I don't want to be anywhere near Jay. *Pleeease* don't make me."

"I won't, baby. We'll have to come up with another plan." Jill buried her face in Zach's chest. He kissed the top of her head and looked across the room at Dex and Ramona. "We need a plan B, y'all."

"Jill, sweetie, you need to call Jay and ask her for your file." Ramona said calmly. "Tell her your boss needs a copy of your passport and temporary visa. Let her know you've already applied for school, and it's important for you to have your file. That's an honest and direct approach. If she asks you to meet her at the hotel, Zach will go with you. If she brings it to his house, he'll be there also." Ramona looked directly at Zach. "You need to handle your business, *sir*. It's time out for all these games. Tell Jay about you and Jill. Be ready for the battle of your life, but tell her anyway. Dex and I are on your side. We'll do whatever we can to help you two."

* * * * *

The scent of Ayla's expensive perfume lingered in Jay's posh corner office an hour after she'd left. Upset, she drained her glass, and immediately filled it again with Disarrono. Jay needed the strong drink to process the interesting conversation she and Ayla had just had. If the doctor's suspicions were correct,

Jill was a hell of a lot smarter than she appeared. Jay couldn't imagine that being the case. She had deliberately kept her in a fish bowl since she was a teenager, and shielded her from all outside influences, including her family. There was no way possible the student had outsmarted the teacher.

If Zach and Jill were actually having an affair right under Jay's nose, which Ayla swore they were, it would be the worst act of betrayal between siblings since Cain murdered Abel. Zach wasn't a murderer, but he damn sure was no saint either. Ayla said he'd been jerking her chain for almost two years now with no plans of making her an honest woman. She'd had two abortions for him, and he'd given her Chlamydia once. Jay was pissed that Zach had refused to let her borrow the four grand she'd asked for, especially now that she'd learned Ayla was his sugar momma. That's why he could roll around the ATL in a Mercedes SUV and Plymouth Prowler and live in the suburbs. His selfish ass had allowed Ayla to basically pay for his master's degree from Georgia State University while she was struggling to pay off student loans she'd accumulated in medical school.

Jay needed proof that Zach was sleeping with Jill. She had to know if he had the balls to do some foul shit like that to his only sibling. And Jill would be a sneaky, ungrateful bitch if she was fucking Zach after all Jay had done for her and her dysfunctional family. The thought of them together in bed was too much for Jay. Yes, she would take Ayla's advice. She would catch them in the act. She had to see it with her own two eyes. And once she did, she would destroy them both.

* * * * *

Jackie Dudley Brown could be called a million things, but *stupid* wasn't one of them. The tension around her dining room table was extra thick. She had cooked a midweek meal of meatloaf, mashed potatoes with gravy and fresh turnip greens. It was a smart combination of Zach and Jay's favorites so she'd invited them both. Her homemade cheesecake was baked with Jill in mind. She loved it covered with fresh pureed strawberries. Now that the family was gathered, and eating in complete silence, Aunt Jackie wondered if dinner had been such a good idea. The atmosphere was awkward, and she wanted to lighten the mood.

"How is work, Jay? Is it what you expected?"

"The pay is excellent, but the hours are much longer and more demanding than I'd expected. I work sixteen to eighteen hours a day sometimes. My personal life is suffering. I'm not even sure what is actually happening before my very eyes most days."

"Oh…well…um…what about you, Zach? Is there anything interesting going on at the hospital? Tell me about your new babies."

"I've got three. They're all boys. Dr. Schwartz said the smallest one won't make it through the night. He was born with gastroschisis which means his intestines formed outside of his little body. I wish you could go pray for him,

Auntie. He's a beautiful baby."

"I'll pray for him and his family. How is dance class, Jill?"

Jay cut her eyes at Jill and held her gaze. Aunt Jackie sensed the friction mounting between them. Neither woman appeared intimidated by the other. Their stares sliced through each other. Jill finally looked away to face Aunt Jackie.

"It is wonderful! I'm teaching, but I am also learning a lot. You must come to our Christmas production, Auntie. It will be on the fifteenth of December."

"I hope you're sending some of your hard earned money back home to your family. I know they'll be looking for it." Jay snickered. "They *love* money."

"Ms. Faye and Mr. Orville called yesterday. They and their children are doing fine. It's funny. They've never asked me for one thin dime," Zach snapped.

"It's dessert time," Aunt Jackie announced. She was determined to keep order in her house. "I'll go and get it."

When she was out of earshot, Zach glared at Jay. "I'm gonna follow you to the hotel after dinner so I can get Jill's passport and other documents. She needs them for her job and school. My friend said you haven't even applied for temporary alien residence on her behalf, Jay! Why did you lie?"

"Go to hell, Zach! You go straight to hell!" Jay slammed her hand on the table. "Why are you so worried about Jill's status in this country anyway? She came here with *me*. If I didn't know better, big bro, I'd swear you and Jill were screwing around behind my back. But that's ridiculous because Jill would never do that to me. I'm the only person who has ever loved her *unconditionally*." Jay locked eyes with Jill. "When your father denounced you as his daughter and called you a bucket of trash, I took you in and cared for you. I gave you a better life than you could've ever imagined."

"And the Academy Award for best actress goes to *Jayla King*! You are good, sis. Can you even spell love? You never loved Jill. You owned her! What about all your other honeys on the island? Remember, I was there. I saw *everything*. Now I want Jill's passport!"

"And I want *you* to kiss my ass." Jay pushed back from the table, knocking her chair over, and stared Zach down.

"Hold up!" Aunt Jackie shouted, returning to the dining room. She put the cheesecake and topping on the table. "There will be none of this in my house. Sit down, Jay."

"I'm leaving. I gotta get outta here."

"You ain't going nowhere. Sit down! I'm about to serve dessert. It's cheesecake, and I know it's your favorite."

Jay took her seat while Aunt Jackie went back to the kitchen to get the plates and forks. When she returned, she began to serve her family. No one said a word until Jay realized the dessert topping was strawberry and not raspberry.

"Damn it! Why would you make strawberry topping, Auntie? You know I *hate* strawberry!"

"I'm sorry, baby. I forgot."

"How could you forget?" Jay hopped up. "From the day Uncle Bubba told me strawberries were Wallace's favorite fruit, I swore I would never eat them again. I was nine years old. You should've remembered!"

Jay ran from the dining room in the direction of the front door.

"Jayla Simone, come back here! Come back here, I said!"

The door slamming shut shook the house. Aunt Jackie starred at it for a moment before she turned her eyes to rest on her nephew. "Okay, Zachary Sean King, I want to know what is going on between you and your sister. But first you need to tell me how long you've been in love with Jill."

Chapter Twenty-Three

Two weeks before Thanksgiving, Faye called Zach to discuss the condition of Oliver's eyesight. The doctors at the Johnson Medical Center said he needed a cornea transplant in his left eye. A group of American ophthalmologists would be traveling to Jamaica to provide services to some of Kingston's most needy patients. Oliver had been listed among them. He'd been matched with a donor, and was scheduled for surgery next week.

"Can you please send Jillian home, Zachary? Oliver is terribly afraid. Orville is away on the ship, and won't be home until Christmas. I am here alone with my children. I cannot take care of them and Oliver. Please, Zachary, send Jillian home. I need her. She will return to you when Oliver gets well."

"I'll call you tomorrow, Ms. Faye. There're some things I'll have to work out first. I promise to call you tomorrow. Give all the children my love."

Zach ended the call and conveyed his conversation with Faye to Jill.

"I must go, Zachary. Oliver needs me. I will take care of him while my mommy takes care of Angelina and the other boys."

"Jay has your passport. You can't travel without it."

Jill ran upstairs. She returned wearing her black leather coat. "Take me to the hotel. I will get my passport from Jay. Oliver needs me, and I must go to Jamaica, Zachary."

* * * * *

Zach had called Dex on his way to the Seven Seas to let him know what was about to go down. As his best friend, Dex reminded him of one of the top ten rules for survival in the hood. He advised Zach to come up with a plan B pronto, and to take backup.

When Zach pulled his SUV into Aunt Jackie's driveway, Jill became confused. "Why are we here, Zachary? We must go to the *hotel* and get my passport from Jay."

"We are, baby. Just wait here. I'll be right back."

When Aunt Jackie joined Zach and Jill in the vehicle, they sped away en route to the Seven Seas. The ladies listened carefully as the man with the plan briefed them on what he believed was the perfect strategy.

* * * * *

"Well, this must be my lucky day. Come on in, baby." Jay swatted Jill on her ass when she passed through the doorway.

Jill stood in the middle of the floor and looked around the suite. It was nice and ornately decorated. The furniture was top of the line, but overall, the suite was a far cry from the lavish penthouse at the Island Paradise Resort. It was much smaller and less extravagant. The suite could actually fit inside the penthouse.

"Have a seat. I don't bite…*anymore*." Jay laughed and stretched out on the couch. "Sit down, baby and relax."

Jill sat down at the bar on one of the tall stools, and placed her purse in her lap. She took a deep breath before she went into her spiel. "Oliver's left cornea is diseased. He is in need of a new one. Some American doctors have made arrangements for a transplant. They're traveling to Jamaica to perform the surgery next week." Jill lowered her head and closed her eyes. "My mommy needs me to come home for a few days. I must go to Jamaica to take care of Oliver while she stays home with the other children."

Jay sat up and planted her bare feet on the carpet. "So you came here because you want *me* to send you home? Zach brought your unappreciative ass all the way to my spot so you could beg for money to buy a damn ticket to Jamaica?"

"I don't need money, Jay. All I want is my passport so I can travel home *please*. I'll only be there a few days then I'll return to Atlanta."

"What are you coming back for? I know it ain't for *me*. Is it to work at that damn dance school or are you rushing back so you can continue to be Zach's little *whore*? Yeah, I know he's hitting that. I can't prove it, but I know my lowdown brother." Jay walked to the front door and opened it. "Get your ungrateful ass outta my damn suite!"

Jill ran out of the room and nearly collided with Aunt Jackie. She kept running until she reached Zach's open arms. He was at the end of the hallway waiting.

Jay had just poured herself a glass of Disarrono and lit a cigar when she heard another knock at the door. She stormed over and snatched it open. "What the hell do you want now?"

"Hello Jay, may I come in?"

"Um…Aunt Jackie, I thought you were…"

"You thought I was *Jill*. I know. Come, baby girl. Let's sit and talk."

* * * * *

Oliver gave Jill a half smile when he opened his right eye and saw her, Zach and Nahima. He touched the patch on his left one and moaned. Slowly his eyelid closed again as he drifted off to sleep. Zach stepped away from the bed, pulling Jill along with him.

"Nahima is worn out, baby. We're gonna catch a cab to your mom's house. I think we'll spend the night there with her and the children instead of at the hotel."

"Are you serious, Zachary? The house is so small and hot. You and Nahima will not be very comfortable there."

"Nahima and I will be fine at your family's home." Zach gave Oliver a kiss on his moist forehead. "Come walk us to the lobby."

Hand in hand Zach and Jill walked down the hall of the small medical clinic. Nahima was sleeping draped over her uncle's left shoulder. Jill pulled the handle of their rolling overnight bag behind her.

"Have a safe cab ride. I'll see you both tomorrow."

"We'll be here bright and early," Zach said and placed a kiss on Jill's lips.

* * * * *

"Sister Clark told my assistant Sunday school teacher, Brother Thorpe, that Zach's aunt announced to the choir's soprano section that he went to Jamaica. He and his pretty girlfriend are on some kind of medical mission. They took his god daughter along for her birthday." Ida Bell paused for her second wind during her Monday morning gossip report. "They say that cute little Jamaican gal can really dance. Reverend Broadus asked Zach's Aunt Jackie to talk to her about starting a youth praise dance troop at the church when she comes back."

Ayla hurried from the break room to the doctors' lounge with newfound motivation. The universe was in her favor after a lonely weekend with just her dependable Peanut Vibe Plus, a pack of Energizer batteries and a couple of bottles of Moscato. Thanks to Ida Bell's big mouth, he-said-she-said, church gossip, the mystery surrounding Zach's sudden leave of absence had just been solved. Ayla typically pranced around the hospital with the poise and grace of a prima donna, but her anxiety level had skyrocketed. She did a clumsy jog toward the lounge to make an important phone call. After dialing the number repeatedly over the weekend in an unsuccessful attempt to make contact, she now knew it by heart. She scrambled to the phone on the wall, thanking God she was alone.

"Ms. King, this is Dr. Fitzpatrick." She paused when the phone line began to buzz and make a crunching noise as if someone had placed their hand over the mouthpiece. Frustrated and impatient, she talked over the annoying sound. "Ms. King, are you still there?"

"Yeah, I'm here," Jay said, wiping whipped cream from her mouth and chin. She shoved Nina's wide hips to the side and motioned for her to have a seat on the bed. "What can I do for you, Dr. Fitzpatrick?" Jay leaned over and stuck her tongue in her playmate's right ear. She teased the woman's nipple with the pad of her thumb."

"Why didn't you tell me Zach was in Jamaica? When we last spoke, you promised to keep me abreast on him."

"What do you mean he's in Jamaica? Only um…*Ms. Bessette* was authorized to travel." Jay ran her fingers through her curly cropped hair. "Dr. Fitzpatrick, I had no idea. This is new information to me."

"Well, your Aunt Jackie told somebody at church, who told somebody else, that Zach is in Jamaica with Jill and Nahima. They're on some medical mission."

"Is that so?"

"Yes, Ms. King, apparently it is."

"Let me call a few of my contacts in Jamaica and see what I can find out. I'd like you to come by my office later this afternoon so we can discuss my findings. Is that possible, doctor?"

"It's very possible. I'll see you shortly after five."

* * * * *

Venus and Charles missed Nahima's laughter and animated chatter around the house, but their uninterrupted time alone was long overdue. Having been at the brink of going their separate ways only a few weeks ago, Venus had to pinch herself to make sure she wasn't dreaming. She was happy and at peace for the first time in five years. All had been forgiven and the plans for an early January wedding were well underway. Lying to Charles about Nahima's conception and withholding her infertility issues had nearly cost Venus the love of her life. Compassion and understanding had overcome fear and dishonesty. She was grateful that she and Charles had weathered the storm and she was dedicated to being the best wife she could to him for as long as she lived.

Venus hurried toward the front of the house when she heard the door open and close softly. "Charles?"

"It's me, baby. I've got a surprise for you." He smiled, hiding both hands behind his back.

Venus stopped a few feet away from her man. What had she done to deserve him after all the pain she had caused him? "You bought me another treat? Charles, this is too much."

"Hush and close your eyes."

She did as she was told, and sighed when Charles took her in his arms. Venus loved the way he made her feel. He tied something around her waist.

"You can open them now."

"A grass skirt? Where would I wear this?"

"I hope you'll wear it on our honeymoon in *Hawaii*." He waved a white envelop in the air. "We're going to Honolulu for seven days and nights."

Venus couldn't hold back the tears. "Thank you, Charles. You're too good to me."

"I know, but I can't help it. You deserve it, Venus. After all you've been through I never want you and Nahima to have worry about anything ever again."

Chapter Twenty-Four

"**G**ood afternoon, ladies, isn't it a fabulous day?"
A hush fell over the break room with the exception of the television. Brooke and Ridge were engaging in their weekly lovers' quarrel on "The Bold and the Beautiful." Ida Bell and her entourage watched Ayla sashay over to the drink machine, smiling like she had struck oil. She inserted some loose change in the coin slot and made her beverage selection. She faced the table where the ladies sat burning holes through her with their distrustful eyes. Ayla smiled and they looked at her like she was insane.

"Have a great afternoon, ladies," she said with too much cheer in her voice, right before she left the room.

"What was that about?" Sheila, a nurse's assistant asked. "She spoke to us. That's a *first*."

"I don't know, but something ain't right. Ms. Thang was too doggone friendly. It was almost like she was mocking us. Dr. Fitzpatrick is up to something, y'all," Ida Bell said. "I'm gonna pray for her because God don't like ugly."

"You go ahead and pray, Ida Bell. The rest of us are gonna keep our eyes and ears open. If Dr. Prissy is up to something, it has everything to do with our favorite nurse. We gotta have his back. You know how she tried to show out on him last time in here. If she messes with Zach again, I'm gonna whip her ass!" Sheila cackled and so did the other women at the table.

* * * * *

"Right this way, sir." The customs clerk handed Zach's passport and Nahima's back to him and waved them through. Good afternoon," he said to Jill and reached for her passport. The tall and slender man opened it and examined it thoroughly. His fingers floated across the keypad of his computer a couple of times before he picked up a walkie talkie and spoke into it.

"What's the problem, sir?" Jill asked. She looked at Zach and Nahima watching her from the other side of the partition. Her heartbeat sped up slightly. She smiled nervously and waved at Nahima.

"Come on, Ms. Jill! We gotta catch the plane."

Two uniformed, male security guards approached Jill and the customs clerk. The short and stocky one touched her arm. "You must come with us, ma'am.

There is a problem with your passport. You will not be allowed to travel to the United States until the issue is resolved."

"What is the meaning of this?" Jill snatched away from the guard. "I *must* travel today!" She looked at Zach who was making his way toward her. "Zachary, please tell this man I am with you."

"Calm down, Jill and let me talk to him. Sir, what's the problem?"

"It does not concern you, sir. Please proceed to the boarding area."

"I'm not going *anywhere* until someone tells me what the hell is going on!"

"Uncle Z, what's wrong? Why are you yelling? Why is Ms. Jill crying? Is she going to jail?"

"Zachary, help me! Please Zachary, you must fix this!"

* * * * *

Zach exited the elevator, and followed the arrows directing guests to the rooms on the eleventh floor. He headed for suite eleven-twenty-nine with a purpose. He was extremely exhausted and totally pissed off, having just landed in Atlanta. He'd come close to being thrown in jail in Jamaica for acting the fool in the middle of Sangster International Airport. He and Nahima had been forced to leave Jill behind because of a bunch of bullshit he was willing to bet his bottom dollar that Jay was responsible for. If Zach had not promised Venus and Charles he'd have Nahima home in time for her fifth birthday, he would have stayed with Jill until she was cleared to return to Atlanta with him. He had explained as much to Jill just as five security guards escorted him and his screaming niece onto the plane, while two other men pulled her in the opposite direction. He wasn't sure who had cried and begged louder for them to leave together, Nahima or Jill.

Zach banged his fist on the suite's door with his full strength. The fact that it was after midnight didn't discourage him one bit. "Jay, if you don't open this damn door I swear I'll kick it in!" He banged harder, repeatedly. Several guests peeped outside their doors to see what the ruckus was all about. "Jay, folks are crowding around your door! *Let…me…in*!

The door swung open. Jay stood under the threshold with an unlit cigar between her teeth, wearing a pair of argyle print boxers and a white tank top. "What's up, bro?" She asked calmly and stepped aside to let him enter the suite.

Zach stood directly in front of Jay when the door shut behind him. "Why the hell did you do it? Why did you tell those people at the immigration department that Jill was here illegally? Why would you do that, Jay?"

She lit the cigar and flopped down on the couch. "I have no idea what you're talking about."

"Jay, don't fuck with me right now! I know you did it. I just wanna know why? You don't love Jill. You treated her like shit while y'all were together, and…"

"What do you mean by that? I thought Jill and I were still together. I don't recall us breaking up. I definitely would've remembered that conversation. Is there something you need to tell me, *big brother*?"

"Yeah, you crazy ass bitch! Jill doesn't want you! She's in love with *me*, Jay. And I love her too, damn it! Get used to it. You never treated her the way she deserved. What you call love ain't love at all. The price is too high. Jill came to me because she knew I could love her better than you."

"Now, *you're* the one who deserves an Academy Award. You don't love Jill. You just wanted her because she was mine. You sick son of a bitch, I hate you! Get outta my damn spot, you dirty bastard! Get the hell out!"

"Jay, what's wrong? Why are you screaming, honey?" Ayla ran into the sitting room. She screamed when she saw Zach, and ran back into the bathroom butt ass naked, dripping wet.

Zach chuckled a little and shook his head. "Listen, I'm gonna let you get back to your friend. But I want you to know the stunt you pulled won't keep Jill and me apart. She'll be back here. I'll do whatever I have to do to make that happen." He walked to the door and grabbed the knob. "I suggest you get a strap on for Doc," he threw over his shoulder. "She *loves* dick, and she'll return to it sooner or later just like Venus did."

* * * * *

Dex took off work the next day to drive Zach around the city. He had a few stops to make, and they all had something to do with getting Jill back to Atlanta. They arrived at the U.S. Citizenship and Immigration Services at eight o'clock sharp and it was already crowded as hell. They asked to see Clive Dooley, and had to wait close to two hours before he was able to see them.

"Sorry y'all had to wait. If you had called me at the crib last night, I would've moved some shit around to accommodate you earlier. I take it you're here to apply for a temp status on behalf of the young lady you were telling me about. You should've brought her with you."

"That's just it Clive. Jill is in *Jamaica*. I took her home to visit her family, and she got stuck over there. The U.S. is denying her reentry because they claim she came here illegally, but that's bullshit, Clive! Jill came over here with my sister on a ninety-day visa. Jay was supposed to have applied for an extension, and worked on her alien resident status, but she never did it. Then while we were in Jamaica, that bitch contacted someone in *this* office. She told them Jill had abandoned their home, and she had no idea where she was or how she was supporting herself. Talking about she didn't wanna be responsible for her if she was out prostituting or doing some other illegal activities."

Clive tapped a pen on top of his cluttered desk and looked at Zach then Dex. "I need any documents you have on Jill. Did she bring a birth certificate or school records with her? Maybe she brought her driver's license or a government issued

ID from Jamaica. Anything you have will be helpful."

"Jay has everything. All I have are her school records. Her boss has her dance profile and some pictures. We're gonna go see her as soon as we're done here. Clive, what can you do to get Jill back here, and how long will it take? I want her in Atlanta for Christmas."

"I'm not sure, Zach. I'm really not sure. Jay made some pretty serious accusations. The government is cracking down on illegal aliens, so they aren't blinking at anything. This is gonna be a tough one to turn around." Clive leaned forward and placed both elbows on his desk. "What aren't you telling me, Zach? Something isn't adding up here."

After Zach gave Clive the inside scoop, he and Dex went to Umoja Academy and spoke with Mrs. Scott. She was sad to hear about Jill's woes with the immigration department and promised to do all she could to help get her back to Atlanta. She then gave Jill's dance profile to Zach. There were more pictures in it than before. The one of Jill doing an instructional performance almost brought Zach to tears. Dex removed everything from his hands and guided his buddy out of the school.

Aunt Jackie's house was the next stop on their agenda. She was dressed in a brown jogging suit sitting in the den watching Jerry Springer when Zach and Dex arrived.

"I never thought I'd see the day when you and Jay would be at odds. I raised y'all to love one another and always have each other's back. Now Jay says she hates you, and she's mad with me. All of this foolishness is because of a *woman*. Zach, you were wrong to touch Jill."

"Auntie, I didn't mean…"

"I don't care, Zachary King. Jill was Jay's lover. You should've resisted all urges."

"Yes ma'am, I know. You're right. Why is Jay upset with *you*?"

"She blames me for making it possible for you and Jill to travel to Jamaica together. Remember, it was *I* who left Jay's suite with that passport. Your sister accused me of knowing you'd be going to the island with Jill. Of course I didn't, and I told Jay that, but she didn't believe me. Then she had the gall to tell me I knew all along you were sleeping with Jill. That heifer called me a liar and a hypocrite. That's when I gave her a piece of my mind. I'm praying for that girl and I'm praying for you too, Zach. This mess ain't over. I've got a feeling Jay is just getting started on you and Jill."

Chapter Twenty-Five

"Zachary, I am unable to eat or sleep. I am very weary. I now know what it means to be lovesick. It is terribly painful. Oliver is sleeping in the bed with me. He sang songs to cheer me up until he fell asleep. He would hate to know that his songs were of no assistance to me. I will never tell him, though. The boy admires you, Zachary. Although he loves having me home, he'd much rather I return to America to be with you. He says my broken heart makes him sad, and only you can repair it."

Zach lay flat on his back and stared into the darkness while he listened to Jill. She had summarized her meeting at the immigration department in Jamaica where Roy had taken her to apply for a new passport. The official had told her it would be six weeks before she'd be granted a hearing in front of the council. Her voice was weak and scratchy as if she'd been crying for hours. Zach was determined to be strong for her. He did an excellent job keeping his emotions at bay. But silent tears escaped from the corners of his eyes and streamed down his cheeks. They dampened the pillow case he'd vowed not to wash again until Jill came home. It was covered with the scents of ginger and lilac.

He refused to tell Jill that things weren't going well with the immigration department in Atlanta. Jay had submitted an affidavit reiterating her original claim. She'd also given the officials a copy of her rental contract from the Seven Seas, insinuating she'd been living there since moving to Atlanta. Jill had been listed as her domestic partner whom she had brought to America to live with her. Jay claimed Jill had abandoned their suite, without warning, several weeks ago. She swore she'd had no idea where she was until Zach came to the hotel after his trip to Jamaica, and confessed she had been living with him. Jay went on to tell the official at the immigration department that Jill had only used her to get to Atlanta so she could study and teach dance. She reported that she had recently learned she'd been working at Umoja Academy before leaving Atlanta to visit her family. Mrs. Scott was now under investigation for employing an illegal immigrant.

Even if Zach had wanted to tell Jill what was happening on his end, he didn't think he'd be able to repeat all the lies and garbage Jay had alleged. How could anyone be so wicked and deceptive? Right now, he just wanted Jill to know he and Dex were working hard to get her back on American soil and that he loved her.

"You'll be in my arms by Christmas. Dex and I are busting our asses to make that happen. I'm sorry you won't be able to perform at Umoja Academy's big production, but Mrs. Scott and your class miss you. They all can't wait for you to come back."

"I miss them too, but I can live without them. It's *you* I can't live without. I'm going insane, Zachary! Please do something. I won't make it much longer here. I need you."

"Hold on, Jill. I'm trying. Close your eyes and think about me. Reflect on all the good times we've shared. Do you see us at Chuck E. Cheese's with Nahima? You ate two pork chops the first time I took you to dinner at Aunt Jackie's house." Zach wiped his eyes and nose with the back of his hand. He rolled over onto his side and inhaled the pillow case. "Think about that night we danced until the morning at the reggae club in Buckhead. You wore *panties*," he said and laughed through his tears. "We made love that night like it was our final day on the planet. Jill? *Jill?* Are you still there, baby?"

Zach hushed and lay perfectly still. He could hear Jill's soft breathing on the other end. She had fallen asleep to precious memories. He wished he could do the same. He pressed the phone's power button, turning it off. He buried his face into the pillow, and inhaled Jill's scent. He imagined her lying in his arms. The phone rang, shattering his vision. Zach it answered quickly.

"Son, it's Wallace. You were on my mind. Something told me you needed to talk. Please tell me what's wrong. I'd like to help if I can."

* * * * *

Zach's depression over being separated from Jill spilled over into every aspect of life. Thanksgiving, Christmas and New Year's had all passed with only one appearance from him amongst his family and friends. He had hoped, against hope, to fly to Jamaica for a few days after Christmas with Nahima, but the twenty-one days he'd taken off in June and the additional days in November canceled out his leave request. Plus, nurses with families got first dibs at holiday leave, and Zach was without chick or child. So he'd spent most of his time locked up in his house with his sorrows. Nahima had been the lone soul he'd allowed inside his world of solitude, and he hadn't been able to fool her.

Zach ran his fingers through Nahima's Shirley Temple curls, and adjusted her big purple bow. He choked up at the memory of how hard she had tried to cheer him up on Christmas Eve. A very wise and attentive child, she had sensed that Zach was quite melancholy without Ms. Jill. Nahima had danced, sang and told cute little jokes in her attempt to make her uncle feel better.

"Uncle Z, how do I look? Am I pretty yet?"

"You're always pretty to me, pumpkin." Zach handed her the white, satin, hand basket filled with purple and gold flower petals. "You're gonna be the most beautiful flower girl ever today in your mommy's wedding."

"And I'm gonna be a beautiful *princess* flower girl in your wedding when you marry Ms. Jill."

"Who said anything about me getting married to Ms. Jill?"

Nahima made a cute little "duh" face at Zach, and put her hand on her hip. "*I* did, silly! You love Ms. Jill, and Ms. Jill loves you. So you gotta get married like Mommy and Daddy Charles."

Zach pulled the child by her hand, and led her to the holding area outside the chapel. Janice, her mom's best friend and matron of honor, was sitting with Charles's best man. They both made a fuss over how beautiful she looked in her purple velvet and lace gown. Nahima blushed, to Zach's surprise, at Janice and Ernest's compliments. The organist started playing softly inside the tiny chapel. The wedding coordinator burst into the room nervously carrying a clipboard.

"Five minutes to show time!" She said firmly.

Zach got down on one knee to meet Nahima face-to-face. "Pumpkin, Uncle Z is about to go take his seat. Don't forget to smile and sprinkle the petals. You gotta smile and sprinkle just like you did at rehearsal last night, okay?"

"Okay."

* * * * *

The ceremony was short and sweet. Zach was happy for Venus and Charles, and he wished them the best. But at one point during the wedding, he felt like wailing like a mourner at a funeral. His emotions had betrayed him sitting on the pew, witnessing the union of one of his closest friends and her soul mate. Zach had thought he was losing his mind right there in the middle of the nuptials. He welcomed the stiff drink he was now nursing at the reception. It was his fifth whiskey sour. Instead of sitting at the table he'd been assigned to, he had settled his depressed ass at the bar.

Janice waddled her six months pregnant figure over to the bar, and took a seat on the stool next to Zach. "I'm gonna drive you and Nahima home, and Ernest is gonna follow me in your car. We'll hang around until the little princess falls asleep, and make sure you're both alright. You're a wonderful man, Zach. I know what you're going through. It's gonna get better, my friend. Before you know it, Jill will be back in Atlanta, and you'll be planning *your* wedding. Now get your drunk ass up so you can go home and sleep it off. These twins are kicking my ass."

* * * * *

No one seemed to recognize Wallace at his old church after twenty-eight years. His appearance *had* changed drastically. He was completely bald now and fifty pounds heavier. No one in Atlanta had ever seen him a wear a beard before, and the one he was sporting now was white as snow against his caramel skin. It had been a smart idea for him to wait several minutes inside the SUV before he entered the sanctuary alone, to sit in the back of the church. Sitting with Zach and Nahima on their pew near the front would've blown his cover for sure. Refuge Pentecostal Temple wasn't the same church Wallace had pastored all those years ago. The address hadn't changed, but the building was a lot bigger, and the membership had grown. The fundraiser he'd launched by pledging the first five hundred dollars had obviously been successful. Those pesky gravel stones they used to park on were gone. A smooth and even parking lot was now in its place.

One thing was still the same as Wallace had remembered. Refuge still had an awesome choir with Jackie, Leland and Betty Dudley's baby girl singing lead with her golden soprano voice. She hadn't lost her touch. Wallace fought hard to stay in his seat to avoid the risk of being noticed, but Jackie was putting it in. The spirit was high, and the saints were up on their feet all over the sanctuary clapping, jumping and dancing to the heavenly sound of the choir. Wallace soon gave up the fight and joined in the praise along with the other energetic worshippers. To him it was just like old times at the church he had once called home.

Chapter Twenty-Six

"I told you no one would recognize you." Zach handed Wallace a bottle of Texas Pete hot sauce, and sat down at the table next to him. "I don't think *I* could've picked you out of a lineup after all this time."

"It *has* been a while. There were times when I thought I would never see you or your sister again. When I was in prison, I used to sit and imagine what the two of you looked like. Until you sent those pictures last year, my vision of Jayla was still that of a bright-eyed toddler sucking her thumb. She blossomed into a beautiful woman. You're not so bad looking either, son." Wallace smiled and turned affectionate eyes on his only grandchild. "And this precious angel is a blessing. Thank you, Zach, for allowing me to meet her, and please thank her mother for me. Will you?"

Zach nodded. "Venus is a good woman. She never would've denied Nahima the opportunity to meet her grandfather. You're the only living grandparent she has."

Zach and Wallace continued eating their Sunday takeout meal over light banter. They mostly talked about the changes in Atlanta over the past two decades and politics. Once in a while they'd pull Nahima into their conversation, asking her about school and her Heritage World doll collection. She'd described all twelve of her friends in detail while she pushed green beans back and forth across her plate. When Zach realized what she was doing, he gave her permission to leave the table. Wallace followed her with his eyes until she was out of sight.

"She's the spitting image of Jayla. I can't understand why she doesn't wish to be a part of her life. You and your sister were all I could think about over the years. I prayed to God every day for a chance to see my children again. It was painful not being able to watch you grow up. I knew you were in good hands with Jackie, but I wanted so desperately to be there. I wanted to teach you about girls, how to shave and drive. I was supposed to have tucked Jayla in every night and taught her to pray. I robbed the two of you of your mother, and I cheated myself. My crime cost me the opportunity to do all the things with my children that Jayla has refused to do with Nahima."

"Jay is Jay. There ain't much more I can say about my sister that I haven't already told you. She's more selfish and superficial than ever. She's heartless."

"That's my fault," Wallace said. "She never got to know Belva Jayne. Her daddy was in jail for murdering the mother whose love she never experienced. It must've been hard growing up under such circumstances."

"That's not an excuse, Wallace. *I* made it. Don't you think it was difficult for me too? It was actually *worse* because I did know my momma. I remember the sound of her voice, her flowery scent and her smile. She used to sing "You Are My Sunshine" to me every night before I went to sleep. I have memories of the good times you and I shared too. I remember us washing that old, green Buick Regal and playing hide and seek. I would stand outside your office door and listen to you practice your sermons on Saturday evenings. *I* suffered more for what you did than anybody else, but I ain't a victim anymore. I used to run from love and commitment because I didn't wanna be like you. And now, I'm in love for the first time in my life because of you."

Wallace got up from his seat at the table and enfolded Zach in his arms as he released twenty-eight years of pain and frustration. He had wondered a million times how it would feel to hold his son again. To Wallace, at that moment, it felt like heaven had opened its gates and let him in. As he had done many times when Zach was a boy, he rocked him. "It's okay, son. It's okay."

"I finally let my guard down and opened up my heart," Zach said, sniffling. "I had to give love a fair chance. I wanted to know how it felt to love a woman to death, and now I know. I'll probably never use my gun, and I don't believe Jill would ever be unfaithful to me. But right now, I'm willing to move and heaven and earth to get her back to Atlanta where she belongs. I'd lay down my life for her, Wallace. I swear I would."

"I'm gonna keep praying, son, and you continue to work with the folks at the immigration department. Harass them if you have to. Jill is coming back. Believe that."

* * * * *

Ida Bell's gossip had hit the bull's eye once again. Jay had to leave the senior member of the marketing team in charge for the remainder of the day after she'd received a disturbing phone call from Ayla. She was sobbing and throwing back a full bottle of Disarrono, standing on the terrace outside her suite. It was a chilly day in mid-February, but she needed the fresh air to clear her head of homicidal thoughts. Based on what Ayla had overheard, Wallace had been in town over the weekend visiting Zach and Nahima. That Negro had had the nerve to take his ass to church, and sat like a spy among the people he had once pastored. He'd executed great discretion according to Sister Juanita Grant, the lead usher on third Sundays.

Ida Bell told her gossip partners that Evangelist Mary T. Tucker had gotten a phone call from Sister Priscilla Hall after she'd left Lizzie's Soul Food Café Sunday afternoon. Deacon Freddie Collins, the second oldest member of the church, and his son Freddie Junior were there, telling the church's musicians that they'd seen Wallace in service. Freddie Junior had spotted him first. He used to play baseball with Wallace as a child and he claimed he'd recognize him anywhere. That bald head and gray beard hadn't fooled him. To confirm their suspicions, Deacon Collins had asked Freddie Junior to put him and his wheelchair in the car several minutes before the benediction. Together, father and son scouted the parking lot like a pair of private investigators. Wallace was the first person to emerge from the church's double doors, five minutes ahead of everybody else. He hurried to Zach's SUV with a key to wait inside for him and Nahima.

Evangelist Tucker called Brother Bonner who told his wife Marvella. She called her best friend Gigi who works the night shift at Chauncey's Storage and Thrift with Sister Grant. She broke the news to Ida Bell. The rumor had spread like hot lava around Refuge Pentecostal Temple, and its members couldn't get enough of it. While they were burning holes in each other's ears and blowing up their phones, Jay was having an emotional melt down. She was angry, sad and confused. She wondered why Zach had allowed Wallace to come to Atlanta to visit him, and how long had they been in contact. Didn't he remember what the man had done?

"You're so damn *evil*, Zach!" Jay spiked the empty bottle to the concrete floor of the terrace. Glass and drops of liquor splattered everywhere. She staggered back inside the suite, and slumped down to the thick beige carpet. "I hate you, Zach! I hate you!"

* * * * *

"Mr. Orville?" Zach glanced at the digital clock on the nightstand. It was five-fifteen in the morning. He never rose before eight o'clock on Saturdays unless it was a special occasion. With Jill still in Kingston after four months of fighting with the immigration department, nothing was special anymore.

"Yes, it is Orville, Zachary. I need to tell ya about Jillian."

"What's wrong with Jill?" Zach sat up and wiped his eyes. "I spoke with her last night. She told me she was fine." He reached forward to pull Nahima from the foot of the bed, and placed her under the covers. "She wasn't very talkative, though. I assumed she was tired."

"Jillian is very depressed. Roy drives her to the immigration services and consulate every other day. When she learns there have been no changes to her travel papers, she becomes *vexed*. Jillian's crying spells keep coming. She refuses to eat, and she only drinks a little. Her mother and I are fretful, Zachary. We are asking you to come to Jamaica for a visit. Even a short one could lift her spirits."

"I'll try to make arrangements at my job for an indefinite leave of absence. My friend Dex will continue the process with the immigration department here while I'm away. Hopefully, I can call you and Ms. Faye Monday afternoon with my travel agenda. But please don't mention anything to Jill about my visit until you've spoken to me, sir. She would be devastated if my plans fell through for some reason."

"I will do as you have asked, Zachary, but please make haste. I am very worried about my daughter."

Chapter Twenty-Seven

With a shortage of nurses experienced in neonatal care on staff, Zach had to wait a week before he was cleared to leave for Jamaica. And in that short time span, Jill's mental state had worsened. Zach's had too. He had spoken to Oliver while he sat on the plane waiting for his flight to take off. The boy said Jill had not been out of her room all morning. She hadn't eaten, drunk any liquids or taken a shower. The only way they even knew she was still alive was by breaking into her small bedroom to check her pulse and heartbeat. Oliver told Zach he wanted to tell Jill that he was on his way to Jamaica, but he couldn't wake her.

Zach looked down at the crystal blue ocean as the plane began to make its descent on the island. He was anxious to be reunited with Jill, but more concerned about her mental and physical health. He cursed under his breath just thinking about how Jay had so casually tampered with his and Jill's lives like she was playing a damn board game. Zach was convinced that his sister was demon possessed. The measure she had taken to have Jill detained in Jamaica was something you read about in a novel, or watched play out in some horror movie on the big screen. Normal people didn't do the kind of things Jay did. As soon as the passengers were given the go-ahead, Zach exited the plan and trotted down its steps with those thoughts in mind.

"Zachary King! Zachary King!" Roy yelled and waved both hands in the air eagerly. He had singled Zach out the moment he entered the airport.

"My buddy Roy, how ya doin', mon?" Zach teased and slapped him on the back.

"I am well. How was ya flight, eh?" Roy removed Zach's carry-on bag from his shoulder and slid it onto his.

"It was fine. I wanted to sleep, but I couldn't. I guess I was too worked up."

Roy led Zach in the direction of the baggage claim area. They weaved in and out of the heavy human traffic. It was very crowded and busy in the airport.

"Give it to me straight, Roy. No chaser. No bull. How is Jill?"

"Mmm, she is not well. She's much too thin and she whines and frets all the time. I am glad you are here. You came to make her smile again, eh?"

"I hope I can, Roy."

"If you cannot do it, my friend, no one can."

Roy helped Zach retrieve his three pieces of luggage and a big cardboard box before they exited they airport and headed to the van. They stopped at a supermarket on the way to Kingston so Zach could buy juice, bottled water, meat, eggs and snacks for Jill's siblings.

Faye met Zach and Roy on the porch when they arrived. "Zachary, thank God you are here. Please come in." She fell into Zach's embrace. "Jill is sleeping. Go and wake her."

Zach made his way through the house to Jill's bedroom. As soon as he saw her rail-thin body lying across the bed he knew something was terribly wrong. She appeared lifeless.

"Wake up, baby. It's me, *Zach*. I came to take care of you." He touched Jill's back. It was warm and soaked with sweat. "Open your eyes, baby."

Jill heard his voice and the scent of his cologne that she loved so much filled her nostrils. She felt Zach's hand stroking her cheek. She opened her eyes, but she couldn't move. Her body was too weak for her to even lift her head from the pillow. Zach gently rolled her onto her back so she could see his face. Jill began to cry when she realized she wasn't dreaming. Zach was there with her.

"I'm here now. You don't have to worry about a thing. I've got you." He pulled her into his arms, and she melted into his strength. "You're gonna be okay.

Zach bathed Jill, brushed her teeth and combed her hair. Ms. Faye gave him a freshly washed night gown and underwear to dress her in. He carried her into the kitchen and sat her at the table so he could feed her.

"I want you to eat. You've lost too much weight. Drink this," Zach said and held a bottle of orange juice to her lips.

Jill drank the juice slowly and smiled at Zach. "I thought I would never see you again. I felt like I was dying. Don't ever leave me again, Zachary. I wouldn't survive."

"I'm not going home any time soon. I'm on extended leave. But whenever I decide to leave, you'll be with me. We're going to the immigration department tomorrow. I made the appointment earlier this week. I'm gonna fix the mess Jay made so we can go on with our life together."

* * * * *

After refusing to eat for three days Jill was famished. She and Zach enjoyed Faye's delicious meat pies and fruit salad at the small kitchen table while they listened to her brothers discuss soccer. Christian and Angelina were playing with wooden blocks in the middle of the floor. Zach loved the closeness of the Bessette family. The six children loved each other dearly. There was a time when the King children were inseparable. Zach reflected over those times as he ate and watched Jill's siblings interact. Strangely, he missed Jay and the bond they'd once shared. After all the evil things she'd done, Zach still loved her very much.

Jill slyly rubbed her bare foot up and down Zach's leg under the table. Their eyes met and latched when she raised it to rest on his lap. It had been four months since they'd made love, but they would have to wait. Zach had rented a villa at the Blue Lagoon Resort in Montego Bay for his extended stay on the island. But he wasn't scheduled to check in until tomorrow. On his first night in Jamaica he would share a room with Oliver and Edgar. He refused to touch Jill in her parents' house. He respected Orville and Faye, and they were fond of him. It would be twenty-four hours before he and Jill could unleash all their pent-up passion on each other after a forced four-month stint of abstinence.

* * * * *

"What's up, Dex?" Jay smiled and extended her hand. The other one was hooked around the waist of her attractive dinner date.

Dex reluctantly shook Jay's hand after Ramona prompted him with a pinch on his back. "What's going on Jay?"

"I felt like eating oysters and crab legs so we ended up here." Jay tilted her head. "This is Nina. Nina, meet Dexter Cruz and his wife."

"This is my wife Ramona. Ramona, this is Zach's sister, Jay."

The two women shook hands. Ramona made a repulsive facial expression when Jay raped her with her eyes in the middle of the popular seafood restaurant. Dex had seen it too, and it pissed him off.

"How is my brother these days?"

"Humph, he's *your* bother. Shouldn't you know how he's doing?"

"Let's not bullshit each other, Dex, you know Zach and I don't speak. He slept with Jill while we were together. What kind of brother does that to his sister?"

Dex held up his hand. "Zach didn't mean for that to happen. It just did. He never meant to hurt you, but *you* retaliated with the intention of destroying him. What you did to him and Jill is unforgivable, Jay!"

"Come on, Dex. Let's go, baby." Ramona tugged at his arm. "You're getting upset, and people are beginning to stare."

"As always, you're gonna hold your boy down even though we both know he was dead ass wrong. You're a good guy. You've settled down with your fine ass wife, and got a baby girl. That's real love. Zach on the other hand, has strung that beautiful doctor along for two years, and took all her money. He forced that chick to abort babies…"

"What the hell are you talking about? Zach has never taken a dime from Ayla. And if he had ever been stupid enough to knock her up, she would've *gladly* had the baby. That helpless kid would've been her lucky charm." He shook his head. "Is that why you slept with Ayla? You felt sorry for her after hearing a bunch of lies? She's sick, and so are you. You two deserve each other." Dex's stormed off with his arm around his wife's shoulders. He could hear Jay and her date arguing.

Honey

"You told me you never slept with that doctor!" Nina shouted.

* * * * *

"Jill, come on." Zach knocked on the bathroom door. "Your breakfast is getting cold."

"I'm too nervous to eat, Zachary. What if something goes wrong in our meeting?"

"We have to show up first. If you don't hurry we'll be late. Roy's friend will be here soon."

"Go ahead and eat. I'll join you in five minutes."

Zach returned to the kitchen to finish eating his breakfast. Faye had been kind enough to prepare ackee and salt fish for him and Jill. The Jamaican Blue Mountain coffee had a wonderful flavor like none other Zach had ever tasted.

Faye sat next to him at the table. "I'm so glad you came. Jillian is so much better now." She looked toward the bathroom door, and then leaned closer to Zach. "Can you take her to see a doctor at the medical clinic?"

"Sure I can, but why?" Zach placed his coffee mug on the table, and waited for Faye's explanation.

"Jillian is feeling good now, but as her mother I feel something is not right. Have a doctor check her over please. It would make me happy."

"I'll take her today, Ms. Faye. As soon as our meeting is over we'll go straight to the Johnson Medical Center."

"Thank you, Zachary. You are a very good man."

DERANGED Love

Chapter Twenty-Eight

The meeting with the immigration officials in Jamaica was very productive. A kind woman named Esther Barrington returned Jill's passport, and updated her and Zach on her status with the United States government. An investigation had proven that Jill hadn't committed any crimes while she lived in Atlanta, and she had not violated the terms of her temporary visa. Clive had informed Mrs. Barrington that more than likely, Jill would receive clearance to travel to the United States in thirty days.

Pembrick, Zach and Jill's driver for the day, drove directly to the Johnson Medical Center after they'd eaten lunch at an ocean front restaurant. He'd been given the instructions to do so while Jill was in the ladies' room. Zach kept a straight face when the old model Toyota 4Runner pulled in front of the gray stucco building.

Jill pressed the back of her hand to Zach's head. "Are you sick, Zachary? What is wrong? Are you in pain?"

"I'm not sick, but your mother thinks *you* are."

"Me, eh?" Jill laughed. "I *was* sick before you came and made me feel better. I will be even better tonight. You will see when we're alone."

"Um...Jill," Zach said, pointing to the back of Pembrick's head.

Jill blushed and lowered her eyes. "Oh, please forgive me. But really, Zachary, I am fine. I was too depressed to eat, and sometimes my tummy griped and rolled because I was hungry."

"I promised your mother I would bring you here to be examined by a doctor, and I'm gonna keep my word. Let's go."

The cool air from a row of ceiling fans greeted Zach and Jill when they entered the clinic. Crying babies and pregnant women made up more than half of the crowd of patients waiting to be cared for. The clerk, an older woman with a funky attitude, told Zach it would be three hours before Jill could see a doctor. He executed a move from Jay's playbook by pulling out a crisp green bill with Benjamin Franklin's face on it. Within five minutes, Jill was sitting on an examination table having her blood pressure taken by a young a nurse. Dr. Harry Johnson had ordered a series of standard test to rule out any health problems. He also did a thorough examination of Jill's body. He entered the room to give her a summary. Leaning his tall, slender frame against the wall, he smiled at Jill.

"You're healthy, my dear. I don't like your weight. You need to eat more in your condition."

"What condition is that?" Jill asked.

"Where is your husband?"

"He is in the waiting area. His name is Zachary King."

Dr. Doctor Johnson turned to his nurse. "Get Mr. King for me."

Jill began to panic. "If it is a bad condition, it came about because I could not eat or drink. I was so depressed. You see…"

"I'm Zachary King." Zach rushed into the room and wrapped his arm around Jill's shoulders. "What's wrong with her?"

"Nothing is wrong. Your wife is pregnant, about sixteen weeks along."

* * * * *

"She's been cleared to come back to the States. I tried to delay it, but the computer kept rejecting my request. The orders came from the top. Mr. Dooley's hands were all over this one." Nina dropped the stack of documents on Jay's desk.

Jay shoved the papers and they fell to the carpet. "This city is big, but it ain't big enough for Zach, Jill *and* me. I ain't leaving. I'm gonna torture them so much they'll relocate to the other side of the world."

"Leave them alone, Jay. We're together now and we're happy. I thought you said you were never in love with Jill. I'm starting to think you lied." Nina rounded Jay's desk and sat on the edge of it facing her. "Forget about her."

"I *wasn't* in love with Jill, but that's not the point! Zach is my brother. He slept with my woman behind my back while we were still together. He showed no remorse when he finally admitted it. He's a cocky bastard." Jay laughed. "He had the nerve to say he loves Jill. Zach has never been serious about a woman in his life. He'll hit it and quit like he's always done. And Jill will come crawling back to me. It'll serve her right. I took that bitch out of a four-room shack in the heart of Kingston. I taught her ass how to dress, speak proper English and I introduced her to fine dining. She didn't have a decent pair of shoes when I met her, but now she's all about Prada and Gucci. I made that bitch and I'm gonna break her!"

* * * * *

As soon as they entered the villa, Jill searched Zach's eyes, trying to read his mood. They hadn't been able to discuss her pregnancy since leaving the clinic. Pembrick had driven them to her parents' house to pack their things and then straight to Montego Bay. Now that they were alone, the air needed to be cleared. Jill took a seat next to Zach on the loveseat.

"I'm so sorry. If you don't want me to go through with the pregnancy, I won't."

"We're not gonna kill our baby. That's not an option."

"I don't have a job or an education. I'm not sure…"

Zach laced his fingers through Jill's. "You have *me*. I'm gonna take care of you and our child. Don't you know how much I love you?"

"I know, Zachary, but this was so unexpected. How could I have not known?"

"It was probably because of the stress of us being separated. And you've never been pregnant before. You had no idea how it felt. That's not so strange. Now that you know you're carrying my baby, you've gotta eat and take better care of yourself. I want a healthy wife and child."

Jill blushed and lowered her eyelids. "I only told the doctor you were my husband because he assumed I was married. It was just a little white lie."

"If you'll have me, Jill, it won't have to be a lie at all."

"I don't want you to marry me because of the baby," she cried. "You don't have to do that, Zachary."

"Jill, I wanna marry you because I *love you*. I'd been thinking about it anyway. I promised myself whenever I got you back to Atlanta I would never let you visit Jamaica again until after you became Mrs. Zachary King." Zach wiped Jill's tears with the back of his hand.

Orville would be home from the merchant's boat in three days. Therefore, Zach and Jill decided they would wait to tell him and Faye together about the baby. They agreed to have a small wedding on the island at the tiny Baptist church the Bessette family had been members of since Jill was a little girl. April twenty-first, her birthday, seemed like the perfect day for a wedding. It gave them a little more than a month to plan the ceremony. Zach would send for Aunt Jackie and Nahima, and he would call Dex in the morning to see if he and Ramona could come also. He'd purchase their rings online and have them sent to his aunt. She would bring them with her for the ceremony.

"Where can you find a wedding dress here? I want you to have something special."

"There is a seamstress in Port Maria. Her name is Gwendolyn Hayes. She travels all over Europe and brings back expensive fabrics, beads and crystals. She can create *anything*, I tell you. But you may not like her, Zachary."

"She sounds amazing. Why wouldn't I like her?"

"Gwendolyn is a very good friend of Jay's. She has sewn many suits and dress shirts for her."

"So what? I still like her and I'm gonna pay her to create your wedding dress."

Chapter Twenty-Nine

"I think you and Jill made that baby right there in Jamaica, man. Y'all were supposed to be over there taking care of little Oliver, but I think you were taking care of each other. You're a nasty son of bitch. Anyway…congratulations to you and Jill on the baby and the wedding. Ramona and I will be there. We'll leave Abriah with Felecia. Hell, we might do like you did and make us a baby in Jamaica too."

"It's the perfect place to make one. If Jill wasn't already pregnant, she definitely would be this morning. We made up for the four months of separation last night, *all night*. She's still sleeping. I'll wake her up once room service brings our food."

"Jill is young, Zach. I hope she doesn't give your old ass a heart attack."

"She almost did around three o'clock this morning. Whenever she does kill me, make sure she buries me in my brown Oscar de la Renta suit. Speaking of dying, I need to change my will and beneficiaries on my life insurance policies. I've gotta add Jill to my health insurance too. Man, I gotta go and handle my business, and you need to take your ass back to work."

"I know, but I need to tell you something first."

"Talk to me."

"I saw Jay."

Zach sat silently and listened to Dex's recap of his run-in with his crazy ass sister. He couldn't believe how far out she was dragging her beef with him. If he thought it would do any good, he'd be willing to meet with Jay so they could hash out their differences. When Dex mentioned the foul shit Zach had supposedly done to Ayla, he screamed so loud he woke Jill. She rushed into the sitting area of the villa to see what was going on. The food arrived right after that, and Zach ended the call, promising to touch base with Dex later that evening. He had a few more wedding preparation details to run pass him. He hadn't wanted to, but Jill insisted that Zach tell her about his conversation with Dex over breakfast.

"None of that shit about Ayla is not true, Jill. I've worked hard for every penny I've got, and I made wise investments over the years with the money from my mother's insurance policy. My grandparents left Jay and me a lot of money when they passed, and I invested my share of that as well. Aunt Jackie used to threaten me so much when I was young about getting a girl pregnant that I never once had unprotected sex. You may not believe me, but it's true."

"Oh, I believe you, Zachary."

"It wasn't until I discovered you in my linen closet in the middle of the night that I lost myself for the very first time. And I've been lost ever since with no regrets. Ayla was never pregnant by me. Any baby she may have aborted wasn't mine."

"I don't wish to discuss this anymore. It's meaningless. You must call Aunt Jackie now and tell her about the baby and the wedding."

* * * * *

Zach called Aunt Jackie and told her about the baby and the upcoming wedding. She sounded happy, but he detected a little apprehension in her voice. Obviously, the origin of Aunt Jackie's unspoken concern was *Jay*. The news that Jill was expecting and would soon be returning to Atlanta as Zach's wife was going to cause another round of fireworks. Aunt Jackie expressed her thoughts.

"I'll tell Jay. I wanna sit down face-to-face with my sister and lay everything out on the table. I owe her an apology, so that'll come *first*. Like you told me that day at your house, I was wrong to lay a finger on Jill. Jay needs to hear me say that. Afterwards, I hope she'll be able to forgive me so we can all move on. I'm tired of this foolishness. I love Jay and I miss her."

"I'll be praying for a miracle. Give Jill and her family my love. I can't wait to see you, and I'm sure Nahima feels the same way.

Aunt Jackie hung up the phone and glanced around her den. On every wall and shelf there was a memory of the sweet pair of siblings she'd raised as her own children. Pictures, certificates and trophies they'd received for their academic and extracurricular accomplishments at church and in the community were everywhere. They confirmed that she had done a decent job parenting them. Warm tears stung her eyes when she saw Jay's senior prom picture. Zach had come home from college to escort her because she didn't want to go stag. And the school had discouraged all gay and lesbian students from attending as couples. Jay looked absolutely breathtaking. She was proud to be on her big brother's arm. That was the last time she'd ever worn a dress, high heels and makeup.

"God, it's in Your hands. It's too much for me. I need You to fix it as only You can. Please Bring Zach and Jay back together in peace and in love. Amen."

* * * * *

Ayla was not to be ignored by Zach or Jay. They'd both cut her off without even a courtesy call or a post card. Pride would not allow her to be dismissed. Zach was on extended leave from the hospital, and no one seemed to know where he was. The break room gossip association had been cold as of lately. The only thing they'd been talking about was Dr. Tidwell and how many nurses he had smashed in the doctors' lounge. Two weeks ago, when she'd greeted Dex in the parking lot and tried to strike up a friendly conversation with him about Zach, he called her a vicious liar. Then he suggested that she make an appointment to see Dr. Capone. He was one of the psychiatrists at the hospital.

If only Zach had been honest about his relationship with Jill from the start, Ayla wouldn't have felt so rejected. She'd known from the first time they ever hooked up that marriage was not in the cards for them, but she didn't expect to get addicted to his dick. *Mr. Wonderful* was like a drug. The feel, the taste and sight of it was sketched in her memory. Even after many months since their last tryst, thoughts of Zach caused her to squirm in her own juices on her black satin sheets. Whenever she thought about Jay's rough style of pleasing her with her tongue and hands, her body reacted the same way. The King duo was sexually talented. Ayla slid her hand down her flat belly to the moist apex between her thighs, imagining a ménage a trios with Zach and Jay.

They were taking turns licking Ms. Kitty in her daydream. Ayla increased the pressure and speed on her love bud, dipping two fingers in and out of her dampness. "*Mmm Zach*," she moaned, but it was Jay's face she saw. Writhing and panting through the wave of self-inflicted satisfaction, Ayla vowed to have just one more night with Zach no matter what the cost. And she planned to wiggle her way back into Jay's bed too, as soon as she figured out what she had done to piss her off.

* * * * *

"I never approved of your relationship with Jay, sweetheart. You were much too young and pretty to be with a woman so worldly and promiscuous. She was only a client with lots of money to me. Lift your arms away from your waist, dear." Gwendolyn, the fashion designer, stuck several straight pins carefully along the seams of white lace to ensure a snug fit to Jill's slender body.

"So does this mean you will not tell Jay that I am getting married?"

"I most definitely will not. You are my client now. I do not discuss my clients' affairs with others. That is my very strict policy. Besides, I have not had any contact with Jay for several months. When she lived on the island I only saw her when she hired me to do work. We never had a personal relationship."

"I see. Thank you. I appreciate your confidentiality, Mrs. Hayes."

"You're very welcome. Okay, that should do it." Gwendolyn stood from the foot stool and took Jill by her hand. She guided her over to the full-length mirror in the corner of the small storefront boutique. "What do you think, Madame Jillian?"

Jill took her time to examine the bright crystal beads in the bodice of the simple white sheath. Hundreds of white faux pearls and sequined appliqués covered the lace from the neckline to the bottom of the ballroom length skirt. She spun around to see the dip in the back of the bodice that stopped right above her butt. Gwendolyn's suggestion to do away with sleeves had been brilliant. "I think it is magnificent! Zachary will be pleased."

"Very well, take it off, and I will have it finished in five days. Will that do?"

"Five days it is, Mrs. Hayes."

Jill hurried behind the curtain to change from her wedding gown back into her floral sundress. She was satisfied with Gwendolyn's work, and was relieved by her promise of confidentiality. In many ways, the seamstress reminded Jill of Aunt Jackie. They were about the same height and robust weight and they shared a gentle spirit.

"Thank you again," Jill said placing her wedding gown in Gwendolyn's hands. "This means a lot to Zachary and me."

"It is my pleasure, darling. I will see you in five days."

The two women embraced to celebrate the creation of a masterpiece and their new professional relationship. Jill hurried to the van where Roy sat waiting with the air conditioner on full blast. He'd promised Zach that Jill would be in good hands with him at all times. He was determined to keep his word. Roy waited for a voluptuous woman wearing a colorful broad brimmed hat to sashay past them. Then he pulled out into traffic, headed back east toward Montego Bay.

Chapter Thirty

The bell above the door rang, alerting Gwendolyn that another customer had arrived. Charlotte walked in and removed her big hat. She fanned her face and wiped the moisture from her brow.

"Welcome to Gwendolyn's Originals. How may I help you?"

Charlotte looked at the lovely wedding gown the shop owner had spread out on the sewing table. Only a tiny bride could fit into it. She'd recognized Jill leaving the shop. Charlotte was sure the gown belonged to her. "I'm browsing for now ma'am. Thank you. What a lovely wedding dress. Who on earth could fit into something so small?"

"You like it, eh?" Gwendolyn smiled with pride, and ran her hand over the expensive piece. "It is an original for a very beautiful young lady. Her fiancé paid me top dollar to create it for their wedding. In fact, she just left here. This gown fits her perfectly."

"What is the bride's name?"

Gwendolyn furrowed her brows, and planted her hands on her wide hips. "That is *confidential* information. All of my clients have a right to privacy. State your business here or leave at once!"

Charlotte removed the slip of paper bearing Jay's measurements and some instructions from her straw bag. She had called and said she'd gained weight since moving back to Atlanta. She needed six new custom-made shirts in various colors. Charlotte gave Gwendolyn the paper. "This is an order for my friend. She...*he* needs new shirts. I have the money," she said, pulling several American bills from the bag.

Gwendolyn read the sizes and description of the shirts. "Tell your friend to come and try on the shirts three weeks from today."

"There is no need for a fitting. The measurements are accurate. I will come for the shirts in three weeks. Thank you."

Charlotte slid her cell phone from her straw bag as soon as she exited the shop. She dialed Jay's office number at the Seven Seas and got her voicemail. "Jay, sweetie, I have seen your precious Jill. You will be surprised to know that she is engaged to be married. Her fiancé contracted Gwendolyn Hayes to design a very beautiful wedding gown. I saw it with my own two eyes! Could this man Jill is about to wed be your *brother*? Please call me back, baby. I'm missing ya. Muah!"

* * * * *

"Hello, Auntie, how are you?" Jay pecked her aunt on both her cheeks. "May I come in?"

Aunt Jackie ran her fingers through her sister locks nervously and stepped aside to give her long lost niece clear passage into the house. "I'm fine, Jay. This is a surprise. I'm expecting company."

A sly grin crept across Jay's face. "Is a *man* on his way here to court you this evening?"

"Oh no, baby, I'm not seeing anyone. I'm waiting on the Lord to send me another mate."

"Well, I won't stay long. I stopped by to apologize. The last time I was here I acted like a fool. I accused you of some things that I shouldn't have. I'm sorry."

"It's okay, baby. All is forgiven. I know you're having a difficult time accepting what's going on between your brother and Jill. I want you and Zach to sit down and talk. You two love each other. I raised y'all to be close. Time is too short to be holding grudges. Will you talk to him please?"

"I don't know, Auntie. I've gotta think about it." Jay hugged her aunt again. "I'm gonna get outta here. Enjoy your company."

"I love you, Jayla Simone."

"I love you too."

Jay hurried to her car parked across the street from her aunt's house. The blinking light on her cell phone alerted her that she had some messages. She had been out of the office all day. Early that morning, she'd gone to Zach's house to get the rest of her things while he and Jill were at work. Then she'd spent hours at Nina's house where she'd gotten a lecture about making amends with Aunt Jackie and Zach. Her dear aunt had deserved an apology, but as far as Jay was concerned, her brother could go straight to hell. Ayla had called and left messages begging Jay to return her call. She deleted them, not wanting to hear a damn thing her crazy ass had to say. The last message was from Charlotte and it was not good news.

"That evil bastard!" Jay hit the steering wheel with her fist. Her eyes wandered over to Aunt Jackie's driveway where she saw Venus walking, carrying a pink overnight bag. Nahima was skipping ahead of her. Jay started her engine and peeled away from the curb at top speed.

* * * * *

The Bessette family was very excited about Zach and Jill's upcoming wedding. Initially, Orville had some choice words for his future son-in-law for getting his daughter pregnant before he made her his wife. But after Zach asked for his forgiveness, and promised to be a loving and faithful husband to Jill forever, all was forgiven. Orville was just happy that Jill had fallen in love with a *man* and a good one to boot.

With just five days before the big day, Orville and Faye welcomed Jill back home. She'd decided to spend her last days as a single woman with her family. It was for the best because Aunt Jackie and Nahima would arrive early tomorrow morning, and they were going to stay at the villa with Zach. Jill figured he wouldn't be too lonely with them there to keep him company. And Dex and Ramona were scheduled to fly in two days after that.

"Come and walk me to the door." Zach took Jill by her hand. "I can't believe you're abandoning me. You could've at least waited until after my folks arrived."

"Are you a *baby*? Do you need me there to take care of you?" Jill teased.

Suddenly Zach's countenance became unreadable. Jill had never seen his eyes darken before. He pulled her to the edge of the porch where the moonlight shined directly over them. His hands eased down to her belly where his child was growing and developing inside. "As long as I can see you, I know nothing can happen to keep us apart. It's when you're out of my sight that I worry. Four months is a long time. We survived it, but I don't ever wanna go through anything like that again."

"Zachary, I am safe here with my family in our home. Papa is here, and I have been cleared to leave the island with you."

"I know. Maybe I'm paranoid. I'll call you when I reach the villa. Wait by the phone for my call."

* * * * *

"Aunt Jackie, are you sure you're gonna be okay?"

"What did I say?" She pushed her empty breakfast plate away and wiped her mouth with a napkin.

"My papa is nice, Nana. You'll see."

"Finish eating your oatmeal, pumpkin. Uncle Dex and Auntie Ramona are waiting for us in the lobby."

The discussion around the breakfast table had been all about Wallace. He was on a flight en route to the island to attend Zach and Jill's wedding. Aunt Jackie had known before arriving that there was a strong possibility that he would make the trip. Zach had told her a few days after he and Jill set a date that he'd extended an invitation to Wallace and his family to come to Jamaica for the ceremony. Now that he was on his way, Aunt Jackie was experiencing a myriad of emotions, but she claimed she'd be fine.

"Auntie, if you're having second thoughts about being around Wallace, now is the time to speak or forever hold your peace. He's prepared to sit the wedding out, and spend time with Jill, Nahima and me in private. I can make sure your paths never cross."

"I *have* to face Wallace. It's been twenty-eight years since Belva's death. I need closure, and if that means I have to rub elbows with Wallace, then so be it. It's not about *me* anyway. We're all here to celebrate with you and Jill."

Zach helped Nahima from her chair and wiped her face and hands with a baby wipe. "Okay, we're about to leave. We'll swing by and pick you up on the way to Jill's parents' house for the party. Wallace will be with us. He's probably nervous about seeing you too, but I think you'll both be fine."

Chapter Thirty-One

The moment Ayla entered Jay's suite, she unbuttoned her mint green swing dress and let it drop to the carpet. She walked over it, kicking her feet free from her white leather mules, and turned to Jay butt naked. "I knew you'd call sooner or later. Ms. Kitty has been waiting." She kissed Jay softly on the lips.

Jay allowed Ayla to press her back against the wall. The aggression turned her on. She grabbed Ayla's ass with both hands, and started a slow grind against her crotch. Jay broke the kiss and began a trail downward with her tongue. She licked and nibbled Ayla's neck, dipping lower to her chest. Her lips latched on to one of her erect nipples. Jay alternated her attention between both full breasts. Ayla squirmed, moaned and begged for more. And when Jay knew for sure the lying ass doctor was under her sexual spell with no defense, she shoved her away with force.

Ayla stumbled backward and nearly fell. "What's the matter, Jay? You sounded like you were in need of a fix over the phone," she said through uneven breaths. She closed the distance between them and tried to rekindle the fire with a kiss.

Jay slapped her hard across her face. "Stop it! We've got a crisis. There'll be plenty of time for that later. Right now we need to stop a wedding. Zach and Jill are in Jamaica getting ready to get married. I don't have the details. My contacts on the island don't know *shit*!"

Ayla rubbed her face in the spot where she'd been slapped. "I had no idea where Zach was. He's been on leave for close to a month. That's why I've been calling you. I wondered if you knew where he was. Damn it! I should've known he was in Jamaica with that *bitch*. How did you find out?"

"A friend of mine called. She saw Jill leaving a boutique after a fitting with a seamstress for her wedding gown. Zach hired a well-known designer to dress that slut. His punk ass is over there tossing money around like Trump."

"It's probably some of my damn money."

"Bitch, why don't you stop lying?" Jay looked at Ayla like she wanted to yank her hair out. "None of that shit you told me about Zach taking your money and forcing you to have abortions is true! You didn't have to lie to make me hate him. He took care of that the moment he fucked Jill.

Ayla turned a fiery shade of red with embarrassment. Jay had called her out and she had no comeback. She folded her arms across her bare breast. "What are you going to do? How do you plan to stop the wedding?"

"I'm flying to Jamaica first thing in the morning. I'll do whatever I have to do to keep Zach from marrying Jill."

The sound of Jay's voice and the haunting look in her eyes made Ayla's flesh crawl. She shivered when different dreadful scenarios popped inside her head. Sure, she was bitter that Zach had dumped her for Jill. She was a sore loser too, but was it worth flying to Jamaica to crash their wedding? Ayla thought not. She was about to express her opinion to Jay when she was snatched by her hair and slammed against the wall. Jay bit down hard on her bottom lip, drawing blood. All thoughts faded when Ayla felt a finger enter her drenched well. She lost all power over her body and mind. Jay's pleasurable sexual assaults robbed her of her senses every time.

* * * * *

"Did you hear the good news, mon?"

Roy inched past Rowland, the evening concierge, on his walk to the resort's lobby. He was all decked out in his black Sunday suit and matching striped tie. The senior driver was on his way to Born Again Baptist Church in Kingston to attend Zach and Jill's sunset wedding. "And what good news might that be?" He asked.

Rowland followed him. "Ms. King is on her way to Montego Bay to visit us! She called and asked that *you* pick her up from the airport, but you were out. I sent Littlejohn in your place."

"Has Littlejohn left the resort already?" Roy stopped midstride and looked at his watch in a panic.

"I don't think so. He said he wanted to clean the SUV before he made the trip to the airport. You remember how vexed Ms. King can become if she sees a dirty vehicle."

"I do," Roy said, feeling more uneasy by the minute. He looked at his watch again. It was a gift from Zach for his kindness to him and Jill. "I will go to the service quarters garage to make sure Littlejohn cleans the SUV properly for Ms. King's arrival."

Roy hurried through the resort's lobby and out to the parking lot. When he reached the van he jumped inside and drove across the lush, green grass to save time on his mission. He had to stop Littlejohn from going to the airport.

"Wait! Wait!" Roy blew the horn frantically to get his coworker's attention.

Littlejohn was backing out of the garage when he heard the loud beeps. He put the SUV in park and waited. Roy exited the van and tapped on the window. Littlejohn lowered the glass.

"You don't have to pick up Ms. King from the airport." Roy was out of breath and perspiring heavily. "I just spoke to her. She wants *me* to come. She told me to give you this for your trouble." He gave Littlejohn one of the crisp U.S. twenty dollar bills Zach had given him that morning. "Take it. You've earned it, my friend. Now go have yourself some fun."

With that said, Littlejohn returned the SUV to the garage, and Roy sped away toward Sangster International Airport. He had no idea what he would say to Jay or how he would explain his actions. Quite frankly, Roy didn't have a plan at all. But there was one thing he knew for certain: Jay would not stop Zach and Jill's wedding. He would handle his former boss by himself. There was no need to upset the bride or the groom with the situation. After the wedding he would tell them the great tale of how he'd kept Ms. King from ruining their special day.

Chapter Thirty-Two

Roy realized he was acting hastily under the assumption that Jay had come to Jamaica to spoil the wedding. Obviously, he had no proof to substantiate his suspicions. He was relying totally on his instinct and snippets from various conversations he'd heard over the past few weeks. He'd been told that the ceremony would be a *private affair*. If they had invited Jay, wouldn't he have known about it? And wouldn't she have arrived with the rest of the family and friends from Atlanta? It didn't take a tea leaf reading to know that there was bad blood between Zach and Jay because of Jill. No one would take too kindly to their sibling stealing their lover.

No, Roy didn't know Jay's intentions for certain. He was operating on gut and theory. If he was wrong, he'd take his punishment like a man. But if his speculations were correct, and he had prevented Jay from disrupting the wedding, he would become a hero in his own right.

When he reached the airport parking lot he immediately removed his suit coat and tie. He reached inside the glove compartment for his chauffer's hat. He put it on, and attached the resort's employee badge to the left side of his dress shirt. It was time to get inside of Jay's head.

* * * * *

"Roy, my man, how have you been?" Jay hugged her former employee and patted his back.

"I am well, ma'am, and you?" Roy took Jay's suitcase and turned away from her.

"I'm great. I came to the island to relax and enjoy the *wedding*." Jay watched Roy closely for a reaction of any sort. He gave her none. She followed after him.

"Whose wedding are you speaking of, Ms. King?"

"My brother is getting married here today. Haven't you heard?"

"Your brother is in *Jamaica*? It is not possible. I have not seen Zachary at the resort."

Jay and Roy continued their trudge through the airport in silence. As usual, the traffic of rushing bodies was thick. It was spring time and visitors from all over the world had flocked to the island to enjoy its sights and culture. Once they were outside, Jay took out her cell phone and dialed.

"I'm here. What do you know?" She paused and listened quietly as the person on the other end of the call spoke. She continued to trail Roy through the parking lot. "In other words, you know nothing, huh?" Jay shook her head, disappointed before ending the call.

Roy took her suitcase and put it in the back of the van. She climbed in the front passenger's seat and they zipped out of the parking lot in the direction of the Island Paradise Resort.

After some time, Jay looked at Roy. "What is the name of that little church up in the hills you took Jill and me to for Angelina's christening?"

"Are you sure it was *I* who drove you, ma'am?"

Jay studied Roy's profile. She honestly couldn't recall who had driven them to the church. All Jay remembered was she didn't want to be around Jill's family that day, and it was raining. "Maybe it wasn't you. I sure would hate to miss my brother's wedding. He called and begged me to come. He's marrying Jill, my ex. I gave them my blessing. I'm surprised you hadn't heard any of this."

Roy kept his eyes on the winding roads before him. "I have not seen Ms. Jill. I thought she was in Atlanta with you. Everything you have told me is a very big surprise."

When they reached the resort Jay asked Roy to wait in the van while she went inside to check on something. Seconds after the double glass doors closed behind her, he removed her suitcase from the vehicle and entrusted it to Rowland before he sped away. All of Roy's suspicions had been confirmed. Jay had not been invited to her brother's wedding, and she had indeed come to Jamaica with ill intentions.

* * * * **

"By the power bestowed upon me by the almighty God and the sitting government of the island of Jamaica, I now pronounce you man and wife. Zachary, you may kiss your bride."

Zach took Jill into his arms and kissed her like there was no one else in the tiny sanctuary except the two of them. Not even the applause and voices of the small choir singing in the loft behind them could break the kiss. It was Aunt Jackie's loud, fake coughing that made Zach come up for air. And even when he did pull his lips away from Jill's, he kept her in a tight embrace. Reverend Baldwin, the Bessette family's longtime pastor, led the well-wishers in a boisterous round of applause.

Roy slipped inside the church undetected at that moment, and thanked God the wedding had proceeded without mishap. He clapped his hands and joined the small gathering of family and friends singing "Love Lifted Me" as Zach and Jill dashed up the aisle. Roy removed a handkerchief from his pants pocket and wiped his sweaty brow. He would be in hot water with the resort once Jay reported what he'd done to the new executive manager, but he didn't care. Right now, he wanted to enjoy some delicious food and fellowship at Zach and Jill's outdoor reception. Then he would drive them to the Blue Lagoon where they would spend their first night as husband and wife in the honeymoon chateau on the beach. Roy's friend, Pembrick, would drive the newlyweds to the airport the next morning to catch their flight to an undisclosed destination.

* * * * *

Zach sat at a table with Wallace under the white tent that housed the small wedding reception. They were smiling and watching Jill dancing with her little brothers. Oliver, the oldest had started the timeless tradition when he tapped Zach on his shoulder to cut in on his dance with the bride. From there, Jill danced with the other three Bessette boys according to their ages.

"She's very beautiful, son. There's a sweet innocence about her that draws you in. Now I understand why things happened the way they did. Jill is enchanting and she adores you, Zach. I have no doubt that she'll be faithful to you."

"I know she will."

Zach clapped his hands, threw his head back and howled. Orville was doing a smooth trot out onto the dance floor, bouncing and bobbing his head to the rhythm of the music. He stopped in front of Jill and did some fancy, side-to-side foot action while snapping his fingers. Everyone started clapping in time, encouraging the father and daughter dance, and they responded. Jill shimmied and rolled her hips with her hands in the air, and Orville pranced around her. Then he wrapped his arms around his daughter and held her close. They rocked to the music holding each other lovingly.

After another hour of dancing and the traditional bouquet and garter tosses, Zach and Jill cut their modest three-tier wedding cake. They fed each other to the applause and cheers of their family and friends. Zach licked icing from Jill's fingers. The two-carat, heart-shaped diamond on her left hand twinkled under the torch flame near them.

"They're not gonna stop dancing any time soon. Look at your parents." Zach tilted his head toward the dance floor. "They're having a good time. Dex and Ramona are too. Let's go. Nobody will miss us."

Jill took in the dozen or so couples still dancing to the Deejay's eclectic repertoire. He had slowed the music down. Percy Sledge was crooning his greatest hit of all time, "When a Man Loves a Woman." The lovers had taken to the floor.

"If you're ready, my dear *husband*, so am I."

"The van is this way, Mr. and Mrs. King." Like magic, Roy appeared at Zach's side as soon as he took Jill by the hand.

"Okay, we're ready."

Honey

* * * * *

A group or Orville's friends and shipmates were taking down the tent and clearing the church's lawn when the brown taxi pulled up. Jay rolled down her window and watched the men discard pastel pink bows, streamers and disposable table cloths into large garbage bags. They shouted out wishes on behalf of Zach and Jill then released the pink and white balloons into the air. The dark sky swallowed each one as they floated toward the heavens. The men's laughter and chatter about the festive wedding that had just taken place was as irritating as finger nails scratching a chalkboard. Jay's empty belly rumbled and jerked from nausea. She had been so engrossed in finding out when and where the wedding was that she'd neglected her hunger.

Tears, perspiration and snot slid down Jay's face and onto the neckline of her white t-shirt. Reality had hit her like a ton of bricks. Jill was Zach's *wife*. They had pledged their lives to each other, leaving her alone and out in the cold to nurse her wounded pride. Their betrayal had caused her great pain. But Jay had come to her senses, and decided against stopping the wedding by the time Charlotte called her with the accurate time and location. She only wanted to show her face and scare Zach and Jill shitless. There was an urgent need to show them they hadn't outsmarted her with their secret wedding. And more than anything, Jay had intended to send them a warning message that vengeance was on its way.

Time and circumstance had caused Jay to miss the ceremony. She wasn't sure if it had been a blessing or a curse. Maybe seeing Zach and Jill in all their wedding bliss would've been too disturbing, and sent her spiraling over the edge. Jay would never know now. She only hoped the newlyweds would enjoy their honeymoon, wherever the hell they were spending it. No doubt they were relaxed and content in their own little love cocoon. And that's exactly what Jay wanted. She had plans for Mr. and Mrs. King once they got back to Atlanta. In case they hadn't heard: Payback was a *bitch*.

Chapter Thirty-Three

"You don't have to leave, Wallace. This restaurant is big enough for the both of us. And this pretty girl has been asking for you." Aunt Jackie tugged the little hand she was holding.

"Good morning Papa." Nahima blew Wallace a kiss.

Wallace reached over from his seat at the table and picked her up. He placed her on his lap. "Good morning beautiful, how are you?"

"I feel fine. I'm hungry, though."

"Let's see what Papa can do about that." Wallace motioned for a server.

Aunt Jackie winked at him. "I'll leave you two alone to enjoy breakfast."

"That's nonsense, Jackie. There're two other chairs at this table. We'd like you to stay unless *you* don't want to."

Aunt Jackie took a seat and looked around. The server came to the table and took their orders. The adults chose the breakfast buffet, and Nahima wanted pancakes and bacon.

"Thank you." Wallace whispered and smiled.

"What are you thanking me for?"

"Thank you for raising my children, and treating them like you had given birth to them. Zach has told me about the sacrifices you made as a young woman for him and Jayla. Thanks for your forgiving spirit. You have every reason to hate me, yet you don't."

"I *used* to hate you because it was easier to do that than accept the truth. Belva was no saint, but you loved her in spite of it. You looked past her imperfections, and Lord knows she had many. Before our mother died, she warned Belva that her greed and impatience would get her in trouble one day."

Wallace waited until the waiter had served them their coffee and Nahima a glass of apple juice. "I didn't mean to do it. Oh, I meant to wound Claudius Henry, but not my Belva Jane. That woman meant the world to me. I wanted to die along with her. My heart stopped the same day hers did because *she* was my heart."

"I know. That's why I was finally able to forgive you. It took a whole lot of praying, but I did it with God's help. And seeing you for the first time in twenty-eight years has given me the closure I needed."

* * * * *

Honey

On the early afternoon flight to Grand Cayman Island, Zach handed Jill a gift wrapped in shiny silver paper. "Open it."

"And what have I done to deserve this?"

"With all the excitement of the wedding, I forgot to give you your birthday gift. I know your family had a breakfast in your honor yesterday, but as the groom, I was banned from it. And last night..."

"I know," Jill blushed. "There was no time for it."

Zach tapped the box. "Open it."

Jill took her time opening her birthday gift, and was pleasantly surprised. It was a gorgeous, fourteen-carat gold charm bracelet. A church with a tall steeple was the lone charm dangling from it. She kissed Zach's cheek, and wiped away the coral lipstick smudge it left behind. "Thank you, Zachary. I love it, but I'm not sure if I understand why there is a church on it."

"We started our life together as husband and wife at your childhood church. For every milestone we reach, I'll add a charm symbolic of it. A baby rattle is next."

"That is very thoughtful. Thank you again."

When the plane landed twenty minutes later, the honeymooners disembarked with one thought in mind. They wanted to spend every minute of their time alone on the island enjoying each other while making lasting memories.

* * * * *

Mr. Carlton Vincent, executive manager of the Island Paradise Resort was disturbed by the complaint he had received about Roy Feagin. The young Brittan who had been hired to replace Jay was very fond of his senior driver. He praised him often for his work ethic. Roy had been an employee at the resort since it first opened its doors fourteen years ago. His record was impeccable. Mr. Vincent had done a little investigation into the four-year relationship between Roy and Jay while she had supervised him. Each employee he'd spoken with told him the driver and manager had gotten along well. They'd had mutual respect for one another. But, as in most work environments, there had been pieces of gossip weaving about which painted a different picture.

Rowland, the concierge, had made it a point to mention that Roy and Jay had once been close. But over some time, the dynamic in their working relationship shifted. At times, Jay had taken advantage of Roy and misused him for personal reasons as it related to her lover. And it was her now *former* lover Jillian Bessette, whose name appeared to be the source behind Jay's complaint. Although Jay had never mentioned her name or anything about the wedding all the resort's employees had been whispering about; Mr. Vincent was inclined to believe most of what he'd heard was true. He didn't think Roy had done anything worth being terminated for, but as his boss, he had to question him and report his findings on the matter to Jay.

Mr. Vincent had left a message with the clerk in the service quarters for Roy to report to his office at ten o'clock. It was eight minutes till. He placed Jay's sloppy, handwritten complaint on top of Roy's employee file. She had left a ten minute rant on his voicemail, so it baffled him when he found the note on his desk Monday morning. There were three quick taps on the door.

"Come in," Mr. Vincent said in his distinguished British accent. He stood behind his desk and extended his hand. "Have a seat, Roy. How are you?"

"I am well. Thank you, sir." Roy greeted his boss with a handshake and a nervous smile.

Mr. Vincent reclaimed his seat and placed his palms flat on the desktop. "Do you have any idea why I requested this meeting, Roy?"

"Yes, sir, I suppose I do. Ms. King is probably upset that I was not available to drive her around the island Saturday evening. I was off work with permission to keep the van in my possession. You can check the schedule and request records. I went and picked up Ms. King from the airport anyway and brought her here safely. Then I left although she'd asked me to wait for her. I never agreed to be her chauffer for the evening, Mr. Vincent, *never*."

"That sounds like a cut and dry recollection, Roy. You're an honest man, and I believe everything you just said. But what *haven't* you told me?"

Mr. Vincent watched Roy's facial expression as he toiled over his situation. There was definitely something more to be said. What was so difficult for him to reveal? His job was secure. Mr. Vincent had hinted as much. Nothing the other employees had already told him about the relationship between the driver and his former boss would change that. All he wanted was the full history in Roy's own words.

"I will tell you everything, Mr. Vincent, so you will understand why I behaved as I did. This will not be a pretty picture at all, sir."

"I'll be the judge of that, Roy. Please do tell."

Roy's journey down memory lane and up to Saturday evening did indeed shed light on the situation, and afterwards he still had his job.

Chapter Thirty-Four

Five fabulous days and nights on Grand Cayman Island had come and gone much too fast for Zach and Jill. The night club dancing, sunset strolls on the beach and passionate love making at the break of dawn would forever be remembered. They'd made enough wonderful memories to last a lifetime. But now it was time to return to reality. Their first stop would be Montego Bay and on to Kingston to spend three more days with Jill's family before bidding them farewell. Zach had spoken with his buddy Clive at the U. S. Immigration Department in Atlanta. Jillian Josephine Bessette had been granted clearance to return to the United States. Her marriage license bearing her new name would have to be shown to airport officials, along with a document from the United States government, before she could board their flight. It had already been faxed and was waiting for them at the Blue Lagoon Resort.

"Welcome back, newlyweds!" Roy was excited to see his friends. "How was the trip?"

"It was *wonderful*. I am the luckiest woman alive!"

"My wife and I enjoyed our honeymoon, my friend. I could get used to married life."

Zach helped Roy load their luggage into the back of the van after Jill climbed into her seat. She was still wearing her bridal glow. Marriage definitely agreed with her.

"I must speak with you privately, Zachary. There is something I think you should know, but please not a word to Jill. She is too fragile in her condition. We must speak as soon as we reach the resort."

Zach grabbed Roy by his arm. "It sounds serious. Is Ms. Faye or one of the children sick?"

"They are all well. Please, Zachary, let us leave at once and we will talk at the Blue Lagoon."

On the drive from the airport to the resort all kinds of scenarios crossed Zach's mind. He did the process of elimination, but came up with nothing. He had spoken to Aunt Jackie and Nahima twice while he and Jill were on their honeymoon. They were fine. He had checked in with Dex and Ramona, and Wallace had called him last night. Zach was clueless and curious. As soon as they reached the Blue Lagoon he checked in and retrieved the fax from the front desk clerk. Once Jill was settled in the villa, Zach hurried to meet Roy downstairs.

"Talk to me."

Roy motioned toward two wingback chairs in the posh resort lobby. "Come, let's sit. Zachary, your sister was here."

"Jay was in *Jamaica*? When and why?"

"My friend, she arrived the day of the wedding. She knew you and Jill were to be married, but she had no idea about the time or place. I drove her to the Island Paradise and left her there. She was very angry I tell you! She tried to have me terminated from my job because of it, but I told my boss the whole truth. Ms. King left the island Wednesday going back to Atlanta. Littlejohn, another driver told me so."

* * * * *

Multiple bottles of Disarrono, and sex with Ayla one day and Nina the next, became a pattern for Jay over the next few weeks. She'd lost more than ten pounds due to her poor appetite. To say she was depressed was an understatement. She was battling to maintain her sanity. Her inability to concentrate was being displayed in her work. Manny, her senior marketing team member was basically running the department. Aunt Jackie had been trying to reach Jay for days, but she'd refused to take any of her calls. She wanted nothing to do with her aunt or any other member of her family.

Ayla had suggested that Jay get some professional help. She'd recommended her colleague Dr. Capone. Jay blew off her concern, and told her in time she would be fine. Then she'd asked Ayla questions about Zach and his attitude on the job since he and Jill had gotten married. Ayla lied and said she hadn't seen him, but she had. She and Zach had actually spoken briefly. She had apologized for the lies she had told on him, and for acting so irrationally when their affair ended. Ayla even congratulated Zach on his marriage. And out of concern for Jay, she'd encouraged him to make contact with his sister because she was experiencing some serious emotional issues.

* * * * *

Jill met Zach at the door as she did every evening when he got home from work. He was two hours late because Aunt Jackie had asked him to come by her house so they could talk. Jill was anxious to hear about their conversation. She followed Zach into the den and sat down next to him on the sofa.

"What did your aunt want to talk about?"

"She thinks it's time for me to talk to Jay. I agree with her, but what do you think?"

Jill closed her eyes and rubbed her belly which had expanded tremendously. She had been stuck in the house for over a month, only venturing out to go to doctor's appointments and the occasional dinner date with her husband. Fear had kept Jill in hiding, but she was ready to reenter the real world. She missed church and shopping. She'd also been eager to visit Umoja Academy.

"It is time. You should visit Jay at the Seven Seas, but I must go with you. We both owe her an apology."

"Nah," Zach said, shaking his head. "You're not going anywhere near Jay. Have you forgotten how she treated you when you went to ask for your passport? You are in no condition for that kind of abuse, Jill. You didn't deserve it then and you sure as hell don't now. Let me go alone. You can apologize to Jay in a letter or over the phone. This is a war between my sister and me, and I'm ready to wave the white flag."

"Are you going to tell Jay we're expecting a child?"

"Why not?" Zach rubbed Jill's baby bump and kissed her on the cheek. "I might as well lay everything out on the table to get it over with. Whatever happens after that is all up to Jay."

Zach called his sister, and she agreed to meet him in the second floor bistro at Seven Seas tomorrow at six o'clock.

* * * * *

Jay pressed the power button to end her surprise call from Zach. She grinned at his humility. She'd detected a tinge of sincerity in his voice. It was *almost* convincing. There wasn't much for them to talk about as far as Jay was concerned. If Zach had any balls, he would've initiated a conversation with her months ago, and he never would've married Jill. If he thought he could offer Jay some half-ass apology, and they'd join hands and sing a couple of verses of "Kumbaya", he was sadly mistaken.

Jay picked up the phone again and dialed Nina's number. She felt like drinking and playing cards at her spot. Things were always hot and popping over there. Jay was a little leery of some of the characters Nina hung around, but for the most part, she could deal with them with both eyes wide open.

Nina answered on the first ring, and immediately Jay heard folks talking smack, and music blasting in the background. "What's up, baby? It sounds like a Thursday night party going on over there."

"Yeah, it's something like that. A game of dominoes, some liquor, and Negroes talking shit. You know the usual. What's up with you?"

"I'm about to roll over there and kick it with y'all. After the crew leaves, you and I can have an after party."

"That's a plan."

* * * * *

Zach had left work an hour earlier than usual. He'd needed the extra time to collect his thoughts and prepare for his meeting with Jay. When he'd called Jill, she sounded nervous for him. She knew how stubborn and callous his sister could be. Jill didn't want Zach to get his hopes up only to have Jay crush them. Aunt Jackie had told him she'd be praying and hoping for resolution because the entire situation was taking its toll on her. She hadn't been sleeping well at night worrying about her children. Aunt Jackie advised Zach to be as humble and apologetic as he could to win Jay's forgiveness.

As Zach sat at the reserved table for two, sipping a whiskey sour, he had a weird feeling in the pit of his stomach. Jay was already twenty minutes late for their meeting. She hadn't called nor had she answered any of his calls and text messages. Zach wasn't down for any bullshit. He had come to get to the bottom of things with Jay, but it appeared she wanted to play games. He had just thrown a few bills on the table to cover his drink and stood to leave when Jay entered the bistro. Her tailored navy suit and light blue custom made shirt made him feel like a bum. He was rocking a pair of green scrubs covered by a black suit jacket.

"What's up, big brother?" Jay pulled out the chair opposite Zach and smirked.

Zach picked up on her cynicism right away. "Hey Jay, how are you?"

"I'm great. How is the family?"

"Aunt Jackie is fine, but she'd be better if you'd answer the phone when she calls."

"And how is the *wifey*?" Jay smiled, but it was so insincere. It was more like a taunting scowl.

Zach was ready to go there if it was what Jay wanted. At this point, he felt he had nothing to lose. "Jill is fine. We're happy, Jay." He rubbed his goatee out of habit and tried to maintain his composure before he spoke again. "Jay, I'm sorry…"

"Hold that thought, Zach." Jay signaled for a server who was busy at another table. "I need a drink for this."

A cute blonde girl came to the table and took Jay's order for her signature drink and an appetizer platter. Zach asked for a glass of water.

"Go ahead, Zach. What were you about to say? It sounded like an apology."

The words *humble and apologetic* resonated in Zach's mind. He took a deep breath. "I'm sorry, Jay. I take full responsibility for what happened between Jill me. I was wrong for allowing my heart to get the best of me. I had no right to make emotional or physical contact with Jill while or even after you broke up. I want you to forgive me."

"You're right. You had no right to *fuck my bitch*."

Zach gritted his teeth and tried to maintain control. "Jay, I'm making every effort to be civil, but you're crossing the line."

"Nah, Zach, *you* crossed the line! What you did was cold-blooded. I never would've done that to you! Yeah, I slept with Ayla after the fact, but you didn't give a damn about her. Hell, I don't either."

"You didn't love Jill," Zach said calmly. "But that isn't the issue here. The reason I asked you to meet me this evening was so I could apologize to you for getting involved with Jill and causing your breakup. I didn't plan it. Things just happened, Jay. I swear."

The server returned with their drinks and appetizer platter. Zach just stared at his glass of water. Jay drained her drink.

"So, how is it supposed to work now, huh? You married my ex. Are we supposed to get together for the holidays and family cookouts? Maybe we could vacation together. We all love *Jamaica*."

"It'll definitely take some time for us all to get used to the situation. But can't we at least try? It's all about forgiveness and moving on, Jay. I know what I'm asking won't be easy, but it is doable. I've forgiven Wallace. We have a good relationship now. It didn't happen overnight. It took time and effort on both our parts. It's possible for us as well."

Jay shook her head. Rumors about Zach and Wallace reconciling was one thing, but to hear his confession was a slap in her face. "You can embrace the bastard who killed our mother, but you stab me in the back. That's cold, Zach."

Zach reached across the table and held Jay's hand. "I'm sorry for hurting you and I'll do *anything* to make things right between us. Just tell me what I have to do."

"That's easy." Jay snatched her hand away from Zach's hold. "Have your marriage to Jill annulled. Then send her ass back to the streets of Kingston."

"I can't do that. I love her and I ain't living without her. And…um...wow…this is hard for me tell you. But I'm just gonna give it to you straight. Jill is pregnant. We're expecting our first child in August."

Chapter Thirty-Five

““I knew Jay would not accept your apology, Zachary. She can hold a grudge forever, ya know?" Jill looked at the letter she had written to Jay. Zach had given it to her, but she crumpled into a ball and threw it at him. "She didn't even bother to read this. It's a shame because I meant every word I wrote. I'm truly sorry for betraying her."

The sound of heavy raindrops pounding against the house and earth filled the den. Jill wondered what Zach was thinking. Did he regret falling in love with her? Had their coming together cost him Jay's love forever? And would he blame her if that was the case? Jill lifted her head from his chest and stared at him eye to eye. He had been holding her on his lap for several minutes in complete silence.

"Before you even ask, Jill, the answer is *no*," Zach said as if he had read her mind. "I love my sister and I miss her, but I have no regrets."

* * * * *

Jay guided her Beamer down the street deep in the hood. She was looking for the address that Fudge, one of Nina's homeboys, had scribbled on a sheet of paper the other night. In all her years in Atlanta, she had never been to this particular section of town before. There was a liquor store on every damn corner, and the number of abandoned homes outnumbered the occupied ones. Half-naked prostitutes, with big jiggling asses, were on the stroll in broad daylight, and it seemed perfectly normal. Drug dealers were bold as hell too, making transactions in wide open view. Jay couldn't believe she had sunk so low, but Zach had started this shit. And she was about to end it.

She spotted the address, but the house was boarded up like most of the other ones on the block. Vulgar graffiti covered the chipping wood on the front of the abandoned residence.

"I'm overdressed for this neck of the woods," Jay complained. She made sure her doors were locked, and activated the alarm. She double checked the number on the house. It was the address alright. "Where the hell is he?"

Fudge appeared out of thin air and scared the shit out of Jay. She patted her chest and panted for air. He stepped closer, his tall and stocky frame decked out in a blue and white Adidas sweat suit. Face to face, they looked like an odd couple with Jay sporting a navy pants suit, starched white shirt and a pair of spectator pumps.

"Chill baby. You're cool. Hop back in your whip and let's roll out."

Jay and Fudge walked to her car side by side. She looked around the forgotten neighborhood. Music was booming from all directions, and the stench of weeks-old trash soured the air. It was hard to believe that only a few blocks away in the opposite direction, there were condos, lofts, high-end boutiques and restaurants that catered to Atlanta's rich and famous.

"I'll drive." Fudge removed Jay's keys from her hand.

She nodded her head in agreement, and walked around to the passenger's side. As they pulled away, a little voice inside Jay's head warned her that she was about to make a big mistake. It was as simple as asking Fudge to turn the car around, but her mind was made up.

"You sure you wanna do this?"

"Yeah, I'm sure." Jay wondered if Fudge had read her mind.

"You got the money?"

Jay reached inside the breast pocket of her suit coat and pulled out a white envelope stuffed with cash. "Here is half like you asked for. You'll get the other half when the job is done. And I want proof."

Fudge merged into the left turning lane cautiously. "Where is the picture of the cat? And I told you I need his schedule. I'll have to study his pattern for a few weeks."

Jay pulled out a picture and a sheet of paper with information written all over it. Fudge studied the picture for a few seconds and handed it back to her.

"Who is this dude you want me to take out for you?"

"He *used* to be my brother. His name is Zachary King."

* * * * *

"Is this where my brother lives, Daddy?" Wallace Junior asked.

Wallace sat in his car admiring Zach's beautiful two-story home. It was located in East Emerald Estates which was a quiet subdivision in North Atlanta. All the residents shared a clubhouse, pool and recreational facility. Wallace was proud of his son's success. "Yes, this is where Zachary lives. Are you ready to meet him?"

"Yes sir."

Zach and Nahima greeted Wallace, his gorgeous wife Patricia and Wallace Junior at the front door. They'd been planning for their visit for two weeks. Zach wanted to make sure his father and family were comfortable and well entertained. Jill had outdone herself, practically cooking right up to the minute they arrived. She'd prepared lots of Jamaican dishes both spicy and mild.

Zach hugged Wallace and slapped his back. "I'm glad y'all made it safely. Come on in." He stepped aside and allowed the group to enter the house.

"We're glad to be here." Wallace reached down and scooped up Nahima. He kissed her cheek. "How is Papa's pretty girl?"

"I'm fine. Is that your little boy?"

"Yes, he is. His name is Wallace Junior. He's your *uncle*." Wallace placed his free arm around Patricia. "And this good-looking woman is my wife Patricia."

"Hi," Nahima said bashfully, and buried her face in her grandfather's shoulder blade.

Zach hugged his little brother. "I'm happy to finally meet you." He and Patricia embraced before he led everyone into the spacious den where Jill sat waiting for them.

"Wow! Aren't you prettier than an angel? You look absolutely stunning, Jill. Give your father-in-law a hug." He placed Nahima on her feet.

Jill met Wallace in the middle of the room and hugged him. He introduced her to Patricia and Wallace Junior and everyone sat down to talk. The children took control over the seventy-two-inch television. After a while, Jill excused herself to the kitchen to check on the food.

"Now that your wife has left the room, there's something I'd like to discuss with you." Wallace squeezed Patricia's hand, which was resting on his knee.

"Talk to me."

"I wanna reach out to Jayla while I'm in town. I know you said she wants nothing to do with me, but I can't let that deter me. She's my only daughter, and I have to at least make an attempt to reconcile with her. It's the Christian way."

"It's a bad idea. Jay hates you almost as much as she hates me. I'm totally against it, but it's your decision."

"Lunch is served," Jill announced from the doorway.

* * * * *

Zach tapped on the driver's seat window of Wallace's silver, Chrysler 300C to get his attention. The older man looked up with tears in his eyes. His thoughts had been a million miles away. He hadn't seen Zach exit the house. He unbuckled his seatbelt, and got out of the car.

"You've been sitting out here long enough, old man. Let's go inside. I don't even wanna know what happened. I know Jay. I'm sure it was a terrible experience for you."

Wallace threw his arm casually over Zach's shoulders. They walked up the driveway together, neither uttering a word. They both had felt Jay's wrath. It was nothing they cared to discuss.

Patricia saw them coming from the window in the formal living room. She hurried to the front door and opened it. "It's okay, sweetheart. You tried," she said to her husband. "There is nothing else you can do." She threw her arms around him and squeezed tight.

Wallace accepted her comfort. "She slapped me," he mumbled, through tears.

"And she spit in my face. At first she didn't recognize me, but once she did, she attacked me like a wild animal. All of the vile cursing and insults I could handle. I even understand why Jayla hates me. But the way she ordered hotel security to drag me out of her office like I was there to do her harm was unnecessary. It was hurtful. I felt so ashamed."

"That's exactly why I didn't want you to go." Zach looked at his father with sympathy. He turned and walked to the den with Wallace and Patricia following him. "Jay is evil and selfish. Her heart is closed to you, Jill, and me. We hurt her, but we tried to fix things. I don't know about you, Daddy, but I've gotta keep it moving without Jay. I have a life with Jill now, and we have a baby on the way. We can't entertain Jay and her foolishness. You should forget about her too."

"I can't do that just yet, Zach. I feel somewhat responsible for the bitter and cold person Jayla has become. She's my only daughter. I want her to know how sorry I am for taking your mother away from both of you and that I love her very much. I won't give up on my child."

Chapter Thirty-Six

"**S**urprise!" the group of ladies shouted.

Jill's eyes widened from the shock. When she saw the faces of the few friends she'd made since moving to Atlanta, she covered her eyes with both hands and began to cry. Aunt Jackie slid her chubby arm around her waist and guided her into the house. Ramona, Felicia, Zariah and Mrs. Scott were there smiling and clapping. They all huddled around Jill and rubbed her protruding belly. Most of the silver foxes from her dance class had come out to celebrate the upcoming birth of her first child. Ida Bell and a few other ladies from Refuge Pentecostal Temple were in attendance as well.

Jill looked back at the front door for Zach. It was closed and he was nowhere in sight. Her husband had tricked her to get her out of the house on a Saturday afternoon with the promise of lunch and a movie. But as Jill took in all the lovely yellow decorations with a sunshine theme, she didn't care.

"Let's get this party started!" Ramona said. "It's game time!"

Felicia led Jill to a chair covered in bright, yellow bows and flowers. As soon as she was seated comfortably, the shower got underway. The mother to be, watched her guests compete for prizes in all sorts of games. There was a race to see who had the fastest hands in changing the diaper on a baby doll. Ramona won that one with seconds to spare. Ida Bell proved to be the champion of taste after she was able to name every yucky baby food sample she and the other ladies put to their lips.

While Jill watched the other women competing and having a good time, Venus watched her. They had never met, but they had a lot in common. Both women had been romantically involved with Jay, and had experienced her wrath and survived it. Now, they were wives of men who loved them unconditionally. And from what Zach had told Venus, Jill was just as happy as she was. Both their paths had led them away from Jay's controlling grip to joy and contentment. When the games had ended, and lunch was being served, Venus approached Jill.

"Hello Jill, my name Venus Morris. I'm *Nahima's* mother. It's a pleasure to finally meet you."

Jill looked up from all the goodies piled high on her plate. She placed it on the TV tray on the side of her chair. She attempted to stand. "I am so very happy to meet you, Nahima's mommy!"

"Don't get up, sweetie. That's not necessary." Venus placed her hand on Jill's shoulder. "Relax. I just wanted to introduce myself. It seems unfair that I know so much about you, yet all you know about me is that I have a daughter and I was once involved with Jay." She didn't miss the chilling affect the mere mentioning of that name had on Jill. She actually shivered like she'd felt a sudden gush of cold air. Venus touched her shoulder again. "It's okay. I feel the same way too sometimes. After all these years, I still find myself looking over my shoulder thinking, Jay may be lurking around watching my every move. I'm sure it's scarier for you in your delicate condition."

"It is at times," Jill confessed. She looked Venus directly in her eyes. "When will it end? When will I stop being afraid of her?"

Venus pulled an empty folding chair from a nearby table and moved it next to the Jill's recliner. She sat down and exhaled. "I thought it was all over when Jay left the country. She swore before she left that she would *never* move back to Atlanta. I was relieved, and I began to enjoy the new experience of motherhood. Soon, after that I met Charles and my life couldn't have been better. My dream turned into a nightmare the moment Zach told me Jay was moving home. If it hadn't been for Charles, she would probably still be bullying and harassing me today. But I don't think you have anything to worry about, Jill. Zach loves you and he will do whatever it takes to protect you, and your baby, from Jay and anyone else."

* * * * *

Jay was pissed off with Fudge and he knew it. He'd had her five thousand dollars for over a month now, yet Zach was still walking around living a happy and content life with Jill. Fudge had given Jay his word that he'd been on the job. He said it took time to set up the perfect hit. Last week when they'd met at Grove Park in Bankhead late at night, Fudge promised Jay he would have good news the next time they hooked up. She was back in the park waiting for an update. Her cell phone rang.

"Where are you?" she asked.

"I'm right behind you, boo." Fudge flashed the headlights on his midnight blue Escalade. "You need to chill. Come back here and hop in. I've got something I think you'll be glad to see."

The only thing I want to see is a picture of Zach's corpse. That was what Jay wanted to say. She got out of her car, and made the quick walk to Fudge's vehicle parked a few feet behind hers.

"I'm tired of this bullshit waiting game," Jay said, settling in the passenger's seat. "I gave you the upfront money on the hit a month ago, but Zach ain't dead. What's up?"

Fudge handed Jay a big brown envelope. When she opened it, she was pleasantly surprised to find a stack of black and white pictures of Zach in various locations. There were shots of him leaving his house dressed in scrubs heading for work on different mornings, and returning in the evenings. He'd been secretly photographed going to the gym alone, and to church with Jill and Nahima. Fudge had even captured Zach at a pricey maternity store in Lennox Square Mall, no doubt shopping for the wifey. The one of him and Jill kissing across a candle lit table at Kyma, an upscale restaurant in Buckhead, made Jay's stomach churn.

"So you've been watching him. When are you gonna smoke his ass?"

"You're a cold ass bitch, Jay," Fudge said, blowing out a stream of cigarette smoke. "Has anyone ever told you that?"

She laughed. "Yeah, I've been hearing that shit most of my adult life. It doesn't even faze me. When and how, Fudge? That's all I wanna know." She put the pictures back inside the envelope and placed it on his lap.

"Next Thursday evening, when your brother is leaving the gym, he's gonna catch a bullet to the back of the head from a nine-millimeter Glock 19 at midrange. *Pow*! If that don't take him out, then his ass ain't human."

"It better take him out! You want the other five grand don't you?"

"Hell yeah, I want my damn money!"

"Then take my brother out!"

* * * * *

"Zach, can I talk to you for a minute?" Ayla walked fast trying to catch up with him. Her heels clicked hard against the freshly mopped floors outside the NICU nursery.

"Um…not right now, Doc. My supervisor just paged me to her office." He kept trekking with Ayla chasing him.

"It will only take a minute."

Zach looked down at Ayla's flustered face. Lately she'd been very cordial to him, and he no longer felt the need to avoid her. "Walk and talk, Doc, I gotta see what Nancy wants."

"It's about Jay."

"I'm not about to get caught up in a lovers' quarrel with you two."

Ayla reach out and tugged at Zach's arm to slow his pace. "It's not *that*. I loaned her a large amount of money over a month ago, and she promised to pay me back in thirty days. Now she won't take my phone calls. She hasn't responded to my emails or text messages. I've been to her suite several times, but she's never there. If you see Jay or even hear from her, would you please tell her to get in contact with me? I need my money."

Zach stopped and faced Ayla. He felt sorry for her. She had fallen prey to Jay like so many other women before her. She wouldn't be the last. Ayla was just another link in Jay's pathetic chain of fools.

"Doc, I'm sorry, but I doubt if I'll run into my sister anytime soon. Let's just keep it real. Jay and I aren't speaking and you know why. The best advice I can give you is to get an attorney and sue her ass. You did make her sign a lender's agreement before you handed over the money, didn't you?"

"That's about the only smart move I made dealing with your sister. She's psychotic, Zach. You and your aunt need to have her ass committed."

"Jay does have issues. Anyway, I gotta run. Call your lawyer, Doc!" Zach said jogging backwards.

Chapter Thirty-Seven

"Come on in, Zach and close the door behind you," Nancy said and gave him an uneven smile.

Zach walked further into his supervisor's office, and noticed two men in dark suits standing near her desk. He pulled the knob to shut the door, and wondered what the hell was going on. "What's up Nancy?" He took a seat across from her and eyed the two men suspiciously.

"Zach, these two gentlemen are detectives from the Atlanta Police Department. There is an important matter they need to discuss with you and..."

"Has something happened to my wife?" Zach jumped up. "Please don't tell me something is wrong with Jill."

"Nothing has happened to your wife or your aunt, sir," the black gentleman assured him. "I'm Detective Joel Franklin and this is my partner Detective Ed Ortega."

Zach watched Nancy scurry around her office, gathering some of her belongings and her purse. She was nervous. He picked it up easily because he knew her well. For the past eight years he had reported directly to the middle-aged, African-American mother of four. He and his coworkers had attended social functions at the home she shared with her husband, Donald, on many occasions. Nancy Jackson was a kind woman and an extraordinary nurse. Her demeanor was usually calm. Zach had never seen her fumble or sweat before.

"Hey man, you said my wife and my aunt are fine. What about my *sister*? Is Jay alright?"

Neither man answered Zach right away. It wasn't until Nancy had left the office that Detective Franklin turned his attention directly to him.

"Your sister is fine too, Mr. King, for *now.*" He folded his arms across his chest

"What the hell is that supposed to mean. What's going on with Jay?"

"Ms. King is in a world of trouble," Detective Ortega said. "She contracted a hit on someone. Your sister paid five thousand dollars to a man who she believes is a professional killer. She wants him to murder someone she no longer wants around."

Zach rubbed both hands over his face, trying to wrap his mind around what he'd just heard. Then his thoughts drifted to the conversation he'd had with Ayla on his way to Nancy's office. Jay owed her a large sum of money, and she hadn't paid it back. Zach was having difficulty grasping the reality of the matter even with the two detectives staring in his face. It all seemed so surreal.

"I don't know what to say. My sister is a little crazy, but hiring a hit man to take somebody out is over the top, even for Jay. It may be against department regulations for you to answer this question, but I'm curious as hell. Who did Jay put out a hit on?"

The detectives looked at each other. Then they faced Zach and answered simultaneously, "You."

* * * * *

"Your sister Jayla King wants you dead. I'm sorry, but she does, Mr. King. She paid one of our undercover officers, known to her as Fudge, five G's in cash on May the thirty-first at approximately 12:26 in the afternoon. She'd met him in front of an abandoned house on West Grand Avenue as he had instructed her to. Our photographer was there." Detective Ortega handed Zach a stack of pictures of Jay inside and outside of her car parked in front of the abandoned house.

"I've never seen this cat before," Zach said, holding up a picture. Jay was standing with Fudge outside her BMW. "I wonder where the hell she met him."

He flipped through more shots of his sister and the undercover cop talking inside her car. "I don't see no money exchanging hands in these shots. How do y'all know she paid him and what she paid him for?"

Detective Franklin removed a Dictaphone from the breast pocket of his navy suit coat and pressed the play button. Jay's voice, telling Fudge that Zach *used* to be her brother, blew his mind. He also heard another conversation in which she described Jill as an ungrateful bitch who deserved to die too, but that she couldn't afford to pay for a hit on her. When Fudge told Jay he wouldn't kill a pregnant woman under any circumstances, Jay laughed and said, *"I ought to take that bitch out myself."*

"Turn that shit off! Turn it off!" Zach sprung from his chair and started pacing the floor in Nancy's small office.

The tape continued to roll despite his request. Another conversation could be heard. Zach shook his head from side to side in an attempt to erase the sound of Jay's voice somehow. Her words were venomous. Zach kept pacing with both fists clenched at his sides. Tears fell from his eyes unchecked. The heartless tone of Jay's voice combined with the hatred she'd expressed for him and Jill was heavy and eerie.

"I'm tired of this bullshit waiting game. I gave you the upfront money on the hit a month ago, but Zach ain't dead. What's up?"

Zach froze when he heard those words, and stared at the Dictaphone in Detective Franklin's hand. The sound of paper moving was followed by silence.

Zach's heartbeat accelerated during the moments Jay and Fudge remained quiet. He didn't know what to make of the hush, followed by the sound of paper swishing and rattling. Zach was about to take his seat. He thought the conversation was over, but Jay's voice broke the silence.

"So you've been watching him. When are you gonna smoke his ass?"

"You're a cold ass bitch, Jay. Has anyone ever told you that?"

She laughed. "Yeah, I've been hearing that shit most of my adult life. It doesn't even faze me. When and how, Fudge? That's all I wanna know."

"Next Thursday evening when your brother is leaving the gym, he's gonna catch a bullet to the back of the head from a nine-millimeter Glock 19 at midrange. Pow! If that don't take him out, then his ass ain't human."

"It better take him out! You want the other five grand don't you?"

"Hell yeah, I want my damn money!"

"Then take my brother out!"

Zach broke down completely after he heard Jay's demand. He was still crying. Each time the meeting with the detectives replayed in his head, it shook him up. He'd been driving around downtown Atlanta in a daze for close to an hour. He didn't want to go home to Jill in his emotional state. It would be hard to hide his feelings from her because they were too raw. He needed time to pull himself together although he would have to tell her everything before the night was over. He had to in order to be in compliance with the authorities. In the next two days life, as they knew it, would change forever.

The detectives had given Zach detailed instructions that he was mandated to adhere to. He had begged them to allow him an opportunity to confront Jay about everything. Zach wanted to spare her from the charges she would face if she did not call off the hit on him. Detective Ortega had said it was too late. He'd explained to Zach that the moment Jay gave Fudge the five thousand dollars and the information to track him, a crime was committed. They had enough evidence to arrest her already, but they wanted her to be prosecuted for the crime of murder for hire. And the only way they could ensure that was to let it all play out.

Zach had mixed feelings about helping the authorities bring Jay down. What she had done was wrong, and it tore his heart into a million pieces, but he didn't want her to go to prison. His sister needed psychiatric treatment, not imprisonment. Only a mentally ill person, in Zach's opinion, could do some of the things Jay had done over the past five years. Hiring a hit man to smoke him was by far the worst of all her devious schemes. If he hadn't heard her voice, seen the pictures, and recognized her distinguished penmanship on the note to Fudge, Zach wouldn't have believed Jay had ordered the hit. But she had, and she expected him to be murdered in cold blood in forty-eight hours.

Chapter Thirty-Eight

Jill peeped out of the window continuously, hoping to see Zach's SUV pulling into the driveway soon. It was five minutes until seven o'clock, and he had not come home from work yet. He hadn't called to say he'd be late and she knew for sure he didn't go to the gym on Tuesdays. Jill didn't want to call Zach's cell phone because she didn't want to scare him. With her due date only three weeks away, he would think something was wrong if she called him now. She waddled back to the kitchen to lower the heat under the pot of peas and rice, and to check the chicken in the oven. The phone on the counter startled her when it rang.

"Zachary, where are you? Do you want me to have a heart attack and go into labor with your child, eh? You know I worry about you. I…"

"Jill, this is Wallace. What's wrong, honey? You sound upset."

"Forgive me, Papa King. It's just that I am so *vexed* Zachary has not come home from work yet, and I have not heard from him. He usually calls if he's running late."

"I called because I was thinking about him, and you, of course. Patricia and I were talking earlier about driving down in a few weeks around your due date."

The chirp of the security system and the sound of the door closing pulled Jill's attention away from the conversation. "That would be wonderful. Zachary is home. Could you hold on a minute?"

"Sure, I'll hold."

"Zachary, where were you?" Jill yelled and hurried to the door as fast as her extra weight would allow her to. "I was worried that maybe…" Jill stopped talking the instant she noticed Zach's teary eyes. She rushed to him and wrapped her arms around him. "What is wrong, baby? What has happened to make you so unhappy?"

Zach pulled Jill's body closer to his and cried in her arms. His sobs frightened her. She didn't know what to do. Then she remembered Wallace was on the phone waiting for her to return.

"Zachary, sweetheart, your father is on the phone he wants to speak with you. Come."

Jill walked Zach into the kitchen, rubbing his back and wiping his tears. She lifted the receiver and pressed it against his chest. She could here Wallace on the other end calling her name. He wanted to know what was going on. He had obviously hearxd his son crying. Zach finally took the phone from Jill.

"Daddy, I…I…"

"Zach, I'm on my way. Put Jill on the phone. Son, I need to talk to Jill. Please give your wife the phone."

"Papa King," Jill whispered. She too was crying now, but she had no idea why. All she knew was Zach was in pain and she shared it with him. "I don't know what is wrong with my Zachary. I am so afraid."

"Jill, I'm on my way to Atlanta. I'm not sure if I'll be driving or flying. Just know that you'll see me before sunrise."

* * * * *

After hearing the details of Zach's unexpected meeting with the two detectives, Jill felt numb. Never in her wildest imagination would she have foreseen Jay doing something so scandalous. Jill clearly understood Zach's outpouring of emotions. He was hurt, shocked and very upset that his only sister wanted him dead. There was no way possible Jill could relate to that. She sympathized with Zach, and promised that she would be cooperative and supportive of him working with the detectives on the case. Then she climbed the stairs, and went to their bedroom.

"Are you okay?" Zach walked out of the master bathroom naked. He went to the chest of drawers in search of a pair of boxers.

"I'm fine and so is our child. He's kicking like he knows his father is fretting over something."

"*He*? How do you know it's not a girl? Remember *you* didn't wanna find out." Zach crossed the room in a pair of brown boxers and sat next to Jill on the bed. He rubbed her stomach and she placed her hand on top of his.

"I'm just hoping it's a boy. Don't you?"

"It doesn't matter to me as long as the baby is normal and healthy. Either way, our child will be born into a cruel world. We're gonna raise him or her to love God first, and family next, no matter what."

"Isn't that the way Aunt Jackie raised you and Jay? Didn't she teach you to love one another no matter what happens between you?"

Zach nodded thoughtfully. "Yeah, she did, but…"

"But I came along and ruined it, didn't I?"

"Jill, you didn't do anything. If Jay wants to blame somebody for what happened between us, I'm her guy. That's why she wants *me* dead. She realizes you weren't at fault. I have apologized and asked for her forgiveness, but Jay isn't interested in reconciling with me. If having me killed is her way of moving past it, then she's sicker than I thought. I just hate that I couldn't save her."

"She didn't want to be saved, Zachary, and it is not your problem anymore. Let the police deal with Jay."

"I don't have a choice in the matter. Do you understand everything I told you we'll have to do? This is some serious shit that's about to go down. It's just you and me, Jill. We can't tell Aunt Jackie or Dex and Ramona. Detective Franklin said we can't say a word to anyone."

"I understand, Zachary. What about your father? He's on his way here. He's going to ask you what has happened. Will you be truthful with him?"

Zach stood and stretched. "I don't know, baby. I haven't made up my mind yet. I want you to go to bed and stop worrying about this crap. The detectives promised me that you and I will be safe. They said my life was never in danger because of Jay." He pulled the covers back on the bed. "Go to sleep now, baby."

Jill lay down on her side and Zach covered her. He kissed her on the lips. She watched him remove a t-shirt from his underwear drawer. Then he went to the closet and pulled out their special blanket. He headed toward the door after he snatched a pillow from the bed.

"Zachary, where are going?"

"I'm gonna wait for my dad downstairs. And I need some time to clear my head. I'll be tossing and turning and you don't need that. Get some rest, baby. I love you."

"I love you too."

* * * * *

Wallace managed to catch a flight out of Raleigh at 10:45 that night. He'd called Zach from Raleigh-Durham International Airport just before he boarded the plane, and Zach immediately agreed to meet his father at the airport in Atlanta. Wallace had no idea what was going on with his son, but his paternal instincts told him it was very serious and should not be taken lightly. Zach had been weeping liked a child and unable to speak on the phone. That alone was alarming. Whatever had happened to upset him, Wallace was committed to helping him get through it.

Zach honked the horn in his Plymouth Prowler and flashed the headlights. Wallace smiled and waved. He liked the canary yellow sports car. It was small, but sharp.

"You need a ride, old man?" Zach teased when he stopped at the curb.

"I sure do."

Wallace took his time sitting down in the car. He'd only brought an overnight bag with him for his brief stay in Atlanta. Judging from the compact interior of the car, he'd made a wise choice.

"Are you hungry? We could stop at a fast food joint or a 24-hour diner."

"I'm not hungry, son. I came here to see about *you*. You were an emotional wreck on the phone. Tell me what's going on. Is it Jayla?"

Zach stole a glance at Wallace out of the corner of his eye. "I'd rather we wait until we get to my place. I don't think I can talk about it while I'm driving."

Honey

* * * * *

Zach and Wallace found Jill in the kitchen drinking a cup of chamomile tea when they reached the house. It was after one o'clock in the morning. They joined her at the table so Zach could relive his horrifying meeting with the detectives all over again. He cried just like he had done in Nancy's office and on his way home from work. Only this time, his father was present to comfort him and Jill. She was battling her own emotions, as well as hormones.

"We will get through this," Wallace said. "I know it's going to be tough over the next two days and in weeks to come, but we'll survive. I'm partially responsible for Jayla's mental state, but I refuse to own her selfishness and need to destroy the people around her. I owe her empathy and I've extended it to her, but she didn't want it. I hope the judge will see that she's mentally disturbed, and order her to go into long-term psychiatric treatment instead of prison. What have the police instructed you to do, son?"

* * * * *

Jill went to bed and allowed Zach and Wallace time to talk alone. She didn't want to hear another word about Jay and her plot to have her husband killed. As she climbed the stairs, she heard Zach telling Wallace the plans they would have to follow over the next two days. It was going to be mentally taxing on them, but in the end, Zach would still be alive and Jay would be behind bars where she belonged.

Chapter Thirty-Nine

"**Y**our brother is dead, boo. He died at the scene."

"Prove it." Jay took a long swig of her drink, and lowered the volume on the stereo.

"Damn it, Jay! I'm gonna give you the proof, but I can't just yet. Stay put and lay low. Wait for a visit or a call from the police. You know the routine. They have to notify the next of kin which is his wife. She won't know what the hell to do. She'll probably call your auntie, who'll then call you and so on and so forth. After that it'll hit the news and…"

"Hell nah, Fudge, I ain't gonna wait that long! I want proof *now*!" Jay stood and screamed with the drink in her hand. "Bring me the proof, and I'll give you the balance of your fee. Make it happen!"

Jay rushed and dressed in a white t-shirt and a pair of well-worn jeans. She grabbed her Atlanta Braves baseball cap from the coffee table, and walked over to the mirror. The face staring back at her was blank. All its dominant features were similar to Zach's. They both looked like Wallace, and so did Nahima. The smooth caramel complexion, naturally curly hair, and dark brown eyes were all inherited from the man she hated almost as much as she hated Zach. She wished she could afford to have his ass knocked off too.

Jay went to the safe on the wall in the sitting area, and entered the combination on the keypad. A white envelope filled with money was inside. She removed it and stuffed it in her pocket. Ayla's lawyer had sent her a letter, threatening to take legal action against her if she didn't pay her back the five thousand dollars she owed her in thirty days. The hotel had no idea she'd hit them for the other five grand.

There was a knock on the door. Jay closed her eyes and composed herself. Her reaction to the news of Zach's death had to be on point. He'd called her an award-winning actress before, and she wanted to make sure she lived up to his compliment. She opened the door, and was surprised to see Fudge on the other side, looking like Rick Ross, the rapper. He dapped into the suite cool and calm, without a word. Before Jay could ask, he handed her a big brown envelope. They sat down on the loveseat. She stared into space as if she were in a trance.

"Ain't you gonna open it?"

"I'm about to. What's the rush?" Jay asked nervous as hell.

"I want my damn money so I can get outta here. I ain't used to no high-class joint like this. Y'all got chandeliers everywhere and elevator attendants and shit.

You balling, boo." Fudge thumped the envelope. "Open it and give me my cash so I can roll out."

Jay opened the envelope and saw Zach lying flat on his stomach on asphalt. A pool of blood surrounded his head. He had died with his eyes wide open. An up-close shot showed the bullet hole in the back of his head with blood gushing out. Jay covered her mouth and gagged like she was about to vomit. The last picture was a full body shot. Zach had on a pair of black gym shorts and a purple tank top. His Adidas gym bag was upside-down on the ground next to his body. The right, black Jordan cross trainer was missing from his foot.

"Here's your cash." She handed Fudge the envelope.

"Thanks baby girl. I'm out." He stood and looked down at Jay. "Are we cool?"

"Yeah, we're cool. Thank you. I'll call you later."

Jay flinched when the door slammed shut behind Fudge. A bundle of emotions hit her at once. She was relieved that Zach was dead, but there were no bells and whistles or confetti like she had expected. Had she made a terrible mistake? Would her life be better now that Zach was dead? Jay continued flipping through the three pictures for several minutes, all while keeping a close eye on her watch. Anxious, she went to the wet bar, and opened a new bottle of Disarrono. Her nerves were so shattered, she turned it straight up. If the police had already informed Jill about Zach's death, it wouldn't be long before they contacted her. The voice inside her head told her to call Aunt Jackie. But that would appear suspicious since she hadn't spoken to her in months. It would be best if she waited it out.

* * * * *

Jill sat restlessly between Wallace and Aunt Jackie in a small room at the morgue. They knew Zach was alive and well, but the sting of death still radiated around them. Detectives Franklin and Ortega had just left to go pick up Jay after updating them on the status of the case. Jill and Aunt Jackie had lost it when the police photographer showed them the pictures she'd taken of Zach. He really looked lifeless lying on the ground. The makeup artist and graphics expert had done an awesome job transforming a living person into a corpse. And Zach had definitely earned the Oscar Jay had said he was worthy of, for his perfect portrayal of a dead man.

Wallace rubbed Jill's back. "They should be back soon, honey. Are you going to be alright? Remember, if you start feeling overly anxious, and the baby shows any signs of distress, you can back out of this."

"Wallace is right, Jill. The detectives said they can proceed with this phase of the case without you. You're thirty-seven weeks pregnant. No one would blame you if you pulled out at the last minute."

"*No*, I want to be here. I must be here when Jay realizes her evil plan to have my husband killed has failed." She laced the slightly puffy fingers on her right hand through Aunt Jackie's, and squeezed Wallace's hand with her left one. "I thank God the two of you are here with me. I will be fine. I'm staying."

* * * * *

"Show time," Jay said as she made her way to the door.

The persistent knocking had disrupted her sleep. She had dozed off after drinking a third of the bottle Disarrono while waiting to hear from Aunt Jackie or the police. She looked through the peephole, and saw two men dressed in dark suits. Jay pasted a fake smile on her face, and opened the door.

"Ms. Jayla King, I'm Detective Joel Franklin from the Atlanta Police Department and this is my partner Ed Ortega. Both men flashed their badges. "May we come in, ma'am?"

"Of course, but what is this about?" Jay turned and walked back into the sitting area. The detectives followed her.

"Unfortunately, we have some very disturbing news about your brother Zachary," Detective Ortega said.

"Has something happened to Zach? Oh my God, please tell me what's up with my brother!"

"He was shot in the back of the head this evening around 6:30 in the parking lot of Man's World Athletic Club."

"Nooo!" Jay slumped down onto the loveseat and wiped her eyes. "Is he *dead*?"

"I'm afraid he is. He died on the scene," Detective Franklin said. "I'm sorry."

"This can't be happening! I can't believe someone killed Zach! Some bastard shot my brother? Why?"

"A team of detectives are investigating that as we speak. Mr. King's wife has been notified, and so has your aunt, Jackie Dudley Brown." Detective Ortega sat next to Jay on the loveseat. "Both women are terribly upset right now, especially your sister-in-law, Jill. As you know she's pregnant. We don't think it would be wise to have her identify her husband's body in her fragile state. We were hoping *you* could."

"You want *me* to do it?" Jay looked at Detective Ortega sitting next to her, and then she peeped at Detective Franklin standing a few feet away. "Why me?"

Ortega touched Jay's shoulder lightly. "Mrs. Brown can't. She fainted before they could remove the sheet from Mr. King's face. We need you to identify your brother's remains."

Jay left her suite with the detectives, and slid into the back seat of their blue, late-model sedan. The fifteen minute ride downtown seemed much longer than usual. Jay was under a serious amount of anxiety. She'd been anticipating this moment for weeks, and now it had finally arrived. The detectives led her into the building. As they walked down a long, dim hallway, Jay's heart began pounding hard inside her chest at maximum speed.

Honey

Detective Ortega placed his arm around her shoulders, and stopped in front of a closed door. Detective Franklin continued down the hallway. "Your family is in this room. Please wait here with them while I inform the attendant that you're here."

Jay opened the door and saw Jill crying hysterically in Wallace's arms. Aunt Jackie was trying to console her through her own grief. Jay walked over to the huddle and stood speechless as seconds passed. They didn't see her until she spoke.

"I'm so sorry, y'all. The police promised me they'll work day and night to find out who did this to Zach."

"Can they bring him back, eh? Can they bring my husband back?" Jill screamed. "I want my *husband*! I don't care about anything else!"

Jay kneeled in front of Jill's chair and took her hand. "Zach is gone, but I'll take care of you. It's what he would've wanted. Whatever you and the baby need, I'll make sure you have it."

Jill rested her head on Wallace's shoulder, and eased her hand out of Jay's grasp.

"I can't think of anyone who would've wanted Zach dead," Aunt Jackie said softly. "He was a wonderful young man. I just don't understand!"

"The police said it was a random shooting. It may have been gang related," Jay lied smoothly. "You know. Maybe it was an initiation type of thing. I swear kids are so stupid these days."

"People are wicked and cold," Wallace spat, his eyes burning a hole straight through Jay.

There was a light tap on the door before it swung open. "Are you ready, Ms. King?" Detective Franklin asked.

"I'm ready." Jay stood and adjusted the baseball cap on her head.

Wallace cleared his throat. "Would you like for me to go with you, Jayla?"

"For what? I've made it through twenty-nine years without your trifling ass! I think I can go another hundred."

When Jay had left the room with the detective, Jill lifted her head from Wallace's shoulder. She made direct eye contact with him. "Your daughter is *deranged*!"

* * * * *

Jay entered the dark room behind the detectives. It was freezing cold, and the scent of harsh chemicals made it hard for her to breathe. The door slammed shut behind her. Then suddenly bright, blinding lights illuminated the small room.´

"Hello Jay."

She squint her eyes against the brightness, and gawked at the figure sitting on an examining table.

"What the fuck?" she screamed and lunged toward Zach.

Chapter Forty

"Jayla Simone King, you're under arrest for murder for hire, conspiracy to commit murder, contributing to…"

"Let go of me! Take your damn hands off of me! This is a bullshit setup!"

The detectives restrained Jay from attacking Zach. She heard the Miranda rights being recited to her as any icy pair of handcuffs clamped shut around her wrists.

"Why Jay?" Zach stammered with tears trickling down his face. "Just tell me why."

"You dirty, lowdown *motherfucker*! You helped these bastards sting me!" Jay fought aggressively against the two men and the handcuffs. She jerked and screamed in Zach's direction. "I hate you, you evil bastard! I should've smoked your ass my damn self!"

"Let's go, Ms. King," Detective Ortega said, shoving her out of the room.

"I want a lawyer! I have the right to speak to a lawyer! I want a motherfucking lawyer right now!"

* * * * *

"Sshh, it's over now, Jill. Hush now, it's all over, baby." Zach could feel the fear, shock and rage warring throughout her body as he rocked her in his arms. "I'm alive, Jill. I was never in any danger. It's okay now. Let it go. All of this crying and fussing will only upset the baby. You don't wanna do that."

"She *touched* me! She had the nerve to say she would take care of me and our baby. I wanted to behead her!"

"Jay is gonna get exactly what she deserves. Trust me."

"That's right. The Bible makes it plain. You will surely reap whatever you sow, honey." Aunt Jackie threw her stubby arms around Zach and Jill. "Everything is gonna be alright."

"Come on, son. Let's go find out if we can take Jill home. She's had a full day of drama, and she's worn out."

Detective Ortega walked into the room. "You're free to go now, Mr. King." He extended his hand to Zach for a firm handshake. "Do you plan to attend the hearing in the morning?"

"Am I needed?"

"No sir, we have more than enough evidence to keep your sister in custody. I don't think any judge will set bail for her. And if one does, it'll be too high for her to post. Your sister is dangerous and very unstable, Mr. King."

"I know. I hope she'll get the help she needs."

* * * * *

"This evening a murder-for-hire scandal was uncovered, and now a young Atlanta woman sits behind bars awaiting her first appearance before a judge tomorrow morning. Jayla Simone King, age thirty-one, was arrested for allegedly paying an undercover police officer ten thousand dollars in cash to gun down her brother, Zachary Sean King, in the parking lot of an Atlanta athletic club earlier today. Mr. King, the alleged victim, is a thirty-six-year old neonatal intensive care nurse at Grady Memorial Hospital."

Zach turned off the television, and tossed the remote control on the night stand. Jill snuggled closer to him on the bed and rubbed his chest. The phone began to ring. The buzz of Zach's cell phone charging on the dresser added to the noise.

"Zach, should I answer the phone, son?" Wallace tapped a few times on the closed bedroom door.

"Nah, come in here with us, Daddy."

Wallace entered the master bedroom, and took a seat at the foot of the bed. "This is a nightmare. God only knows how long it will be before you and Jill experience a sense of normalcy again."

Both phones continued to ring.

Zach sat up in the bed and carefully pulled Jill up with him. "I didn't even consider the media coverage this case would draw. I really didn't have time to think about anything except cooperating with the police and keeping Jill and the baby out of harm's way. I guess we'll have to lay low for a while. Please don't feel like you have to stick around for this circus, Daddy. Patricia and Wallace Junior have been patient and understanding long enough."

"What are you talking about, boy? They're flying to Atlanta tomorrow evening. I hope you and Jill don't mind if they stay here."

"We don't mind at all, Papa King. We are a family. It will be good for all of us to be together right now."

The chime of the doorbell rippled through the house. Wallace got up and peeped through the blinds. He scratched the top of his bald head. "There're two media vans outside, son. About six or seven people are dragging cameras, microphones and other equipment out. Uh-oh! A husky guy with a beard just hopped out of a champagne Ford Explorer. Whoa! He shoved a reporter carrying a camera to the ground *hard*. This guy is pretty ticked off. He's yelling and waving his fist at another reporter. He's a mad man!"

"That's my best friend, Dex." Zach laughed. "Let me go get that fool before he catches a case."

Zach threw on a pair of sweat pants and dashed down the steps, skipping two or three at a time. He disengaged the security system, and flung the front door open. Bright lights blinded him, and a Britney Spears looking chick thrust a microphone in his face.

"Mr. King, I'm Rebecca Arnold from WXYS Channel 7 here in Atlanta. We'd like to know…"

"Fall back, Goldilocks!" Dex slapped the microphone out of the reporter's hand. "Get them damn cameras outta his face! I'm gonna smash them. I swear I will."

Zach snatched Dex by his green FAMU t-shirt, and pulled him inside the house. They cracked up when they slammed the door on some bold, black female reporter who'd tried to barge her way inside. Her foot almost got crushed in the act.

Dex stopped laughing, and stared at Zach. He grabbed his buddy in a bear hug, and slapped him on his back. When he let him go, he released a breath and shook his head.

"I wanted to tell you so bad, man, but I couldn't. The police wouldn't even allow me to tell Aunt Jackie. The only reason I was able to tell my dad was because he swooped in from Raleigh on a whim. I refused to have him come all this way and be left in the dark.

"Jay is psychotic as hell! That bitch is possessed with a million demons. I love her, and I'll always remember the sweet teenager she *used* to be. But I don't ever wanna see her crazy ass again."

The house phone and doorbell continued to ring and chime nonstop. Zach walked into the kitchen, and Dex followed him. He removed two ice cold bottles of Heineken from the refrigerator. And like they had done for the past eighteen years, they sat down to work through a problem over their favorite beer.

Chapter Forty-One

Ayla swerved, barely missing a truck in the right lane when she heard Jay's name mentioned on the radio. She increased the volume and listened as the news reporter released details about her arrest in a murder-for hire-case. Ayla reached for her cell phone when she learned Zach had been the hit man's target.

"That crazy bitch borrowed money from me to have her brother killed!" she screamed while she waited for her lawyer to answer his phone. The call rolled over to voicemail after five rings. She pressed the number two on her speed dial list. It was still assigned to Zach after all this time. The man was happily married, and expecting a child, but she still hadn't downgraded his status in her phone. He wasn't answering her call either. Ayla fired her engine and sped toward the hospital.

* * * * *

"I knew her when she was an itty bitty thing," Ida Bell whispered. "I was at her momma's funeral in the third pew on the left side of the center aisle. Honey, Reverend King baptized me when I was seventeen years old. I know the whole family history. I remember when Jay started liking girls. She propositioned my Tina." She rolled her neck, and popped her lips for dramatic effect.

One of the nurse's assistants leaned in closer to the table and lowered her voice. "Is it true that Zach's wife came here from Jamaica with Jay as her lover? That's what *I* heard."

"Mmm, mmm, it's true. Jill was Jay's woman first. They came over here, and were staying at Zach's house until they could find a place. Jay wanted to buy a condo at the Seven Seas, but she couldn't afford it. They're *expensive*. Anyway, Zach and Jill started doing the hoochie coochie behind Jay's back. Before long, they fell in love. Jill dropped Jay, and Zach kicked Dr. Fitzpatrick to the curb, honey."

"Ms. Ida Bell, I would appreciate it if you'd refrain from discussing my personal business at our place of employment. And you ladies sitting around here taking it in are just as messy as she is. I should report all of you." Ayla approached the table with her hands on her hips. "I thought y'all liked Zach. You call him your *favorite* nurse all the time. If that's the case, you should respect his privacy, and pray for him during this awful time he and his family are facing."

The housekeepers, nurse's assistants, and the one LPN scattered, leaving Ida Bell at the table alone, looking sheepish.

* * * * *

Zach walked downstairs early the next morning just as Wallace was about to leave the house. He'd given his father permission to drive his SUV the night before. Wallace had a few errands to run downtown.

"You never did tell me where you were going this morning. Is it a surprise or just none of my business?"

"I didn't tell you on purpose. I wasn't sure how you'd react, son." Wallace walked toward Zach with his hands in the pockets of his gray suit pants. "If you must know, when I leave here, I'm going to visit Belva Jane's grave."

"Aren't you a little overdressed for that? That's a nice suit you're rocking."

"After I leave your mother's grave, I'm going to the courthouse. I want to speak with Jayla's attorney, and offer some of our family's history. It's the right thing to do. I'm her father, Zach. Some, but not all, of what she's become is my fault. I want that to go on the record."

"You could've told me this last night. I wouldn't have been upset. I actually understand because I'm suffering with my own guilt." Zach looked into his father's eyes. "I hurt Jay too, you know? I guess I didn't realize how much. But I love Jill, and I don't regret getting her pregnant or marrying her. I just hate how it all went down. I never meant to hurt my sister. Can you tell her attorney that for me?"

"I will, son. I'll see you later."

* * * * *

Jay wasn't sure if she could wiggle out of her legal troubles by playing crazy, but she damn sure planned to give it her best shot. The first person she had to convince was Mr. Alan Rice, her court appointed attorney. In their first meeting she told the man she couldn't remember very much about what she'd done. Jay described herself as a very depressed alcoholic who'd been dumped by two women she once loved deeply. Both breakups happened over a five-year period, leaving her very distraught, she'd claimed. Then she put on an Oscar-winning performance with tears, hysterics and lots of drama. Jay cried and screamed over the death of her mother at such an early age like it had just happened. The devastation she described about growing up without a father was her trump card.

Then all of a sudden she started rambling about *Ayla*. She named her as her conspirator in planning the hit on Zach. Jay claimed the doctor had lured her into a sexual affair after the end of her four-year relationship with Jill. At that time she was extremely vulnerable. Allegedly, Ayla had used her to get back at Zach for dumping her for Jill. Mr. Rice's confused expression was comical to Jay. The poor man had a hard time keeping up with who had slept with whom and when. Jay broke it down for him. She described the way she and Zach had swapped lovers as a *love square*, and then she started laughing like a damn fool. Then, without warning, her mood became very somber as she recounted the night she was given five thousand dollars to hire a hit man to kill her brother. According to Jay, Ayla had somehow convinced her that Zach deserved to die for wrecking both of their lives. He had disrespected them and betrayed them by sleeping with Jill.

Hopefully, for Jay's sake, Mr. Rice had bought her story, and would be able to build a strong case to defend her at trial. Until then, she wanted a bond, and she had her fingers crossed that it would be low enough for Nina to post. Her drug-dealing cousins in Mexico had promised to help her raise the money to pay Jay's bond. Then they were going to get her and Nina out of the country somehow.

* * * * *

"It's time to go to court, Ms. King." An overweight, female deputy unlocked the cell. She pulled Jay's arms behind her back to secure them in handcuffs. "Are you ready?"

"I guess so, ma'am. I wish I didn't have to wear this ugly orange jumpsuit, though."

"It's standard, honey. If your family wants to, they could always bring you a nice Sunday dress or a business suit for your court appearances. Ask them whenever they come for a visit. Let's go now."

"You think the judge will set a bond for me today?"

"I'm not so sure," the woman said leading Jay down the hall. "You'll have to wait and see."

Chapter Forty-Two

"Thanks for the information, Reverend King. I'm sure some of it will be helpful in establishing a solid defense for your daughter." Mr. Rice reached out his hand to end their impromptu meeting. He looked up the courthouse corridor just as Jay was being escorted toward the holding area. "Look, Reverend, here comes Jayla now. I could arrange a brief meeting with the three of us before the hearing if you'd like."

Wishing to avoid an explosive confrontation with his daughter, Wallace blew Mr. Rice's suggestion off. "I'm sure she's nervous right now. Maybe it's best that you two meet alone. I'm going to go find a seat in the courtroom." He turned and walked away.

"Daddy? Oh Daddy, I'm so glad you're here!" Jay shouted. "I want my daddy…ah…ah…*Daddy*!"

Wallace turned and stared at Jay screaming and trying to break free of the deputy's hold. She doubled over and cried like she was in pain. He felt Mr. Rice's hand touch his back. Jay's pleading cries had escalated. She was completely out of control. The deputy struggled to keep her on her feet.

"Wait here, sir," the attorney said. "I'm going to request a private room in the holding area so you can tend to your daughter. She needs you right now, and there's plenty of time before the hearing. Wait here."

"Don't go, Mr. Rice. Help me! I want…my…*daddy*! Oh my God, I want him! I want him! I want him! *Daddy*!"

Wallace stood motionless, watching his child in shock. He imagined she had cried for him many times while she was growing up without him, but he had been in no position to help her then. But it was a new day, and his circumstances were different. For the first time in twenty-nine years he could be a real father to his daughter. Wallace refused to let the opportunity slip through his fingers. Jay continued her outburst as passersby gawked and whispered.

"Right this way, Reverend King." Mr. Rice had returned to the corridor. "You'll be allowed three minutes alone with Jayla inside a four-by-four room. She'll be in handcuffs, and two armed deputies will be directly outside." He held up three fingers. "That's the best I could do."

Wallace followed the attorney down the corridor. They stopped outside a heavy, metal door just left of the courtroom. Mr. Rice displayed his security badge, and stepped aside for Wallace to enter the room.

"Have a seat. They'll bring your daughter here shortly."

Wallace took a seat in the folding chair facing the door. It was one of three pieces of furniture occupying the tiny drab space. A small table and another chair identical to the one he now sat in were the others. When the door opened, Wallace watched a female deputy force Jay down into the vacant chair. Then she removed two chains from her pocket and secured her arms and legs to the seat.

"Three minutes," the deputy reminded them before she shut the door.

Wallace got up immediately and hugged Jay and kissed her on her cheek. She didn't respond. He took his seat again and waited for her to speak.

"Thank you for coming, Daddy. I never wanted anybody to kill Zach. You gotta believe me. This is a big mistake. It was Ayla Fitzpatrick. She's Zach's crazy, jealous ex. She's a doctor. They work together at Grady. She was pissed that he had left her for Jill. She tricked me into talking to the guy about the hit. She even gave me the money! Please help me, Daddy. I don't wanna go to prison."

Wallace listened quietly as Jay continued to ramble on. Nothing she had said so far made any sense. He studied her eyes and body language. There was no doubt in his mind that Jay was lying and blaming this Ayla character for what *she* had done. But even so, he wanted to support her as best he could without giving her false hope. The detectives had hard, cold, undisputable evidence against her. They'd searched her suite with the authorization of a warrant after her arrest, and found the manufactured pictures of Zach's corpse. They'd also stumbled on the lender's agreement between her and Ayla for the five-thousand-dollar *loan*.

Besides that evidence, there were dozens of pictures of Jay and Fudge together. The prosecution had two hours of audio taped conversations of them planning the hit. The ten-thousand dollars had Jay's fingerprints all over it as did the interior of Fudge's Escalade. A conviction was a certainty as far as Wallace was concerned. Even without Jay's hotheaded statement to Zach upon her finding out he wasn't dead, Wallace was pretty sure Jay would be convicted. Telling her brother that she should have killed him herself, in front of Detectives Franklin and Ortega, was simply the icing on the cake. It was a strong inference to the crime she had been accused of committing.

"Jayla," Wallace finally interrupted. "I came here to help you, sweetheart, but you'll have to be totally honest with me. Did you order a hit on Zach?"

Jay's eyes narrowed to slits. "Are you kidding me? Didn't you hear a damn word I just said? I didn't do it!"

"I heard your voice on the audio tapes. You said you wanted Zach dead. There are countless pictures of you and the undercover officer together on three or four different occasions. Your fingerprints were found on both stacks of money, Jayla. If Dr. Fitzpatrick wanted to have your brother murdered, why didn't she take the initiative? A lender's agreement found in your suite after you were arrested proves the five thousand dollars she gave you was a *loan*. You were supposed was supposed to have paid her back in thirty days. According to Zach, Dr. Fitzpatrick has been trying to reach you. She wants her money. How do explain any of this, honey?"

Jay leaned forward in her chair as far as the chains would allow her. "Why the hell did you bring your punk ass here if you're already convinced that I'm guilty? Don't you think you've caused me enough pain by killing my mother? You did this to me!" Jay started jerking and twisting in the chair. "*You* ruined my life! I hate you, you coldhearted son of a bitch! I hate you! Get the hell outta here!"

A male deputy burst into the room. "Your time is up."

Wallace left the room with the sound of Jay's cursing and hatred ringing in his ears. He didn't bother going to the courtroom. He had seen and heard enough. There was nothing more he could do for Jay other than pray for her. She was a classic example of a woman who had lived through unfortunate circumstances because of the actions of others. But instead of using her pain and sorrow as motivation to fight and beat the odds against her, she'd misused it to abuse others. Jay wore Belva's death as a badge of sympathy and a crutch to get whatever she wanted from whomever she'd been lucky enough to swindle it from. Venus, Jill, Zach and even he had been her victims.

Wallace was tired now and fresh out of ideas on how to win Jay's love and forgiveness. The "Daddy is so sorry, baby girl" game he'd been playing with her over the years had come to an end without a winner. They'd both lost. Jay was on her way to prison, and Wallace would never know the joy of being loved by his only daughter. But he was cool with that. He still had a beautiful wife who loved him in spite of his past, and his two sons respected him. Nahima saw no flaws when she looked into his eyes and called him Papa. And in just a few weeks he would experience the birth of a brand new grandchild.

"Reverend King?" Mr. Rice jogged behind Wallace as he made his way to the elevator. "What happened back there? Why is Jayla so flustered? No one can calm her down."

Wallace looked at the well-dressed white man all decked out in a two-thousand-dollar designer suit. His face was flushed with a pale red hue, and he was out of breath after tussling with Jay. Wallace wondered how much the state of Georgia was paying him to represent his mentally ill daughter. Whatever the amount, it wasn't worth the man's time. She was going to string him along with lies and excuses like she'd done everyone else in her life.

"I'm leaving, Mr. Rice. Jayla doesn't want me here. You have my numbers and email address. If there is anything I can do to assist you with her defense, feel free to call me. Otherwise, I don't think you'll be hearing from me. Thank you for representing my daughter. Expect that check from me within a few days. I'll be praying for you because you're gonna need it."

Honey

*****

Venus volunteered to drive Nahima over to Zach's house for the weekend. He was keeping a low profile lately because of the media frenzy surrounding Jay's murder-for-hire case. The hoopla was dwindling off slowly, but his face had become recognizable in Atlanta. Besides church, and taking Jill to the doctor every other day, he stayed at home. Wallace and his family were there for support, and Aunt Jackie spent a lot of time there as well. Dex and Ramona dropped by every day to run errands for him and Jill and to entertain them.

"Are you sure she won't be a bother, Zach? You have a lot going on." Venus handed him Nahima's pink overnight bag. He eased the long strap onto his shoulder.

"I need her." He scooped the child up in his arms, and kissed her on the forehead. When he placed her back on her feet, she took off running into the house, calling for Wallace Junior. "Come in and stay a while, Venus."

Venus walked into the den and took a seat next to Zach on the sofa. "I still can't believe it. Jay is a certified fool if I've ever met one. I've been having nightmares since the story broke. I can only imagine what you and Jill have been going through."

"It's been *rough*. Jill wakes up at night sometimes crying, and it pisses me off. She knows Jay is in jail, but she's afraid to go anywhere. She doesn't feel safe anymore. Can you believe she suggested we move to Jamaica?"

"My heart goes out to Jill. I can relate to what she's going through. We share a firsthand experience that's almost impossible to describe. Jay's claws dig deep. A few years ago I could've been her target. Jill could've easily been next. But I never would've thought she'd turn on *you*."

Zach stared off into space and rubbed his goatee. "I may have deserved her resentment for what I did, but Jay had no right to arrange my death. She tried it, though, and now she's in jail for it. I don't plan to go anywhere near the courthouse in the event of a trial, and I don't wanna testify against her. All I want is for Jay to get the professional help she needs to deal with her issues."

DERANGED Love

Chapter Forty-Three

"Zachary, I'm not sure, but I think my water has broken." Jill shook Zach gently as she slept in his arms.

He didn't answer. He shifted positions, and patted Jill's back. He was snoring slightly with the smell of Heineken on his breath. Zach didn't get to bed until after midnight. He and Dex had been watching a baseball game on television, and nursing a case of their favorite brew.

"Zachary, I think the baby is coming." Jill shook him more forcefully this time, and sat up. She could feel the warm trickling of fluid pooling in her panties. A sharp pain hit her when the baby kicked a few times. "Zachary, wake up! The baby is coming."

"I'm up. Be calm, okay?" He lifted his body into a sitting position in the bed. "I'm gonna call Dr. Doctor Nwizu, and get you cleaned up. Are you having contractions?"

"I am, but they are bearable."

Zach called and left a detailed message with Dr. Doctor Nwizu's answering service, and showered with Jill. He helped her dress in a comfortable red caftan. As they headed for the staircase, Zach tapped on the guest bedroom door.

"Hey, Jill's water broke. We're on our way to the hospital. We'll call with an update as soon as she gets settled."

Wallace opened the door. "Do you need me to go with you?"

Zach chuckled even as Jill squeezed his hand tight. "That's not necessary. It's 5:20 in the morning. Go back to sleep, old man. I'll call you."

En route to the hospital, Zach called Faye. She became very excited by the news that her first grandchild was about to be born. Zach promised to call her later. Then he went on to call Aunt Jackie and Dex.

* * * * *

"Go to sleep, Ms. King, or I'll have the doctor come in and give you a sedative! I refuse to put up with your racket this early in the morning. It's not even six o'clock yet. Shut your mouth and lay down!" Deputy Hall warned. He'd had enough of all the screaming, cursing and crying.

"I hear voices! I wanna die!"

"Well, lie down and close your eyes! Maybe God will grant your wish."

Jay hadn't anticipated the time and effort it would take to convince the court, law enforcement and the psychiatrists that she was crazy. It was a fulltime job. Threatening to kill herself had become her mantra ever since the judge had set her bail at a whopping one hundred and fifty thousand dollars. It was why she was under a seventy-two-hour suicide watch, *again*. It was her fourth time. The tiny cell closest to the deputies' surveillance room, housing nothing but a cot and commode, had become her home. She was allowed no contact with other inmates because of suicidal tendencies and erratic behavior.

"Just look at her crazy ass." Deputy Hall and a female deputy were watching Jay on the monitor. She was on her knees in the middle of the floor howling like a wild animal.

"I think she's faking. You know how dramatic we women can be."

"I *know* she is. I've read her record. She has a master's degree in business and once managed a five-star resort in Montego Bay, Jamaica. The woman has no history of mental illness. The undercover officer she hired to snuff out her brother was a dude she'd met at a bootleg house in Ridgewood. He was supposed to be a friend of a friend of her lover's. Dude said she was desperate to have the job done, and was willing to pay top dollar. Do you think a crazy person could've set that up?"

"Hell no, I don't. She can keep her little loony act going for as long as she wants to, but she's going to prison. I'd bet my rent money on it."

* * * * *

"How do you feel?"

"I am so tired, Zachary. When will the baby be here?"

"Not much longer. Our kid is a stubborn little rascal. He won't come down. I'm gonna spank his little ass as soon as he gets here for putting you through all of this hell."

Dex snapped a picture of Zach and Jill holding hands while they waited for Dr. Nwizu and her team to deliver their baby via C-section. They'd been at the hospital since six o'clock in the morning. It was after eleven at night. Jill had been a trooper during her seventeen hours of labor. It was Zach who'd done all the whining and complaining. At one point, he became frustrated and threatened the doctor. He told her if she didn't take Jill to surgery he was going to sign her out of the hospital and take her to another one where he could find a doctor who would. Thanks to Dex, he settled down and went to the cafeteria to eat and let off some steam. That had been six hours ago.

Jill's drooping eyes were closing from exhaustion. The epidural had kicked, in and she was drifting in and out of sleep. "I'm so sleepy, Zachary. Where is Dr. Nwizu?"

"I'm right here, my dear." She entered the operating room with a cheerful smile on her face. "Are you ready?"

"Mmm, mmm, I've been ready since this morning."

Zach held Jill's hand, and watched Dr. Nwizu and her team prep for surgery. The anesthesiologist made sure the patient had the proper amount of pain medication for the procedure. Then like an expert, the Nigerian-born doctor made an incision just below Jill's belly at the bikini line. Dex didn't care to watch that particular part of the process. His face was turned away from the operating table. He promised to resume his photographer's duties once the pediatric nurse accompanying Dr. Nwizu gave him a cue.

"Oh my, this is a *big* baby. Not much longer now, Jill. You've been a champion, darling. Your patience is to be commended. Ah, at last he is here!" Dr. Nwizu lifted a crying and flailing baby boy from his mother's womb.

Flashes from Dex's camera covered him with several quick shots. The nurse took the baby, and invited a teary-eyed Zach to help with her post-delivery duties.

"You did it, Jill." Zach kissed her damp face. "You did a great job. Thank you." He kissed her again. "I'll be back. I've gotta go meet our son."

Jill nodded as her eyes slowly closed. "Mmm, mmm" she hummed before sleep overtook her.

Chapter Forty-Four

Zach couldn't help but think about Zachary Junior every time he held one of his little frail patients. He was at home with Jill healthy, thriving and slightly overweight. But the baby girl he'd just given a steroid injection to help strengthen her lungs faced a grim prognosis. Zach cradled her fragile, three-pound body in his palm a little while longer for comfort.

"Be strong, little momma. I want you to live and grow up to be the first female president of the United States. I'll tell everybody I once held you in one hand. You've gotta fight to live, pumpkin." He kissed the baby on her forehead and returned her to the incubator.

Someone outside the NICU nursery tapped on the window. Zach looked up and frowned. Detective Ortega smiled, and motioned for him to come out into the hallway. Zach signaled with his index finger that he'd be with him shortly. It had been weeks since he'd heard anything about Jay's case, and he had hoped it would remain that way. He'd forbidden Aunt Jackie and Dex from telling him anything they'd heard on the news or read in the newspaper. He and Jill were enjoying parenthood, and wanted no negative distractions. The last six weeks had been like heaven for them with their new baby boy.

"I'll see you later, princess. That ugly man out there came to harass me." Zach covered his little patient with a pink blanket. He removed a pair of latex gloves from his hands, and washed them before leaving the sterile nursery.

"Mr. King, how are you, sir?" The detective smiled, and extended his had to Zach.

"I was doing great until I saw you." He shook Ortega's hand. "Talk to me."

"Is there someplace private we can go?"

"Let's go back to the place where we first met."

Zach led the detective to Nancy's office. She politely left so they could talk privately. When they were both seated, Zach motioned for Ortega to start the conversation with a shrug of his shoulders.

"Your sister's attempt to play crazy due to post traumatic distress is holding the case up. Her court appointed lawyer and his defense team are milking it. She's been evaluated by a psychologist of their choice and one chosen by the state."

"And this has what to do with *me*?"

"Well, um…we were hoping to get a deposition from you."

Zach rose to his feet shaking his head. "Nah, I'm done. Y'all don't need me to prosecute Jay. This is some bullshit, and you know it. Y'all have audio tape, pictures and fingerprints. Isn't that plenty?"

"We're only trying to cover all bases, Mr. King. We need a security chip just in case your sister's psycho act works. She's throwing folks under the bus left and right. She implicated your ex-lover, Dr. Ayla Fitzpatrick, as the mastermind behind the hit. That poor woman was mortified when she came in for questioning. She brought *two* attorneys with her."

"How did it go?"

"Nothing your sister said stuck. The pretty doctor walked away in the clear. "

"I'm glad to know that." Zach sighed and dropped back down in his chair. "What do you need from me, Ortega?"

"Just come down to the station, and tell us your side of the story. Give us anything you feel will show that Ms. King carefully planned to have you murdered. Help us build on the motive we've already established. We know your sister was angry, and acted out in a jealous rage against you for stealing her lover. But the prosecution has to prove, beyond a reasonable doubt, that she was in her *rational mind* and premeditated the hit on you. Fill in the blanks for us. What triggered this chain of events?"

Zach knew exactly what Detective Ortega was talking about. He and the DA were fishing for the key factor or the crux, the straw that broke the camel's back. The State needed to know the single most significant act that had sent Jay spiraling over the edge. It was the news about Jill's pregnancy that had turned his sister's world upside down. The inner battle between his heart and mind over whether or not he should provide the prosecutor with that tiny speck of information waged. Zach was partially to blame for Jay's problems. He had no desire to pour water on his drowning sister's head.

The way he saw it, Jay would be locked away somewhere for an extended period of time no matter what. Either she was going to prison or a mental institution; with or without his input. His father had been in touch with Mr. Rice, and he'd admitted that he and his team were fighting an uphill battle to defend Jay. There was no evidence indicating that she was mentally insane on the actual day she ordered the hit or during subsequent meetings with Fudge. Her conviction seemed like a slam dunk. But obviously, the prosecutor wasn't one hundred percent sure, and he didn't want to take any chances.

Zach clapped his hands together hard once, and Ortega gave him his undivided attention. "Let me think about it. I'll get back to in a few days."

"Have it your way, but the prosecution could always subpoena you, and drag you into court as a hostile witness during the trial. Trust me. It would be easier and less stressful if you would just cooperate in the pretrial stages. Who knows? Something you say may prove to be so indisputably imperative that the defense will fold. It might pull a confession out of Ms. King, and this case would be one for the history books."

Zach stood and walked toward the door. He opened it wide, dismissing Detective Ortega and his comments. "Like I said, let me think about it. Remember I'm not a criminal. I have options."

He walked out of the office leaving the detective standing in the middle of the room.

* * * * *

"I wish I was Zachary Junior. He sees your breasts a helluva lot more than I do." Zach leaned over Jill and kissed his son's chubby face. He sat next to his wife on the sofa and watched her nurse the baby. Jill shuddered when he leaned in and blew in her ear. "When our son goes to sleep tonight, I want to *play* with his momma."

"And his momma would like very much to *play* with his papa. How was work?"

"It was cool, but I had an unexpected visit from Detective Ortega. He asked me, on behalf of the prosecutor, to go downtown for an interview. Jay is pretending like she was insane when she paid the officer to kill me. Her legal team is rolling with it. So the State wants me to help them add muscle to their already strong case."

"Can Jay avoid prison if you don't speak with these people? Because if she can, you owe it to your son to make sure that does not happen. I am so very sick of your sister using innocent and harmless people like *babies* to justify her wickedness. Nahima and this little one in my arms have not committed a single ill act against Jay. Yet, she blames them for the evil she's done. It is rubbish, Zachary! You *must* speak with those people in your son and Nahima's honor, if for no other reason. I married a good man who should tell the prosecutor whatever he needs to know."

* * * * *

"They grilled my ass. I felt like *I* was being accused of something in there. Thank God it's over. Assistant DA, Dale Lugar, seems to think I sealed the deal. Detective Franklin thinks so too. I hope they're right because I'm not bringing my black ass back down here even if there is a trial."

Dex matched his buddy's gait, step for step. He'd waited outside the District Attorney's office a little over three hours while Zach was being deposed. He wanted to be close by while his friend faced the legal vultures. "Did you tell them *everything*?"

"*Hell yeah*," Zach snapped. "I put it all out there. Jay had painted an ugly picture of me, man. She basically told her attorney I pursued Jill like a *pimp*. It was embarrassing. Mr. Rice was under the assumption that I went to Jamaica with the intention of stealing Jill from Jay. Then I lured them over here to live with me."

"I told you Jay is a cold piece of work. You should be glad you came down here to set the record straight. There ain't no way a real psychiatrist is gonna say Jay was insane at the time she paid dude to off you. A crazy person wouldn't be able to twist and distort facts the way she did. Jay is *vicious*!"

Zach and Dex reached the Ford Explorer in the parking deck. They got inside the vehicle and drove to the attendant's booth to pay the fee. As they eased out into the downtown traffic, Dex saw an attractive, plus size woman in a red dress strutting toward the courthouse. Her face looked familiar. He had seen those pouty lips and wild auburn curls before. He slowed his vehicle down, and tilted his head in the woman's direction.

"Who is that chick? I've seen her somewhere before."

Zach leaned forward and studied the woman. "She's kind of exotic looking. Where would you have seen her? The only time you go out is with Ramona or me. You damn sure weren't with me when you met that chick."

A horn blowing loud behind them prompted Dex to move on. "She looks familiar. We've met before. That I know for sure. I feel like we had a conversation. It'll come to me sooner or later."

Chapter Forty-Five

"**S**tate your name for the record, ma'am."

"Nina Celeste Lopez," she said in a shaky voice. The group of three men and one woman sitting around the table watching her made her very uneasy.

"Do you know Jayla Simone King, also known as Jay King?" Mr. Lugar asked.

"Yes, I know Jay. I told the two detectives that when they came to my house."

"Ms. Lopez, my name is Alan Rice. I'm Ms. King's attorney. Do you mind describing your relationship with her? Were the two of you friends, associates or *other*?"

Nina exhaled as her eyes skidded around the massive oval shaped table. She felt like jumping up, and running out of the room. If only she'd hired a damn attorney, but she didn't have money for one. All of her extra cash had been put on Jay's books. And now she was sitting in a stuffy room, with three suits and a skirt, like she was some kind of evil criminal.

"Please answer the question, Ms. Lopez."

Nina rolled her brown eyes to the ceiling. "Jay and I are...well, *were* lovers."

Mr. Lugar, the young, hotshot assistant district attorney slid a manila folder across the table. It stopped right at Nina's bulging pair of breast. He smiled, and his blue eyes flashed with intimidation. "Is that why you tampered with Jillian Bessette's records at the immigration department? That is where you work isn't it?"

"Yes, I work there. But I only..."

"Did you, or did you not, alter information in Ms. Bessette's record; denying her reentry to this country back in November of last year?"

"Go to hell, you white bastard! I ain't saying another damn word until I get me an attorney up in here!" Nina shoved the file away without ever opening it.

"Why do you need an attorney, Ms. Lopez? You came down here on your own free will. You weren't coerced."

"Hell, I didn't know *my* neck was gonna be on the chopping block. Those detectives told me Jay's attorney needed me to help him with her defense. This right here," Nina said, pointing to the four pairs of eyes staring her down. "It's a bullshit setup. Get me a damn lawyer or I'm walking!"

Honey

*****

Aunt Jackie had volunteered to babysit Zachary Junior and Nahima for Zach and Jill. They'd gone out to dinner and dancing on a Friday night. It was the first time since the baby's birth that they'd gone on a date. The little fellow was three months old now, and the spitting image of his father. Aunt Jackie thought he was a wee bit too plump for his age, tipping the scale at twenty pounds already. Jill had lost all her baby weight since giving birth, and had started talking about dancing and teaching again at Umoja Academy. Mrs. Scott had assured her she'd always have a place at the school whenever she decided to return.

Nahima rested her knees on the thick, black carpet in the den, and searched the channels on the big screen television. She paused and wrinkled her pretty face when she saw a picture of Zach on the WXYS evening news. In the background, there was rolling footage of Jay being escorted by a female deputy into the courtroom in handcuffs. The anchorwoman stated her full name and Nahima, a very intelligent kindergartner, now recognized *King* was also her Uncle Z's last name. As the report progressed, the camera zoomed in on Jay's face. Nahima inched closer to the huge screen mounted on the wall.

"Nana, who is that lady on TV?" The child pointed to Jay's face. "Her last name is King just like Uncle Z, Auntie Jill and Little Zachary."

Aunt Jackie looked up from feeding the baby his bottle and gasped. "Nahima Angelique, please change the channel *now*, sweetheart. Little children don't need to watch the news."

"But who is she, Nana? And why was she on the news with Uncle Z's picture? Is she his friend?"

"Turn to the Disney channel, sweetie. I want to watch it with you. A good movie is probably on."

"But Nana…" Nahima whined.

"Turn to the Disney channel, little girl…right this minute!"

*****

Nahima fell asleep during a movie about children spies. She had grown too big for Aunt Jackie to carry up the stairs. She woke the child, and guided her up to her room where she undressed her and put her to bed. Zachary Junior had been asleep in the nursery for a couple of hours since his healthy bottle of rice cereal. When Aunt Jackie was alone in the guest bedroom, she was assaulted with a very troubling reality. More than half of what Nahima believed about her existence wasn't true. Yes, Venus was her mother technically and legally, but not biologically.

"The truth is gonna come out one way or the other." Aunt Jackie shook her head as she reached over and turned on the radio on the dresser. "I just hope it won't destroy that precious baby."

DERANGED LOVE

* * * * *

"Thanks for meeting me, Zach. I know this may be a little awkward for you."

"It's not a problem, Doc. We're associates and coworkers. Ain't no law against two people sitting down, having a conversation over lunch. I'm cool with it. Why are you trippin'?"

Ayla looked around the popular deli located a few blocks away from the hospital. "You're married and we do have an *interesting* past," she smiled slyly.

Zach smiled back. "Yeah, it was pretty interesting. It's funny how quickly life changes. This time last year, I was in Jamaica with Nahima and Jill for a short visit. I was single, with no children. Now I'm a husband and father. I never knew life could be this sweet."

"Well, my life was screwed up back then, having just gotten involved with your crazy sister. It's still screwed up today. I've made a lot of bad mistakes, Zach. I'm working on rebuilding my life. Some much needed changes are in order. For one, I'm leaving Atlanta. That's what I wanted to talk to you about. I was wondering if you'd write me a letter of reference. I don't have very many friends here in Atlanta, especially not in the medical field."

"Of course, I'll do that for you, Doc. Where are you going?"

Ayla laughed dryly. "You're not gonna believe me." She laughed again, and rubbed her hands together.

"Try me." Zach bit into his Philly cheese steak. "I'm waiting. I ain't got all day."

"I'm going to *New Mexico*. I have an opportunity to help the less fortunate while making good use of my Morehouse medical degree. Imagine me, on an Indian reservation. I'll be second in charge. It's almost a sure thing. I just need a few references."

"Cool," Zach said, reaching across the table. "I'm proud of you. Congrats Doc."

Ayla shook Zach's hand. "After the mess I made of my life here, I need a fresh new start. A new city and a new job seemed like good moves. Maybe I'll get lucky and fall in love like you did."

"Don't look for love. Let love find you. I was a sworn bachelor for life. You know that, Doc. But there was something about Jill that robbed me of my player's card. I wasn't looking for love. It honestly found me, and now I'm the happiest man alive."

"I can tell. Hell, *everyone* can!" Ayla looked around the deli. "Let's just hope Ida Bell's gossiping ass is nowhere around here because she'll make sure your wife hears about our lunch meeting. That old woman will make me out to be a home wrecking hussy."

"Jill already knows we're having lunch. I called her as soon as I hung up with you." He smiled at Ayla's surprised expression. "I tell my wife *everything*."

"And what did Mrs. King have to say about you meeting me here today?"

"She actually told me to say hello to you from her and our son. Jill is not a jealous woman at all, and she has no reason to be. She's very secure. My wife knows that she's the only woman for me because she holds a brother down."

"She's one lucky woman. I wanna be just like her one day. I'm gonna to take your advice, and allow love to find *me* in Cibola County, New Mexico. I want to be loved and cherished."

"Which team are you on, Doc?"

"About that…it was just a phase…the absolute *worst* of my mistakes in this city. God, I don't know what was wrong with me!"

"Jay has confused many before you. She has a way with women from all walks of life."

"Tell me about it. But that's in the past. I'll be starting over in New Mexico."

Zach raised his glass of strawberry lemonade. "To new beginnings!"

"Yes, to new beginnings," Ayla agreed and raised her glass filled with diet soda to touch his drink.

Chapter Forty-Six

"No Zachary, let it ring! *Pleeease* don't stop!" Jill wrapped her long, dancer's legs around Zach's waist to hold him in place, and thrust her hips upward. All nine plus inches of his rigid manhood slid deeper inside of her. "Oh yes, *Zach-a-ryyy!*"

The phone stopped ringing, and the passion resumed at a more intense level. But the caller seemed to have been on a mission to rob Zach and Jill of their midnight lovemaking session. The ringing only ceased momentarily only to start all over again. The persistent distraction caused Zach to slow his strokes.

"Oh no Zachary, you cannot stop! You can't! Don't stop!"

"What…what...um…what if it's Aunt Jackie? She's got Zachary Junior."

Jill squeezed her legs tighter around him, refusing to let him abandon the ride. The phone had become annoying, messing up their flow. She reached up and pulled Zach's face to hers, and covered his lips in an aggressive kiss. Jill accepted his tongue sliding in and out of her mouth, mimicking the action going on under the sheets. Her body stiffened when the first ripple of pleasure struck. All ten of her toes curled as her racing heart skipped a few beats. Rhythmic spasm after spasm racked Jill's entire body, eliciting a high-pitched soprano note that could've shattered glass.

"*J-Jill!*" was Zach's response when his body toppled over the edge and landed on cloud nine.

The phone continued to ring off the hook, but neither Zach nor Jill could move at the moment. He had collapsed on top of her, basking in the aftershock of their mind-blowing lovemaking. Their bodies covered by beads of sweat were still joined. Breathing didn't come easy and energy was nonexistent. The pair of satisfied lovers inhaled the sweet scent of sex in the air, and listened to the phone disrupting their peace.

"Can you reach it?" Zach asked. He eased off his wife's body, and rolled onto his back.

Jill shook her head, and gulped air into her lungs. "No."

Zach extended his arm until it touched the nightstand. His hand roamed around until it landed on the cordless phone. He picked it up. "Hello?"

"Zach, it's your father. I'm sorry to wake you."

"Daddy, what's wrong?" He sat up and rested his back against the headboard.

"Your sister tried to commit suicide a couple of hours ago by slitting her wrists. She's in the hospital. I can't get down there before the weekend. Can you or maybe Jackie go and check on her for me? Whichever one of you decides to go, I'll have to provide verbal consent to the authorities in advance. I'm listed as next to kin. So nothing can be done without my permission."

Zach looked at the clock on the nightstand. It was almost two o'clock in the morning. He was scheduled to be at work by seven, and Jill had a ten o'clock dance class to teach at Umoja Academy. That's why Zachary Junior was with Aunt Jackie overnight.

"Jay doesn't want to see me, Daddy. To be truthful I'm not really feeling her right now either. And won't it look strange for me, the victim to show up at the hospital to visit the sister who paid somebody to whack me?"

"That's just it, son. Jayla is your *sister* no matter what she's done. Both of you are my children. I'd be on my way to Atlanta this very minute so I could tend to my daughter if that were possible. But it's not. I came to see about *you* when you needed me, and I owe Jayla the same kind of support."

"You think so, huh?" Zach felt his temper rising. "So you've put *Jay* on the same level with *me*? After the way she's cursed you, spit in your face and told everyone how much she hates you, you still look at us with the same eyes? Damn! I'm glad to know how you really feel."

"Zach, please don't look at it that way. I'm her *father*. She doesn't have anyone else. I know I told you I'd washed my hands with Jayla, but suicide is a very serious matter."

"And homicide is a walk in the park? She paid ten grand to have me killed!"

"Okay son, you don't have to go to the hospital. I'll call Jackie and ask her if she'd be willing."

"That ain't gonna happen. She's got Zachary Junior with her. Jill has to work this morning." Zach closed his eyes and gritted his teeth. "I'll go, but don't ever ask me to do anything else pertaining to Jay again. Which hospital is she in?"

Zach peeped down at Jill. Their eyes met and locked under the moonlight. He listened as Wallace gave him all the information about Jay and the person he needed to speak with at the hospital. He ended the call and lay back down on the bed. He eased behind Jill and held her in his arms. For several minutes they rested contentedly in the spoon position in silence.

"You're a good man, Zachary. I don't know anyone else like you."

* * * * *

Jay had somehow gotten her hands on a razor blade and slit both her wrists. She'd lost a lot of blood, but not enough to have died. The psychiatrist believed it was an effort to get attention more so than an attempt to take her own life. Either way, she had been admitted to the psychiatric ward at a South Atlanta hospital and it was all over the news. Zach stood outside Jay's hospital room after showing the security guard his ID.

"You can go in now, Mr. King."

"Yeah, I know. I just need a minute," Zach said, stroking his goatee out of habit. "I don't know why the hell I'm here. I must be a sucker for punishment," he murmured under his breath.

He blew out a long stream of wind, and turned the door knob and pushed. He hadn't expected to see Jay handcuffed to the hospital bed, but it made sense. She *was* a criminal, and a very smart one at that. The fact that she was in a comfortable bed in a hospital room instead of in a shitty jail cell proved that. Jay was too proud and strong willed to commit suicide. She'd much rather stick around to make his life a living hell even if she'd never see the light of day again. It was kind of amusing that she was still running game even while she was in lockup.

Jay's eyelids lifted slowly. Zach could tell she was struggling to focus on him as he closed the distance between them. Her eyes closed again. Zach stopped at the foot of the bed with no desire to be any closer to her. He had been asking himself since he'd received the phone call from Wallace if he even loved his sister anymore. Now looking at her in her weakest and most helpless state, he still wasn't sure.

"Jay, it's me, Zach." He shook her right foot. "I came to check up on you. The doctor said he gave you something to make you sleep so I won't stay long."

"Thank you for coming." She lifted her drooping eyelids again. "I'm sorry for everything I tried to do to you, Zach. Please forgive me."

Zach wasn't sure if he'd heard Jay correctly. She was mumbling and under the influence of powerful medication. The doctor had told him she'd be in and out of sleep for several hours. More than likely, any apology she offered was a result of the meds. Humility had never been a part of Jay's character. Even when she was a sassy mouth little girl, it had often taken an act of congress or a good old fashion ass whipping from Aunt Jackie to get her to apologize for anything.

"What did you say, Jay? I didn't hear you." He moved closer to stand by her bedside.

She tried to reach out and touch Zach's hand, but the cuffs and chains restricted her. "I'm sorry." Tears spilled from her half opened eyes. "What I did to you and Jill was wrong. Will you forgive me?"

Zach weighed his options. Could he forgive Jay for all the evil shit she'd done to him and Jill? Or would he hold on to bad blood, walk out of her life forever and pretend he'd never had a little sister. What should've been an easy decision required some deep thinking because his life was no longer his alone. He had Jill and Zachary Junior to consider. Everything he did now affected them too.

Zach's heart was tender when it came to Jay, and it had always been that way. He had nurtured and protected her since she was a baby. There were thousands of precious memories tugging at his heart. But his mind was working overtime, warning him not to be a sucker for Jay again. She was cold, manipulative and undeserving of his mercy. The night he'd begged for her forgiveness for his affair with Jill was now blazing in the front of his mind. He could hear her mocking laughter and the words "I hate you."

"Zach, I know it's gonna be hard, but I need you to forgive me." Jay closed her eyes and yawned. "I'm so sorry. I want Jill to forgive me too. I've done some things to her that I'm ashamed of."

Zach's mind had been in deep contemplation when Jay made her second plea for forgiveness. He almost missed it. The mentioning of Jill's name is what snatched him from his emotional tug of war. For the first time ever, Jay had admitted to mistreating his wife while they were lovers back in Jamaica. For some unexplainable reason, he needed to hear it again.

"Why were so cruel to Jill? She didn't deserve it, Jay. How could you have treated her like crap when you claimed to love her?"

"I…I was selfish, and I wanted her to belong only to me. I was afraid she would leave me like Venus did. That's why I kept her at the resort away from her family and friends. I shouldn't have done that. I hope she'll forgive me someday and that you will too."

Subconsciously, Zach took hold of Jay's hand and squeezed it gently. "I forgive you, Jay. Something deep within my psyche is telling me I'm a damn fool to do it, but I love you and I miss you. I'm sorry for causing the beef between us in the first place. But I don't regret falling in love with Jill and marrying her. I'm a complete person because of her and our son. I only hate *how* she and I got together. It hurt you and I'll always carry the guilt of that."

"I forgive you, big brother. I forgive Jill too. I want you both to forgive me." Jay's head flopped and her face fell to rest against her pillow.

Zach watched Jay sleep for a while with all kinds of thoughts running through his head. They had wiped the slate clean on their troubled relationship. Their future was uncertain in light of her present situation, but Zach still had hope. He would stand by Jay in any way he could from now on. Everything else was in the hands of a judge and jury.

Zach tucked his sister in snuggly as he'd done many times when she was a little girl. He kissed her forehead. "I love you. Take care."

Jay's eyes popped wide open the second after she heard the door close. She sucked her teeth. "I hate you, you stupid ass, gullible bastard. That's one down and two more to go."

Chapter Forty-Seven

With Jay's jailhouse suicide attempt all over the news, Zach decided against going to work. He went to Aunt Jackie's house to chill with her and his son after dropping Jill off at Umoja Academy. He used the key he'd been given to let himself in. He could hear Keith 'Wonderboy' Johnson singing his hit "I Just Wanna Be Right" from the radio in the kitchen. Aunt Jackie loved her gospel music.

"Auntie, it's me! I didn't wanna scare you."

"I'm in the kitchen, baby!"

Zach found Aunt Jackie at the table with her glasses on reading the bible. The baby monitor was sitting on the table right next to a cup of steaming hot coffee. Zach sat in the chair to her immediate left and kissed her on the cheek.

"Why aren't you at work, boy?" Aunt Jackie pressed her gold bookmarker in the crease of the bible and closed it.

"I guess you haven't seen the news."

"Yes, I have. I watched it early this morning. And my radio has been on ever since the baby went back to sleep around seven-thirty."

"Well, you should know why I didn't go to work."

"Jay slits her wrists and you can't go to work? So whenever your sister does something stupid, will it always affect you?"

"No, it won't. My dad called and asked me to go to the hospital to make sure Jay was okay."

"And did you go?"

Zach nodded his head and waited for the fireworks and lecture.

"Well, tell me what happened, chile!"

Zach filled Aunt Jackie in on his visit with Jay without skipping any details.

"It's okay to forgive, Zach. In fact, you're *supposed* to. It's the Christian way. But sometimes it's good not to *forget*. I'm not advising you to hang on to the bad memories forever, and let them keep you stuck in the past. I just want you to be careful when dealing with Jay. Be very mindful of what she's capable of doing, and how far she'll go to make it happen."

"I hear you, Auntie. I hear you, but Jay was sincere. I saw it in her eyes. She was humble and apologetic. That's your formula, ain't it?"

"Yeah, it is, but Jay has *never* used it before. I'm having a hard time believing she wasn't faking it this time. Promise me you'll be careful."

"Don't worry. I will."

Later that afternoon Zach had the same conversation with Jill over lunch. After he picked her up from the dance school, they stopped at Houston's restaurant on Peachtree Road. Jill echoed Aunt Jackie's sentiments, but with a more serious warning. She didn't want Zach to have anything to do with Jay firsthand. It would be fine for him to offer her moral support from afar, but Jill was against him making any personal contact with her. She was afraid Jay would misuse Zach's trust, and maneuver her way inside his head. Jill's heart told her that Jay's intentions were insincere and self-serving. But Zach, blinded by love and the guilt from hurting his sister, refused to see it that way. He was determined to give their new relationship a fair chance. And he didn't want any interference from Jill or anyone else.

Out of love and respect for her husband, Jill chose not to argue with him. She was very hurt and shocked that Zach had so readily opened his life, *their life,* back up to Jay after all the pain she'd caused them. The latter part of their lunch date went along in an awkward and quiet standoff. On the drive to Aunt Jackie's house, the silence continued. The radio filled in the gap. Once they arrived, Jill jumped out of the SUV, slammed the door and hurried inside to get their son. When she returned to the vehicle, she sat in the back seat with the baby while Zach chauffeured them home.

* * * * *

"Jill called me last night. I agree with her, Zach. I think you're screwing up. Jay is the devil and she's got something up her sleeve. Don't fall for it, dude. I'm warning you."

Zach held up his empty Heineken bottle, and waved it in the air. Floyd, the bartender quickly swapped it out for a brand new one. Zach had guzzled down eight already, and he felt like shit. It was Saturday afternoon, and he and Jill were supposed to be at an arts festival downtown with Zachary Junior and Nahima, watching a puppet show. But when he woke up, his wife and the children were gone.

"I…I…I love my baby sister and…and all y'all need to just fall the hell back," Zach slurred.

Dex snatched the bottle from his hand. A little of the brew sloshed on Floyd's spotless bar counter, and he wiped it down on the spot.

"What the hell is wrong with you, Negro? Are you gonna let *Jay* come between you and Jill after how hard y'all had to fight to be together? That woman has gone through hell to be with you! While Jay was stealing and dropping big bucks to have your ass killed, Jill was by your side scared and pregnant with your child." Dex pointed his finger in Zach's face, inches from his nose. "You're gonna mess around and push Jill away. You'll wake up one morning, and she and my god son will be gone. The next time you see your little boy, he'll have dreadlocks down to his ass, smoking some gunja and asking you, "What's up, mon?"

"Nah, Jill ain't gonna leave me. She knows I love her. I...I...um...gotta make her understand that I can love her and Jay at...at...the same time."

"You're a fool! And right now I can't stand you." Dex dropped some cash on the counter to cover his and Zach's tab. He whistled at Floyd to get his attention, and pointed to the money. "Get your sorry, drunk ass up so I can take you home."

* * * * *

As Jay's luck would have it, a psychological evaluation deemed her sane and competent on the day and subsequent days she plotted to have Zach murdered. A psychiatrist appointed by the court concurred with the evaluation team. The doctor concluded that Jay's actions were that of a rational person who premeditated the act of murder for hire out of jealousy and revenge. However, the psychological evaluation performed on Jay by a team of experts hired by Mr. Rice and company yielded conflicting results. It was determined that she had suffered from post-traumatic stress after learning Zach and Jill had secretly married, and were expecting a child. They believed alcoholism intensified her impulsive behavior as well as the misfortune from her childhood. The untimely death of her mother and the extensive incarceration of her father had damaged Jay emotionally.

After reviewing both psychological summaries, and hearing arguments from Mr. Lugar and Mr. Rice, Judge Rudolph Elway declared Jay sufficiently competent to stand trial. The defense had hoped their claim of temporary insanity would've helped her avoid a date with judicial destiny. But Mr. Rice had been forthcoming with Jay about her chances. He'd advised her that the audio taped conversations between her and Fudge were quite damaging, notwithstanding the pictures and handwritten instructional note. That kind of evidence was very difficult to defend, Mr. Rice had noted, but Jay wanted to try her luck. She'd outright refused to agree to a plea bargain.

Judge Elway set Jay's date with fate for January thirtieth at Mr. Rice's request for a speedy trial. When she got word of it, she set her plan into motion. Zach, Wallace and *Nahima* would all be pawns in her scheme. They would help set her free.

Chapter Forty-Eight

"Jill, baby, how long do you plan for us to live like this? I don't wanna go into a new year with this year's baggage."

"I don't know what you are talking about, Zachary." Jill spooned apple sauce into her son's mouth and smiled at him.

"You don't talk to me, and you spend most nights on the daybed in the nursery. And when you do come to our bed, you sleep far away from me, and I'm not allowed to touch you."

"And why do you need to touch me, Zachary?"

"You're my *wife*." Zach placed his fork on the edge of his plate. "We're married or did you forget?"

"Oh, so now you want to remember you married me, eh? When you're at the jailhouse, visiting your evil sister that paid someone to take you away from me while I was pregnant with your child, you forget you have a wife. When you write her long letters, and send her money, do you remember me, your wife?" Jill removed Zachary Junior from his high chair with tears pouring down her face. "I heard you whisper to her on the phone that you would not willingly say anything to hurt her on the witness stand, ya know? Were you thinking about your wife when you made that promise?" Jill's voice grew louder with each word, and her tears continued to fall. "After she makes a *fool* of you, then and only then will you remember you have a wife!"

Jill took the baby upstairs to give him a bath. Zach was left with her words resonating in his head, mixed with Aunt Jackie's and Dex's warnings. He looked down at his plate of half-eaten food. He was starving when he'd first sat down at the table, but his appetite was gone. Everyone was against him. No one, including Wallace, wanted him to have contact with Jay. If he could forgive her for what she had done, they needed to do the same, and stay off his ass.

* * * * *

"My brother will say whatever I ask him to say during his cross-examination, Mr. Rice. He feels guilty about the way he and Jill betrayed me. I have letters he wrote admitting in a roundabout way that he was partly to blame for my breakdown. Why do you think he keeps putting money on my books? We talk twice a week, and he visits me every Saturday morning. He's a State's witness, but he'll do right by me."

"I hear your predictions, Ms. King. But will your brother say in a court of law, under oath, that he believes beyond a shadow of a doubt that you were insane at the time you ordered a hit on him?"

Jay leaned back confidently in her chair, and stuck out her chest. "I know he will. Trust me. He'll say it or some family secrets will be leaked to the media."

"And what is it that you think Mrs. Venus Morris will say?"

"Oh, V will say I've had mental issues for a long time. And she'll admit that her pregnancy and our breakup contributed to it. We've got history. There's a little secret that Mrs. Morris wouldn't want to come out in court. You can count on her to be very cooperative."

Mr. Rice scribbled something on his legal pad. "Is Reverend King aware that he'll be asked to delve into his criminal past? When he shared it with me, I got the distinct feeling he didn't like to talk about your mother's murder or his incarceration. He said he had only come forth to help you."

"Well damn it, he better get ready to help me again."

"Ms. King," Mr. Rice said, removing his glasses from his eyes. "I want you to understand that even if these witnesses say exactly what you believe they will, we are still at a disadvantage. The State has a real strong case against you. As your lead attorney, I must advise you that a plea bargain is the best way to end this. You're facing felony charges. I can work out a deal with Mr. Lugar wherein you'll be looking at seven years, but you'll only serve five at the most. But if we go to trial and lose, you'll be sentenced to twelve to fifteen years. And believe me; you will serve twelve to fifteen years."

"I'll take the gamble."

After Jay's attorney left, the wheels inside her head began to turn. She could only imagine the look on Zach's face once he learned she had been using his ass. He would have a choice to make. He'd have to go along with her scheme in order to protect his precious Nahima or be responsible for the exposure of her true maternity. Venus and Wallace were about to catch hell too. But they would cooperate to cover their asses.

* * * * *

"What is it, Zachary? Who was that man?" Jill tried to peer over his shoulder to read the papers he'd just removed from a big brown envelope.

Zach closed the front door, and brushed past her. Jill followed him into the den with Zachary Junior in her arms. Something was terribly wrong. Since yesterday when Wallace had called to say he was coming to Atlanta early next week, Zach had been on edge. He hadn't shared anything with her about the private conversation with his father, but she could tell from his facial expression and mannerisms that things weren't quite right. Nothing was normal in their family now that Zach had committed himself to becoming Jay's super hero. Jill was about to take a seat on the sofa next to her husband when the doorbell rang for the second time in five minutes.

"I'll get it." She hurried to the door and opened it. Venus stood on the stoop with bloodshot eyes, holding a brown envelope just like the one that had just been delivered to Zach. "Come in, Venus. Oh my goodness, you seem upset. Zach is in the den. Come with me."

Jill became very worried and wanted to scream. Something was going on, and she had no idea what it was. She left Venus and Zach alone in the den so they could have a private discussion about the papers in the mysterious envelopes. Jill sat at the bottom of the steps quietly rocking Zachary Junior to sleep. Venus was visibly shaken, and had been crying before she'd arrived. She was still crying now as she spoke to Zach. Jill decided to go upstairs and wait for her husband to come and tell her what was going on.

* * * * *

Zach was surprised to find Jill in their bed when he finally came upstairs a few hours later. He had gone to the nursery first looking for her so they could talk. "Jill, wake up, baby. I need to say some things to you." He sat on the side of the bed close to her.

"What's the matter, Zachary?" Jill sat up and searched his face. "Tell me what is wrong."

"You were right. Every warning you gave me about Jay was on point. She *was* using me."

"What did those papers say?"

"It's a witness profile summary. Jay wants me to alter my testimony on her behalf so it won't be so damaging. She gave her defense team some information she wants me to say to help her. It's some bullshit I won't feel comfortable saying."

"What exactly are you talking about, Zachary?"

"Jay wants everyone to know she's Nahima's biological mother, and that her birth caused her to suffer from depression. She wants to drag Venus and me into court to confess that crap in front of all those damn strangers! And what she wants to do to my father is unforgivable after all he's done for her crazy, ungrateful ass! Jay expects Daddy to take total responsibility for her state of mind because he accidentally killed our mother. Why would she want him to rehash that nightmare?"

"Don't do it, Zachary. You, Papa King and Venus need to be strong, and refuse to do what Jay is asking. Where I come from, we call what she's doing *blackmail*."

"Jay is smarter than that. She didn't issue a direct threat to either of us, and neither did her attorneys. The information was mentioned in the narrative summaries we each received as a warning. All of our family's secrets are gonna come out in court somehow. Whether we testify or not, Jay's defense team will use the information in any way possible to help her. It's a no win situation for our family, especially *Nahima.* All of her life we've protected her, and now it's gonna come down to this."

"God will protect Nahima. Do not worry about her at this time. You, your father and Venus need to hire an attorney to represent you. Let him advise you of your options. A good attorney can guide you in the right direction." Jill hugged Zach tight trying to take away some of his pain.

"Aren't you gonna say it?"

"What am I supposed to say, Zachary?"

He leaned back in her embrace to look into her eyes. "Say it. I told you so."

Jill shook her head, and kissed him tenderly on the lips. "I will not say that, but you should always listen to the woman who loves and respects you. I would never tell you anything wrong."

Chapter Forty-Nine

Christmas and New Year's Day passed without much fanfare. Zach and Jill spent most of their first holiday season together as husband and wife in the comfort of their home with their son. They celebrated Christmas Eve at Aunt Jackie's house, surrounded by uncles, aunts and cousins laughing and talking over a traditional holiday meal. Not a soul mentioned Jay or the upcoming trial. Everyone focused on good times and hope for better days in the New Year. The atmosphere was peaceful, relaxing and full of cheer.

But Jay experienced a staggering loneliness in the confines of her jail cell. For the first time in her life she was forced to face her demons. Every person whom she'd ever loved was no longer a part of her life. They had all left her behind to build new lives with new lovers, leaving her all alone. Jay felt the throb of being abandoned by her family with Zach leading the way, and Aunt Jackie trailing right behind him. Mr. Rice had informed her a few days before Christmas that he had not spoken to Wallace in weeks although he'd been making every effort to reach him.

The therapist Jay had been seeing three times a week since her release from the hospital had given her an assignment. She'd asked her to take inventory of her character flaws, and entertain the possibility that she had pushed certain family members and loved ones away. That advice had fallen on deaf ears. Jay had been playing the victim for so long that it was impossible to view herself in any other way. In her mind, it was now her against the world in the fight of her life to avoid a prison. Come hell or high water, she planned to stick to her claim that Zach and Jill's betrayal had driven her insane to the point that she'd ordered a hit on him. And she hoped God, the judge and the jury would have mercy on her.

* * * * *

Zach, Wallace and Venus sat in a row of identical scroll back chairs watching Kirk Orowitz review their subpoenas and witness profile summaries. He strummed his finger tips on top of his cherry wood credenza as he flipped through the stacks of papers. It was Zach's first time meeting the young, Jewish attorney, and he liked him already. Venus and Charles had assured him, and his father, that Kirk was just the man to help them kick Jay's ass once and for all.

"Well, well, well, Ms. King and her legal team think they're pretty damn smart, do they?" Kirk shuffled the documents into a neat stack and pushed them to the right side corner of his desk. "I happen to think I'm a hell of a lot smarter. You see, girlfriend failed to mention to Mr. Rice that there is a restraining order in place forbidding her to have contact with Mrs. Morris. That includes even through a third party. That subpoena is invalid. Honey, you ain't even gotta show up for the big dance."

Venus smiled and looked at Zach and then Wallace. "So how do we keep them from mentioning anything about Nahima being Jay's biological child?

Kirk snapped his fingers and gave Venus a big smile. The brilliant diamonds in his pinky ring sparkled under the overhead light. "I've got a combination of things working for us on that one. Let me break it down for y'all. For starters, Nahima is off-limits because she's covered under that same restraining order. Then we have the closed records law and the medical confidentiality act. Thank God for the Health Insurance Portability Accountability Act. Hallelujah!" Kirk threw both his hands in the air. "The DA will not let Mr. Rice and his posse go there. Know what I'm sayin'?"

"How will all that protect Nahima?" Zach asked.

"Ms. King has done a poor job keeping her dream team up to speed. She has no records whatsoever to prove that Nahima Lawson is her biological child. They simply don't exist. She could probably get her hands on her medical records to prove that she had some eggs extracted from her girlie parts, but then what? The other half of the process is under Mrs. Morris's medical records. And *bam*! In your face! HIPAA forbids them from going there."

"What if Jayla's attorney petitions the court for a DNA test to be done on my granddaughter?"

Kirk popped his lips and put on a somber face. "It ain't gonna happen Papa, and I'll tell you why. This is a criminal case, not an episode of the Maury Povich show! Who gives a damn about DNA? Mr. Lugar will argue that it has no relevancy whatsoever to the criminal proceedings. How can a child you abandoned five years ago, and refused to keep in contact with, cause you mental anguish? Honey *pleeease*!" Kirk waved his hand. "I have the transcripts from the case that settled the custody issue when Nahima was an itty bitty baby. Ms. King was MIA. She threw up deuces and bounced."

"Yeah, she did and never asked to see Nahima again. Jay's been in Atlanta over a year now, and she's only seen that little girl one time by mistake at my house before day one morning. She went completely off on me for having my niece in *my* house."

"Don't worry my good people. None of this crap will make it inside the court room. I'll confer with Mr. Lugar and his crew and we'll eighty-six all of it during pretrial motions." Kirk shot Wallace a forlorn look. "Unfortunately for you, Papa, you'll probably have to take the stand. I don't see any way around it. You see, the information you provided voluntarily to Mr. Rice on your daughter's behalf is considered a confession. He can call upon you to repeat it before the jury. You're not guilty of doing anything wrong, sir. You've paid your debt to society a long time ago. I think you're a wonderful father to have come to Ms. King's rescue the way you did. I don't think she deserved it, but we can't change that now."

"I don't regret telling Mr. Rice about my past. It's accessible by public records anyway. He could've easily researched my case and learned some things. What I offered him was insight into how my crime affected my daughter. If I have to repeat it in court, I will."

Kirk smiled at the trio sitting across from him. Then his blue eyes settled directly on Zach. "You, *my brother* will be hit hardest of all. You're the victim in this disaster, but they'll try to villainize you. Yeah, man, they're gonna make every attempt to force you into confessing that you pushed your sister over the coo coo's nest. It sounds whack, but it's a fact, Zach."

"I don't give a damn. So long as Nahima comes out of this crap unscathed, I don't care. But you better believe me, I'm not gonna take responsibility for Jay's actions. I'll tell the truth. Yes, I betrayed her by having an affair with Jill behind her back. I hurt her deeply; humiliated her even, but I *did not* deserve to die. I tried to make things right between us, but Jay wasn't interested. She wanted my blood."

"And since then he's reached out to her. He's been visiting her in jail, and sending her money." Wallace patted Zach's shoulder. "Tell him, son. Your marriage was on the rocks because you tried to support Jayla."

"I initiated contact with my sister after she tried to take her own life. We talked at least once a week after that until she pulled her latest stunt. My marriage did suffer because of it, but Jill and I are back on track now."

"All of this will show how vindictive and manipulative Ms. King is. It'll poke holes all up and through her little psycho act. Don't worry about a thing, my good people, because Kirk O has got y'all. Mrs. Morris, you're free to leave, darling. I'll be in touch. King and King will have to hang with me a little while longer so I can school them on a few things about the witness stand."

* * * * *

Attorney Rice had sent Paul Ford, one of his young associates, over to the jail to update Jay on her case. The last time he had met with her personally, they'd ended up in a shouting match. Her already weak insanity claim was now on life support, and Mr. Rice was pushing her to cop a plea deal. But Jay was hell bent on going the distance. Out of the group of witnesses she'd handpicked to testify in her defense, only one stood a chance of scoring any points on her behalf, and that was her father. And even his testimony alone wasn't enough. Jay's entire legal team had warned her that Zach and Fudge were going to be almost impossible to trip up during cross-examination because their hands were basically clean. Mr. Rice had expressed his concern that a jury would not be impressed with him badgering the murder target on the stand, but Jay totally disagreed. She wanted him to twist her brother's neck until he accepted some responsibility for driving her insane.

Mr. Ford didn't have any good news to report to Jay on his visit one week before her trial. And she was pissed off with him, Mr. Rice and her entire defense team.

"Let me get this straight. Y'all ain't gonna cross-examine Zach?"

Mr. Ford shook his head and flipped nonchalantly through the case file. "We will, but not the way *you* want us to."

"Why can't y'all ask Zach about his trip to Jamaica to visit me and Jill? Make him tell you how he seduced her in our penthouse while I was working like slave! When we moved here and were living in his house, Zach and Jill were having sex behind my back, but smiling in my face. That's enough to drive anyone crazy. My brother came into our bedroom one night while we were making love, and stopped us because he said we were too loud. He's a freak! Zach betrayed me, and it messed with my head. What he and Jill did to me is unforgivable! They drove me crazy!"

"Ms. King, there is an in-depth psychological evaluation that says you are indeed *sane*. A psychiatrist with over thirty years of expertise in criminal behavior is going to testify on behalf of the State that you are no more crazy than I am. His report supports a theory that you are a conniving, manipulative, self-absorbed criminal who carefully orchestrated murder for hire on your brother. How the hell do you suppose we get around that, Ms. King? And why didn't you tell us that you stole five thousand dollars from the Seven Seas? Didn't you think that would come to light at some point?"

Jay had forgotten about the money she'd *borrowed* from her job. She hadn't expected them to discover it until their next audit in March. By then, she had planned to have paid it back. "I don't recall taking money from the Seven Seas," she said point blank. She crossed her legs and glared at Mr. Ford.

"Well, we have evidence that you took five thousand dollars from a special event's account. No one else could have done it besides you. Here is a copy of the transaction slip where you transferred the money from the account to another one; right before it was reported missing by the accounting department." Mr. Ford held the paper out to Jay.

She folded her arms across her chest and looked away. "I don't know anything about that."

Mr. Ford shook his head, and released a breath. "Have it your way, but you're digging a hole so deep that you're going to need a bulldozer and crane to pull yourself out. We *will* lose this case, and it's going to be your fault. I suggest you enter a plea before it's too late."

"I suggest that you, Mr. Rice, and the whole damn team do your fucking job and get me off!"

Chapter Fifty

"I'm not sure how I feel about Aunt Jackie going to court this morning. I suppose she should be there. She did raise Jay and me. I consider her to be our mother, and I've always treated her with the utmost respect. Jay, on the other hand, would get mad with her for any little thing, and would go weeks without speaking to her. She hasn't been in contact with Aunt Jackie since the day she found out you were pregnant. Jay called her and cursed her out for not telling her we were expecting. That was the last time they spoke to one another."

"Maybe your aunt wants to show Jay her support regardless of their estranged relationship. She loves your sister very much despite the fact that she is very wicked. You can love a person, but hate their behaviors. Don't you think that's possible?"

Zach leaned across the green blanket he'd spread on the floor in the den. He gently pushed Zachary Junior's diaper clad bottom, encouraging him to crawl. He'd been scooting around on his knees while his parents relaxed on the blanket next to him.

"I guess it's possible. I still love Jay, and I want what's best for her, but I no longer want her in my life. After I testify later this week, I never wanna see her again."

* * * * *

"I don't blame Zach one bit for taking a leave of absence during Jay's trial. He didn't even come to church Sunday. Reverend Broadus asked his auntie to come to the front of the church so he could lay hands on her and pray for Zach in his absence. Honey, I felt the power of that prayer all down in my bones!"

"What are folks around the church saying?" Sheila asked Ida Bell.

All the women leaned forward in their chairs with their hands on the table.

"All the saints at Refuge want Jay to go to jail for hiring someone to kill Zach. Nobody could believe she did something so cruel to her own brother. I hope she rots in jail."

"Amen," Sheila said.

Ida Bell looked toward the break room's door to see if anyone was coming. "Jay is claiming she's crazy, and doesn't remember what she did. Her lawyer is gonna try to get her off on temporary insanity. That chile ain't crazy. She's just mean and evil. I hope the judge throws the book at her."

Honey

* * * * *

Zach made direct contact with Jill from his seat on the witness stand where he sat tensely, sweating bullets. Kirk and Mr. Lugar had been quite thorough in preparing him for cross-examination, but Mr. Rice's technique was far more aggressive than either of them had anticipated. He was on the warpath, and had been since he'd started questioning Zach two hours ago. He'd hammered away at his and Jay's relationship as children, teenagers and as adults. Mr. Rice had just asked Zach to describe the circumstances surrounding his initial sexual encounter with Jill, and Zach had paused to look at his wife regretfully for the answer he was about to give. It would open up their personal life to a world of strangers who had no right to know anything about them.

"It was the latter part of August, year before last," he stated and lifted his chin.

Mr. Rice pressed his palms flat on the wooden slab separating him and Zach and grinned. "Where was your *sister*?"

"I'm not sure. She had just left my house."

"I see," Mr. Rice said, smiling as he adjusted the glasses on his long nose. "You pounced on your sister's lover of four years as soon as she left your home headed back to her brand new, stressful job. Are you sure it was your *first* time sleeping with Ms. Bessette? You see, I find it hard to believe that she willingly fell in the sack with you only moments after Ms. King had left your house. I mean, did you court Ms. Bessette? Did you promise her anything? Did you *pay* her?"

Kirk was sitting directly behind the prosecutor's table. He sent Zach a message with his eyes to keep his cool, and answer the question.

"I did not pay my wife to be intimate with me."

"She wasn't your wife *then*, now was she? She was your sister's lover. Was she not?"

"Yes, she was."

"I didn't hear you. I'll ask you again. The first time you had sexual intercourse with Jillian Bessette, was she, or wasn't she, your sister, Ms. Jayla King's lover?"

"I told you already! She was Jay's lover at the time."

"What about the second time and third time you slept with Ms. Bessette? Wasn't she still romantically involved with your sister?"

"No, they weren't *really* involved after the first encounter Jill and I had."

Mr. Rice faced the jury box where the seven men and five women of different races and ethnicities sat listening attentively to Zach's testimony. "How do you know that Ms. Bessette wasn't *really* romantically involved with Ms. King as you continued your secret love affair with her? Was there an official breakup? Did Ms. Bessette move out of the bedroom they were sharing in your home into another one or into *yours*? Explain to the judge, this fine jury, and me exactly what you mean."

"My sister was basically living at the Seven Seas hotel, and she didn't call or visit Jill for several days. I know for a fact that after the first time my wife and I were intimate, she discontinued her sexual relationship with my sister." Zach loosened the knot in his silk gray necktie and leaned forward.

"You most definitely would know that now, wouldn't you? You crept around the door of their bedroom while they were making love one night, didn't you? You became insanely jealous! You couldn't stand that Ms. Bessette was having sex with her lover, your sister, when you wanted her for yourself! You became so enraged, Mr. King that you burst into the room and stopped them!"

"That's not how it happened," Zach whispered, struggling to maintain his composure. "Jay didn't tell you the whole truth."

"Well, please enlighten us, Mr. King." Mr. Rice inched closer to the witness stand wearing a sinister smile, taunting Zach. "This is a courtroom where truths are supposed to be revealed. We'd like to hear *your* truth."

"I heard Jill screaming that night. She sounded like she was crying. She screamed, and asked Jay to leave her alone. There was fear in her voice. I tried to ignore it, but Jill kept crying like she was in pain."

"So you entered the bedroom unannounced while your sister, Ms. King, and her lover Ms. Bessette were in the throes of passion? That's a gross invasion of privacy! How dare you? What gave you that right?"

"Don't answer that question, Mr. King!" Mr. Lugar stood and shouted. "He's badgering the witness, Your Honor."

"Answer me, Mr. King! You were out of control with envy that night. Weren't you?"

"Keep quiet Mr. King!" Mr. Lugar demanded.

Zach felt himself about to snap. He could clearly see the scared look in Jill's eyes that night in his memory, and hear her shaky voice telling him what Jay had done to her the next morning. Judge Elway was banging his gavel against the bench to silence the opposing attorneys. Spectators were whispering. The courtroom was in chaos with Mr. Lugar and Mr. Rice shouting alternately.

"Order in the court!" the judge shouted.

Mr. Lugar jabbed his index finger hard into the air. "I object to this line of questioning, Your Honor! Mr. King is the *victim* in this case. He is not on trial here."

Jill closed her eyes, and lowered her head. Aunt Jackie reached over and clutched her hand and Dex grabbed the other one. Zach watched it all from his seat. Jill was upset over how Mr. Rice hurled accusations at him about the very private details of their life. She had been adamant about coming to court today to support Zach, and now he wished he had followed his instincts and insisted that she stay home. Wishing very much to get past the long cross-examination, he faced Mr. Rice, man to man.

"Like I said, Jill sounded like she was crying, and I distinctly heard her ask

Jay to leave her alone. I apologized to both of them for intruding, and left the room. Minutes later, I heard my sister leave the house and I didn't see her again for several days."

"How many times did you have sexual relations with Ms. Bessette after that?"

"I'm not sure."

"When did you finally come clean with your dear sister about your affair with Ms. Bessette?"

"I think it was in November of that same year after returning from a trip to Jamaica. I had accompanied Jill to the island to tend to her little brother's medical needs. On the day we were to return to the States, she was detained by airport security. My sister, the woman who *claimed* to have loved her, had reported some false information to the U.S. Department of Immigrations. I had to leave Jill in Jamaica. Upon my arrival in Atlanta, I went to my sister's suite at the Seven Seas, and told her that Jill and I were in love."

"How did Ms. King take the news? Did she congratulate you? Did she laugh, cry or faint?"

"She was very upset as I expected she would be. She cursed at me and threw me out of her suite."

"And then you topped that by marrying Ms. Bessette months later in a secret wedding in Jamaica after she became pregnant with your child. How did your poor sister take *that* news?"

Zach looked at Jay. She was cool as a cucumber nestled between Mr. Ford and a female attorney at the defense table. Her countenance was flat. She wore a nice black pants suit, and her short curly hair had grown out several inches. Without a doubt she was enjoying Mr. Rice's attack on him, but she was doing a good job suppressing it.

"Jay was very angry when I told her Jill and I were expecting a baby. Again, she cursed and screamed. Her reaction caused an embarrassing scene in the bistro where we'd met to talk. She vowed to never forgive me, and she told me Jill and I would get what we deserved someday."

Mr. Rice made multiple attempts to coax Zach into saying his marriage to Jill and the news about her pregnancy had pushed Jay over the edge. None of his tactics worked. In fact, Zach boldly told everyone in the courtroom that he didn't think Jay was crazy at all, and that only her pride had been damaged by his relationship with Jill. He repeated her bone chilling wish to have killed him herself on the evening she discovered he hadn't been murdered. A stir of mummers and gasps filled the courtroom, and once again Judge Elway had to demand order.

Chapter Fifty-One

Aspontaneous trip to Raleigh turned out to be the perfect getaway from all the courtroom drama and media blitz. Wallace was pleasantly surprised when he'd found Zach, Jill, Zachary Junior and Nahima on his front porch. Patricia and Wallace Junior had been expecting them. Zach had called to speak with his father earlier that week after his cross-examination, but he was at his church teaching bible study. Patricia had insisted that they come up for the weekend to surprise Wallace, and surprise him they did.

Jill and the baby joined Patricia in the spacious sunken den in the middle of house. It was close to the play room. They sipped tea, and talked while Wallace Junior and Nahima made lots of noise playing together. Zach and Wallace were on the golf course.

"This is the happiest Wallace has ever been. Not even the trial has been able to steal his joy. He's in a good place now that his son and grandchildren are a part of his life."

They both watched Zachary Junior babbling and playing with his toys on a blue blanket in the middle of the floor.

"When I first met Jay, she spoke very little about her parents. All she'd ever said was her mother was dead, and her father had left them to be raised by their aunt. It was Zach who told me the whole truth. As painful as it was, he shared everything with me. The one thing he stressed most was his father's intentions. Zach felt it was crucial that I know Papa King didn't mean to kill their mother."

"No, he didn't," Patricia said. "When I was first introduced to Wallace he was a broken man. One of my friends, a fellow attorney who had been my mentor since I graduated law school, had represented him during his murder trial. His name is Grady Vaughn. He brought us together during the time Wallace was trying to become a school teacher here in Raleigh. He was fighting a battle with the school system because of his criminal record. I took the case on and won. While we prepared for court, we became close. I was much younger than him of course, but I saw his spirit. It was gentle and calm. It was hard for me to imagine him killing anyone."

"Love causes us to do things we aren't proud of sometimes, I suppose. It was only because my father-in-law loved his wife that he attempted to wound his friend for having an affair with her. That was not the case with Jay. She wanted

Zach dead because she felt he had taken something that belonged to her. I was her property as far as she believed. Jay had controlled me for four years. She never imagined I would open my naive eyes to the reality of our very toxic relationship. And she never thought I would open my heart to someone else, especially not her brother. Zachary didn't take advantage of me, ya know?"

Patricia chuckled lightly, and the dimples buried in her smooth brown cheeks made an appearance. Her long thick ponytail swayed from side to side when she shook her head. "I didn't think he did. When I first met you, I noticed a passion in your eyes for Zach that reminded me very much of what I have for Wallace. When most of my family members called me crazy for marrying a much older, convicted murderer, and former client, I ignored them. I followed my heart. I know how it feels to fight for love."

"I know how Zachary and I came together may be frowned upon by others. We've both admitted it was wrong, but look at us. We are so very happy. Our son means the world to us. We are a family. I don't believe God will punish Zach and me because we fell in love. He has forgiven us, and that's the most important thing. We both sought Jay's forgiveness, but she refused us."

The front door slammed followed by the hum of male voices. Wallace entered the den with Zach right behind him. The children must've heard the men, because Nahima ran from the play room with a handful of Lego building blocks. She waved to her uncle and grandfather before she dashed back into the room.

"I hope you two are hungry. Jill and I prepared a spread."

"I don't know about Daddy, but I am." Zach leaned over and pecked Jill on the cheek.

She pinched her nose. "Zachary, you smell dreadful!" She pushed him away. "Please do not touch the baby!"

Zach knelt down at the edge of the blanket, and Zachary Junior squealed and crawled briskly in his direction. His meaty arms and legs moved in perfect coordination toward his daddy. Jill made a clever interception, and carried the baby to the sofa. Wallace and Patricia laughed.

"Do I stink that bad that I can't hold my own son?"

"Yes, Zachary, you are quite smelly. Please go and shower while I heat up the food."

"I guess I better do the same before Patricia starts complaining too."

"Thank you. I was about to suggest that, sweetie."

* * * * *

"Welcome back, Zach. How are you?"

"I'm okay, Nancy. I got plenty of rest and quality time with my family. Now I'm ready to work. I wanna stay as busy as possible. What do you have for me?"

She handed Zach three charts as they walked down the hall toward the NICU nursery, side by side. "They're all little girls and *fighters* too. The smallest one has lots of spunk, but she's a crack baby. Her maternal grandmother is here around the clock. Make sure you talk to her because she likes to know everything that's going on with the baby. Her name is Lizzie Carter."

"No problem. What's the buzz around here? Are folks talking about me? Is the trial still a hot topic?"

"You know how it is, Zach. Some people live just to gossip. I guess it makes them feel important. But to answer your question, yes, the trial is hot as jalapeño peppers. Everybody is reaching and pulling for every tiny detail. The newspaper and all the local news channels are covering it daily."

"I know. The entire state of Georgia knows me as the brother who stole his sister's Jamaican lover, knocked her up and married her in a secret island wedding. I bet everybody thinks I'm a lowdown son of a bitch."

"Nobody around here feels that way about you. We know the *real* Zachary King, and we love him. Screw Jay's stupid attorneys. She ain't crazy. *They* are, for believing her nonsense. I don't want you to worry about the gossipers, Zach. Just do your job the same way you've done it all these years. Your little patients need you." Nancy looked up and saw Mrs. Carter making steps in their direction. "Here comes that grandmother I was telling you about. Introduce yourself to her. I've gotta run to a meeting."

* * * * *

Dex tried to hide the newspaper when he saw Zach approaching their table. At the last minute he crumpled it, and threw it on a chair behind him.

"What are they saying about Jill and me today?" Zach sat down and shook a bottle of guava juice before he opened it.

"You caught me, huh?"

"You know damn well I did. Why do read that shit anyway? You know the whole story inside and out."

"I'm curious about all the lies Jay fed her lawyers. That's all."

"Well, I can't wait for the verdict. At this point, I don't care if Jay is found innocent. I just want my life back. With this trial hanging over our heads, Jill and I can't fully relax and let our guards down. The sooner it's over, the better. I feel like the whole world is watching me."

"Ain't nobody watching you, man. You're paranoid."

"Maybe I am, but I can't wait for this case to be over. If it's not soon, I may pack up my wife and son and move to Raleigh. Nobody knows me up there except my dad, Patricia and Wallace Junior."

"So you'd just up and leave like that?" Dex snapped his fingers. "Jay hires someone to kill you. She's on trial for it. Her defense is weak by Attorney Rice's own admission. Sure, some of your dirty laundry is being aired out, and it's foul. But *you're* the victim, man. Why the hell would you leave your aunt and *Nahima*? Forget about me, your best friend and Abriah, your god child. We'll be fine. But that pretty, little, innocent girl who looks up to you would be devastated. How would you explain to her the reason you're leaving her behind? Stop acting like a punk! You made some choices, Zach, and now you're living with them. I thought you said you didn't regret falling in love with Jill. You told me if you had it to do all over again, you wouldn't change a damn thing."

"I wouldn't." Zach stuffed the remains of his sandwich in his lunch bag. "It's just hard walking down the hall knowing folks are whispering about you. A waitress at Pappadeaux recognized me the other night. It was strange, man."

"People will forget all about the entire case after awhile. Just hold your head up and keep it moving."

Chapter Fifty-Two

Mrs. Scott watched Jill performing with her senior women's class through the studio window. She admired her graceful and fluid movements. It was remarkable how she had bounced back so physically fit and energized after her pregnancy. The older women in Jill's class loved her patience and creative edge. Mrs. Scott considered her a rare jewel, and she wanted to reward her with a proposition. She walked into the room quietly, and stood in a corner in the back. Jill and her mature students were executing a simple routine in a very unique and complex formation.

"Bravo, ladies, you were simply magnificent!" Mrs. Scott applauded after their final move and standing pose. "They were incredible, Jill. You've done an amazing job with them. I'd like to showcase my *silver foxes* in our spring production. It'll be a first for them."

Jill smiled and turned to the women who were talking and taking a water break. "Did you hear that, divas? Madame Helena wants to show you off at the spring production! It's a *big* deal, ya know?"

The ladies clapped and cheered. Jill liked their response. "Rejoice now, but it will require lots of hard work and dedication."

Mrs. Scott looped her arm through Jill's. "Let's go to my office, sweetie. There's something I'd like to discuss with you."

"Please do not tell me the immigration people are bullying you again. I have legal documentation that says I can work here, ya know? I'll become an American citizen soon."

Mrs. Scott felt the tension in Jill's muscles as she pulled her along down the hallway. "It's not that. We're in compliance with those goons. What I'd like to talk to you about is something *wonderful*. Come on in." She unlocked her office door. "Have a seat and relax."

Jill followed her boss's instructions. She watched her round the desk to take her seat behind it.

"Jill, from the first day I met you in this very office, I fell in love with your gift and your passion for it. You promised not to disappoint me and you've kept your word. We missed you like crazy when you went home and stayed for a while. You're an asset to Umoja Academy. In addition to your senior women's performance, how would you feel about choreographing the advance young women's finale for the show? It pays a pretty penny."

Jill pressed her palm to her chest. "I…I would love to do that! Thank you. I will not disappoint you, Madame Helena. All I need is the music and timing, and then I'll get started right away."

Mrs. Scott laughed and held up her hand to stop Jill from saying more. "*You* will select the music for the five-minute routine. You'll also have final say on the costumes, props and lighting."

"This is unbelievable! Zachary will be so very pleased."

"Hold up, my friend. There is one more thing."

"Oh?"

"I applied for a prestigious dance seminar on your behalf. A colleague of mine will be facilitating an exclusive, six-week training camp in Atlanta this summer. He's internationally renowned and has trained some of the best dancers in this country. Are you familiar with Sir Max Ebu?"

"Oh my God! Every dancer has heard of him!"

"He has agreed to grace our city to work with a select group of twenty-five men and women who wish to pursue dance as a profession. One of those two-thousand-dollar slots belongs to you, Jill. I've secured your fee with a grant for international students."

Jill ran around the desk and wrapped her arms around Mrs. Scott. "Thank you so very much. This is like a fairytale!"

* * * * *

"I bet you ain't ever had it that good before. I know your old man can't make you feel like *that*." Jay shimmied back into her county-issued panties. She looked over at her latest victim resting limply on the cot with her back propped up against the wall. There was a sparkle in her green eyes. That was a sure sign to Jay that she had worked her magic on the young woman. The stupid bitch was *hooked*. Jay smiled and slid her arms through the sleeves of her ugly orange jumpsuit. She stood to her full five-foot-six-inch height, and secured the buttons in the front of it. She nudged Bethany hard on her pale flabby thigh. The shiny gold badge attached to her uniform shirt on the floor twinkled like a giant star. "Don't you think you need to be getting dressed? What if someone catches you in here spread-eagle in your birthday suite?"

"Stop worrying. Ain't nobody coming down here. I turned off the security camera 'cause they don't give a rat's ass about you. They all think you're evil as hell. And remember, I'm on the stroll before my break." Bethany raked her fingers through her wild red curls and giggled. "I ain't never been with a woman before you. I been curious, but I ain't have no idea what to expect. The first time when we were in the shower made me come back for *more*. Tonight was even better." She ran her hand up Jay's leg, and fondled her crotch through the orange fabric. "Hell, I think I'm in love."

Jay smacked her hand away jokingly. But she really wanted to snap her neck and throw her white, trailer trash ass out of her cell. She was nauseous and on the verge of vomiting. "Come back in here whenever you need to, but remember it's gonna cost you."

"I know. I know." Bethany stood up, and started putting her uniform back on. "What else do you need besides the aspirin, liquor and prepaid cell phone?"

Jay reached under her cot's mattress, and pulled out a sealed stamped letter. It was addressed to Nina. "I need you to mail this to my cousin from anywhere but here. I don't want any records on file that we've been in contact. You understand?"

"Got it," she said, stashing the letter inside her shirt. "I'll be back Wednesday night with the stuff you want." She leaned in and kissed Jay full on the lips. "And I expect you to have the stuff *I* want."

* * * * *

Zach turned off his Bluetooth and stared at the slow moving traffic ahead of him. Jay was going to prison for twelve to fifteen years. That's what his father had just told him. Mr. Rice and his team were taking a brutal beating in court. They couldn't win. The jury seemed aloof and bored to death with the defense team's entire presentation so far. Wallace's testimony hadn't scored the punch they'd expected. A few grade school teachers, her high school guidance counselor and few of Jay's childhood friends had taken the stand. All they had offered were basic stories, mostly things she'd shared with them about her family over the years. The only expert witness was the psychologist, and Mr. Lugar had torn his assessment of Jay to shreds during cross-examination with notes from his team of specialists. Nothing Mr. Rice and company had presented to date had helped Jay. They now wanted her to plead and strike a deal with the State before it was too late. But she wasn't having it. Her stubbornness had become a thorn in her attorney's flesh and he had reached out to Wallace for help. Mr. Rice wanted him to try to persuade Jay to throw in the towel. Otherwise, she was going to end up in prison seven to ten years longer than she had to.

Needless to say, Wallace had no influence over Jay whatsoever, and he'd told Mr. Rice as much. He then asked him to make one last appeal to her about the plea deal with hopes that she'd finally see the light. If she was smart, Jay would confess and take the lighter sentence. If not, it would be her loss.

Zach parked in front of Umoja Academy with Jay's situation heavy on his mind. He turned on his Alpine stereo system, and reclined his seat. Smooth jazz floated from the speakers. Zach wanted it to erase all thoughts of Jay, the trial and her inevitable prison sentence. The possibility that she'd spend the next decade or so locked away for ordering a hit on him was not his problem. But why did it bother him so much?

"Why the hell do I care?" Zach yelled.

"Zachary?" Jill opened the front passenger's door, and slid inside the SUV. She touched the side of Zach's face. "What is it? Do not tell me it's nothing because I'm not stupid. You're upset about something. Talk to me."

Zach pulled out of the parking lot. "Jay is going to prison for a very long time."

"Mmm, is that so? I never knew the trial was over. How many years did the judge sentence her to serve?"

"The trial ain't over. Her attorney called my dad this afternoon and told him there's absolutely no way possible he and his team can win Jay's case. That means she'll be convicted and serve at least twelve years in prison. But if she were to shut down her damn crazy act right now, and admit what she did, she could reduce her time to maybe five to seven years."

"After all Jay has done to us you still love her, and care what happens to her. I admire you. I don't understand it, but I accept it. Do not allow this to affect you negatively, Zachary. Jay will *never* confess to her crime because she is much too proud and stubborn. She'd rather lose in court, and endure prison than to admit any wrongdoing. That way she can maintain her false innocence and blame her attorney for losing her case. No matter what happens, *you* are still the victim, and you're not responsible for what Jay did."

Chapter Fifty-Three

Crying was uncommon for Jay. She didn't consider herself one of those butchy type lesbians with pseudo masculinity, but she was no punk either. She was tough and emotionally sturdy. The brick wall she'd built around her heart was meant to protect her from pain and disappointment. She had only let her guard down once, and that was when she fell in love with Venus. Any tears she'd cried as an adult were because of that relationship. But today she couldn't blame Venus or Nahima for her emotional breakdown. Her tears were those of defeat. Every muscle in Jay's body stiffened when Mr. Rice placed a timid hand on her shoulder

"Do you understand what we're saying, Ms. King? We simply don't have what it takes to win this case. If we proceed on the rocky path we're now on, you'll be convicted. I'm sorry. Our best efforts to defend you under temporary insanity are failing, and miserably so. If you plead guilty now, you will serve five to seven, instead of twelve plus years in prison. It's all up to you."

Mr. Ford remained silent as he placed a prepared confession statement on the table in front of Jay. He held a stainless steel Montblanc ballpoint pen before her bowed head. Jay used the white handkerchief Mr. Rice had given her to wipe the fresh flow of tears tricking down her face. She ignored the paper and pen that had been offered to her.

"I need time to think about this."

Mr. Rice and Mr. Ford looked past their client who was seated between them to stare at each other. Jay's head remained down as she skimmed over the confession lying on the table.

"You don't have any more time, Ms. King," Mr. Rice said, clearly frustrated.

"It ain't your ass on the line! It's *mine*. I need to sleep on this. Don't I have that right?"

Mr. Ford nodded, and raised his hand to cut off Mr. Rice's next statement. "Of course you do, Ms. King. But we need you to understand that tomorrow is the deadline. We will allow you to weigh your options overnight, but in the morning we'll expect your decision *before* we walk into that courtroom. Do you understand?"

"Yeah, I got it. I ain't stupid."

Honey

* * * * *

"Her pulse and heart rate are dropping fast!" The emergency medical technician yelled over the wailing siren. "And so is her blood pressure!"

Jay's limp body began to jerk and shudder spastically. The female medic restrained her against another bout of convulsions. She'd had three episodes since leaving the jail. The deputies said that's how they were alerted that something wrong was going on in her cell. By the time they reached Jay she had fallen off her cot, and was having a seizure in the middle of the floor.

The ambulance swerved, changing lanes in its race to the hospital. "We're almost there!" The driver informed his crew.

"I hope so because she just threw up some more blood, a hell of a lot more." She pried Jay's eyelids open with her fingers, and pointed a pen light directly at her dilated pupil. Her cool and clammy body continued to tick involuntarily as blood oozed from her mouth and spilled down her chin. The paramedic eased Jay carefully over to her side to keep her from choking on her own blood. "Stay with me. We're almost there."

"How the hell does an inmate on trial for murder for hire get her hands on liquor and a bottle of aspirin?" The driver asked, pulling in front of the emergency room.

"How the hell am I supposed to know? I've never been to jail before. I wonder what possessed her to take the whole damn bottle of pills."

The driver shrugged his shoulders, and exited the vehicle. Together the three medics removed the gurney from the back of the ambulance with Jay lying nearly lifeless on it. They rushed her through the double glass doors of the emergency room where they were approached by a team of nurses and a doctor.

* * * * *

Zach arrived at the hospital an hour before his shift to check on Jay. When Wallace called him around ten-thirty the night before to tell him she'd attempted suicide again, he thanked him for calling. He outright refused to rush to her bedside again like he had the first time. Zach swore he was done playing games with Jay. But now, standing outside the glass door of her intensive care room, he wasn't sure if he'd made the right decision. Jay was in bad shape, but she was stable. The lining of her stomach was totally destroyed which had caused internal bleeding, and poisoned her system. Her sensitive liver, spotted by heavy alcohol consumption over the years, had sustained severe chemical damage. Zach was convinced that Jay had really meant to end her life this time. That realization opened the floodgates, and he was now wrestling with guilt once again.

Health monitors beeping with flashing graphics were no big deal to Zach. He saw them every day. But usually his tiny patients fighting for their young lives were hooked up to them, not his only sister. Jay preferred death over prison. And she had wanted Zach dead rather than allow him to be happy with Jill and their son. But she had no right or authority to choose who should live or die or be happy. No human did.

"Are you going in there, man?"

Zach had been so wrapped up in his thoughts that he didn't realize Dex had walked up beside him. He shook his head to clear it. "Nah, I'll pass. I can't get caught up in this madness with Jay again. Ain't no room for her in my world anymore. It's all about my wife, our son and the people who love us. I just wish Jay the best, whatever the hell that is."

* * * * *

"Sister Brown, how are you, darling?" Reverend Broadus greeted Aunt Jackie with a hug after Sunday morning service.

"I'm well, Pastor. How are you?"

"I won't complain. You tore the church up this morning with that anointed voice!"

"Thank you. You preached up a storm. I hope Mother Finney finds that pretty silver hat of hers. It flew off her head when she jumped up and started dancing in the spirit."

The pastor and the church songbird shared a genuine laugh. Reverend Broadus looked at the long line of members waiting to shake his hand. He put his arm around Aunt Jackie's shoulders, and escorted her a few inches away from the young couple behind her. "How is Jay doing?"

"She's doing much better. Thank you for asking. She's in a standard room on the psychiatric ward getting the professional help she needs. The doctors are gonna assess her Wednesday to see if she'll be able to go on with her trial some time soon. It's been on hold for three weeks since she's been in the hospital."

Reverend Broadus looked at Aunt Jackie with compassionate eyes. He knew the family history. They had endured a lot over the years. Through it all, Jackie Dudley Brown had never lost her faith even up to now.

"I'm praying for that girl. I'm praying for you and Zach too. Please call me if you need *anything*. Sister Broadus and I will be there for you and the family anytime."

"I know, Pastor. Thank you from the bottom of my heart. I'm sure Zach and Jill will appreciate your prayers too. They took the children up to Pigeon Forge for the weekend. The trial and Jay's suicide attempt have been rough on my nephew. He needed to get away from Atlanta even though it's just for a little while."

As Aunt Jackie walked down the church steps toward the parking lot, she saw people whispering and staring at her. She heard their snickers too. It brought tears to her eyes, but her pride wouldn't let them fall. She was a *Dudley*, and they were strong, confident, brave people. She'd held her chin up in the face of loose tongue gossipers and haters when Belva died in that hotel room twenty-nine years ago.

Honey

What Jay was putting her through now was like a block party compared to that.

* * * * *

"For a redneck, you're smart as hell! I didn't know you had it in you. Are you sure this is gonna work?"

"Does horse shit stink?" Bethany jumped up from the futon, and peeped out of the window. She was alone in the trailer she shared with her boyfriend Todd and their two children, but planning Jay's escape made her paranoid.

"It stinks like hell. All shit stinks," Jay joked.

"Trust me. It's gonna work. Is your cousin on board? A lot of this depends on her."

"Nina is in all the way. She knows exactly what to do."

"Then, we're all set. This time tomorrow you'll be a free woman, baby. We'll be on our way to Miami and from there on to *Jamaica*!"

After Bethany ended her conversation with Jay she went to her bedroom to finish packing. She'd never been out of the state of Georgia before. Moving from the mountains of Dahlonega to Atlanta had been the highlight of her life. With her recently issued passport and a duffle bag full of brand new Walmart outfits, she was prepared to take up residence in the Caribbean. Todd was going to shit bricks once he found out she had left him. But she didn't care. She wasn't going to miss his abusive, alcoholic, unemployed ass. Leaving her babies wasn't going to be easy, though.

Bethany peeled the Christmas picture of her daughters from the mirror where she had taped it. She held it to her chest. "Momma's gonna miss her angels," she whispered on the brink of tears. She flipped the picture over, and looked at Becky and Carley. "Granny's gonna take good care of y'all."

Bethany's girls meant the world to her, but she couldn't afford to take them to Jamaica with her. Jay had promised that she would make arrangements to have the children join them on the island after they got settled. The girls would only slow them down during their travels. It was just too risky. So Bethany had written a letter to Todd's mother Louise, asking her to take care of Becky and Carley until she sent for them.

None of Bethany's family members or friends would ever suspect she'd run away with some inmate she'd fallen madly in love with. Where she came from gays and niggers were worse than Satan himself. But none of them knew how Jay made her feel inside and out. The way she called her beautiful and smart all the time made her believe she was more than just a fat piece of white trash with only a GED. For the first time in years, Bethany felt special and needed by someone other than Todd or her girls. She was in love, and she didn't give a damn what anybody thought about it.

Chapter Fifty-Four

"*Daaamn*, you hit him hard! I hope you didn't kill him." Jay held out her arms for Bethany to free her of the handcuffs. Then she squatted, down to check the sergeant's pulse. Jay placed her hand on the left side of his chest to feel his heartbeat too. "Nah, he ain't dead, but I bet he's gonna have one of those hangover headaches whenever he wakes up."

She and Bethany struggled to lift Sergeant Abernathy from the floor of the hospital's parking deck to place him into the driver's seat of his patrol cruiser. With adrenaline pumping, increasing their strength, they managed to do it quickly and unnoticed. The middle-aged man never saw it coming. Bethany had crashed the butt of her department-issued firearm to the back of his head, and knocked him out cold. She disarmed him, and destroyed his radio. And then with *his* handcuffs, she and Jay locked his wrists to the steering wheel before placing his hat on his head. His pale face and grayish blonde hair were saturated with perspiration. The stiff heat underneath the layers of concrete in the parking deck was almost unbearable.

"I'm sorry, Sarge," Bethany said to her victim. "You never should've trusted me." She popped the trunk, and grabbed the two duffle bags she had stashed inside unbeknownst to Abernathy.

She and Jay laughed as they ducked in and out of the rows of cars, dodging the security cameras. Ray Hood, one of Nina's homeboys had done a good job casing the map of the entire multilevel deck. He used to be a security guard at the hospital. He'd pointed out every camera, and explained the timing schedule. Because of him, they were completely hidden so far. The area where Sergeant Abernathy had parked the patrol car was designated for specialty vehicles such as military, fire fighters and obviously, law enforcement.

After Bethany and the sergeant went to the psyche ward to sign Jay's medical release papers, they escorted her in handcuffs to the parking deck. They were supposed to have secured her in the back of the patrol car and transported her back to jail. But a secret escape plan was now underway as had been carefully planned without Abernathy's knowledge. It was unfortunate for the twenty-two-year veteran. He'd been lured into the trap of a coworker sprung by new lesbian love. Bethany had made herself available to Sergeant Abernathy to assist with Jay's transportation. And he, a sucker for the full-figure redhead, had gladly taken her up on her offer.

Bethany used a flashlight to read her watch. "Where the hell is your cousin? She's late. All hell is gonna break loose when Sarge wakes up. We should be on the road *right now*."

"Pump your breaks. Nina will be here. She's just a few minutes behind schedule as usual."

A medical transportation van and a few cars whipped around the corner. Jay and Bethany dropped to the ground, and covered their heads. They stayed on their knees while other vehicles drove past them. After several moments of silence, Bethany raised her head to check out their surroundings.

"I see a dark green car coming this way. Could that be your cousin?"

"Yeah, that's Nina. But let's wait first for the signal to be sure."

Nina flashed the headlights once, twice and then a third time. She'd told Jay that would be the signal that she was definitely behind the wheel of the car, and the coast was clear.

"Let's roll," Jay told Bethany, and trotted toward the car. She kept her head low as she weaved through a row of cars.

"I'm right behind you, baby."

Jay slid in the front seat of the car, and lowered her head to rest in Nina's lap. Bethany hopped in through the back right side passenger's door, and sprawled out face down on the seat. She tossed the duffel bags on the floor and opened one.

"Cover up," Bethany whispered and threw a brown blanket over the back of the seat. She removed another one just like it from the bag, and covered her entire body before she dropped to the floor.

"I hope y'all are ready because we ain't stopping until we get to Valdosta."

"Just drive, Nina. Get me the hell outta Atlanta, baby."

* * * * *

"What the hell am I supposed to do to protect my wife and son? Jay tried to have me killed once. This time she may come at Jill and me herself. This is so *fucked up*!" Zach snatched the baseball cap from his head, and threw it as far as he could across his den. "It's been three days, and not even the FBI can find her! How hard can it be, Ortega?"

"You know as well as I do, that your sister is a very intelligent woman. She's attractive, charming and confident. Women are drawn to her like bees to honey. I'll bet she could hook and reel in any given *man* if she wanted to. Ms. King's escape was meticulously planned down to the tiniest detail. It wasn't some spur of the moment idea. Everything was well organized and executed. Unfortunately, certain elements worked against us in the first twenty-four hours of her disappearance."

"What elements are you talking about?"

"Sergeant Abernathy's inability to remember anything initially was very unfortunate," Detective Franklin explained. "The female deputy who had been assigned to accompany him to the hospital to transport Ms. King back to the jail said they'd agreed to meet at one-thirty that afternoon in the garage at his cruiser. When Deputy Phaedra McMillan went to her locker to prepare for the transport, she found a note from the sergeant informing her that he'd been instructed by his supervisor to go to the hospital earlier. Another female deputy went with him."

"The funny thing is Sergeant Abernathy's superior knew nothing about the time change on your sister's transportation. Someone had sent the sergeant a message from Major Lonnie Jefferson's employee email address making everything look official." Detective Ortega sighed. "We're working with the FBI and the Fulton County Sherriff's Department to find out who that person is."

Zach started laughing. "Jay had some inside help. My sister put her mojo on one of those female deputies, and she helped her escape." He stood to his feet, stroking his goatee. "Well, I don't expect any of y'all to give a damn about me or my family. For all we know Jay could be laying low somewhere planning our massacre. I ain't about to let that happen."

"Wait a minute, Mr. King." Detective Franklin walked over to Zach, and stood toe to toe with him. "We don't need any assistance from you. Let us do our job. There's a national manhunt for Ms. King. She'll be found. You need not worry."

"You must think I'm a damn fool!" Zach left the detectives alone in the den while he went into the foyer to search through the closet. When he returned, he brandished a good-looking, nine millimeter handgun. "If my sister comes anywhere near this house I'm gonna bust a cap in her ass. Then I'll call y'all." Zach shook his head. "I ain't gonna kill her. I can promise you that, but I'm gonna make her wish she was dead."

* * * * *

Jay couldn't sleep on the plane. She had too much shit on her mind. She felt pretty secure now that she and Nina were on their way to Jamaica. Getting out of the country hadn't been as hard as she'd thought it would be. Nina had promised her she had everything under control. From their passports to money and disguises, everything had gone according to plan. Jay couldn't deny it. She was one sexy bitch in the getup Nina had put together for her. She almost didn't recognize her own reflection in the mirror. The Fashion Fair makeup, long hair extensions and big ghetto earrings had transformed her into a *hottie*. The body-hugging red dress put the icing on the cake. And the matching four-inch stilettos added the cherry on top.

Jay reached over and squeezed one of Nina's meaty thighs. She swatted her hand, and mumbled something before she started snoring again. Thoughts of Bethany filled Jay's head. There was still some guilt lingering because of what she'd done to her, but not much. Life was a risky game, and only the strong survived. Bethany had fallen in too deep,˙ and it had cost her. Maybe she'd get lucky, and make some friends in the South Florida trailer park. It was her hillbilly ass who had found their doublewide hideout and reserved it online. She'd basically planned and financed Jay's entire escape. Too bad she had been blindsided like the old sergeant. Karma had paid Bethany a visit. This time she was the one left out of the loop. Jay had had no intention of ever taking her to Jamaica. She'd only used her to escape her sentencing. And after the unassuming deputy had served her purpose, they drugged her with some white power Nina had brought along. According to the dealer, it wouldn't kill her, but she'd be out close to twenty-four hours.

Chapter Fifty-Five

"Mmm…my head hurts like hell!" Bethany rolled over on her pallet in the middle of floor. "Jay, where are you? Jay?" She pulled her herself up to sit on her knees. "Jay? Nina?" She swiped her long hair away from her face and coughed.

Bethany looked down at her flabby body covered with sweat. She was completely *nude*, but she couldn't remember taking off her clothes. Her head was throbbing. She reached up and massaged her temples for relief. The small room started to spin when she tried to stand. Snippets of the night before drifted back to her. She specifically remembered drinking a few beers, and begging Jay to take her to bed, but she'd acted shy and uninterested in front of her cousin. Bethany wasn't sure what Nina's problem was, but she'd behaved moody and unfriendly toward her.

"Jay, where are you, baby? Her second attempt to stand was successful. Bethany searched all four rooms of the trailer on wobbly legs. There was no sign of Jay or Nina anywhere. When she looked out the front window and discovered the truck she'd rented on her credit card was gone, her knees buckled. "What the hell is going on?"

Bethany rushed back to the room where she'd slept. She grabbed her duffle bag so she could get dressed. The only thing she found was her loaded .45 handgun. All of her money, credit cards, passport, license and clothes were missing. There wasn't even a pair of panties in the bag.

"*Nooo*!" She screamed and collapsed to the floor. "Oh no! Dear God, help me! What have I done? What the hell have I done?"

Bethany sat on her knees rocking and rubbing both arms with her hands. Warm tears clouded her vision. The realization that Jay had left her out in the middle of nowhere hurt like hell. Her cell phone had been attached to the jeans she'd worn the night before, so she had no way of contacting anybody. There was no one she could call for help anyway without implicating herself. Visions of Becky and Carley smiling and playing outside their trailer began to play like a movie in her mind's eye.

"My babies…I miss my sweet babies…uh…uh…" Bethany whimpered. She could hear Todd's voice cursing and shouting vulgar insults at her about her weight and lack of common sense. It made her shudder. She could actually see him laughing and raising his hand to slap her. "You used me, Jay! You worthless *nigger*! You evil monkey bitch!" Bethany crawled over to her duffle bag, and grabbed her pistol. She held it up to her head. With tears saturating her face, she pressed the muzzle to her right temple and screamed, "I'll see you in hell, bitch!"

The single shot rang out all over the secluded trailer park. A few stray dogs howled and barked in response. Blood and cerebral membrane instantly splattered across the room onto the dingy white wall. It dripped down on the carpet. The tragic end of Bethany's life would be ruled a suicide by the authorities, but if the walls could talk, they'd call it a homicide in every way.

* * * * *

"It's beautiful up here, ain't it?"

Nina rolled her eyes to the sunny sky, and scrunched up her nose. "It's okay, but I thought you said we would be living in a nice hotel or some a beach house." She turned around to look at the old wooden shanty where she and Jay had been hiding out for the past four days. "This house is a piece of shit, and you know it. I didn't sign on for this, Jay."

"Damn it, Nina! I told you we gotta lay low for a while. I'm working on some shit. This is the best I can do for now. Thanks to Charlotte, we've got food and running water."

"It's *cold* running water." Nina threw her cigarette butt to the ground and stomped it out. "I swear if I had known it would be like this…"

Jay jumped off the porch, steps and landed right in front of Nina. "Go ahead and say it. If you had known we would have to slum it for a while you would've stayed home. You've been complaining ever since we got here. Stop your bitching, Nina! As soon as the coast is clear, Charlotte will find us a better place. Maybe I should've left *you* in that damn trailer instead of Bethany."

Nina stretched her eyes, and her jaw dropped. She burst into tears. "After all I've done for you, how could you say some foul shit like that to me? How could you, Jay?" Nina pushed Jay and stomped up the three steps onto the porch. She pulled the handle on the screen door to go inside, but Jay reached over her and pressed both hands on it to keep it closed.

"I'm sorry, baby. I didn't mean it. You know I love you, Nina." She kissed the back of her neck, and started massaging her full set of breast. "I shouldn't have said that to you. I love you."

Like butter, Nina went soft at the sound of Jay's voice and the warmth of her touch. Her breath got caught in her throat when the hem of her skirt went up, and a single finger began teasing her clit. Like the breaking of a dam, Nina's love juices gushed forward. Jay removed her finger and slid it inside her mouth. She sucked and moaned.

"It's sweet just like I like it. Let's go inside and finish this," she whispered seductively in Nina's ear.

"Okay. Do you really love me, baby?"

Jay eased her hand back under Nina's skirt and traced the lips of her pussy with two fingers and blew in her ear. With her other hand, she applied pressure on her right nipple with her finger tips.

"Let's go inside and I'll *show* you."

* * * * *

"Zachary, it is the third time the police have called this house. Don't you think we should answer the phone?"

Zach ignored the constant ringing. He checked his tie one more time in the mirror, and looked down at his son relaxing in Jill's lap. He smiled at his little plump face. Zachary Junior was the spitting image of him. Zach reached down, and lifted his mini twin from his mother's arms. Nahima smiled when the baby cooed and kicked.

"Zachary?"

"*What Jill?*" He snapped, "We're already running late for church! I'm not gonna talk to Franklin or Ortega on the Lord's Day." Zach looked around the bedroom for the baby's diaper bag.

"It's downstairs." Jill stood from the bed and pointed a finger at Zach. "You are my husband and you are the head of this family. I have always been submissive to you. I respect you as the father of our son. I have been by your side even when I did not agree with you and I seldom complained. But hear me, Mr. Zachary Sean King; do not *ever* speak to me in that tone of voice again. Do you understand me?"

"I'm sorry. I…"

"Of course you are, Zachary." Jill took the baby from his father's arms and walked toward the bedroom door with Nahima following behind her.

Zach had seen tears in his wife's eyes when she spoke to him. She was sniffling even as she walked out of their bedroom. He had hurt Jill's feelings, but he hadn't meant to. "I've gotta get my shit together," he said to himself. "I'm about to lose my damn mind."

Jay had been missing for two weeks now. It was as if she had vanished into the atmosphere undetected. The mystery of her whereabouts was messing with Zach's head. The last location Jay was known to have been was outside of Miami in a trailer park of all places. Zach dropped down into the recliner and looked out the window. It was a bit cloudy. The weatherman had said there was a thirty percent chance for rain in the late afternoon.

Out of habit, Zach stroked his goatee as he thought about the poor female deputy who had run off with Jay. She'd left two little girls behind to be with a woman who didn't have a heart or conscience. Although the authorities in Florida had ruled the deputy's death a suicide, Jay might as well have pulled the trigger herself. That white chick was another one of her victims. She had been used, abused and played. After Jay turned her out, she was like a druggie itching for a fix. And she obviously did whatever she could to get it which included helping her escape, leaving her children motherless. Deputy Bethany Hardy was dead because like so many before her, she had fallen in love with the wrong woman. Jay had caused that poor chick to lose her mind, but Zach wasn't going out like that.

"Jill!" He got up and hurried out of the room. He trotted down the stairs. "Jill, I'm sorry, baby."

Zach found her and Nahima in the den. Zachary Junior had fallen asleep lying on his mother's lap. The television was on the Disney Channel. Nahima was singing the Handy Manny theme song, but stopped when she saw her uncle. Jill was relaxing quietly on the sectional sofa with her eyes closed.

"I'm sorry, Jill." Zach sat down next to his wife, and wrapped his arm around her shoulders. "I was wrong to yell at you. It's just that I'm so worried about you, the baby and Nahima. Nobody knows where Jay is, and it is driving me *crazy*. Ortega and Franklin call me every day with the same old bullshit. Talking about the FBI is on the case, and she's still hiding out in Florida somewhere. I won't feel that you and the children are safe until they catch that psychotic bitch."

"You mustn't curse in front of the children, Zachary. I'm concerned as well, but we cannot stop living because Jay is at large. Do not take your frustrations with her out on *me*. When we return home this evening, I think you should call the detectives and listen to whatever they have to say. What if they have an update on Jay's whereabouts, eh?" Jill gave Zach his sleeping son, and she rose to her feet. "I'm ready to go now." She reached out her hand. "Come, Nahima, let's go to church, sweetie."

Chapter Fifty-Six

Detectives Franklin and Ortega exited Nina's house with more than just a suspicion that she was with Jay wherever she was. She had been on a two-week vacation from her job, and was due back tomorrow morning. Her roommate, Rick, didn't know where she was and he hadn't heard anything from her. He was sure she wasn't in California with her family because her mother and step sister had called several times asking for her in recent days. Mrs. Lopez seemed worried that she hadn't spoken with Nina in a while.

Ortega slid behind the wheel of the dark sedan and started the engine, but he didn't pull out of the driveway. Franklin scribbled more notes on his pad, and flipped through several pages before he looked at his partner.

"They're together," Ortega said. "Those two are somewhere in Florida hiding out in that trailer park or close by. Someone is helping them."

"Why are you so sure Ms. Lopez and Ms. King are together?"

"I have a hunch right here." Ortega patted his stomach. "Ms. Lopez is head over heels in love with Ms. King. She's *sprung*, and that's a damn shame. Nina Lopez is a *very* sexy woman. I'd gladly spend some time with her if I wasn't a happily married man."

Franklin laughed. "I'm just as happily married as you are, but I'd *fuck* her just to show her what she's been missing. She's too damn fine to be sleeping with a woman instead of a man. Anyway, do you honestly think they're together in South Florida?"

"That's exactly what I think, and if the FBI doesn't find them soon, it'll become more difficult for them to be found. Ms. King is no ordinary woman. She'd make her way across the country, settle down and establish a new identity with Senorita Lopez." Ortega put the sedan in reverse, and backed it out of the driveway.

Franklin took out his cell phone. "I'm gonna call the Florida authorities to put some heat under their asses. They must be stupid down there. It blows my mind that they can't sweep through a trailer park full of hillbillies and thugs and find a couple of dykes. And what the hell is going on with the FBI? Ms. King is probably sitting back laughing at them."

"She sure is…with Ms. Lopez sitting on her lap smiling pretty."

Honey

*****

Keeping Nina and Charlotte apart was becoming more stressful and *expensive*. Jay was burning the candle on both ends, and it was running her ass ragged. But because she needed both of her women, the queen of players had to hustle to keep them satisfied. So twice, sometimes three times a week, Jay left the seclusion of the tiny hideaway up in the hills above Kingston to spend the night with Charlotte at her apartment. She lived east of Runaway Bay. Her place was modest, but clean and a hell of a lot more comfortable than that shitty shanty. The problem was, whenever Jay left Nina alone, it was under the pretense that she was going to work as a bartender at one of the local watering holes. And each morning when she returned home from *working* all night, Ms. Lopez expected her lover to have some money or anything money could buy to make her happy.

On most mornings after leaving Charlotte's warm bed, Jay would have a small wad of cash in her pocket *if* she'd had a hot hand at the casino the night before. She would sit for hours at the roulette table taking her chances with lady luck, puffing Cuban cigars at Coconut Grove Club & Casino. It was an upscale nightclub in Ocho Rios where Charlotte had worked as a hostess for years. When Jay's hand was hot it was hot, but when it wasn't, the cab ride back to the fruit stand at the bottom of the hill from the shanty was a long and dreaded journey. This particular rainy morning was one of those days. The slow windshield wipers swished and swiped, making the most irritating noise as the cab rocked over potholes and debris on the dirt roads outside Kingston.

Jay loosened the elastic band on the big bundle of braids at her nape. She hoped it would help relieve her dull headache. She would never get used to having so much hair on her head. The braids were a part of her new look. Lots of people that she knew when she'd lived on the island before had passed by her without recognizing her face. Jay was happy about that because she didn't want anyone from her past to know she had returned to Jamaica besides Charlotte. She was the only person she trusted. Anyone else would more than likely turn her in to the authorities, and she'd be extradited back to the States.

"Can I stop at the supermarket and grab a few things?" Jay asked the cabbie. "It won't take me long. I'll pay you for waiting."

"No problem, ma'am," the driver said, winking at Jay in his rearview mirror. "No problem at all."

Jay did some quick calculating in her head. They had vegetables in the cooler and lots of fruit too. Nina had been riding her ass about meat which did not include the fried fish she often bought from the dread headed brothers further up in the hills. They fished and sold their catches by day, and fried the excess in big barrels and smoked gunja by night. Jay had just enough money to buy a whole chicken, some rice, cigars and a bottle of Disarrono. She would have to hide the liquor from Nina, though, so she wouldn't start bitching about wasting money. And on top of that, she would go into a long lecture about Jay's liver and stomach. Both were in bad shape because of all the booze she'd guzzled down over the years.

"I'll be right back," Jay told the driver when he pulled in front of the supermarket.

"And I'll be waiting right her, ma'am. No worries."

Jay scurried around the supermarket gathering the few items she needed. She was on her way to the checkout line when she saw a pretty little girl with big bright eyes sitting in a shopping buggy. The child was sucking her thumb and twirling one of her ponytails around her finger. *Angelina*! Jay recognized the cute little face. She ducked behind a stack of cereal boxes and watched Faye toil over the decision to buy oatmeal or cream of wheat for her family. She looked well and her cart was nearly filled to capacity.

Zach must've been working hard to take care of the Bessette brood. That was the only way Faye could have that much damn meat in her shopping cart. She, Orville and their little crumb snatchers were feasting high on the hog, while she and Nina were eating like miserable paupers. Jay's hate rose to another level when Faye dropped two canisters of oatmeal *and* a big ass box cream of wheat into the buggy. She stomped off toward the cashier shaking her head and cursing like a sailor under her breath.

* * * * *

"What did Franklin say?"

Aunt Jackie returned her cordless phone to its cradle, and looked at Zach and Jill. "He thanked me for calling and promised to file a report." She stood up and started pacing nervously between the couch and coffee table. "There's nothing they can do, Zach."

"Say what? This ain't 1955. We're living in the twenty-first century. With all this modern technology, digital this, solar that, GPS devices and microchips, you mean to tell me they can't trace Jay's call?"

Aunt Jackie shook her head, and reached down to lift Zachary Junior from Jill's arms. "That's exactly what the detective said, baby. Nothing showed up on my caller ID screen. We didn't talk for very long. Jay could be anywhere."

"I know, and that's what scares the hell outta me. She could be right around the corner or clean across the country." Zach rubbed his hands down his face. "This is a nightmare."

"Everything is going to be fine, sweetheart," Jill said, rubbing her husband's back. She watched Aunt Jackie pacing and bouncing the baby in her arms. "Please have a seat, Auntie. You must relax."

Zach, Jill and Aunt Jackie sat quietly on the sofa; each buried deep in their thoughts. The only sounds in the den were from the television and Zachary Junior laughing and clapping his hands to a cartoon song.

"It was probably Jay who called us twice in the middle of the night and hung up. Something told me it was her."

"Someone called and breathed in my ear shortly after you left for work this morning, Zachary. I thought nothing of it."

"Why didn't you tell me?"

Jill laced her fingers through his and squeezed. "I told you. I didn't think very much of it. Now I believe it was Jay."

Zach turned to Aunt Jackie. "Please tell me one more time exactly what Jay said. How did she sound? Was there any familiar noise in the background?"

"Like I told you three times already, it was a very short conversation. I answered the phone, thinking it was a telemarketer because nothing registered on the ID screen. As soon as I said hello, Jay started talking. I was too shocked to notice any background noises. She told me she was fine and she misses me. I asked her where she was, but she refused to say. Then she told me that she loved me and to take care of myself."

"And then that bitch had the nerve to tell you to say hello to Jill and me before she ended the call."

"Watch your mouth, nephew. You're not too old for me to take my belt to your behind."

"Don't I get a pass? I'm stressed out! I'll shoot Jay if she comes near my family, Auntie. She's crazy as hell, and the police think she's *dangerous*. Plus, she's desperate right now. Ain't no telling what she'll do to stay outta jail."

"You would actually kill your own sister, Zach?"

"No, I would try to *wound* her to keep her from killing my family or me. It was Jay who wanted *me* dead, remember? Her plan fell through and I don't wanna give her another opportunity to make it happen. She told me she wished *she* had taken me out. I'll never forget that or what she told the undercover officer she wanted to do to my wife. If Jay messes with my family, Auntie, I'll shoot her. I'm sorry, but I swear I will."

Chapter Fifty-Seven

Wallace hung up the phone and stared at Patricia standing at the sink washing dishes. She turned to face him, and dried her hands with a hanging dishtowel. She was anxious to know what Zach's plans were. Patricia was too young to be his son's step mother or a granny to Zachary Junior, but she loved them just the same. There was a strong bond between Zach and his father's wife. They were close and Jill was very much a part of their relationship.

"What did Zach say?"

"He's going to take Jill to Jamaica to celebrate their first wedding anniversary. Then after a few days, he's going to leave her and the baby there with her family. He'll send for them *after* Jayla is apprehended and put back behind bars.

"How does Jill feel about that?"

"He hasn't told her yet. She's busy preparing for a major dance performance scheduled for this weekend. He plans to tell her about the trip to Jamaica and her extended stay after that."

"That sucks. Jill won't be happy about that at all. I know Zach is only doing what he thinks is best for her and the baby. But he can't make important decisions about their marriage without first discussing them with his wife."

"That's exactly what I told him, but he believes his way is the *only way* to deal with the situation. He doesn't want to ruin Jill's show. She's been working hard. That's why he decided to wait to tell her about his plans. They've been getting those aggravating phone calls around the clock, especially at night. Zach is convinced it's Jayla torturing them. And because he's uncertain of her whereabouts, he feels Jill and the baby will be better off in Jamaica for the time being."

"Maybe Zach is right, but I still think Jill should have some say in the matter. Being separated from her husband indefinitely, for *whatever* reason, won't be easy. I wouldn't want you to take me somewhere and dump me off on a few days' notice. I'd be mad as hell."

"I would never send you away. I'd be too miserable without you."

Patricia smiled and turned to the sink again to resume washing the dishes. Wallace admired her figure from behind. After fifteen years of marriage, the mere sight of her still turned him on. Healthy eating and Pilates three times a week kept Patricia's perfect size eight body in great shape. Even at sixty-two, somehow

Honey

Wallace was still able to hang with his gorgeous wife who was twenty years his junior. They took long walks together regularly, and shot eighteen holes of golf from time to time. Their sex life was amazing and even in her prime, Wallace was proud he still had the stamina to satisfy Patricia at least three nights every week. He didn't need Viagra or any other drug either.

He tiptoed across the kitchen to stand behind Patricia. He slid his hands around her slender waist and kissed her neck. He felt her shudder in response to his affection. Patricia moaned when Wallace's hands found their way under her purple tank top to tease her hardened nipples. His erection came instantly, and pressed against her firm backside. Patricia turned around, sloshing warm soapy water all over the floor, her aroused husband and herself. When she raised her wet hands to caress Wallace's shoulders, his mouth sought hers out and the mating of tongues began, intensifying the passion stirring between them.

Patricia gasped when Wallace suddenly broke the kiss to lift her. He placed her on the counter top next to the sink.

"Where is Wallace Junior," he asked and planted a few quick kisses on Patricia's neck.

"Um…he…he's with my sister and her boys. He'll be home by eight."

Wallace wedged his body between Patricia's smooth thighs, and pulled her forward on the counter. He moved his lips from her neck down to her breast and lifted her shirt. He yanked it up over her head and flung it on the countertop. "We have thirty minutes," he announced, tugging at the drawstring on Patricia's cotton shorts. He relieved her of them easily, along with her red lace thongs.

Wallace let out a low growl when Patricia massaged his erection through his gray sweat pants seconds before she snatched them down. They dropped to his ankles. He took off his t-shirt and let it fall to the floor.

"I don't think you need these boxers, Reverend King." Patricia smiled. "Let me help you get rid of them so I can make you shout hallelujah." In one motion, she pulled down Wallace's plaid boxers, exposing the part of his anatomy that made him all man.

"Mmm, welcome home, Reverend King," she whispered hoarsely when she felt her husband ease inside her, filling her sweet spot completely. She began a slow and methodical grind right on the cool granite countertop much to Wallace's approval.

He closed his eyes as his body answered with fluid, purposeful strokes. "Hallelujah!"

* * * * *

"Who are you calling, Jay? I see you dialing the phone all the time, but I've never heard you to talk to anyone. What's up with that?"

Jay slid the cell phone back inside her jeans pocket. "I'm trying to remember the number at my old job. I'm thinking about getting us a room there for the weekend. I really want you to see the place. It makes the Seven Seas look like a Motel 6. It's fabulous. All the restaurants are classy. I wanna take you to a romantic dinner at Café Rhapsody."

Nina was miserable, wrapped in a floral sarong secured snuggly around her big boobs. She'd lost a sizable amount of weight since living on the island in hiding, but she remained top-heavy. Her hair was brittle and dry due to lack of proper conditioning. The mosquitoes up in the hills had a fondness for her deeply-tanned skin. Every day, in Nina's eyes, Jamaica looked more like a scene from Survivor: The *Caribbean Hell Hole* rather than the tropical island paradise Jay had boasted about before they arrived. There were no rich and beautiful sights, sounds and activities of Jamaica up in those damn hills. Life had been so rough that Nina had been thinking about reaching out to her cousin Juan in Mexico. He could help her abandon Jay and their horrible living conditions. At least there she would have a decent place to live with him and his partners in crime, and she damn sure wouldn't be starving.

"Yeah, if my tips stack up tonight, I'll book us a basic room at the resort for two nights. We'll eat well and make love in a *real* bed. You'd like that wouldn't you?"

Nina snapped from her wishful thinking. She fanned her face with her hand and pulled long and hard on her cigarette. She blew out a stream of smoke. "Anything would be better than this fucking match box. If you'd let me get a job, maybe we could find us an apartment or a small house and move out of this dump. Shit, I'll clean houses or wait tables. I just wanna get away from these damn mosquitoes and crickets. I'm tired of being poor. I didn't sign on for this, Jay."

"I know, baby. Be patient with me. Things are gonna get better. Wish me good luck tonight so I can make enough money to treat you to a nice weekend at the resort. Now give me some sugar." Jay leaned over and smacked Nina's lips with hers. "Let me get down to the fruit stand to catch a cab. I'll see you tomorrow."

Nina waved her hand and sucked her teeth to dismiss Jay. Without a television, the little radio was her only entertainment. Every now and then she would hang out with the friendly pot smoking fishermen up the hill at one of their nightly fish fries. She'd flirt with them, and drink lots of their liquor. On occasion, after taking a few hits of the strong gunja from their bong, Nina would dance until her high faded away. Then back down the hill she'd go to the lonely shanty and the raggedy radio hissing and crunching over reggae classics.

Chapter Fifty-Eight

"Jill, if you weren't already my wife, I'd make a move on you tonight and try to woo you, baby. You were sexy as hell up on that stage. I was mesmerized. I want you to do that *split* for me when we get home."

Dex pushed Zach out of the way so he could hug Jill and kiss her on both cheeks. Then he handed the woman who had fascinated the audience with her moves a bouquet of colorful fresh cut flowers. "You brought the house down tonight. I didn't know you could move like that. Great job, sweetie."

"Thank you Dex." Jill inhaled the flowers. Her hands were already clutching two dozens of long stem red roses from her hubby and son. "They smell so good."

"*Girrrrl*, you shut it down tonight! Oh my God, Jill! Zariah told us you were an amazing dancer, but you were *unbelievable* up there. And what you did with those older women was out of this world!" Ramona threw her arms around her friend.

"You were awesome," Felecia whispered with tears in her eyes. She pecked Jill on the cheek. "You took my breath away."

"This little boy is very proud of his mommy and so am I." Aunt Jackie smiled and shook her head as she bounced Zachary Junior in her arms. "I thought I was going to explode when you did that running leap thing and landed on your toes. The audience went crazy!"

When the baby reached for Jill, she gladly exchanged him for the flowers and kissed him on his little nose.

"Auntie Jill, I wanna be a dancer like you. You gotta teach me how to spin and jump in the air."

Jill looked down and winked at Nahima. "I will teach you how to dance for sure."

Zach checked his watch. "Hey, y'all, we need to hit the road. We have 9:15 dinner reservations at Geno's in the Alley." He took Zachary Junior from Jill and heaved him over his shoulder. Clutching his wife's hand, he said, "Come on, Mademoiselle, your husband is gonna take you and your fan club out to celebrate your kick-ass performance. I've got something special for you when we get home."

"Don't fall for that trick, Jill. My boy ain't got nothing special for you. He wants something *from* you. I hope my god son stays up all night long to block him."

"Shut up, Dex! You always…"

"Jillian, my dear," Mrs. Scott approached the group and interrupted. She honored Jill with a low graceful curtsy. "You were magnificent! There are some people I'd like you to meet."

Jill looked at everyone around her, still holding Zach's hand. "My family and I were about to leave for a late dinner. My husband made reservations at a restaurant."

"Go ahead with your family, sweetheart. I've scheduled a ten o'clock meeting at the academy Monday morning with you and some very important people on the Atlanta arts scene. They thought your performance was spectacular and your choreography too. Those gold lame palazzo pants you designed for the young women were a huge hit. The creative heavyweights in this town think you're the total package, darling. They're dying to talk to you."

"I'm so very flattered. I don't know what to say." She looked in Zach's eyes after he gave her hand a slight pull. "Monday morning it is, Madame Helena."

It was fine dining at its best and the atmosphere was festive. Zach was extremely proud of Jill. For weeks he'd heard her bouncing and humming around the house, practicing for the academy's spring production, all while taking care of their home. It was a special night for her, and he wanted more than anything for her to enjoy every minute of it with the people she loved most. The two new charms he'd purchased for her bracelet to congratulate her would top off her big night. Then he was going to make love to her for the last time ahead of the storm he knew was on the horizon. Zach almost choked on a buttery lobster bite, when he realized that tonight could very well be his last time making love to Jill *ever*. His plan to leave her and the baby in Jamaica for a while had the potential to ruin their marriage. He drained the champagne in his flute, and reached for the bottle chilling in a bucket of ice on the table. He poured himself a refill.

"To my beautiful wife," Zach announced, raising his flute. Everyone around the table followed his lead with their beverage of choice in hand lifted in a toast. "Jill, you were poetry in motion tonight. I'm a blessed brother to have such a talented and *fine* wife. You're a great mother to Zachary Junior and there isn't a dancer in the universe who can work it the way you do. Congratulations on an awesome performance, baby. Our son and I love you to death."

"Here, here!" Dex yelled.

Felecia was way past tipsy. She threw her champagne back and grinned. "Yeah, you worked it, girl!"

Glass touching glass chimed all around the table. The whole crew spoke words of congratulations to Jill in some form or the other. Even Nahima raised her glass of orange juice in a toast to her auntie.

"Thank you," Jill said before she leaned over and kissed Zach on his lips a little longer than she'd intended to. He held her in place with his arm secured around her tiny waist. She managed to wiggle free. "There are others at the table, Zachary. Let us not be rude."

"He can't help it. He's been rude since the day I met him back in college. Zach ain't thinking about nobody but you, Jill. Everything he does is all for you and my god son. Always remember that."

* * * * *

The thrill of going back to Jamaica for a short visit with her family made it hard for Jill to sit still in her first-class seat. Just thinking about her parents' initial reaction to meeting their first grandchild excited her. In just thirty minutes, the plane would land in her home country where she would be reunited with her family after exactly one year since their last visit. The trip would also include a small party to celebrate hers and Zach's first wedding anniversary.

"Your mommy is one blessed woman, little one," she bounced Zachary Junior up and down on her lap. He giggled and babbled. "I'm going home to see my mommy, papa, all my brothers and baby sister. They are going to love you. Yes, they are! Then we will dance and eat good Jamaican food to celebrate our wedding day. It falls on my twenty-fifth birthday. Sounds like lots of fun, eh?"

"Your son is mighty handsome, ma'am. How old is he?"

Jill smiled at the handsome flight attendant. He didn't look a day over twenty-one. "He is eight months old. He eats a lot, ya know? That is why he is so *round*. He appears to be much older, eh?"

"He's a bit chubby, but he's a good-looking fellow." The young man smiled at Jill before he walked away.

"Give me my son." Zach was wide awake. He pried Zachary Junior from Jill's clutches. "How're you gonna flirt with that young dude with your husband sitting beside to you?"

"Eh, Zachary, do not be ridiculous! I was not flirting with him at all. He noticed what a handsome son we have who happens to look just like his *father.* He only wanted to know the child's age, and I told him. Are you *jealous*, my dear husband?" Jill placed her hand over her mouth to stifle a laugh.

"Hell yeah! I'm getting old and fat and you're young and sexy. Punks like him are bold to step to you with me sitting right next to you thinking, I'm your big brother or uncle. He had to know we're together. Little Zach is a miniature version of me. He was flirting with you, and I don't like that shit."

"It doesn't matter how old, fat or bald you become, Zachary. I will always love *you* and nobody else but you. There isn't a man alive or to come who could steal me away from you, sweetheart. Don't you know that?"

The knowing look he gave Jill when he reached over subtly and rubbed her thigh sent a crystal clear message to that part of her that only *he* was privy to. The wink that followed caused her to writhe in her seat.

"I know you love me and you're faithful to our marriage," Zach said sincerely. "I'm just not down with other brothers checking you out. I don't want them fantasizing about doing things to you that are reserved only for me. You're clueless about the affect your presence has on men, baby."

"I don't care about other men's opinions of me, Zachary. They see me with their *eyes*. You see my heart, which will belong only to you until the day I die. Put your jealousy away. There is no need for it here."

Chapter Fifty-Nine

Dex thought about Zach and Jill on their first wedding anniversary. They were celebrating with their family and friends in Kingston. They'd mentioned a fish fry up in the hills near the small Baptist church where their ceremony took place. The same beach chateau at the Blue Lagoon would be their home for the next few days.

Abriah ran into the den giggling with Ramona chasing after her out of breath.

"Whoa! What's up, little mama?" Dex patted his baby girl's back when she jumped into his arms. She laid her face on his chest.

"Come on here, little girl! It's past your bedtime."

Dex waved Ramona off. "Give her a few more minutes, baby. She wants to spend some time with her daddy."

Ramona fell onto the sofa next to her husband. "I want her to go to sleep because *I* was thinking about spending some time with *her* daddy tonight."

"Good night princess." Dex lifted Abriah from his chest. "It's past your bedtime." He kissed her cheek and handed her to Ramona. "Daddy will see you in the morning."

Ramona licked her lips and winked at her husband. "I'll meet you in the Jacuzzi in fifteen minutes."

As Dex made his way upstairs to his and Ramona's love nest, his thoughts of Zach and Jill resurfaced. He hated it, but after tonight, all of their celebrating and romantic moments in Jamaica would come to a screeching halt. Zach hadn't told Jill that he'd be leaving her and Zachary Junior on the island for their safety while he returned home. The timing never seemed right in the days leading up to their trip. Plus, Zach would've had a hard time getting Jill on the plane if she'd had the slightest idea they would be separated at the end of their vacation. Dex closed his eyes and released a deep breath as random scenarios of how Jill might react to the news played out in his head. They all were pretty ugly.

It didn't even matter now. Zach was prepared for the fallout, or so he thought. He was going to do what was best for his family. The mysterious calls had increased. And the fool had started hitting Zach up on his cell phone early in the morning before work and in the evenings. Everyone was convinced it was Jay now, even Detectives Franklin and Ortega. But that theory didn't mean shit because they couldn't determine where the calls were coming from. Zach was looking forward to a long overdue meeting with FBI agents the day after he was scheduled to return home. They'd hinted around about possibly installing a high-tech tracking device on both his phones to detect the origin of the calls. It was technology used by the U.S. military, CIA, FBI, and the Department of Homeland Security. It would require top-ranking government approval before it could be used in an ordinary civilian case.

Dex stripped down to nothing, and turned on the water in the Jacuzzi. After he'd secured the drain and adjusted the temperature to warm, he reached for the papaya and cherry scented bath crystals on the shelf. The combination of fruit and chocolate was fitting for every episode of intense foreplay. So he lit three, chocolate aromatic candles before he turned out the lights.

"You said fifteen minutes," he said when he felt Ramona's naked body press against the back of his. "That was more like five."

"Are you complaining?"

"No complaints here, baby. As in the words of the late, great musical genius, Marvin Gaye: Let's get it on."

* * * * *

"It's good for ya, eh?"

Nina coughed hard, and fanned the strong smoke she'd just released from her lungs. The gunja from her fishermen buddies tonight was more potent than any of the other batches she'd ever tried. After just two hits, her mind began to float, giving her an uncontrollable case of the giggles. She passed the gigantic, green bong to Leo, her favorite guy of the group. She nodded slowly to answer his question. The Jamaican herb was *kicking*. Leo was sweet on Nina. Her womanly senses told her so. Whenever she hung out with him and his buddies, he treated her kind. He always allowed Nina the first hit on his pipe, and let her drink all the liquor she wanted. And he never let her walk down the hill alone after a fish fry and dance.

Leo offered Nina the bong again after he took a long, deep pull from it. He exhaled and watched her suck in the powerful mood altering herb. She swallowed hard and closed her eyes.

"This is some *good* shit!" Nina released smoke through her nostrils.

"Yeah, baby, it is *good*." Leo winked at Nina and took her by the hand. "Let's go party! Me friends are fryin' most of our catch at a weddin' party tonight. It's for a native merchant sailor. His pikin and her American husband married for one year ago today. They come back to Jamaica where they wedded to remember that day. Please come with Leo, eh? This poor Jamaican mon wanna dance with a pretty lady tonight."

Nina's fresh high, combined with her need to have some fun, squashed all thoughts of Jay. Jay was constantly warning her about being friendly with the locals. She was afraid it would lead to them being discovered as criminals on the run from the States. The fear of that had held Nina prisoner long enough.

"Let's go, Leo! I deserve to have some fun."

Leo stood and tried to pull Nina up with him. They stumbled back to their seat on a pile of brick blocks and started laughing. They were on cloud nine, feeling mellow as hell. This time, Leo stood alone and reached down to help Nina to her feet. She struggled to stand, still snickering uncontrollably. She looked at Leo through blurry eyes.

"Alright, I'm ready to shake my big sexy ass to some funky reggae, mon!" Nina doubled over and laughed deep from her belly.

Leo wrapped his arm around her waist then eased his hand down to palm her ass. "Yeah, baby, let's go."

* * * * *

"Damn!" Jay sucked her teeth and slumped down in her chair. "This ain't my night." She shuffled quickly through the few bills she had left, counting them repeatedly like they would magically multiply if she did it enough times.

"Are you in ma'am?" The wheel captain asked.

Jay looked at the white dude like he was crazy. He'd watched her wad of cash slowly disappear over the course of three hours. She wanted to spit in his face for trying to lure her into placing a bet she couldn't win. "Nah, I'm out."

Jay removed a cigar from the breast pocket on her yellow dress shirt and wedged it between her teeth. She needed to find Charlotte to beg her for a loan from her pocket full of tips. The club was packed, hot and popping tonight. It was spring, the time of year when tourist from all over the globe flocked to the island for a good time. Charlotte probably had stashes of cash hidden all over her body. If Jay could pin her down for a few minutes, she'd gladly relieve her of the bundle tucked between her titties. She scanned the crowd.

"You searching for me, baby?"

Jay did a brisk about face, genuinely startled by the deep voice that had just whispered in her ear. The warm breath that had tickled her sensitive lobe and neck caused a chill to run up her spine. Her eyes roamed slowly over the baritone stranger from head to toe. He was a tall, dark and handsome one even by her anti-men standards. The scent of his cologne was a combination of woodsy and sweet. It was definitely expensive and possibly rare, and his smile was bright and alluring enough to tilt any woman's world. But this was Jay, and Jay wasn't remotely attracted to any member of the human race who'd been endowed with a *penis*.

"Hi," *Mr. Velvety Voice* greeted, and took Jay by her hand. He lifted it to his lips and kissed the back of it tenderly while his eyes bore directly into hers. "I was admiring your beauty from the black jack table. I take it you're a fan of the lucky wheel. I never did get the gist of that particular game. Would you care to teach me?" He flashed a perfect set of pearly white teeth.

Who does this motherfucker think he's talking to? Jay snatched her hand from his and gave him a fake smile.

"You play and I'll gladly pay," the mysterious stranger added smoothly and displayed a spread of cash. "I could learn by watching you."

The money captured Jay's attention and altered her attitude on sight. "I'd be more than happy to show you around the wheel, um…I'm sorry. I didn't catch your name."

"My name is Pierce Murdoch. And what name does a lovely lady like you go by?"

Jay did a visual sweep around the club. Charlotte was still missing in action. She wet her lips with the tip of her tongue, and batted her eyes; two gestures she hadn't offered a male since Tyrone Williams the third, back in the sixth grade. "I'm *Simone*."

Pierce hooked his right arm, inviting Jay to take hold. "Shall we?"

Jay accepted the arm of Pierce Murdoch, her naïve unanticipated prey, and allowed him to escort her to the roulette table.

Chapter Sixty

"Come on, pretty lady. Leo thought you wanted to dance."

Nina couldn't move. The sight of Zach and Jill dancing inside a large circle of people had paralyzed her. She dug her heels deeper in the dirt when Leo pulled her hand, trying to lead her into the crowd. Everyone was bumping and grinding to the Deejay's music. She yanked her hand free, and leaned against a tree out of view from the partygoers.

"Um…wait a minute, Leo." Nina rubbed her stomach and wrinkled her face. "I feel like I'm coming down with something. Maybe I shouldn't have smoked so much of the weed after drinking all that rum." She leaned her back against the tree, and slid down it to sit on the ground.

"Wait here." Leo patted the top of Nina's head, and turned to walk away.

She latched on to the back of his t-shirt and pulled hard. "Hey, where are *you* going?"

"Leo will bring ya sumtin' to eat. You will feel much better after ya eat sumtin'. Food will soak up the liquor in ya belly. The haze will soon pass over."

"Unh-unh, I don't think I can eat or drink anything right now. I just need to go back down the hill to my house and get some rest." She reached her arms up, and turned on puppy dog eyes for Leo. "I need you to walk me home. I can't make it without you."

Nina was no dummy. She knew her little act was working on Leo. That, along with her feminine charm, was breaking him down. All those moonlight dances they'd shared with his crotch grinding into her ass and V zone, had turned him on. Many nights she'd felt his hard dick pulsating against her body while they partied under the influence of booze and herb. Nina had let Leo get his thrills because he was sweet and harmless. And besides that, she wanted him to remember all those free touches whenever she asked for a favor in return. Nina moaned and frowned again.

"Leo will walk ya home, my dear, but I'll get the food first, eh? You can eat it later." He left Nina resting on the ground under the tree while he fixed her a plate of seafood from Zach and Jill's anniversary party.

Unbelievable! It was the only word Nina could come up with to describe the situation she now found herself in. She and Jay had escaped from the States without a glitch, leaving all their problems behind. How the hell did the two people that were responsible for all their troubles end up in Jamaica too? Nina watched Jill smiling happily, swinging her son in her arms while she swayed from side to side to the music. Zachary Junior was a very beautiful baby, looking just like his father. Zach was behind Jill with his arms wrapped around her waist, doing a two-step to the beat. He whispered something in her ear. Whatever he said had a visible effect on her. Jill closed her eyes, and her smile widened like the words were touching her in private places that lit her fire.

"Ugh!" Nina growled, and kicked at the dirt. She rested the back of her head against the tree's dry bark. "I can't believe they're on the island *celebrating,* while we're here in hiding, living like paupers."

Nina was startled when the crowd at the party started cheering and clapping. Her eyes popped open. The music had stopped, and everyone was singing, dancing and clapping in a big circle around Zach and Jill. The song's lyrics were repetitive and had a traditional reggae vibe. Even the little boys, dressed in cute party outfits, knew the words. They were clapping and bouncing around Zach and Jill too, singing their hearts out. Nina couldn't take another second of the happy scene. It had robbed her of her appetite anyway. She jumped up and ran back down the hill to the house.

* * * * *

"Mmm, your skin is so soft." Pierce fondled Jay's breast through her shirt as they sat in his rental car. When he tried to kiss her lips, she jerked her head away. "What's the matter, baby? I thought you were going to show me a good time." He unbuttoned the top two buttons on her shirt and tried to ease his hand inside to touch her bare breast. She forced his hand down to his lap.

Jay was totally unfazed and bored to death by Pierce's petting. His hands roaming all over her body did nothing to turn her on. But with a stack of cash they'd won at the roulette wheel stashed securely inside her wallet, it was time to pay the piper. Pierce had allowed Jay to keep more than half of their eighteen hundred dollar winnings in good faith that she'd accompany him back to his hotel room for *sex.* It would've been a reasonable exchange if she'd ever had any real intentions of keeping her part of the deal. And it would've been the first time Jay had ever fucked a man. But it wasn't going to happen; at least not willingly so.

More than ready to get the dull event over with, Jay reached over and handled the big, hard bulge between Pierce's thighs. It was thick and rock solid, pushing against the black linen of his expensive shorts. *This bastard is hung like a fucking horse!* Jay discovered as she performed a gentle massage on his dick. It grew bigger with each stroke of her hand. She unzipped Pierce's shorts and released the only button securing them around his waist. He squirmed and moaned when her hand slid under the waist band of his underwear. The dark, smooth flesh covering his manhood was warm. She fully exposed it. Pierce wasn't prepared for her wet, hot mouth when she dipped her head to his lap and swallowed him whole. He groaned and twitched as Jay went to work on him. She took her time giving head with expertise, slithering her tongue skillfully up and down to add the perfect amount of pressure, increasing his pleasure.

"Oooh shit!" His voice had grown deep and raspy. "Yeah, baby, suck Daddy's dick!" He pressed the back of Jay's braid covered head, smashing her face deeper into his crotch. "Suck it, bitch! Suck it! Suck my big, black dick!"

Pierce's entire body stiffened. He wailed like a man about to take flight for the moon. He was out of control about to cum. Jay eased her hand around his waist, and slid his share of the money from his pocket. She decreased the suction her mouth was applying to his dick. He was seconds away from spilling warm semen inside her mouth.

"*Ouch!* Ugh…ugh…y-you…you…bitch…you *bit* me!" Pierce screamed and flopped forward in his seat in excruciating pain. His head hit the steering wheel with a loud thud. "Shit! I…I t-think I'm bleeding! Aaah!"

Jay had bolted from the car already, leaving the door open. She was half way down the street, and still running like the wanted fugitive she was. Behind her she could hear Pierce screaming continuously and cursing in agony. Jay waved down a cab and hopped inside.

"Where ya goin', ma'am?" the driver asked.

"Runaway Bay"

* * * * *

"Where the hell have you been?" Nina asked. She'd been sitting in the chair next to the door all morning listening to the radio, and waiting for Jay to arrive. "It's almost noon."

Jay brushed past her, and dropped down on the lopsided sofa. "I had a long night, baby, and all I wanna do right now is sleep."

"*Sleep*? You ain't about to go to sleep. We've got problems, honey."

Jay lay down on the sofa on her back, and closed her eyes. "We'll talk about whatever problems we have after my nap. She reached into her breast pocket, and pulled out a one hundred dollar bill. "Here, this should make you feel better."

Nina took the money and stuffed it in her cleavage. Then she folded her arms across her breast. "Thanks, but money can't fix our situation. Zach and Jill are in Jamaica celebrating their wedding anniversary. I saw them last night. I almost shitted in my clothes."

"How do you know it was them? I'm sure you only saw them from afar."

"Jay, I ain't no damn dummy! I saw your brother, his wife and their son partying last night with a bunch of people. I went up the hill to get some fish. The guys invited me to an outdoor dance. They had sold some fish to a merchant sailor. He was throwing a party for his daughter and her *American* husband."

Jay sat up and looked at Nina. She was shocked. "You went?"

Nina shook her head and took a seat next to Jay. "I was about to, but I noticed Zach on the spot before I got close enough for him or anyone else to see me. I left."

"Ain't that some shit?"

"It is. We're here trying to survive, and they're over here partying and having fun. Now we've gotta lay low for a while. Ain't no telling how long they'll be here. We can't risk getting caught, Jay. If Zach or Jill sees either one of us, all hell's gonna break loose. And before we know anything, we'll be back in the States serving hard time in the pen."

* * * * *

Jill turned her back to Zach when he rubbed her face. She had slept with Zachary Junior in his room the night before, and they were still cuddling in bed. After celebrating and spending time with her family for five days, Zach had finally told her that only he would be returning home to Atlanta. His flight was scheduled to leave in six hours, and things between them were worse than they'd ever been. Last night, after Zach broke the news to Jill, she threatened to divorce him if he followed through with his plan. But he stood his ground, believing his decision was in the best interest of their safety. It broke his heart when Jill cried and begged him not to separate their family. And his heart was still aching.

"Jill, your breakfast is getting cold. The baby needs to eat too. Don't you think you should wake him so we can have breakfast together?"

Jill lifted the baby and kissed him all over his chubby face. "Rise and shine, little one," she whispered in his ear. "Your daddy wants you to wake up and eat breakfast with him."

"And you too, Jill."

Jill ignored Zach's statement. Zachary Junior squirmed and stretched his little limbs. "Good morning," she said when he opened his eyes and smiled at her.

Zach reached for the baby and Jill handed him over without a fight. Then she lay down again with her face to the wall.

"Jill, please come and eat with us. I don't know when we'll be able to share another meal together." Zach stood above the bed with the baby in his arms and waited patiently for Jill to speak or move. Any reaction, good or bad, would've been fine at that point, but she didn't say a word. "Jill, you may hate me right now, but I still love you no matter what. I'm only doing what any responsible husband and father would do to protect his family."

Chapter Sixty-One

Two men who had been best friends for nearly two decades could always detect when something wasn't quite right in the other's life. When they'd spoken over the phone the night before, Zach had lied to Dex. He told him that Jill wasn't angry about him leaving her and the baby in Jamaica with her family while he headed back to Atlanta. But now that they were together, face to face, guzzling down bottles of their choice brew, the truth was spilling out. Zach's nine-bottle buzz had him testifying like a sworn witness. Dex was sitting across the kitchen table from him just as tipsy, taking it all in.

"W-what...what...what if they never find Jay and that half-Mexican chick? You gonna leave Jill and my god son in Jamaica *forever*?"

"Hell nah!"

"Then what's your plan, smart ass?" Dex drained his beer and started searching through the mountain of ice in the cooler for another one. "I need a fresh bottle for this," he slurred.

"If the FBI doesn't find Jay in three months, I'm gonna put this house on the market, and buy a new one in Alpharetta or Roswell. Hell, anywhere outside of the ATL will do. I'll head north because I gotta keep Jill and the baby safe."

"Did you say three months?"

Zach nodded and closed his eyes. "Yep."

"Jill ain't gonna stand for that. She'll stop being sad and lonely after a while. Then she'll turn bitter and resentful. That's when you'll lose her, Zach. Trust me. Three months is a *long* time."

"I know that. It's a long time for me too, Dex. I..."

"Hold up! Let me finish. Remember Jill didn't wanna be left behind in the first place. *You* made the decision without considering her feelings. Did you forget what happened the last time y'all were separated? Jill was flirting with death. She could've miscarried your child, she was so bad off."

"Okay, you know everything, Dex. You've got all the answers." Zach placed his empty beer bottle on the table, and leaned back in his chair. "What the hell do you suggest I do?"

"I think you should go back to Jamaica and get your family. Rent an apartment for them here, but away from this area in a gated community. Anything will be better than what you've already done. Just think about it, and make a decision as soon as possible before it's too late."

"Before it's too late for what?"

"Look, man. Jay has been trying to make you lose your mind for months now. Please don't allow her to cause you to lose your family too."

* * * * *

Jay ended her phone call and rolled over to stare at Nina's curious face. She gathered her naked body in her arms and started rubbing the smooth flesh on her ass. "They've checked out. Zach and Jill have left the island, baby. Our lives can return back to normal. I can go back to work tonight and make some money."

"Are you sure, Jay?"

"Were you not listening to my conversation with the clerk at the Blue Lagoon? She couldn't tell me when they checked out, but it must've been within the past forty-eight hours. Charlotte's cousin saw Zach, Jill and their son eating lunch by the pool Wednesday. Another maid cleaned their chateau Thursday, and all of their things were still in place. When I called the chateau direct yesterday, no one answered either time. So I called the front desk just now, and the clerk said no one named Zachary or Jillian King was registered at the resort. They're gone. You should be glad."

"I am. But I'm still gonna lay low for a few more days just in case they only changed hotels or something."

"That's up to you. I'm going to work tonight. But while I'm here, why don't we play a little sex game?" Jay rolled on top of Nina and gave her a sloppy wet kiss on the mouth. "You wanna play the mean pimp and the nasty ho?" She grabbed a hand full of Nina's long, thick hair and yanked hard.

"Ow! Ease up, Jay. That hurts!"

Jay pinched one of Nina's nipples with her thumb and middle finger, applying unbearable pressure. "I want it to hurt. That's what you get for being a bad little ho." Jay laughed like a possessed person. She tugged on Nina's tresses again, and slapped her hard on her thigh. It brought tears to her eyes.

"Jay…" Nina croaked. Words escaped her when she felt Jay's teeth clamp down on her other nipple, first gently, then ferociously. "*Yesss*, Jay, that's it!"

It was Nina's turn to yank Jay's hair. She grabbed a handful of her braids when she slithered down her body to bury her face in the moist, hairy place between her thighs. Jay breathed in deeply, taking in the potent scent of Nina's love juice. It was flowing like a water fall. With soft flicks of her tongue and gentle grazes with the edge of her teeth, she teased Nina's hardened clit unmercifully. Nina's moaning and twisting turned Jay on so much that her body almost lost control too soon. She straddled Nina, placing her saturated vagina on top of hers. The grinding began with a slow and smooth rhythm. Hair against hair and wetness to wetness, they mated; creating an erotic dance. Their synchronized climaxes drained all their energy and put them right to sleep.

* * * * *

Zach called Jill twice a day, *every* day to make sure she and Zachary Junior were okay. Being separated from them was painful and stressful, but he still believed he'd done the right thing. Jill and the baby were safer in Jamaica as long as Jay was still on the run. Zach couldn't take a chance with their safety no matter what. Even though the separation had caused a major rift in his marriage, at least his wife and son were out of harm's way. Nothing was more important to him than protecting them. That would always be his main priority.

There was one good thing that came out of the separation. Jill was teaching dance at Royal Rhythms, her childhood studio. She worked alongside her old teacher, Madame Katherine Chapelle. Three days a week Jill taught girls and boys, ages eight to fourteen basic dance poses, moves, routines, spacing and formations. Zach could tell by their daily conversations that she was enjoying working with the children in her home country. Jill made sure no girl or boy was turned away because their family couldn't afford to pay her their fees. She simply paid the money herself. In a nutshell, she worked for free, and paid for the lessons she taught her young students.

The only times Zach could hear the hint of a smile in Jill's voice during their daily calls were when she talked about how well her siblings and Zachary Junior played together and the progress of her dance students. She cherished the time she spent with her family and dance students, but her heart was in Atlanta. Jill wanted to be home with her husband, and she told him that every night before she went to bed. And if the FBI received approval to use the high-tech tracking device in their case to hunt Jay down, Jill's wish could soon come true.

* * * * *

"Say something, Madame Katherine. Don't you think it's a brilliant idea? Sure, it will take weeks of hard work and long hours here creating the choreography, but it can be done. I believe the children are up to it, and I am devoted to preparing them. *Pleeease*, I beg you, give me your blessing."

Jill stood still facing the old woman perched on a wooden cane. There was noticeable hunch in her back from years of dancing and conditioning. Jill held her breath as she watched the woman's facial expression. Madame Katherine, dancer extraordinaire, was considering her proposal to put on a major dance recital. Jill wanted to showcase the talent of the thirty-one students at Royal Rhythms Dance Studio. All she needed was Madam Katherine's approval.

"We don't have the means to produce something as extravagant as what you are speaking of, Jillian. A suitable venue to house the pageant, costumes, and props are not cheap, darling. The profit from ticket sells in a poor country like

Jamaica won't return the money we're bound to spend putting on such a show. We will more than likely end up in the red after all is said and done."

Jill walked in a slow circle around her dance instructor. It would cost a lot of money to put the recital together. She needed to come up with some ideas on how to raise the money. Otherwise, Madame Katherine would not approve of the show.

"I got it! We can *raise* the money to cover the production cost through donations from business owners here and in Atlanta. Dr. Johnson owns his very own medical clinic. Desmond makes lots of money at his nightclub Caribbean Cove and...and...*Gwendolyn Hayes*!" Jill snapped her fingers. "She's the seamstress who designed my wedding gown. Oh, Madame Katherine, she has globs of money. I know she will help us. They all will. I'll set up meetings with these people, and explain to them what we want to do. They'll sponsor our production."

Madame Katherine sat down on the wooden bench in front of a wall of mirrors and handrails. "How are you so sure, Jillian? There are no guarantees in this thing we call life."

"I just believe they will do it for the children. There are good people who are willing to do good things for those in need. The production is for the boys and girls of Jamaica. Who will deny *them* an opportunity to dance?"

Chapter Sixty-Two

Zach left Aunt Jackie's house Sunday evening with a stomach full of good old soul food and a money bag stuffed with cash and checks. Refuge Pentecostal Temple had been the last contributor to make good on its pledge to Royal Rhythms' first ever *major* dance production. Reverend Broadus and the congregation had promised Zach that they would donate one thousand dollars toward the big event. But when First Lady Broadus asked him to join her in the pulpit for the check presentation, his eyes almost popped out of their sockets. The check was for two thousand dollars.

"God had a change of plans, Brother Zach." She'd announced in her prim and proper voice.

He still couldn't get over how much financial support his church had thrown behind Jill's special project in Jamaica. By doubling their pledge, the total of American sponsorship had peaked to fifty-one hundred dollars. Jill had hoped that Umoja Academy, the church, her family and friends could pull in at least three thousand dollars in all. Zach couldn't wait to tell her he had collected much more. She deserved some good news to make her day. But there was just one thing that would make her even happier, and Zach was the only one that could make it happen. He was going to surprise Jill by flying to Jamaica, with his sidekick Nahima, for the dance production. And then he was going to bring her and Zachary Junior home where they belonged with him a few days afterwards.

$$* * * * *$$

"Damn beggars," Jay spat before she crumpled the neatly printed flyer. She threw it to the ground. "They're the worst part of this beautiful island."

Jay was referring to the group of little girls running up and down the street passing out sheets of paper. It was their way of soliciting money, food, clothes or anything free from hardworking Jamaicans and unsuspecting tourists. Jay despised what she called, "poor men's mentality." That's how she described a lot of the locals who panhandled and ran scams for a living instead of finding real jobs to support themselves. At least she *earned* her money, even though it was through gambling. Jay felt justified doing that because she was a wanted woman on the run from the States. She wasn't able to put her education to good use by landing a legitimate job. Bums, like the ones she'd run into begging for loose change or using kids to do it for them, made her sick.

"It is hot as hell this morning." Jay opened a bottle of warm water and sipped it. She'd done okay at the wheel last night, and had spent hours afterwards making Charlotte scream and climb the wall behind her bed. Jay was tired and couldn't wait for a cab to come to take her to the fruit stand.

As if on cue, one of her regular cabbies pulled up to the curb directly in front of her. "Goin' to Kingston, ma'am?"

"Yeah. How fast can you get me there?"

"Hop in. You'll be there safely in no time."

Jay pushed a stack of those pesky flyers onto the floor in back of the cab. Everyone on the island seemed to be distributing them. They were all over the place. Whatever they were advertising didn't mean a damn thing to Jay. She needed all the money she could get her hands on. So she wasn't interested in buying any raffle tickets or making a donation to a school, church or charity. She closed her eyes, and thought about how hard she had to hustle for cash these days. Sucking a man's dick in the front seat of a car was the lowest she had stooped. Luckily, Pierce Murdoch was an engaged American soldier on leave from Stuttgart, Germany. He'd been scheduled to leave Jamaica early the morning after their little rendezvous. That's why she wasn't worried about running into Sergeant Murdoch ever again.

Exhaustion took its toll on Jay during her ride to the fruit stand. A long night of playing too hard had the tendency to do that to a chick. The flyers she'd refused to read were posted on every business shop, abandoned house, church and merchant's stand. Jay didn't see any of them because she was sleeping in coma-like fashion. By the time the cab arrived at the fruit stand, she was snoring like a bear.

"We are here, ma'am!" The cabbie chuckled at his sleeping passenger. "Hello?"

The voice pulled Jay from her sleep. She jerked upright in her seat, and wiped the drool from her face and chin. She paid the driver and exited his cab, longing for her bed. The first thing she saw was one of those damn flyers posted on a tree. The picture of a woman on the front of it grabbed her attention and held it. Lo and behold it was *Jillian Bessette King*. She was in Kingston preparing for a dance extravaganza featuring the students from the Royal Rhythms Dance Studio.

Jay's blood began to boil. A thousand questions crowded her brain at once, but she didn't have an answer for even one of them. She folded the flyer quickly, stuffed it in her pants pocket and hustled up the hill.

"Nina! Nina!" She burst through the door yelling. "Nina, where the hell are you?"

"I'm right behind you. What's wrong? You're screaming like you're crazy." Nina placed the basket of clothes she'd just removed from the clothesline on the floor. She stared at the piece of wrinkled paper Jay was holding in her shaky hand.

"Do you see this shit? Do…you…see…this…*shit?*"

Nina snatched the paper from Jay and looked at it in total shock. "I don't know what to say. Jill is still *here*? Why? I can't believe she stayed in this jungle to do a dance recital with some damn kids. Zach and the baby must still be here too."

"Nah, he's in Atlanta. I know that for sure."

Nina raised her brows curiously. "How the hell would you know that?"

"Let's just say a little bird told me."

Nina stepped to Jay with her hands on her hips. "How come that same little bird didn't tell you Jill was still here on the island too? A bird told you, my ass! How do you know your brother is in Atlanta, Jay?"

"I called his house last night just to make sure. I hung up in face as soon as he picked up." Jay sat down on the sofa. She felt Nina's eyes glued to her. "I needed to know, okay?"

"I guess we're back on house arrest until after the show."

Jay rolled her eyes and sucked her teeth. "Jill ain't gonna put me back on lock down. Jamaica is *my* territory now. I had to come here because of her and Zach. They can have Atlanta, but this island belongs to *me*. Jill needs to stay on her side of town, and I'll stay on mine.

* * * * *

The long hours of practicing and conditioning were taxing on Jill's body, but she was enjoying every minute of it. Then there were the constant meetings with the manager and staff at the Alliance Performing Arts Center in Montego Bay. Every fine detail for the upcoming recital had to be perfect. All the money collected in donations had allowed her to secure the venue and production crew not only for the performance, but also for a week of practices leading up to the show date. She'd also contracted a skillful set designer to build props and create incredible scenes and backdrops to bring the stage to life. With the stylish costumes Gwendolyn Hayes had so graciously designed, the production was going to be off the chain. The seamstress had outdone herself on the dance costumes. They were fit for Broadway dancers. Some of the young girls cried when they looked at themselves in the mirror at the final fitting.

The sixty-five hundred dollars in donations had covered the entire cost of putting the show together with money to spare. Ticket prices had been set at the minimum. Even low income natives could afford to buy them. And for those who couldn't, Dr. Johnson had purchased hundreds of tickets so that anyone that came by Royal Rhythms would not be sent away empty-handed. Now, with just one week before the live production of "Magical Moments in Motion" featuring Kingston's Jillian Bessette King, all that was left for her to do was perfect her solo performance.

Honey

*****

"Just look at that *bitch*, Charlotte!" Jay leaned forward to get a better look. She watched Jill remove a set of keys from her Louis Vitton bag to unlock the front door of the dance studio. A cabbie had just dropped her off and sped away. Students who'd been waiting for Jill followed her inside. "Everyone on the island is catering to that tramp like she's Beyonce or Michelle Obama. That same cabbie drives her here every damn day at the same time. He comes back to pick her up at 6:45 sharp."

Charlotte had no idea Jay had been stalking Jill. Obviously, she'd spotted her ex a few times in town. Royal Rhythms was on a main street. They were bound to pass each other from time to time. But Jay's loose tongue had made an odd confession without her even realizing it. Her hate for Jill had made her a damn *stalker*. Charlotte regretted borrowing her cousin's car to drive Jay to stakeout the dance studio. There was something wrong with the situation. Jay was obsessed with Jill. Her voice shook and dropped in pitch whenever she talked about her. It worried Charlotte. Everything about Jay had changed since she'd learned Jill was back in Jamaica. Charlotte wanted nothing to do with Jay's obsession,

"Jay, you don't need to get all worked up over Jillian. Her time here on the island is short. As soon as her show is over, she'll bid Jamaica farewell, and return home to the States to her husband. Then maybe you can leave the hills so *we* can find a place together. It's our time, baby." Charlotte leaned over from the driver's seat for a kiss.

"Stop it!" Jay turned her face away.

Charlotte started the car's engine and shifted the gear into drive with her foot still on the brake. Jay had pissed her off. Her craziness was out of control.

"Wait a minute, Charlotte. I wanna see something. Who's gonna drive Jill and all those kids to the Alliance Center? Didn't Desmond tell you they were gonna practice there every day until the show?"

"He did, but I'm leaving, Jay. I have grown bored of this…this…this *foolishness*. I won't sit here while you obsess over Jillian. I played second best to her in the past, but I will not do it now. Get out of the car if you care to stay here, but I'm leaving *now*."

Without hesitation, Jay exited the old, red Honda Civic and slammed the door. She kicked it like a spoiled brat before Charlotte stomped on the gas pedal and skidded off. Jay ducked behind an overflowing trash dumpster, and fell to her knees when she heard cars coming. Two white vans were headed down the road in her direction. She sneaked a peek when she heard the doors open and shut. Roy and Littlejohn hopped out to help the young students pile into the two vans. Jay ducked again. A little boy sitting in the front passenger's seat of the first van had spotted her. She stayed out of sight until both vehicles had left, and were far away.

Chapter Sixty-Three

"Mmm, I am in desperate need of a massage, but there is no one here to do it. Then again, because I have no husband on the island to take care of me, I have every right to find a *boyfriend*. I'm over twenty-one now, ya know?" Jill laughed and rolled over closer to her sleeping son in the bed.

"You told me I was the only man for you. Did you lie to me?"

"At the time I told you the truth, but you left me here. Sometimes I feel so lonely and angry. It still hurts very much, Zachary. I've been trying to forgive you, but it's not easy."

"I promise we won't be separated much longer. Like I told you, the FBI installed the tracking device on our home phone and my cell phone the day before yesterday. It's just a matter of time before Jay calls again. No matter where she calls from, it can be traced with certain accuracy. All I have to do is keep her on the line for forty-five seconds or longer, and I know just what to say to make that happen."

Jill yawned. "I sure hope so. I'm exhausted, but I feel much better since my long hot bath. Oliver rubbed my aching feet. He is such a wonderful little brother. He's my personal assistant for the show. He told me something quite funny today."

"And what was that?"

"He swore that he saw *Jay* here on the island hiding behind a garbage container. He says he'll never forget her mean face from the many times she sat in her car outside this house. The woman he saw has very long braids and wears gigantic hoop earrings. Isn't that funny?"

"Yeah, that's funny. Jay wouldn't be caught dead wearing earrings. And long braids are a major no-no. Besides all that, the FBI has her passport. There's no way she could've applied for a new one. And it would've been impossible for Nina to hook her up because she was transferred from that division in the agency."

"Oliver was wrong, and I told him as much. But I couldn't convince him, though."

"That's okay. I don't wanna talk about Jay anymore. What are you wearing?"

* * * * *

Jay walked away from the young thug without a penny to her name. But what she had depleted her prior night's winnings on was more valuable. She loved the feel of the pistol in her grip. It wasn't too heavy or difficult to operate. *Aim and fire*, the dude had told her. He even gave her a simple demonstration. Jay didn't plan to kill Jill. She didn't have the balls for murder. Her goal was to keep her ass off the stage. The show would not go on. Snatching Jill and holding her prisoner for a few days would be easy. Her schedule was like clockwork, branded in Jay's memory. Nothing would go wrong because Jill was too comfortable and care free in Kingston. The chick was clueless and fearless of what awaited her.

Jill had adjusted back into her former environment. Jay had seen her sitting on the front porch of her parent's small home laughing at her son and Angelina who were playing in the dirt. Her four brothers were close by kicking a soccer ball around the clucking chickens and malnourished dog. Jay stood behind an abandoned house and watched Jill for over an hour, even as the sun started to lose its brightness to dusk. She wondered how anyone could be comfortable in a pathetic shanty in Kingston, a five-star resort in Montego Bay and in a suburban community in Atlanta *equally*. Jill was flexible. In contrast, Jay would never get used to the way she was now living, and she had no intention of being poor much longer. Once she kidnapped Jill, she would force her to hand over all of the money from ticket sells and donations for the recital. People all over the island were talking about how business owners in Jamaica and Atlanta had given thousands of dollars to sponsor the event. That money was Jay's ticket off the island. She planned to steal it from Jill so she and Nina could hop on a boat and lay low somewhere for a little while. Then they'd make their way to Mexico and live with Juan, Nina's drug smuggling cousin and his family.

* * * * *

"Okay, Auntie, I'll call you in the morning after I pick up Nahima. I know she'll wanna speak to you before we board our flight. I love you."

Zach placed the receiver in the cradle on the nightstand. He was almost finished packing for his surprise trip to Jamaica. He needed to add a few more t-shirts to his suitcase, but they were in the dryer downstairs. He couldn't wait to see the expression on Jill's face when he showed up at her parents' house unannounced. He hadn't even told Faye or Orville about his plans. The whole Bessette clan would be surprised to see him and Nahima. Only his man, Roy, knew he was coming and Zach had sworn him to secrecy.

He laughed when the phone rang again. Aunt Jackie always called him back seconds after ending a lengthy conversation with him. There was usually something she'd forgotten to say. It was probably some church gossip or something crazy going on in her neighborhood.

"Talk to me, Auntie," Zach answered, still amused by his thought. With the exception of the caller breathing on the other end, there was silence. It was *Jay*.

Every cell in his brain told him so. "I know that's you, Jay. Why don't you get a life and stop fucking with us? You're so damn evil. I can't wait until they catch your psychotic ass. You belong in a jail cell because you're wicked and crazy as hell. That's exactly why Venus and Jill left you."

"Go straight to hell, Zach! Yeah, it's me, *motherfucker*! And ain't nobody gonna catch me. While you're worrying about *me*, you need to check up on your *wifey*. Someone might snatch her ass and make her disappear." Jay broke out in a fit of laughter.

"Hell, I don't give a damn about you! And I ain't worrying about Jill. She's safe and sound and so is our son, you stupid bitch. I just want you to leave us the hell alone. I'm serious as a heart attack. Stay away from me and my family, Jay, or I'll blow your ass away." Zach ended the call with Jay, cursing and screaming like a maniac. Just like he knew he could, he had pushed all the right buttons to make her talk, prolonging the call.

The phone rang again. This time Zach checked the caller ID screen before he answered it. Someone was calling from U. S. Federal Bureau of Investigation.

"Hello?" Zach's heart was beating so hard and fast that it made him dizzy.

"Mr. King, this is agent Adam Wooten of the FBI. We have a location on your sister thanks to you. You did a great job keeping her on the line."

"Thank God. Okay, talk to me. Where is she?"

"She's in Kingston, Jamaica."

G STREET CHRONICLES
A LITERARY DYNASTY

WWW.GSTREETCHRONICLES.COM

Chapter Sixty-Four

Jill squeezed her eyes shut tight, and thought about Zachary Junior. He was giggling, cooing and clapping his little hands when she'd left him in her mother's care earlier that day. Now she wondered if she'd ever see her son again. Even with her eyes closed, tears still escaped and spilled down her face. The ropes Jay had used to tie her wrists behind her back were pressing painfully into her flesh. And whenever she moved, it hurt worse. Jill looked around the small room, hoping to spot a window. If she continued twisting her face and moving her lips, she believed she would eventually loosen the wide strips of duct tape Jay had placed over her mouth.

"What the hell are you looking around for, huh? You ain't going nowhere." Jay squatted next to the chair where Jill sat strapped in by four leather belts. She grabbed a fist full of her hair and pulled her face toward hers. "I'll let you go *after* I get the money. And you can forget about your big dance production, baby. I canceled it."

Jill moaned and shook her head, her tears continuously flowing. The dim room was terribly hot. Sweat poured heavily through her leotards, tights and long skirt. The air was so stale and dry that Jill thought she may pass out at any time. All she could think about was her son and *Zach*. It was him that had insisted that she remain behind in Jamaica out of fear. He thought Jay would somehow harm her and the baby if they had returned to Atlanta. Oh, how wrong he had been about everything. The FBI and local law enforcement believed Jay was still in the States. They had convinced Zach that she was somewhere in Florida. And her daily prank calls had only made matters worse, causing him to separate their family.

Now that Jay had found her, Jill feared for her life and that of her family in Kingston. Jay hated them for no reason. Jill hoped they were okay. All she could do was pray for their safety, especially her baby. She envisioned him in her arms back home in Atlanta with Zach. The front door slammed shut, robbing Jill of her pleasant thoughts.

Nina stumbled in the house, breathing hard. There were a few bags of groceries in her arms. Her eyes bucked when she saw Jill strapped in the chair in the middle of the room. "What the fuck?" The bags slipped from her hold and crashed to the floor. Nina glared at Jay in a panic. "What the hell have you done,

Jay? Why is *she* here? Did you kidnap her?"

Jay rushed toward Nina with her palms held up. "Lower your voice and chill out, baby. It's not what you think. I ain't gonna kill her."

"No, no, no, Jay! I am not gonna be a part of this madness! Jill is a celebrity in Jamaica right now. Her face is all over the place. She was on television last night talking about the dance recital. I heard everybody talking about it in town. The police are probably looking for her right now. How long has she been here?"

Jay reached out to Nina, but she pulled away, shaking her head. Jay gave it another try and was rewarded with a hard slap across her face.

"Get away from me! You're crazy as hell!" Nina started backing away. "You're on your own. I'm outta here." She found a duffle bag and started stuffing clothes and shoes inside of it.

"Where the hell do you think you're going? We're in this together."

"No, Jay, we *were* in this together until you went off and did this stupid shit! No, honey, you are now on your own."

"Look, just relax for now. Wait until tomorrow so I can go to the bank to get the money Jill collected for the show. Then we can hop on a boat to the Caymans, and catch a flight from there to *you know where*."

Nina started laughing, but she kept packing her things. It was a genuine laugh. Jill's eyes moved slowly back and forth from Jay to Nina. Their relationship was unraveling, crumbling by the second. Jay appeared pissed and nervous, but Nina didn't give a damn. It was now a matter of which woman had the stronger will to go through with her plans. Jill would bet her money on Nina.

Jay pulled out the gun. She'd used it to force Jill out of the dance studio and into a cab. This go around, she pointed it at Nina to scare her into going along with her plan.

"Oh, so now you're big bad ass Jay. You're gonna shoot me? I don't wanna be a part of this little kidnapping, and you pull out a gun?" Nina's laughter returned. "You ain't gonna shoot me, Jay." She turned and started toward the door with her purse and duffle bag on her shoulder.

"Sit your ass down, Nina! You ain't going nowhere!" Jay yelled, aiming the gun at her back. "You ain't gonna leave me like…"

Nina spun around. The sudden movement caused the skirt of her polka dot sundress to fan about her ankles. "I'm not gonna leave you like who? Venus? Jill? *Humph*, just watch me."

She left the house without any further drama.

* * * * *

She's in Kingston, Jamaica. Those four words haunted Zach like a ghost. From the moment Agent Wooten identified Jay's location, his stomach had been tied in knots. He was paralyzed for a few seconds, *literally,* before he pulled himself together. Jill, the baby and his in-laws' safety was more important than anything else. The FBI assured Zach that they would be under the protection of the Kingston Police at all times until Jay had been arrested. That gave him a bit of relief, but he wouldn't be fully at peace until he'd heard Jill's voice, and knew that she and Zach Junior were okay. He hadn't been able to reach her by phone because she was practicing with her students for the recital. Jay's statement about someone, *snatching Jill and making her disappear*, played over and over in Zach's head. Looking back on it, he now knew it was meant to be a threat or a warning. They were now back on the island together. Only this time, they were enemies and not lovers. If they happened to run into each other, their reunion would be anything but pleasant.

Zach had only had limited time to change his travel plans, and call Dex to fill him in. He'd been able to secure a late evening, nonstop flight to Jamaica online, but the rest of his duties had fallen into Dex's lap. He was going to call Aunt Jackie, Wallace and Venus to tell them that Jay was in Kingston and Zach was on his way there. He was also the FBI's contact person in Zach's absence. All information on the case would be reported directly to him. Dex would know the exact moment Jay was captured or killed.

"Would you care for something to drink, sir?"

Zach looked up at the older woman and tried to smile. He was surprised to meet an airline attendant with such a matronly appearance. She could've easily been someone's grandmother. "Water please," he said. "Hold the ice, ma'am. A bottle will be fine."

The attendant placed the bottle of water on Zach's tray and he thanked her before she eased down the aisle with her beverage cart.

As had been the cycle since he'd learned where Jay was, Zach began to toil with the guilt of leaving Jill and Zachary Junior in Jamaica. Anger followed. Jay had managed to outsmart the law enforcement agencies in Georgia, Florida and the federal government. Either the trained officers, deputies and agents were stupid, or his sister was a genius. Zach wondered how she had fled the country so easily without their knowledge. The whole situation was a mystery, surreal even.

The last update Zach received before boarding the plane was that Jill had left Zachary Junior with Faye, and had taken a cab to Royal Rhythms. She was to meet her students there. With only two days to go before the show, they were supposed to have a full dress rehearsal with props, lighting and the whole nine yards. All Zach could do was hope and pray that the Kingston police were doing their job keeping her safe. Once he arrived, he would take over from there.

* * * * *

"Don't fret, sweetheart. Leo would *never* hurt ya. You must trust Leo, eh? Come my dear."

Honey

Nina looked around as she entered the small, wooden house high above the ocean. It was surrounded by lots of fruit and palm trees and bushes. There wasn't another house close by for over a mile. Once she walked fully into the faintly lit room, she felt the cool breeze of a ceiling fan. She looked up at the rotating blades and inhaled. Leo removed the duffle bag from her shoulder and placed it on a folding chair.

"Sit, my dear," he said, motioning to a brown sofa across the room. It was facing an old floor model television. An episode of "The Cosby Show" was on. "Have a seat, Nina," Leo offered again. "Let Leo serve ya sumtin' to eat and drink."

Nina nodded and walked across the room. She lowered her full hips to the sofa. It was a sturdy piece of furniture, unlike that crap she'd been sitting on in the house down the hill. Her thoughts drifted back at that hell hole. She hoped Jay hadn't harmed Jill and would set her free like she'd promised. Surely by now Jill's family had reported her disappearance to the police. Every inch of the island would be searched until they found her. Jay was smart and manipulative, but she wasn't the type that functioned well alone. All her allies were gone, which meant she was going to slip up soon.

"Here ya are, my dear." Leo had returned from the kitchen carrying a plate. He handed it to Nina.

"Thank you. You're too kind."

Nina ate a delicious meal of spicy oxtails over rice, steamed cabbage and fried plantains. She washed it all down with cold pineapple juice. It tasted freshly drawn from the fruit. Leo removed the plate from Nina's lap and took it to the kitchen. When he returned, he turned off the television, sat in a folding chair across from her and smiled.

"Nina, ya must tell Leo all about yer troubles. The first day Leo set eyes on ya, he knew there was sumtin' special about ya. Nina is too pretty and nice of a woman to live in that old house. Who are ya hidin' from and why?"

Nina lowered her eyes to stare at her hands. She contemplated on what, if anything, she should tell Leo. What if she told him the truth about her life before moving to Jamaica, and he turned her in to the police? She looked up to search Leo's sun-kissed face. He had honest eyes, and he had always been sweet to her. There were times he could've taken advantage of her while she was high off of his gunja and rum, but he hadn't. Nina took a deep, cleansing breath before she told Leo her story.

Chapter Sixty-Five

Roy was the first person to arrive at the airport. Zach had asked him to pick him up. Time had not allowed him to go into very many details of why he was coming earlier than expected. The only thing he had confided in Roy was that Jay was in Jamaica, and Jill could be in danger.

Now, with Orville standing by his side, having been transported to the airport by the police, Roy was nervous as hell. All six men standing near the door where Zach would emerge from once his flight landed were suffering from anxiety. The four police officers, including the chief were deeply concerned about Jill. No one had seen her since one o'clock that afternoon. It was now ten minutes past midnight. A cab driver by the name of Ian McBride had dropped her off at Royal Rhythms as he had done every day for the past two weeks. He and other cabbies had voluntarily organized a search for Jill all across the island while her family waited patiently for her to be found.

* * * * *

Zach's heart dropped when he noticed Roy, Orville and the four police officers standing at the gate. Each man wore a somber expression on his face. That wasn't a good sign. Zach's feet and legs were heavy as steel as he ran in their direction.

"Where is Jill?"

The police chief extended his hand to Zach. "Mr. King, I am..."

"Where are my wife and son?" Zach shouted, ignoring the policeman. He walked pass the officer to stand directly in front of Roy and Orville. "Take me to Jill and Zachary Junior *now.*"

Roy cleared his throat. "Zachary, that is not possible. We don't know where Jill is at the moment. But the police and volunteers are searching the entire island for her as we speak. Your son is fine, though. He is with his grandmother and the rest of the family safe at a hotel. They're all under the protection of the police."

"Mr. King, I am Chief Phillip Bess. I'm sorry for your wife's disappearance. We're committed to finding Mrs. King alive as soon as possible. If you would allow us to follow you to the hotel where your son is, we'd like to discuss some things with you, sir. Right this way, Mr. King."

Zach retrieved his single piece of luggage, and walked to Roy's van in a trance. He heard his friend and father-in-law talking during the drive to the hotel, but none of their words registered. All he could think about was Jill and how scared she must've been. What was Jay doing to her? Had she hurt her? Had she raped her? The thought of either or both brought out Zach's rage.

The chief had said he and the other officers were committed to finding Jill. That would be the best case scenario, but Zach was prepared for the worst. He reached for his suitcase and rummaged through it. He found his gun case and ammunition. If the authorities found Jill and rescued her from Jay, they would arrest her. She would be extradited back to the States and thrown in prison for a very long time. But if *Zach* got to them first, things would turn out altogether different. To ensure that Jay would never harm another human being, he was going to blow her brains out if given the opportunity.

* * * * *

Nina waited nervously inside Leo's house while he went into town. He had gone to the police with a solid plan to have Jay arrested without affecting her. After talking half the night, disclosing the most personal details about her life, Leo had promised to fix everything and would not allow Jay to hurt her or anyone else again. Nina believed Leo for some reason. Those honest eyes of his, and the way he'd treated her from day one, shattered all doubts. Her heart told her Leo was a man of his word.

Nina had heard Leo showering in the outdoor stall bright and early that morning. He had built it himself. And it ran *hot* water. Last night Nina had enjoyed her first warm shower since being in Jamaica because of the kindness of a stranger. It was the same stranger who had shaved his beard and dressed in a black suit and tie to go into to town. He had one purpose in mind. Leo was going to lead the police to the house where Jay was holding Jill. He'd told Nina not to worry about being arrested because he was going to make sure that never happened.

"Where are you, Leo?" Nina whispered into the cool late morning air. Then she stood and peeped out the window for the one hundredth time it seemed.

Leo's house was small, but it was tidy and homey. It smelled of bleach and coconut. A candle bearing the stringy fruit's scent stayed lit most times. Leo believed it kept the evil spirits away. If anyone could attest to that, it was surely him. He had explained when he'd lived in the lower lands of Kingston with his wife Thelma and their two daughters he had practiced a lot of rituals his grandfather had taught him as a young boy. The old man had come from Dominican ancestry. The milk of the coconut and other fruits and herbs were believed to have healing and protective powers. On one of the few days in his life that he didn't have a single coconut product in his home, was the same day a powerful hurricane had swept his entire family away.

Nina's recollection of that tragic story from the night before faded from her mind when she heard footsteps on the front porch. She held her breath and watched the door knob turn slowly. The sight of Leo entering the house allowed her to breathe again.

"Gather yer things, my dear. Leo must take ya somewhere safe for a few days. My friend will take very good care of ya. Leo will see ya daily, but ya *cannot* be in this house right now. No worries, now. Nina trusts Leo, eh?"

"Yes, I trust you. I don't have a choice. But I don't know your friend."

Leo took Nina by both her hands and squeezed them. The sincerity of his smile and his honest eyes assured her she had nothing to worry about. "I'll pack my things."

* * * * *

Jill was weak from hunger and thirst. Jay hadn't fed her or given her anything to drink since the night before. The afternoon sun was now shining brightly through the dusty window pane. The curry chicken and peas and rice had been warm and tasty. Jill figured Jay had bought it from a restaurant or a friend had prepared it. Regardless of where it came from, Jill ate it like a ravenous animal with the gun aimed at the back of her head. Then Jay applied fresh strips of duct tape to her mouth, and led her outside to pee like a dog. Jill was tired after that. She fell into a restless sleep in the chair. But now she was wide awake, afraid and starving again.

The peace and raw beauty up in the hills above Kingston used to be a fun place for Jill and her friends as children. But as she sat bound against her will, she knew she'd never view it the same again *if* she survived. Jay's behavior was very irrational, and she had that *gun*. If the police didn't find Jill soon, anything could happen to her.

* * * * *

"What did that man just say to you, Roy?" Zach looked back over his shoulder at the young dude who had approached them. He'd spoken quickly to Roy and Orville, and ran away in the opposite direction. Like magic, he had vanished into the crowded straw market where they'd been searching for Jill since sunrise. They each had a picture of her and the flyer advertising the recital.

Roy kept walking. He ignored Zach's question. Orville did too.

"Roy, what did the guy say? Does he know where Jill is?"

"Zachary, the young man has a *suspicion*. That is all. I will call Chief Bess and tell him what he said."

Zach pulled Roy's arm to stop him from walking. Orville stopped as well. Zach would not be ignored. Suspicion or not, he wanted to know what the guy had told them about Jill.

"Zachary," Orville said. "He *thinks* he saw a woman who looks like Jillian on the beach in Negril. I don't believe him because he wanted money before he told us anything. Let us report it to the chief like Roy said. The police will go to the beach to search for Jillian there."

When they reached the van, Roy took out his cell phone to make the report to Chief Bess. He was about to dial the number when the phone rang. Orville's phone began to ring too. Both men answered their phones immediately. Zach could tell by the animation in their voices that something significant had happened. Either Jill had been found or someone knew where she was.

"We must go to the police station at once," Roy said.

"Is Jill there?"

Orville placed his arm on his son-in-law's shoulder. "No, but the chief knows where she's being kept. Your sister kidnapped her. A man has seen Jillian and he told the police where they can find her. We must go and wait at the station. They will bring her to us there."

"Where is she? Where did the man say Jay is keeping her?"

The way Roy and Orville eyed each other told Zach they knew Jill's exact location. He couldn't understand why they didn't want to tell him. She was his *wife*, and he was responsible for her being in danger. As her husband, he had a right to know where she was. Zach trusted the police to do their job, but he didn't trust *Jay*. She was an accomplished, psychopathic criminal capable of doing the unthinkable. If she felt trapped with her back against the wall, she wouldn't hesitate to kill Jill. Zach wanted to be there to stop her by *any* means.

"Roy, I don't wanna wait for Jill at the police station. Take me to her. She needs me. I gotta be there the minute she's found. I won't get in the police's way. I promise."

"No, Zachary, we will go to the police station. The chief…"

"The chief doesn't know Jay the way *we* do! We both know what my sister is capable of. She was your boss for four years. You witnessed her manipulation firsthand." Zach turned to Orville, trying to make him understand. "This is your oldest child we're talking about. I promised you I would take good care of her. It was a mistake leaving her here. Please help me fix it."

"Roy, Zachary is right. We must take him to Jillian immediately."

Chapter Sixty-Six

Jill heard men's voices calling her name in the distance from all directions. It had been twenty minutes or so since she'd first heard vehicles making their way up the winding hills. She had no idea how many men or cars there were, but she imagined lots of them. Heavy footsteps running closer to the house and barking dogs caused Jay to toss and stir in her sleep. She was sprawled out on the raggedy sofa where she'd been for a few hours. Earlier that afternoon, she'd stumbled in the house sloppy drunk, reeking of alcohol and cigar tobacco. In one hand she held a half-empty bottle of Disarrono. A big red apple was in the other. She slurred a few curses and threats at Jill while she led her outside to pee at gunpoint. Then she gave her the apple and a bottle of warm water and watched her gulp it down. As drunk as Jay was, she didn't forget to tape Jill's mouth shut afterwards.

The shouts and pounding feet grew louder. The men had surrounded the house. Jill's heartbeat accelerated. Her eyes fell on Jay again. She was now lying on her back snoring loud with her mouth wide open. Her left arm was hanging over the edge of the sofa, and she had dropped the gun on the floor close by. Jill jumped in her seat when someone tapped on the window. She looked up and saw two police officers staring at her. The silence following that was eerie.

The first kick to the back door was loud and forceful. Jill started twisting and turning in her chair, wanting very much to break free. Jay sat straight up, and looked around confused. Another kick made her fully alert. She grabbed the gun from the floor, and quickly fired off a shot into the ceiling. Dust, broken wood, and pink fiberglass fell down on Jay and Jill. The kicking stopped and so did the shouting.

"I'll blow her fucking brains out!" Jay yelled. She coughed several times as she ran behind Jill and held the gun to her left temple. The dust and debris that had fallen from the collapsing ceiling burned her eyes. More fell onto the floor making a huge cloud of dust. Jay coughed more intensely. "If you bust in here, I'll kill this bitch! Then I'll off myself! *Nobody* will win!"

The tense atmosphere suddenly became quiet. It felt like an eternity to Jill. Sweat trickled down every inch of her body. The dust and debris made it hard for her to breathe. She whimpered, and tears stung her eyes when Jay tugged on a fist full of her curly afro.

Honey

"Get ready to die, you selfish, ungrateful bitch. I'll put a bullet through your skull before I let them take you from me. We're gonna die right here together. You and me, Jay and Jill, ride or die just like old times."

Jill saw four policemen through the front window. Another group had gathered on the side of the house. She could see them through the cracked side window. Jay paid no attention to the activity outside. Her face was buried in the crook of Jill's neck.

"We're going to hell, and it's your fault. You and Zach disrespected me! Now you gotta die."

* * * * *

The scene outside the shanty in the hills became busier as more police officers arrived. Chief Bess was in command. He was adamant that no deadly force would be used against Jay unless it was absolutely unnecessary. The FBI had requested that she be apprehended alive. Agent Wooten was en route to Jamaica, hoping to take her back to the States. The most experienced marksmen on Kingston's police force had a clear shot at Jay from his position outside the cracked side window. All he needed was the official order from Chief Bess to take her out.

Down the hill, Zach had grown tired and frustrated with the chief's passiveness. The small structure he'd described as a shack should've been invaded by the officers hours ago. He, Roy and Orville had been obedient, and stayed at the bottom of the hill several yards away from the scene. A crowd of nosy natives had joined them.

"I'm about to go up there and get Jill! What the hell are they waiting for, huh?" Zach faced Roy and Orville, having asked them the same question repeatedly over the past hour and a half. "Why can't they shoot Jay, and rush in to get Jill? How hard is that?" Zach started up the hill with his hand inside the waist band of his jeans.

Roy pulled him back and restrained him. "No, Zachary, you mustn't interfere with the police. They're the trained ones. Let them do their job. Be patient, my friend."

Zach snatched away from him. He looked up in the sky at the dark clouds that were forming. The sun was still shining, but not as brightly as it had been earlier. There was a hint of fresh rain in the air.

"The rain is coming," Orville said, looking up as well. "It is a good sign."

"How so?" Zach asked, and moved closer to his father-in-law.

"Whenever we are on the sea, the first sign of rain tells us it is time to head for safe cover. No matter what we are doing or how well we are doing it, the dark rain clouds are our sign to end our tasks and practice safety. For twenty-one years now, I have made voyages for the same company. The ship has changed and many of my shipmates have come and gone, but one thing has not changed. The sign of rain is still a good sign. Let us wait now, eh? My daughter-your wife, will return to us safely today. The rain says so."

Suddenly, a group of officers ran toward the back of the house. Zach, Orville and Roy walked closer toward the scene.

"What's going on, y'all? Can either of you tell?" Zach asked.

"No." They answered in unison.

A bolt of lightning crackled across the sky, followed by a deafening clap of thunder. Drops of cool rain fell from the sky. The crowd of spectators began to disperse, but many stayed. More officers ran to the back of the house. Without warning, Zach sprinted up the hill in Chief Bess's direction. Neither Roy nor Orville could run fast enough to catch him.

"What's happening, chief?"

The man in charge turned toward the voice. "Mr. King, you shouldn't be this close to the official scene of an ongoing police operation. Please sir, go back where you were, and wait for us to complete our work here. Your wife will be brought to safety soon."

Zach shook his head as the downpour of rain increased, limiting his visibility. "I'm not leaving. I won't get in your way, but I'm not going back down that hill without Jill."

"Very well, Mr. King, if you insist on staying, please consider yourself advised that neither the city of Kingston, nor I am responsible for your well-being. You're in the middle of an official ongoing police operation without my consent. You could very well get hurt. Your sister is armed and dangerous."

Hell, I'm packing and on the edge too, Zach wanted to say, but he held it back. He fingered the outline of his gun, and leaned against one of the police vehicles parked at the top of the hill. He looked down and saw Roy and Orville watching him anxiously. Zach turned his back, dismissing them.

Chapter Sixty-Seven

By early nightfall, Jill was hungry, and had a full bladder. With the tape over her mouth, she couldn't tell Jay anything. It wasn't like she gave a damn anyway. Aside from the rain falling inside the house through the collapsing ceiling, there was calmness all around. The hushed voices of the policemen and bright flashlights assured Jill that her rescue was still in the making. Jay had guzzled down the rest of the Disarrono, but she wasn't drunk. The liquor had stimulated her instead. She was wired up.

Jay got up and turned the radio on. It filled the small house with static and reggae music. She searched the pockets on several pairs of pants piled high over the back of a folding chair. The gun remained secure in her right hand. Jay smiled at the half-smoked cigar she found like it was a pot of gold. She lit it in a hurry, and blew the smoke in Jill's direction.

"Are you ready to die? You know that's the only way we're leaving here. If we were in Atlanta, I'd be dead by now. Hell, you probably would be too. The ATL Swat Team would've stormed this little house, and blown my damn head off a long time ago. Those motherfucking, Barney Fife, cartoon cops ain't gonna do shit. I'll bet my last cigar they ain't got no bullets in those guns." Jay walked over and peeped out of the front window cautiously. "So you ready to go to hell with me? All my wicked deeds are out there. Shit, I've done it all and then some. But you," Jay said, pointing the gun at Jill. "You're a sneaky and slick one. We thought you were naïve and innocent, but you fooled us. You seduced my brother in my penthouse and fucked him behind my back. Then you left your family and homeland to follow me to Atlanta so you could finish what you started. You're a deceitful little bitch. You're ungrateful too." Jay waved the gun carelessly in the air, and walked over to Jill. "I was good to you, damn it!"

Jay was unraveling, slipping further and further away from sanity. Her countenance had hardened to that of a deranged person on the verge of murder. The louder she cursed and screamed, the more afraid Jill became. She closed her eyes and envisioned Zachary Junior and Zach. What happy memories she could recall of Nahima floated through her mind. Her parents, her brothers and Angelina appeared one by one. Would she ever see them or touch them again? The cool muzzle of the gun brushed against the side of Jill's face. She held her breath and waited for her life to end. Jay yelled wildly and yanked her hair.

Honey

"You, Wallace, Venus and Zach ruined my damn life! I never had a fair chance," Jay cried. "Why did y'all screw me over? I needed someone to love me!"

Jay pressed the muzzle of the gun against Jill's temple with an unsteady hand. Jill whimpered and closed her eyes once again, preparing for the darkness of death to take her away. Into the night, piercing the quietness of the hillside, the blast from the gun made time stand still. Orville fell to his knees, and dropped his face to the ground when a second shot was fired. Roy kneeled and wrapped his arm around him as sobs racked the weary sailor's body. Zach shouted Jill's name repeatedly above the police activity and heavy rainfall. He was surrounded by several officers struggling to hold him in place. He fought them off, and attempted to run to the side of the house after Chief Bess. They restrained him.

"Get off me! Get off me!" Zach demanded, his voice many pitches higher than normal. *"Jiiiiiiill!"*

An ambulance siren blared, the sound growing louder as it sped up the hill. The small crowd of spectators pointed the driver in the direction of the house. Roy pulled Orville to his feet, and guided him up the hill to where Zach stood crying silently. Father and son-in-law embraced. Their tears fell freely down their faces. Roy wept also, but kept a watchful eye on his friends. His attention was divided between them and the paramedics rushing toward the house with a stretcher and medical equipment.

"I need to see her," Zach whispered. "I need to see Jill. It doesn't matter if she's dead. I gotta see her." He tried to break away from the group.

Roy placed his hands forcefully on both his shoulders, prohibiting his movement. "No. Zachary, let the professionals tend to Jill, and give the police time to assess the situation."

Zach nodded and wiped his face with both hands. "This is the worst day of my life. None of this should've happened. I will *never* forgive myself for leaving her behind."

"Zachary! Zachary! Where are you? Zachary! I'm okay!"

Zach adjusted his eyes through the steady drizzle of rain. They followed the familiar voice. Coming toward him was a tall officer carrying Jill in his muscular arms. Chief Bess was behind them smiling.

"Jill? You're alive!" Zach ran to his wife.

Orville fell to his knees once again, but this time he cried, thanking God for sparing his daughter's life. Roy breathed a sigh of relief, and looked into the rainy, starlit sky. He laughed from deep within as the raindrops continued to fall mixing with his tears.

* * * * *

"I *will not* postpone the recital, Zachary. My students have worked too hard.

They're prepared. The show must go on."

Zach hadn't left Jill's side since she arrived at the Johnson Medical Center. He had watched the nurses and staff check her from head to toe until the doctor arrived. Zach was there when Dr. Johnson repaired the cut above her right elbow with fifteen stitches. The shattered glass from the marksman's first shot through the window had sliced her flesh pretty good.

"Let her dance, Mr. King. I insist. The entire island has been looking forward to the dance recital for weeks. As her doctor, I don't want her fans to blame *me* for the cancellation. And as a financial sponsor for the event, I demand to see a show tomorrow night. Mrs. King, you have medical clearance to dance, dear heart," Dr. Johnson said, smiling. He left the treatment room.

Zach looked around. Jill, Orville and Roy were waiting for his answer. "Okay, there'll be a show tomorrow evening, and you can dance. But you've gotta take it easy. You need to rest tonight, but first, I want you to eat and drink a lot of fluids."

"I want to see my son."

"Zachary Junior is with your mother. I just spoke with her. That little dude is wide awake and noisy. He's a smart kid. He knew something was wrong. Let him stay with your parents at the hotel. *You* are going with me to the Blue Lagoon so I can take care of you. Get dressed. We'll wait for you outside."

Roy and Orville followed Zach into the hallway while Jill changed from her hospital gown into a red sundress. Faye had sent it to the clinic by police officers. Chief Bess, Agent Wooten and two other FBI agents approached them.

"Mr. King, gentleman," the chief greeted them. "We need to speak with you privately if we may, sir."

Roy and Orville walked away and took seats in a waiting area down the hall.

"Your sister asked for you before she was taken to surgery," Chief Bess informed Zach. "She was shot in her right hand seconds before she attempted to kill your wife. It's a very serious wound, Mr. King. She won't die, but she lost two of her fingers. The other bullet struck her in her left leg when she tried to escape through the back door."

"Is Jay here at *this* clinic?"

"Oh no, sir, she's at Kingston Public Hospital. I'm sure she's in surgery as we speak. We can have an officer take you to her if you'd like."

"Hell nah, I don't wanna see Jay. Tell her that. I *never* wanna see her again. As far as I'm concerned, I don't have a sister. She's dead to me. Give Jay that message for me, okay?" Zach turned and retraced his steps to Jill's treatment room.

Chapter Sixty-Eight

Mamie, Leo's friend tapped softly on Nina's door before she opened it. She smiled at her sleeping border, and turned to Leo who was standing in the hallway. "She's resting, but I'm sure she'll want to see you. I'll wake her." Mamie entered the room, and approached the bed. She shook Nina gently. "Ma'am, you have a visitor. Wake up, my dear." Mamie nudged her gently.

Nina stirred and opened her eyes slowly. "What time is it?"

"Ah, at last you are awake," Mamie said. "It's half past ten at night. You slept a long time. There is someone here to visit you. Let me get him for you."

Seconds after Mamie exited the room, in walked Leo holding a baseball cap in his hand. He looked around the space where a single candle on a table flickered. "How are ya, Nina?"

Nina sat up, yawning and stretching her arms above her head. "I'm fine. This is a nice place, and Mamie is a great hostess. How much longer will I have to stay here?"

Leo sat at the foot of the bed. "I am not sure yet. The police are wanderin' about the hillside askin' folks lots of questions about yer friend. She is alive, ya know? A sharp shooter shot two of her fingers clean off! Then he put another bullet in her leg. The dancer is safe, though. All thanks to God."

"I'm so glad Jill is okay. I was afraid Jay would do something terrible to that poor girl. She's such an evil person. She's crazy too."

"Yet she was *yer* friend."

"Jay was never really my friend. She didn't care about me. I've been reflecting on our relationship ever since I found Jill in that hell hole we were staying in. No friend would've dragged another into this *bullshit*. If Jay truly loved me, why was it so important for her to get revenge on her ex-lover?"

"Leo has no idea, my dear."

"Why couldn't she forget about her and be happy with *me*?" Nina paused as tears filled her eyes. "I left everything in Atlanta to come here and live like cave woman with Jay. Now I have nothing and nowhere to go. She ain't going down by herself. Believe me. Jay will tell the police and whoever else will listen that I came to Jamaica with her. They're gonna hunt me down like a dog. And when they find me, they're gonna send me back to America, and I'll rot in prison."

"Or they could *not* find ya and my sweet Nina could spend the rest of her life with Leo," he offered with his hand on his chest. "I'll be willin' to take care of ya and protect ya forever. No American or the Jamaican police will find ya if ya just trust yer friend Leo to keep ya safe."

Nina's options were limited. There was no way she could survive in Jamaica on her own. And if she tried to make it to Mexico right now, she'd get caught. Leo had made good on all his promises so far. She had no reason not to trust him now. What other choice did she have anyway? If Leo was willing to protect and provide for her, she would allow him to. But nothing in life came free. For everything worth having there was a price. A chance at freedom and a fresh new start wasn't cheap.

"Leo, you're the only person I have in the world right now. If I reached out to my mother or my step sister, it would cause them all kinds of problems. I can't do that to them. My cousin Juan would help me, but Jay no doubt has already told the police all about him. So I'll stay in Jamaica with you. But I ain't stupid. You want something from me. What is it? Tell me," she said, sliding to sit closer to Leo on the bed."

Leo reached out and touched Nina's face with care. Her eyes fluttered shut, as she welcomed his gentleness. She had forgotten how it felt to be touched by the strong hands of a man. All of her fear about the future and how it would play out disappeared when Leo rubbed her bottom lip with the pad of his thumb.

"Leo wants whatever Nina is willin' to give him for now. In time whatever should happen between a man and a woman will come."

"I understand. Leo will take care of Nina and Nina will take *good* care of Leo. "

* * * * *

"I think she is hallucinating," the nurse whispered to Chief Bess and Agent Wooten. "A very powerful pain medication is dripping through the IV, plus she has a morphine pump. The doctor is very concerned about her liver, though. She has an moderate case of cirrhosis, ya know? And she's been complaining about her belly. I do believe she's a heavy drinker. You may speak with her, but she seems to be babbling. Maybe you can make some sense of her words."

The chief and FBI agent left the nurses' station, and headed down the hall. They greeted the armed policeman outside Jay's hospital room. When they entered, the female police officer inside stood from her chair, and met them in the middle of the floor.

"How is she?" Agent Wooten asked.

"She's been sleeping a lot. Sometimes she cries out in pain, screaming bloody murder." Earlier, she called for someone named Zach and then Nina."

"Zach is her brother," Chief Bess told the officer. "He doesn't wish to see her. I have no idea who the Nina person is."

Agent Wooten shoved his hands inside his pants pockets. "Ah, Senorita Nina Celeste Lopez is one of many in Ms. King's chain of fools. We believe she and our ailing fugitive over there left Atlanta with Deputy Bethany Hardy. Together they hid out on the outskirts Miami, Florida. What happened after that is still a mystery. Deputy Hardy ended up blowing her brains out in their trailer park hideaway. The trail on Ms. Lopez ends there too."

"My officers have been questioning residents along the hillside. They're mostly fishermen and a few farmers and craftsmen. All the men said Ms. King came to Jamaica alone. She was the only person living in the abandoned house. None of them have seen this Nina Lopez. We confiscated clothes, shoes and other personal items. Everything seems belongs to Ms. King." Chief Bess pulled something from the breast pocket on his uniform, and handed it to Agent Wooten. "That is the Jamaican passport she used to travel here from your country. She looks nothing like the picture today, eh? And she used the name Belva Jane Dudley? Who is that?"

Agent Wooten shrugged. "Maybe Mr. King knows this person, and will tell us who she is. Nothing about this case makes much sense to me so far. I wonder when and how Ms. King applied for a *Jamaican* passport from jail. Check out the date on it." The agent angled the booklet so the chief could see it. "She was an inmate at the Fulton County jail when this was issued. It's going to take awhile for us to sort through this case. In all my fourteen years with the FBI, I don't believe I've ever run across anyone quite like Ms. Jayla King."

"Your fellow agents said the same thing to me this morning in my office." The chief chuckled. "I can't recall ever meeting anyone with such a deceitful and manipulative nature either. I think she's a disturbed woman. I'm just grateful that Mrs. King is alive and well. It would've been most tragic had she been seriously injured or killed by her sister-in-law."

Chapter Sixty-Nine

"*No*, Jill, not tonight." Zach folded his arms across his bare chest, and rolled over onto his side away from her. "We agreed to wait until tomorrow night after the show. You've been through hell over the past forty-eight hours. You need to rest. And I don't wanna hurt your arm, baby. Just let me hold you." Zach reversed his position in the bed to face Jill again. He wrapped his arms around her waist, pulling her body against his.

"But Zachary, it's been too long. I'm fine. You heard Dr. Johnson." Jill kissed Zach's lips hungrily and rubbed his chest like a woman on a mission of the sexual kind. "You forced me to eat that huge dinner, and I have all of this energy now. I have missed you. *Pleeease* Zachary…"

"Go to sleep, Jill. Your pain medication should've kicked in by now anyway. Tomorrow is your big day. You're a professional dancer. Show some restraint."

Jill wanted Zach to make love to her. She'd been putting the moves on him. Her seduction started over the seafood feast they'd ordered from room service and heated up in the shower. While Zach made phone calls to their family and friends in the States to report that Jill was safe, she fondled and massaged him all over. His body, especially that certain part of him she'd missed the most, responded to her skillful touches. Zach wanted his wife, but resisted her. He didn't want to put any unnecessary stress on her body after all she'd been through. The cut on her arm was his main concern. He didn't want to risk hurting it.

Zach forgot about Jill's injury when she whispered his name, and eased her hand inside his boxers. Before he had a chance to protest, she pressed her lips against his and snaked her tongue inside his open mouth. He was rock hard and ready.

"Stop that, Jill." He moved back a few inches, interrupting her rhythmic strokes. "You're not playing fair. Go to sleep and rest your body so you'll be able to give your best performance tomorrow night. You may not like it, but I'm trying to do what's best for you."

"First of all, I'm about to do my best performance *tonight*. Secondly, the last time you decided what was best for me, you were dead wrong. I'm more than capable of determining what is best for *me*," Jill teased, and caressed her husband's sensitive spot again.

As much as Zach wanted to be in control, he was helpless. During his absence from Jill, his heart definitely grew fonder, and every other part of his anatomy too. So he stopped resisting the pleasure, relaxed and took his seduction like a real man.

* * * * *

"Go! Go! Go! Go! Go!" Jill ordered her students, waving her hands in the direction of the stage. "Get back out there! Don't you hear them begging for more? This is your chance to do the special routine we added last week. You remember it, eh?"

"Yes ma'am." All the girls answered.

"We know it very well, Madame Jillian. We will make you proud," Wilma, the senior dancer told her.

Jill hugged the young girl. "I'm sure you will. Shoo now. Your audience waits."

The applause and cheers of the crowd swelled when the curtains opened. The thirteen female dancers appeared before them again all dressed in lavender flowing dresses for an encore performance. Jill threw her head back, and covered her mouth to keep from screaming. The entire show had been an amazing success; every performance perfect, captivating the two thousand plus people in the audience. Jill stood behind the curtain watching her students twirling and leaping through the air. They all danced with the grace and precision of gazelles to Miriam Makeba's "Pata Pata." The audience was up on its feet clapping and cheering. Jill couldn't have been more proud.

At the end of the dance, the girls received a lengthy standing ovation. Jill came out on stage and introduced all of her students, including the ones behind the curtains. She presented Madame Katherine to a thunderous round of applause and spoke very highly of her extraordinary legacy at Royal Rhythms. She acknowledged everyone responsible for making "Magical Moments in Motion" possible. Careful not to overlook anyone, Jill read from her long list of sponsors and production team members, including Gwendolyn Hayes. She'd done a superb job on the dancers' costumes. Then through tears, Jill publicly thanked Chief Bess and all of his officers for rescuing her. After an extensive standing ovation, she acknowledged her family and thanked them for their support, especially Zach and Zachary Junior.

By the time Roy's van left the Alliance Performing Arts Center, Jill was too pooped to hold her head up. On the ride to the Blue Lagoon she and Zachary Junior fell asleep, using Zach's body as a pillow.

* * * * *

"Yeah, she sends me a message *every day* by Chief Bess, talking about please come visit her. I don't know why. Ain't nobody thinking about Jay."

"You're not little curious about what she wants to say?" Dex asked.

"Nope." Zach checked his watch. "Jill has her last interview with Chief Bess and the FBI in an hour. After that we're heading to Kingston to have dinner with our family and say goodbye to them. Our flight back to the ATL leaves tomorrow morning at ten. Make sure your ass is at the airport to pick us up by one."

"Negro please, I'm always on time. Just make sure you bring me a big bottle of that strong Jamaican rum."

"I will. And I gotta buy a few bags of Blue Mountain coffee for Aunt Jackie. She reminded me *again* when we spoke this morning. My dad and Patricia want some too. I picked up a bunch of t-shirts for Nahima, Wallace Junior and Abriah. What should I buy Ramona?"

"A coffee mug or one of those spoons with "Jamaica" inscribed on it should do. She collects that kind of stuff."

Zach looked across the room at Jill when he heard her open the front door. She pursed her lips and placed her hand on her hip. Zachary Junior was straddling the other one.

"I gotta go, man. Roy is probably downstairs waiting on us. It's funny how he's a driver for the Island Paradise Resort, but whenever Jill and I come to town, he makes himself available to us. Anyway, I'll see you tomorrow afternoon."

* * * * *

Agents Wooten, Brooks and Paretti were all seated in Chief Bess's office when he opened the door to welcome Zach and Jill inside. Roy was left in the lobby to babysit Zachary Junior.

"Mrs. King." Agent Wooten began, "Ms. King confessed to kidnapping you, and holding you thirty-six hours against your will, but she claimed she didn't act alone. According to her, a woman named of Nina Lopez helped her. We know Ms. Lopez left Atlanta with Ms. King. They ended up in Miami together. Another woman was with them, but she's dead. We have *nothing* to support Ms. King's claim that Ms. Lopez traveled with her to Jamaica, but that doesn't mean much in a case like this. Was there a woman with Ms. King, and did she help her kidnap you?"

The agent wanted the truth, but Jill wasn't so sure he needed it. What good would it serve? Falling in love with Jay was the only thing Nina had done wrong. That wasn't a crime. It was a terrible mistake. In Jill's opinion, Nina, like her and Venus had been one of Jay's victims. She'd been used. Whatever part Nina had played in Jay's escape from jail and her flight to Jamaica had nothing to do with the kidnapping. However, it would be hard to convince the FBI and Chief Bess of that. If they knew Nina was in Jamaica, she would be arrested, and shipped back to the States with Jay. Jill didn't want that to happen. Nina had not harmed her, and she didn't want to harm her either.

She addressed Agent Wooten. "I've *never* met Nina Lopez. Like I told you before, Jay forced me from the dance studio with a gun. She made me put on a big straw hat and sunglasses. We caught a cab that drove us to a fruit stand at the bottom of the hillside. Jay led me up the hill to the house with that gun still pointed at me. Once we got inside she taped my mouth shut, and belted me to a chair like a prisoner. I was inside that house for a day and a half, only allowed to go outside to relieve myself with a gun held to my back. I saw no one else the entire time except Jay."

Agent Paretti, the only female agent, jotted some notes on a pad. Then she spoke to Zach. "Mr. King, your sister traveled here on a Jamaican passport. The face on the picture is definitely hers, but it appears she's wearing a disguise. The name on the passport took us aback. Do you have any idea who Belva Jane Dudley is?"

"That was my mother. Actually, that was her name before she married my father. Belva Jane Dudley *King* has been dead almost thirty years now. I can't believe Jay disrespected our mother's memory by using her name in her mess."

"No one is off-limits when Ms. King is involved," Chief Bess told the group. "A woman in Runaway Bay named Charlotte Gregory has been arrested for aiding and abetting her. She too, was one of your sister's lovers. Ms. Gregory allegedly arranged for Ms. King to hide out in the house up in the hills amongst other things. If everything your sister has told us is true, Ms. Gregory could serve many years in prison."

Zach and Jill answered a few more questions before they left Chief Bess's office. On the way down the hall, hand in hand, Zach leaned in to whisper in Jill's ear.

"You told me you saw Nina in that shack the day Jay kidnapped you. You're a liar, young lady."

"I am not a *liar*. I told a little white lie. Nina didn't help Jay do anything at all to me. Why should I have helped Jay do something to her?"

DERANGED Love

Chapter Seventy

Nina studied her hair closely in the mirror. It *was* different. The new short length and the dark color had totally changed her appearance. She hadn't meant to steal Jill's hair style, but she'd needed something drastically new. And going from long auburn curls to a short black afro was quite drastic. Nina adjusted the straps on the pastel pink sundress Leo had bought her, and smiled. With her thirty-pound weight loss, she almost didn't recognize her own reflection in the mirror. That was a good thing because Nina Celeste Lopez no longer existed.

To Leo and Mamie, she would forever be Nina, but to every other person on the island she would be known as Marta Fox. It was the name Juan had chosen for her when he'd arranged for her Mexican passport. On the picture she was rocking a long, black, curly wig. That had been her cousin's idea too. She had confided in him about her plans to leave the United States with Jay, and asked for his advice. The one thing Juan had insisted was that Nina allow him to get her a Mexican passport instead of asking one of her coworkers to hook her up with one issued from the States. Otherwise, she would've been tracked down by now, awaiting extradition back to the States.

Nina's gaze locked with Leo's in the mirror. He was sitting on the bed behind her watching her examine her brand new makeover. "So what do you think?"

"It makes no difference what Leo is thinkin', my dear. The important thing is what *you* are thinkin'. Leo likes whatever Nina likes."

Nina took a seat next to Leo on the bed. "I don't know what I would've done without you. Thank you for everything, Leo." She placed a soft kiss on his cheek.

"We must be goin' now. Leo moved everything from the old house, and put it all in the new one. It's time to leave the hillside. Nina deserves better."

Never in a million years would Nina have guessed she'd be living anywhere else besides Atlanta, East Los Angeles or Mexico City. But falling in love with the wrong woman had cost her dearly. She couldn't contact her mother or any other relatives out of fear that the FBI was searching for her. Leo was the only person in her life. And because of him, she had a chance to make a fresh new start. It wasn't a perfect situation, but Nina was hell bent on making it work.

"Let's go home," Leo said, standing to his feet. "The cab should be here now."

"Yeah, let's go home."

* * * * *

Honey

"Hello?"

Jay paused before she spoke. The mere sound of her aunt's voice stirred her emotions. "Aunt Jackie, it's me, Jay."

"How are you, baby?" She placed her Bible, purse and choir robe on the kitchen table, and took a seat.

"Well, I'm living in a bootleg Jamaican jail cell with only three of the fingers God gave me on my right hand. I'm still on crutches, and the doctor said my limp is gonna be a permanent one. I guess I'm doing pretty damn great. What do you think?"

"I'm just grateful you're alive."

"The doctors here have released me. I'll be returning to Atlanta some time tomorrow. Can you believe the FBI sent *three* agents over here to escort me back? You'd think I was a fucking sociopath like Jeffrey Dahmer or Charles Manson." Jay laughed, but it wasn't genuine. There was no humor in her situation. She had hit rock bottom. Her life was pathetic, and she had no one to blame but herself.

"Don't take this the wrong way, but you've done some *awful* things, Jay. I'm not judging you, but you have some repenting to do. Zach and Jill hooking up behind your back was wrong. They've both confessed to that. But your plan to make them pay for it was worse than anything I could've imagined. I love you with all my heart, but I can't condone anything you did. All I can do is pray for you."

Jay had expected a spiritual reprimand from Aunt Jackie. Anything else would've been insincere. This was Jackie Dudley Brown. The woman was a saint. Jay had never heard her curse or swear. Everyone in the family said she was a virgin on her wedding night. Jay could testify that no man had ever spent the night at their house when she was a child. Uncle Julius was the only man she knew who had hit it. And that was only after they'd gotten married. Yes, Aunt Jackie was a special woman with a kind heart. Otherwise, she wouldn't give Jay the time of day.

"Yeah, I need prayer alright to fight all these damn charges," Jay said softly.

"I'll put your name in the prayer box at church today. It was good to hear from you, but I gotta run now. Brother Slocomb, our new minister of music, will tear my head off if I'm late. I'm singing "Encourage Yourself" by Donald Lawrence and the Tri-City Singers this morning. I'm so excited, honey. But before we hang up, bow your head, and let Auntie pray with you."

* * * * *

"It was so nice of y'all to put this together for us. Thank you," Zach wrapped his arm around Venus's waist and kissed her on the cheek.

"It was my idea, but Dex, Ramona and Charles deserve most of the credit. They did all the leg work. Look at all that spread. You know I can't cook like that. I was responsible for getting your father and his family down here."

Aunt Jackie walked over to the picnic table with Zachary Junior in her arms. Nahima was right beside her carrying one of her Heritage World baby dolls all dressed in red. "Isn't it a beautiful day for a cookout? I'm glad we decided to do this."

"It's a perfect day." Jill walked over.

"After all we've been through, it was time for us to set aside a day to chill, and enjoy one another." Zach pinched Zachary Junior's nose. "Most of the people I love are here with me."

"Son," Wallace placed his hand on Zach's shoulder. "Come go for a walk with me."

"We'll be right back, y'all."

Zach and Wallace left the table, and walked toward the pond. A mother duck and her ducklings sat afloat on the water. They stopped under the shade of a tree to talk.

"I spoke with Jayla's attorney earlier this week. She has a new one. He's a young black guy. Malcolm Henderson is his name. He thinks he's convinced your sister to plead guilty *but* mentally ill to all charges pertaining to you. She'll serve eight to ten years."

Zach nodded and rubbed his goatee. "What about the escape charges? I know she's gonna serve some major time for that."

"Yes, she has to face those charges as well. It's a long laundry list of offenses, but she's fighting every last one of them. Jayla says Deputy Hardy and Nina planned her escape without her knowledge. She claims they sprung her out of the hospital, and forced her to go along with them."

"That doesn't sound right, Daddy. How did Nina and the deputy meet? They couldn't have been friends. Jay had a sexual relationship with both of them. It doesn't add up."

"It doesn't, but it's exactly what Jayla told her attorney. That's why she insists that Nina be found. She's responsible for the escape to Jamaica according your sister. She even gave the authorities some information about one of Nina's cousins in Mexico. Jayla swears that's where she is, and she wants the FBI to go after her."

"You do know your daughter is a pathological liar, right?"

Wallace nodded his head. Everyone knew Jay had a sharp tendency to lie.

"And you know she's crazy, but nowhere near clinically insane. I wouldn't be surprised if she killed Nina, and buried her body somewhere in that trailer park outside of Miami. I told Franklin and Ortega what I believe. Anyway, Jay needs some help."

"I know." Wallace said with a faraway look in his eyes. "I wonder how she would've turned out if I hadn't gone to the White Cloud Motel that afternoon with my gun."

"We'll never know. By the way, you didn't tell me how you knew Momma was there that day with Claudius Henry."

"I guess it was instinct. He was my best friend, and I knew that's where he took all his women. When Belva Jane left home that day headed for the beauty parlor, she was dressed to the nines. She didn't ask me for the fifteen dollars to pay for her hairdo like she usually did. I got suspicious and the rest is history.

Epilogue

One year later…

Zion's soft whimpers floated through the baby monitor, and greeted Zach as he entered the kitchen. He had just returned home from work. Jill turned around with a dishcloth in her hand. She bumped into her husband on her way to check on their two-month-old daughter. Zach reached out and grabbed her hips to hold her in place. He kissed her lips. Zachary Junior pulled the hem of his mother's dress to get her attention.

"That's enough, Zachary," Jill whispered against his lips. "The baby is crying, ya know?"

Zach released her, and shot her a bedroom promise for later with his eyes. Then he bent down and scooped up his son and tossed him in the air. He caught him and kissed him on the forehead. "We'll go and take care of the baby. Finish cooking. It smells good, by the way," Zach yelled as he ran up the stairs with his son bouncing in his arms.

"Are you wet, little girl?" Jill heard him say over the baby monitor. "Are you hungry, too? Daddy's gonna change you, and take you to your mommy so she can nurse you. Ain't that right, Zachary Junior?"

"Baby wanna eat, Daddy."

Jill smiled at the sound of her son's voice. Life was peaceful with no worries or danger waiting around the corner. Jay's sentencing for her escape from jail had taken place that morning. Jill had no idea of the outcome. If she really wanted to know the details, all she had to do was pick up the phone and call Aunt Jackie. But she wasn't interested.

"Somebody's hungry." Zach had entered the kitchen with Zion in his arms and Zachary Junior skipping behind him.

"Let me fix your plate first," Jill said. She reached down and ran her fingers through her son's curls. "And I will fix yours too. Then I will nurse the baby."

Zach helped Zachary Junior into his high chair and took a seat at the table cradling his daughter. "Jay was sentenced this morning," he said coolly.

"I know."

"Aunt Jackie said she didn't take it well. In fact, Jay showed her ass in the courtroom when the judge gave her an additional seven years on top of the ten she's already serving."

Jill placed a plate of food on the tray of Zachary Junior's high chair, and kissed his face. When she pressed her palms together and closed her eyes, he mimicked her gestures, and bowed his head. Together, mother and son said a short grace.

"Auntie said Jay started cursing and screaming some nonsense about Nina and Deputy Hardy at her attorney," Zach continued, shaking his head. "Then she *attacked* the dude, and swung at the bailiffs when they tried to get her off of him. She threatened to kill the judge, the DA and of course you and me before they hauled her ass outta there clowning like a fool. Auntie was so embarrassed."

Jill quietly placed a plate of piping hot food in front of Zach. She took Zion from his arms after she handed him a fork. Then she began to nurse her daughter. Zach paused and waited for Jill to respond. She felt his eyes on her. Nothing about Jay interested her one way or the other. How long the judge had sentenced her to serve in prison didn't matter. Jill only hoped that Zach had found the closure he needed to move pass what his sister had done to them. She had with no regrets.

"I wouldn't change a damn thing, you know? How it all went down may have been wrong, but I think we were meant to be."

"I know we were, Zachary. There's no doubt in my mind."

"In Jamaica that night when you were tipsy, dancing on top of the bar and on my *lap* at Desmond's spot, I wanted you. But I refused to cross the line. I honored the hood rule, and kept my hands to myself." Zach shook his fork in Jill's direction. "Even after Jay brought you here to live in this house, I fought it. You were her lover, the forbidden fruit."

Jill lowered her eyes to look at the baby still nursing in her arms. "I know, Zachary. You're a good man. I was drawn to you too, but I didn't know what it meant. You made me feel safe and I enjoyed being around you. It felt wonderful to laugh and speak freely about my dreams. You were a kind friend to me."

"And you deserved it. You needed a friend, someone to love you, and treat you special. What happened that night after Jay discovered Nahima here was the turning point. It wasn't an accident or some mishap. It was supposed to happen."

"I'm honestly sorry Jay got hurt. You lost her because of what *we* did. It turned her into a…a…I don't know."

"Nah, baby, it brought out the real Jay; the one she *used* to be able to turn on and off on a whim. It's her dark side. The monster within that had manipulated you, me and everyone else. It was there all the time."

* * * * *

"I ain't bullshitting y'all this time. I'm sick!" Jay shouted through gulps of air. Her stomach rumbled again, causing her body to jerk out of control. The contents of her belly rose up to her throat. She almost choked on the blood and vomit as it gushed from her mouth. She wiped her lips and chin with the back of her hand.

"Damn it, I need to see the nurse! Guard! Please help me, somebody!"

The two deputies manning the security monitors stared at Jay kneeling in front of the commode crying and puking. The female was on the phone catching up on the drama between her ex-boyfriend and the chick that had jacked him from her and their daughter. She placed her hand over the mouthpiece of the phone and turned to her coworker. "You ain't gonna go down there to check on that fool?"

"Hell no! She probably got her hands on some pills again. Let the next shift deal with her crazy ass."

We'd like to thank you for supporting G Street Chronicles and invite you to join our social networks. Please be sure to post a review when you're finished reading.

Facebook
G Street Chronicles Fan Page
G Street Chronicles CEO Exclusive Readers Group

Twitter
@GStreetChronicl

Email us and we'll add you to our mailing list
fans@gstreetchronicles.com

George Sherman Hudson, CEO
Shawna A., COO